THE PRESERVE

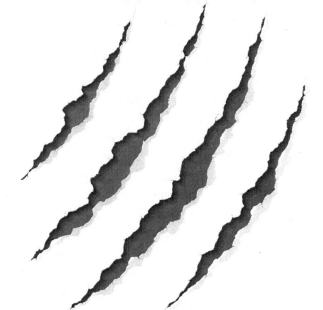

PATRICK LESTEWKA

NECRO PUBLICATIONS
2010

ISBN: 978-1889186665

Book design & typesetting:
David G. Barnett
Fat Cat Graphic Design
www.fatcatgraphicdesign.com

Assistant editors:
Amanda Baird
John Everson
Jeff Funk
C. Dennis Moore

A Necro Publication
5139 Maxon Ter.
Sanford, FL 32771

DEDICATION:

To my Grandfather, Charles

ACKNOWLEDGMENTS:

Thanks to Bob "Pegleg" Strauss and my father for their
diligent editing, and to Dave Barnett for taking a chance.

I was eighteen years old. And I was like your typical young American boy. A virgin. I had strong religious beliefs... My religious upbringing was, God was good. Everything good was what God wanted. Y'know, evil was the Devil's way.

But evil didn't enter it till Vietnam. I mean real evil. I wasn't prepared for it at all...

It was all evil. All evil. I was all evil. Where before, I wasn't. I look back, I look back today, and I'm horrified at what I turned into. What I was. What it did. I just look at it like it was somebody else. I really do.

It was somebody else.

—Unidentified Vietnam Veteran
Achilles in Vietnam, Jonathan Shay

I.
MAGNIFICENT SEVEN
(1967)

War Zone D, South Vietnam
July 15th, 1967. 12:05 hours.

Flanked by a pair of Cobra gunships, the Huey banked around a broccoli-topped mountainside. A cool rotor wash blew through the open cab, tugging at the soldiers' fatigues. Seven men were packed into the nylon mesh seats like so many lethal sardines: the Mobile Guerilla Force, A-303 Blackjack, the blackest of Black Ops units.

Or, as Top Brass dubbed them, the "Magnificent Seven."

The Huey dropped to two hundred feet, into a valley between the green and purple mountain peaks. Triple-canopy jungle unfurled in five shades of green below the Huey's armor-plated hull. The foliage broke and the chopper dropped into the Dong-Nai river basin, the river's brown water scalloped by its whirring blades. The door gunner, all of eighteen, sat impassively behind his M60 machine gun. A pair of Wayfarer sunglasses set on the bridge of his nose reflected a doubled image of the noonday sun, twin fiery discs burning outwards from the smoked lenses. Sam the Sham's voice pumped out of the cab speakers.

Lil' Red Riding Hood, I don't think little big girls should, Go walking in those spooky old woods alone...

The dustoff was two klicks off, an alternate pickup zone and hotter than a motherfuck. A 9th Infantry paratrooper unit on Long Range Patrol had been pinned in position by a patrolling platoon of heavily-armed NVA. The LuRPS had been taking heavy fire for hours, Charlie on them like stink on shit. Intel reported half the unit dead and a lot more wounded. Nobody knew if it was a job for Recon or Graves Registration.

The Blackjack insert team leader, Sergeant Jerome "Oddy" Grant, scanned the six faces staring back at him. He saw no fear or anxiety, only readiness.

Six men, aged nineteen to twenty-three. A year ago they'd been high school seniors and college sophomores and grainbelt farmhands, bank tellers and foundry workers. Two were married, three had steady girlfriends. Five children between them. Most had car loans and mortgage payments, performed volunteer work, attended church on Sundays. In a basement or rec room in six middle-class households scattered across America you would find walls hung with photographs of these men as swaddled infants and gap-toothed grade-schoolers, later as high school football slotbacks and basketball point guards. More recent snapshots show them as robed and mortarboard-bedecked college grads, or fathers dangling infants on their knees. In these same six houses lived the families who missed them, the mothers and fathers, wives and children who prayed nightly for the swift, safe return of their sons.

The pilot barked, "One minute to drop-off."

The exercise was known as an *out-and-in*: Charlie knew there was going to be an extraction but wasn't expecting an insertion on the same flight. The unit would drop in, load any wounded onto the chopper, secure a perimeter, and mount a counter-attack. Intel was murky as to the number of Charlies in the vicinity. Maybe only a few units. Then again, maybe enough to pack the cheap seats at Shea Stadium.

"Huey's gonna buzz us in right on top of them!" Oddy's voice rose above the rotor wash. "We're coming in hot, dump and run, throttle wide open!"

"Bust 'em up!" Daniel "Zippo" Coles bellowed, fingering the trigger of his LPO-50 flame-thrower.

"Bust 'em open!" Alex "Slash" Trimball hollered. The son of a sharecropper, Trimball's barracks cot at Ho-Ngoc-Tao was lined with nine neon dashboard Jesus sculptures. His tongue was black from the Benzedrine tabs he'd been chewing.

You're everything a big bad wolf could want...

The dustoff came into view. The Cobras laid down suppressor fire, strafing the jungle. The Huey pilot brought the bird down to fifteen feet and the men tossed lengths of jute cord from the cab, clipping on and rappelling to the ground. The door gunner laid down a line of cover fire, feet braced on the chopper's landing strut, M60 kicking against his chest. Spent 7.62mm longjacket casings glanced off the bulkhead and skidplates, pinwheeling, falling, reflecting brilliant yellow sunlight filtering through a bank of thin afternoon clouds.

Oddy signaled to the pilot, who tugged on the steering yoke and guided the chopper to a landing site some seven-hundred yards distant, beyond the range of Charlie's mortars. As the Huey rose into the cobalt-blue sky, the young door gunner kept firing and firing, M60 barrel glowing white from the heat. His mouth was wide open and he may have been screaming but his voice could not be heard above the gunfire and scything chopper blades.

"Scatter!" Oddy shouted. "Get these boys up and out of here!"

The men broke apart and pursued separate tangents through wind-tossed whorls of elephant grass. Their tiger-striped fatigues, made from high-tensile parachute nylon, blended with the tropical foliage seamlessly; the soldiers melted into the vegetation.

They reconnoitered two-hundred yards distant, in a circle of tamped grass where the LuRPS were pinned down. The site was partially ringed by a thicket of mangroves, trunks shattered by RPG missiles, branches splintered from AK-47 rounds. In several places the grass and earth had been blown apart in deep craters where mortar rounds had detonated. Beyond the mangroves lay a field of elephant grass pocketed with cypress thickets. The field was perhaps eight-hundred yards long, terminating at a dense glade of breadfruit, cinnamon, and palmetto trees. The sun beat down like a superheated fist, the humidity so intense it felt as though every breath was drawn through boiled fleece.

The 9th was in rough shape. A freckle-faced kid resembling a young Richard Chamberlain squirted blood from his femoral artery. Another man with Lieutenant's chevrons nursed a sucking chest wound, eyes bugged out and glassy; he screamed for someone named "Davey." A black kid lay on a bed of crushed banana leaves *sans* right leg, chest pin-cushioned with so many morphine syrettes he resembled some freakish sort of hedgehog. All three were in shock, their faces ashen, beyond the realm of pain.

A whey-faced medic was slicked to the elbows in blood with his hands buried deep in the belly of a dead Marine. He jerked his wrists up hard, dislodging a jagged star of mortar-shell from the dead man's ribcage. He hurled it into the grass and said, "It's gonna be okay, Hollywood," then rooted through his medical ruck for the Granulex blood coagulant. "I'll have you back on your feet *toot sweet.*" He sprayed Granulex along the raw edges of the wound while the gutshot Lieutenant wailed on and on: "Davey! Davey! *Daaa*–vey!"

Tony "Tripwire" Walker, Blackjack's demolitions expert, leaned over the medic. "Easy, man," he told him. "He's gone. Nothing you can do."

The medic stared up at Tripwire. His eyes were huge, the pupils dilated. His hands continued to push at the dead Marine's guts, pushing with no real sense of purpose or understanding, as though it were somehow possible to jam all the blood back inside. "I gotta get out of here," he said. "Can't hack this shit no more."

"Help me stabilize the others and get them to the Huey," Tripwire said, leading him away, "then you're going home."

Tripwire went over to the black kid. Since being taught basic field medicine at Camp Pendleton, he'd become Blackjack's meatball medic. He unshouldered his M-5 medical ruck and pulled out a bottle of Betadine, a suture kit, a blister pack of Dexedrine tablets, plus several ultra-absorbency Kotex pads. He plucked the morphine syrettes out of the black kid's chest and asked his name.

"D-D-Dale." This kid was seventeen years old, Tripwire guessed. Lied about his age, draft board only too willing to look the other way. His skin was the gray of a rotted potato. "A-a-am I go…gonna b-b-be o-okay?"

"You'll be fine," Tripwire said. It was a lie, but in a conflict built on lies, in a military machine that ran on lies, in a situation where men told lies to keep insanity at bay, this particular falsehood tripped off Tripwire's tongue with slick ease. "Be pumpin' Siagon whores by nightfall."

Tripwire felt around the base of Dale's right thigh. The limb was raggedly severed above the knee. His fingers came in contact with something wet, hard, and slippery: the kid's femur.

Karoumph, karoumph. Two artillery rounds exploded in a cypress grove three-hundred yards distant.

"What do you think?" Tripwire asked the medic.

"Let me check his pulse." Leaning over Dale, the medic found his left wrist. "Racing and weak—165 beats per minute, I'd say."

"You got serum albumin?"

"In my kit."

While the medic set up an IV flow, Tripwire tore Dale's fatigues up to the groin to get a better look at the wound. The meat of his thigh was badly chewed, most of the flesh blown clear off the bone. The femur shone wetly in the crisp sunlight, red muscle encased in a thin layer of adipose tissue. Tripwire saw a white blood vessel sticking out of the mess, blood spritzing from the vein like water from a spigot. "Tourniquet him off high on the thigh," Tripwire instructed.

After the medic had cinched Dale's leg with an M-16 strap and stemmed the blood flow, Tripwire removed a hemostat clamp from the med kit, clamped it to the end of the bleeding vessel, and tied the end off with a piece of black surgical thread. He then padded the wound with Kotex before wrapping the stump in an Ace bandage. While he operated, the medic worked an IV needle into a vein in Dale's hand and pumped in blood-plasma expander. The black soldier smiled slightly, laying back and closing his eyes.

"Good as we can do," Tripwire said. "Let's hoof your Lieutenant to the Huey."

The medic unfolded a portable back-board and together they shuttled the wounded Lieutenant down a speed trail to the Huey's landing zone. The man kept screaming: "Davey! Daaa–*veey*!" Tripwire knew the Lieutenant would probably be dead long before he reached the medical center at Da Nang. The same could be said for Dale and the other one. Maybe it was futile, but that didn't matter. They were Marines. You did everything you could to save a fellow Marine's life, even if it meant dying yourself.

By this time the other six members of Blackjack had moved to the clearing's perimeter, where the remaining LuRPS were positioned. The 9th unit's baby-faced corpsman looked barely old enough to deliver the Sunday paper.

"You got Charlie everywhere!" he screamed. "I mean, *every*–fuckin–where!"

Oddy said, "I can dig it."

"I'm glad you can," the corpsman said, "because I am flaking like fucking tuna!"

"Just chill, son."

"Yeah, pacify." Zippo lit the stub of a Swisher Sweets cigarillo on the shaft of blue flame thrown by his weapon's pilot light. "Cavalry's here to save your sorry asses."

"Zip that lip," Oddy told him. To the corpsman: "Where's Charlie at?"

The corpsman pointed across the knee-high elephant grass to a dense glade. "In there. Don't know how many." He looked around frantically, eyes darting too fast to focus on anything or anyone. "Seems like a fuckin' thousand!"

"LuRPS," Slash said, chewing on the word like it was a turd while scanning the soldiers' shit-scared faces. "I guess someone's been lying to me."

"Who?" a sandy-haired LuRP asked.

"The guy who told me you pussies were hardcore."

"I said *zip* that *lip*."

The low *thoomp* of a mortar being launched was followed by a whistling *sweeee* as it streamed through the air.

"Asses *down!*" Oddy hollered. The soldiers crouched low as the round passed directly overhead, landing thirty feet behind them. The ground shook as shrapnel cut through the grass and thumped into mangrove trunks.

"Charlie's zeroing in," Zippo said, shaking dirt off his collar.

"You and your men diddlybop," Oddy told the corpsman. "Help your medic transport the wounded to the Huey's LZ and send my man forward. Dig me, dogface?"

"You sure?" The corpsman peered up at Oddy from beneath the brim of his piss-cutter helmet. "There's only, what, six of you?"

"Hey," said one of the LuRPS, "the man told us to diddlybop." He looked at the corpsman, then at the big black Sergeant, as if expecting Oddy to experience a sudden change of heart. "He gave us a direct *order*."

"Yeah," said Frank "Gunner" Hardcastle, Blackjack's machine-gunner, 250 pounds of ripped Iowa farm muscle with bad attitude to spare. "Get thee *gone*."

"Okay," said the relieved corpsman, turning to address the remaining LuRPS. "Hustle back to LZ double-time. Jackson, you and Henried hoof Phillips. Samuelson and me got—"

Suddenly there were several loud hollow pops and someone shouted, "Incoming!" Seconds later the first of a half-dozen mortar rounds landed in the grass twenty yards behind the men.

When the sound of the explosions receded, Oddy heard screaming.

A mortar shell had struck the corpsman high on the left arm, just beneath the shoulder. While the deadhead round hadn't exploded, the force of its downwards trajectory was enough to tear the corpsman's arm off. He stood looking down at his arm in the green, green grass, the fingers still twitching, biceps flexing convulsively.

The corpsman made the sounds a baby will make when he is trying to work up the breath for a good scream. Blood spurted from the wound, plastering his face in red sheets. The corpsman's right hand clenched around the butt of his M-16, fingers squeezing the trigger. The clip emptied in a rapid cook-off, slugs slamming into the earth and punching through his shins, feet, kneecaps, toes. The young corpsman dropped onto the grass with a grunting sigh. He fell forward on his face into a clump of small yellow flowers.

"Hightail him back to the Huey," Oddy said.

"Jesus, man," the sandy-haired LuRP said, "he's wormfood!"

"Hoof...him...*back*."

"Okay," the LuRP said, moving toward the body. "You got it."

Tripwire and the medic had loaded the Huey by the time the remaining LuRPS reconnoitered with their dead corpsman. Tripwire helped them onto the bird, receiving their grateful looks and whispered thanks with a curt nod.

The pilot gave Tripwire the thumbs-up before lifting off. As soon as the Huey gained altitude, small arms fire erupted from the glade. The door gunner answered with his M60.

Tripwire hustled to rejoin his unit. Oddy flagged him down beneath a banana tree. The Sergeant pushed a cluster of small green bananas out of his face and said, "Charlie knows they've been trumped. They're royally pissed."

Just then, AK-47 fire erupted from the trees. Tripwire spied a few camouflaged uniforms crouching along the darkened wood line.

Tripwire said, "So what are we gonna do?"

"What we always do, son." Oddy smiled, his teeth stark against the black skin and streaks of olive-green lampblack. "Go to work."

So. The Magnificent Seven got to work.

Sheltered beneath drooping fleshy mango leaves, Blackjack sniper Neil "Crosshairs" Paris scanned the enemy line through the iris of a Gewher scope, sighting down a soldier whose fatigues roughly matched the bark of the breadfruit tree he was perched in. Crosshairs's silenced G3SG/1 sniper rifle made a *tssst* sound and the VC's head snapped back in a mist of red. The corpse slumped over the branch like a noodle on a chopstick. Crosshairs was able to pick off two more before Charlie got wise.

A wave of VC soldiers crept out of the jungle on their bellies, AK's pushing down the elephant grass. Then they reached a semi-circle of M-14 toe-poppers and Bouncing Betties Tripwire had strung fifty feet off Blackjack's position. Panicked shouts were followed by a sequence of muffled explosions; these were followed by a clotted rain of earth and charred cloth and ribboned flesh and enough bone-confetti to outfit a ticker-tape parade.

A second wave charged hard, releasing a pack of attack dogs before them. The dogs, starved and murderous, caught the insert team's scent and rushed headlong, yellow teeth bared.

Zippo rose up from a copse of bushes, thumbing the pilot light on his LPO-50 flame-thrower. "Run along, little doggies."

He loosed a whip of liquid flame that turned the dogs into canine fireballs. They ran through the grass in maddened, helpless circles, fur burned away, flesh melting like candle-wax. They ran in herky-jerk circles, biting at the flames crawling down their throats and igniting their lungs. The smell of them was horrid, a tire fire in July. Soon they lay down, all of them all at once, lay still as stones and burned to black smudges on the grass. Zippo receded into the bush before the Viets could draw a bead.

Now the second wave found themselves with their asses hanging out, exposed in the middle of the field. *Tssst*: one of their number was thrown out of his boots, the back of his head exploding in a spray, a stream of blood plastering his face, executing a graceless backwards-somersault to land facedown in the grass.

Gunner swung around the trunk of a moss-covered tree hefting a Stoner M63A1 light machine-gun. The Stoner's .223-in hollowpoints punched through the VC soldier's uniforms, blowing their combat jackets out in billowy bell-shapes. The exit holes cast a lingering pinkish mist and their faces contorted and they tried to scream, lungs filling with blood. Gunner slipped behind the tree as retaliatory fire slammed into it.

While the remaining VC's concentrated their fire on Gunner, Oddy and Slash jack-in-the-boxed from their hidey holes. Slash took two of the four soldiers out with textbook K-5 shots. Oddy's first shot went high, blowing a crease in the top of the second-to-last soldier's skull. He lowered his aim and drilled a slug straight into the man's face, spewing cartilage and molars out the back of his head. He sighted down the M16's barrel and squeezed off a pair of shots that destroyed the last soldier's kneecaps, dropping him to the dirt, screaming.

Eight-and-a-half minutes had passed since the Magnificent Seven touched down.

They waited to see if the wounded soldier would draw any lingering comrades from cover. The man's screams tapered to moans, then to whimpers and, finally, to a pitiful sort of sniffling.

Oddy whistled. The insert members assembled on his position. The rest of the team covered Gunner and Slash while they humped out to retrieve the wounded soldier.

The second stage of their mission was Recon. Intel reported Charlie was stockpiling firepower at a location near the village of Bu Von Kon. Blackjack was to locate the weapons cache and frag it, killing any and all VC between here and there.

One question: Where were the weapons?

"Answer," Oddy said, once the Viet was secure. "Get on it."

Randy "Answer" Blondeau was twenty years old, tall and gangly with a mess of carroty curls tamped beneath his helmet. He looked like any other grinning, inoffensive adolescent who might be found wandering college campuses in Anytown, USA. Looks can be deceiving: Answer was Blackjack's interrogator, a post at which he exhibited a terrifying proficiency.

Answer knelt beside the wounded soldier. The Viet's face held a simple geometry in profile, flat and sunken, faintly mongoloid. Mucous ran from his nostrils in webby strands, across his upper lip and down the sides of his mouth in a snotty Fu Manchu. The shock had him trembling like a Parkinson's victim.

Answer whispered in his ear. The Viet shook his head.

Answer nodded slowly. Then, with equal slowness, he probed the index and pointer fingers of his left hand through the bloody hole in the soldier's right pantleg, exploring the inner workings of the Viet's shattered kneecap.

The VC's neck tendons bulged out, hands seizing handfuls of dirt.

Answer's fingers twitched inside the wound. He cocked his head to one side, as dogs sometimes do when curious or perplexed. The Viet thrashed, incapable of screaming, the pain a living, all-consuming entity.

Answer pulled his fingers free. They were red to the knuckles. He whispered into the soldier's ear again. The soldier told him something. "He says the cache is southeast, Sarge," Answer told Oddy. "Ten, twelve kliks."

Crosshairs pointed his gun at the prisoner. "So what do we do with him?"

"For damn sure he's never walking again," Tripwire said.

Gunner said, "Call a med evac."

"Med evac for a hobbled Gook?" Zippo said.

"Ever hear of a little something called the Geneva Convention, Zippo?"

"Tell that to the poor fucks Charlie's got rotting in tiger cages."

"Gunner's right," Oddy said. "The enemy poses no threat. Slash, get on the PRC and call in a—"

Before Oddy could finish the med evac order, Answer unsheathed a K-Bar knife and stabbed the VC soldier in the neck.

The man looked mildly bewildered, staring first at Answer and then somewhere beyond him, up into the sky, where a black raven circled. Answer pulled the knife out. Blood leapt from the wound, painting a thick red scar across his fatigue vest.

"Jesus!" Tripwire shrugged off his explosives bandoleer and knelt beside the VC soldier, who was gurgling like an infant, unable to scream or cry out because of the blood spurting from the slit in his neck. Tripwire pressed Kotex pads to the gash but it was futile: the blood pushed through his fingers in thick rivulets, and within seconds the pads were soaked. The soldier grabbed at Tripwire's sleeves, fingers clenching and unclenching like a panicked infant's. He burrowed his head into Tripwire's stomach, mouth opening and closing, as though he wanted to eat his way inside, tunnel in where it was warm and safe to die.

Oddy knocked the knife from Answer's hand. "The fuck you think you're doing?" Gripping the scrawny interrogator's shoulders, he slammed him up against a banana tree; the rough bark made dry scratchy noises, slicing Answer's cheek. Oddy slapped his face once, twice, three times, forehand to backhand to forehand, the sound of black flesh on white flesh sharp as a starter pistol's crack. "That's *not* how we do things!"

Answer appraised his Sergeant through half-lidded eyes. Thin streams of blood leaked from the corners of his mouth and down his face. He turned and spat a tooth into the dirt. "This is a warzone, Sarge," he said. "Different rules apply."

Oddy yanked Answer forward until their noses nearly touched. "Not in this unit. Not under my roof." Up close, Oddy was struck by the blueness of the young interrogator's eyes, a color somehow devoid of pity. *Cold eyes*, he thought. *Cold, dead eyes.* He thrust Answer backwards with a mixture of anger, revulsion, and—the emotion rising quick and unbidden—fear. Answer stumbled gracelessly, tripping over an exposed root, falling on his ass in a puff of red dust.

"Do something like that again and we'll have serious words, dog-face."

Zippo came over and knelt beside Answer. He lowered the muzzle of his flame-thrower until the pilot light's flame touched the sole of Answer's Bata combat boot.

"There's fair and there's fair," he said as the pilot light burned into the boot's rubberized sole, sending up tendrils of stinking black smoke. Answer did not move his foot. "That, my little friend, was not fair. We got to keep our heads, get me? Keep our heads, keep our shit hardwired, and maybe—just maybe—we get through this alive."

By now the flame had melted through the sole. The smell of bubbling rubber was joined by another, thicker smell reminding Crosshairs of sweet pork barbecue. Answer stared up at Zippo with those cold blue eyes, face a mask of composure. Zippo raised the flamer's muzzle with a look halfway between bafflement and grudging respect.

"As long as we're on the same wavelength," he said.

"I'm tuning in on your signal," Answer said softly. He tore a strip off his fatigues and tied it around his injured foot.

Tripwire cradled the VC's head as the man twitched through his death throes. The young man died quickly, quietly. Tripwire rolled the head off his lap and stood up. Low-hanging storm clouds moved over the horizon, blocking out the sun, etching the foothills in clean-edged darkness.

Oddy said, "Let's get humping."

**Excerpted from the *Slave River Journal*,
April 9th, 1986:**

THREE RESEARCHERS MISSING
IN NORTHWEST TERRITORIES

"No Physical Evidence Found as of Yet,"
—RCMP Spokesman Says

By Michael Fulton

Fort Simpson, NWT: A three-member expedition team sent to observe and record caribou migratory patterns in the territory surrounding Great Bear Lake has gone missing. The crew (statistician Carl Rosenberg, cartographer Bill Myers, and Lillian Hapley, another statistician) took off from the Fort Good Hope airport on April 7th in a Cessna 340-S ultralight plane piloted by Rosenberg. Contract workers for the Department of Natural Resources, the trio were scheduled to fly a circuit over Great Bear Lake and outlying areas, recording the movement of the dwindling caribou herds. The last radio communication came at 2:30 p.m., when Hapley radioed the DNR home base to report no caribou sighted. Sid Grimes, Spokesman for the Royal Canadian Mounted Police, issued a statement that a search-and-rescue team is currently combing the presumed crash area, but as yet, "No physical evidence has been located..."

II.
SLAUGHTERHOUSE FIVE
(1987)

20 Years Later

Daniel "Zippo" Coles—Execution Poet
Vancouver, British Columbia.
November 30th, 1987. 12:05 p.m.

Picture this: you're knee-deep in elephant grass, walking point somewhere between the Delta and the DMZ, and you can *smell* the fucking Gooks, smell their stink on the breeze, and fear crawls like fire ants at the back of your throat and you're thinking, *I'm here to change things, make things better*, but all the while it's you who's changing, changing deep inside.

Soldiers deal with this change in different ways.

Me?

I lit the pilot light of an LPO-50 flame-thrower, 50,000 BTUs of Gook-cooking power, and laid down a scar of flame that'd turn a village full of militant Zipperheads into roving, raving, Roman-fucking-Candles in a New York minute.

Talk about your motherfucking catharsis.

Gritty noonday sunlight streams through a west-facing bay window to fall across white satin sheets. I rub sleep-crust from my eyes and stand, naked, to survey the dull vista. Rain falls in endless gray sheets over a horseshoe-shaped metropolis ringing Queen Charlotte Sound. Vancouver's mayor, a huckstering blowhard in a ten-gallon cowboy hat, proclaims the city to be "The Florida of Canada," on account of its lack of snow. The comparison is ridiculous, like proclaiming the seagull the "Bald Eagle of Canada."

After showering and dressing I sit on the balcony, drinking a Carnation Instant Breakfast and reading the *Globe and Mail*. A story on page five incenses me: some of these new-wave fags are *trying* to contract AIDS. It seems there's these homo-lifestyle magazines—*Turdburgling Today* or *Modern Man-Ramming* or I don't know what the fuck—painting a rosy picture of the disease. You've got glossy photos of pillowbiters climbing mountains and hang-gliding, all of them thin on account of the AIDS cocktails giving them chronic diarrhea. So now the disease has become romanticized, the latest must-have accessory, and these fruits are falling all over themselves to catch it. There's these clubs where AIDS-positive men—"gift-givers"—meet up with negs—"bug-chasers"—and then flounce off to shoot ass-darts, passing the disease.

Pisses me the fuck off.

You see, Canada's got socialized medicine. So who do you think foots the bill for these butt-monkeys and their life-prolonging cocktails? That's right: John Q. Public. Specifically, me. Mother*fuckers*. I mean, a bunch of ass-pirates want to off themselves, fine by me. Just have the common decency to ventilate your cranium with a .44 and spare us hard-working taxpayers the expense, huh?

The telephone rings. I answer on the third. "You got Coles."

"Kawanami's in from the airport."

"Where?"

"Princess Gardens. Penthouse suite."

"How much?"

"Fifty large for Kawanami, twenty anyone else."

"Deal."

What's the value of a human life, bypassing the ethics of the question? Human flesh and innards are worthless, unless you happen to know a black market organ farmer or an unscrupulous Chinese chef. Bones can be ground into fertilizer but that's a buck a pound max, so risk outweighs reward. You can sell a decent head of hair to a wig shop but there'd be questions and who wants that hassle? So basically, the human body is worth less than the most worn-out trail nag, which could still net a few bucks as dog food. Ergo, the value of a human life is less, monetarily-speaking, than an animal's. And we slaughter animals by the millions *every day*.

Dig that logic, baby.

I work for Slopes, mostly. Vancouver's lousy with them. They cross the Pacific from Laos, Cambodia, Hong Kong, nailing down stakes on the first patch of soil they wash up on. The city's infested to the point that local wags have dubbed it "Chan-couver." Didn't take the Yakuza and Triads long to migrate. These dudes hold 3,000-year-old grudges against each other; a fellow with my abilities can make a very good living settling their age-old scores.

Truth be told, I *enjoy* killing Slants, except for Japs, who do their best to emulate us by drinking Coke, wearing blue jeans, shaking their narrow yellow asses to Elvis and Bob Dylan—they're making a genuine *effort*. Amazing, isn't it, how a couple Atom bombs can vaporize 4,000 years of stagnant history and tradition?

The fictitious hitman as portrayed in movies and television is just that: a fiction. Guys wearing black leather trenchcoats or flash satin suits, calling attention to themselves with bowler hats or handlebar moustaches, killing with metal teeth or samurai swords or poisoned hatpins?—all bullshit.

Here's the lowdown:

Rule #1: You've got to be invisible. It's about being gray, about hiding in the sunlight. You have to be nondescript. Every aspect of your appearance must repulse attention. You shower, shave, brush your teeth every day. You don't wear cologne or if you do only a hint, you wear off-the-rack suits that render your profession a speculative question—maybe you're a lawyer, maybe a banker, maybe a plumber who spends his toilet-snaking profits on decent threads. If you wear a tie make it dark and cheap, nothing with little golfers or Disney characters. No jewelry, but you want a decent watch, Seiko or Casio. You drive a domestic car between five and eight years old, rust- and dent-free. You do this and, somewhere between here and there, you might just become invisible. Part of the scenery. The last person anyone would peg as a cold-blooded killer.

Rule #2: K.I.S.S.—Keep It Simple, Shithead. Hitmen swiss-cheesing their marks with helicopter chainguns, slicing people to ribbons with razor-tipped nunchuks or sending them into convulsions with blowdarts steeped in poison-toad venom? Only in Hollywood. Anything a real professional needs can be found at the nearest Home Depot: box-cutters, screwdrivers, leather punches, hacksaws. You want to use anonymous weapons, items that can be bought anywhere. If you leave a golden butterfly knife with your initials engraved in the hilt or—God forbid—a *calling card* at the hit scene, you're fucking with Rule #1.

Rule #3: the simplest rule. No wife, no friends, no kids, nothing you can't abandon in the time it takes to pack a duffel bag.

These are the rules of my game.

Kazuhito Kawanami is head of the Shinju Yakuza. He's older than Abe Lincoln's bedpan, but you don't get old in his business unless you stay sharp and *this* particular cat is sharper than a bagful of razor blades. His security team's the equivalent of the '76 Steelers "Steel Curtain" defense: a posse of TEC-9-toting killers trained in urban warfare, dudes who could flatline the 5th Precinct in the time it takes to tie your shoelaces.

They've got one small problem, though.

I'm better.

Here's how it'll shake down:

I am going to ride the elevator down to an underground parking garage where my 1980 Dodge is parked. I will drive down Sussex street and merge with the TransCanada highway, heading north until I reach the outskirts of a town called Naniamo. I will stop at *Stow Away*, a long-term storage facility, storage unit #878. Inside the rental unit are stacks of boxes whose contents are written on the cardboard in green Magic Marker. Inside a box labeled LP'S/MAGAZINES/BOWLING BALL are several dozen jazz records in their original dust jackets, every Playboy spanning the years 1960-67, and a gray bowling ball bag.

Here's the thing: I don't bowl.

Returning, halfway between Naniamo and Vancouver, I will pull off at a Dunkin Donuts, where I'll order a medium black coffee and a honey-glazed. I will take the bag into the restroom and, in the handicapped stall, will remove and load a pair of 9mm Llama pistols with hollowpoint Mausers before screwing on Nambu silencers. I will strap a box-cutter, a Phillips-head screwdriver, four extra clips, and a pound of C-4 explosive underneath my suitcoat, adjusting for comfort and mobility. I will call my wheelman, Fred Jackson, and tell him to be waiting on the third level of the Princess Gardens underground parking lot, zone E-8, in an hour.

Back in the city, I will park at the Finch Avenue subway station. If the weather has improved I will don a pair of tinted mirrorshades and ride the subway four stops, Finch to Wellesley. Exiting at Wellesley, I will navigate a series of underground tunnels until I reach an escalator that will take me into the lobby of the Princess Gardens hotel.

I will cross the brass-and-marble lobby, not hurrying, and enter the elevator. I will pull on a pair of powdered surgical gloves and press the button for the twentieth floor, one below the penthouse. As it rises, I will dislodge a ceiling panel, unlatch the maintenance trapdoor, and hoist myself onto the car's roof. I will replace the panel and wait for the elevator to stop before climbing a maintenance ladder to the penthouse ventilation shaft. Unhinging the grate, I will crawl into the shaft. I will hear voices speaking in Japanese. I will crawl down the shaft until I am directly above those voices, until I can peer through a vent and see their owners' shiny silk suits and yellow skin.

This is what I will do. This is what I did.

And here I am.

Kawanami reclines on a leather sofa with a tumbler of scotch. He's talking to someone via speakerphone. To his left sit a pair of bodyguards decked to the nines in French-cut suits and black wingtips, TEC-9's resting on their laps. Intricate tattoos project above their collars and shirt sleeves. I idly wonder how their skin might look drying on the limbs of a breadfruit tree, yard upon yard of skin inked with intricate designs, dragons and koi and samurai warriors and suddenly the ventilation shaft is very cramped, I feel claustrophobic, flashback to…

…deep in the guts of Phuoc-Long province, walking in darkness through a grove of banana trees. Our boots crush the rotting fruit underfoot, filling the air with their sickly sweetness. Eakins, a Cherry we were escorting to Song-Be, trudged along on a path of flattened elephant grass while the rest of us, keen to VC booby traps, kept to the fringe. Eakins, a beach-bum with a bleached-out brushcut, was singing something by the Beach Boys: "We got this board and we call it a Woody; it ain't too cherry, it's an oldie but a goody…"

Then the ground opened up and swallowed Eakins to the armpits. He was screaming, arms flailing, digging up chunks of loose earth and mashed banana. His body thrashed like he was being fed feet-first through a wood-chipper.

I humped twenty feet up the trail, found the tunnel, dove in head-first. I didn't know Eakins and was fairly certain I wouldn't like him if I did. Didn't matter. He was a Marine and I was going to save him if I could, die if I had to. We were all like that back then, operating at a level above duty or patriotism or friendship: I will die for you and you will die for me. There is a terrible, reckless kind of strength in such a simple code of conduct.

Anytime. Anywhere. Anyhow. I will die for you.

In the tunnel, wet earth pressed against me. Ahead were noises like slabs of raw meat colliding. I triggered the LPO-50's pilot light, producing a narrow finger of flame.

"Jesus Christ…"

A pair of Gooks crouched in the blackness clutching long, sharp knives. Eakins' legs, what was left of them, kicked wildly. All the flesh and most of the muscle, with the exception of his booted feet, was hacked away. The bones of his shins and knees collided wetly, clicking and clacking. His belly was slashed open and his guts had tumbled out. Long bluish ropes of intestine glistened like wet cables and the Gooks hacked at them with gore-streaked blades and the smell of blood was so strong that suddenly the tunnel was the size of a gopher burrow.

The Gooks turned to me and their faces reflected perfect, undiluted hatred and that's when one of them shoved a blade up into Eakins, digging and twisting until something thick and clumped and rank-smelling spewed out of the ragged hole, splattering their snarling upturned faces.

Pulling the flame-thrower's trigger felt like an absolution. The LPO-50 spread a carpet of fire that filled the tunnel with the smell of burning butane and burning flesh. The heat blistered my face and singed my eyebrows to ash but I kept the trigger down. And all the while I'm thinking, "Please someone shoot Eakins, shoot him in the fucking head, end his misery because…"

…Kawanami's off the telephone. He rises and walks to the window. His bodyguards follow. They're all facing away from me.

Rock and roll.

The Llamas kick in my hands as slugs tear through the ventilation shaft, leaving a network of dime-sized holes. Through the vent I see a bullet punch through a bodyguard's neck, just below his hairline. The slug bores through his throat, leaving a fist-sized exit hole where his collarbones meet. He drops to his knees, hands raised to the wound. He appears to be praying.

The other bodyguard takes one slug through the knee and another turns his elbow into red mashed potato. He folds like a pup tent onto the cream carpet, spraying the TEC-9, punching holes through the far wall. I drill a bullet through the left lens of his sunglasses. His head snaps back like it's been nailed to the floor, pulped eyeball oozing around the mirrored plastic.

I smash at the vent with the pistol butts until it swings open and pour myself through to land feet-first on the carpet. Ten seconds have gone by.

Kawanami stands beside the window, drink in hand. He is trembling, but whether this is fear or the palsy of his age I cannot tell. He knows my presence means his life can now be measured with a stopwatch.

"I'm going to kill you, now."

The old man nods. He does not beg, or offer to double whatever I'm being paid. He just nods and sips his drink, eyes never leaving mine. I can only hope, when my time comes, I check out with similar dignity.

The silenced Llamas make a dull mechanic hiss—*snick-snick, snick-snick*—as I double-tap the triggers. Hollowpoints tear through Kawanami, blowing the back of his blazer out. There are only pinpricks of blood on his chest but I'm certain his back now resembles a surrealist painting, bullets leaving massive exit holes. The window spiderwebs and then shatters. His body is thrown backwards, feet propelled from his shoes—I notice a hole in his argyle sock through which one big toe pokes—and his neck is severed clean through on the jags of window-glass. His head plummets twenty-one stories to the sidewalk.

I'm heading to the elevator when I notice a TEC-9 laid across the sofa's armrest. It can't be Kawanami's so that means…

Ssshhht is the sound of my suitcoat splitting as a blade slashes diagonally across my back, shoulderblade-to-hipbone. I barrel-roll to my left instinctively, adrenaline redlined, and catch a glimpse of my attacker. Another cookie-cutter bodyguard wearing shades and a suit, but this one's got a ten-inch Barlow knife and as I face him he lunges at me.

I feint right and the knife slices into the meat of my right bicep, sawing through skin and sinew. I spin on the ball of my foot, rolling off my attacker's momentum, coming through with an elbow that forces his jaw bone into his neck, jamming it into the big cluster of nerves there. He goes down and I cross behind the sofa, pulling the screwdriver and box-cutter from inside my suitcoat.

"Listen," I say to the guy. "Your boss is dead. You lose, I win. What's the use you dying now?"

The dude just snarls at me.

You try to toss these fucking mongrels a bone…

He comes around the sofa, chopping at me with the thick blade. I draw back far enough to avoid a fatal wound but the tip passes through my shirt below my nipples and blood pisses through the slit. I bring the box-cutter around in a hard arc, slashing at his unprotected face, creating a half-moon gash starting at his hairline and terminating somewhere below the jawbone.

He screams and his hand goes up to grab at his face, his hand's trying to press the fatty flap of skin that was so recently his cheek back in place. The box-cutter slips from my right hand as I jerk my left up into the gap between his outstretched arm and chest, screwdriver aimed at a spot beneath his chin. I know this is going to end ugly, ugly and senseless, but these things usually do.

The screwdriver punches through his throat—*thack!*—and blood sprays down in twin brownish geysers, staining his suit. This is accompanied by a horrible hissing noise as his jugular pumps blood around the screwdriver's molded plastic handle. He opens his mouth and through red-streaked teeth I glimpse the screwdriver's tip. He's making this noise, this horrid *gurgling*, and it fills me with a desperate sort of pity so I yank the screwdriver out of his throat and bury it in his left ear. He squawks, eyes blinking, and face-plants on the carpet.

Less than two minutes and I've earned $110,000.

But I'm a mess. In the bathroom, I strip my shirt off to examine my arm. The gash is straight and very, very deep and when I clean away the blood I see things that look like snapped piano wires and I force myself to stop looking and wrap the wound in a towel.

Three suitcases stand next to the front door. I rifle them to find a black Cerutti 1881 shirt and suitcoat. Through the shattered window I hear distant sirens.

It takes forever for the elevator to reach the penthouse. I take it to the third floor before stumbling into the stairwell and descending to the underground parking lot.

Fred Jackson's two-tone Chev is parked behind a pillar in section E-8. I slump into the front seat and Fred—skinny and shrewish with aviator sunglasses and a pencil-thin moustache of a style favored by '70s-era adult film performers—whistles softly.

"Oh, Danny-boy," he says. "You been wrestling grizzlies or what?"

"Just drive."

Fred navigates up a series of ramps, pays the attendant, and angles onto the street.

"Going to need medical attention?"

"Arm's hacked up bad."

"We'll head to your place and call Lois."

Lois is Fred's wife, a registered nurse who administers to the bumps and bruises I absorb in the line of duty. Fred reaches into the back seat and grabs a cell phone, a white behemoth twice the size of the PRC units we hoofed in 'Nam. I close my eyes and when I open them we're at my condo complex.

Fred parks near the service entrance and hustles me up the maintenance elevator. He drags me to my apartment, kicks the bathroom door open, and sets me in the bathtub. He lifts my arm and cinches a belt above the gash. I close my eyes again and when I open them Lois is beside me. Fred's wife is sexy as all hell and I've often wondered what it would be like to screw her, that tight body, that pert can. She injects me with something.

I awake in bed with my arm heavily-bandaged. Fred comes in with an envelope.

"Someone bathe me?"

"Lois," Fred says. "And not just to prevent infection. You reeked."

"What kind of soap she use?"

"Irish Spring."

"I smell like a leprechaun fart."

Fred laughs. "Ninety-three stitches—took a couple yards of catgut to put Humpty-Danny back together again." He tosses me the envelope. "Don't see Ed McMahon's mug on it, so I guess you can't quit your day job."

I tear the letter open with my good hand.

An unsigned check for fifty thousand dollars slips onto the coverlet.

Neil "Crosshairs" Paris-Card Shark
Las Vegas, Nevada.
November 30, 1987. 12:05 p.m.

All that remains clear anymore is the split-second before it all happened: the scissoring limbs and wall of gnashing blood-stained teeth and the smell of flayed and burning children. Then the creature scrambled up my chest, talons hooking into my skin, a brittle crunch, *followed by earth-shattering pain.*

I came to on the jungle floor, my nose—what was left of it— inhaling the stench of rotting vegetation. The left side of my face felt as though it'd been dipped in liquid nitrogen and smashed with a Louisville Slugger. A hand hammered shots of morphine into my chest. Focusing with my remaining eye, I realized the hand was my own.

Then Oddy, his big black skull like a solar eclipse, eased the syrette out of my hand. "Pacify, son," he whispered. "Med evac's on the way."

The dirt surrounding my head was wet and sticky. Noise came from my skull. A horrible pissing *sound.*

Tripwire joined Oddy. He got an eyeful of me and paled.

"Jesus Christ, Sarge. He ain't going to make it."

"He's one tough fuck."

"Shit, Sarge, half his fuckin' head's missing—"

"Zip that lip, soldier." Oddy propped a balled-up flak jacket under my head and wrapped a shredded blanket around my face. "Gonna be fine as cherry wine."

Footsteps came near. "Gunner and Slash are dead." Zippo's voice.

Oddy said, "What happened?"

"It was…that thing. *Slash's spine is torn out, bits of him scattered across half the fucking warzone. Found Gunner's head, but that's it."*

"This is royally fucked up," said Tripwire.

"Christ Sarge, Gunner's a fucking head," *Zippo said.*

"I'm dying," I said weakly.

Oddy said, "Shitcan that talk, dogface. Where's Answer?"

"Here, Sarge." Although I could not see him, I knew Answer had made his usual entrance: materializing silently from the undergrowth, the epitome of Blackjack's "Swift, Silent, Deadly" credo.

"We got med evac rendezvous one klick down this speed trail," Oddy said. "Answer, scout ahead. Trip and me hump Crosshairs. Zippo, you tail."

We raced breakneck through the midnight jungle. Oddy's hands were hooked under my armpits, Tripwire had my ankles, my body slung like a hammock between. The Thing that had slaughtered Gunner and Slash and had nearly punched my ticket, the Thing we found hunched and gibbering in a hut full of skinless Viet villagers, was still out there. We'd hurt it, and badly: I'd personally drilled it with five .303 copperjackets before it stole my face. But it was still alive, still lurking in the bush.

"Go go go!" Oddy hollered.

Soon I heard the drone of the Huey's Pratt & Whitney engine. I passed out…

…and awoke in a field infirmary near Duc Phong with an IV drip suspended above my head and a heart-rate monitor beeping at my side.

I could not feel my body.

I wasn't paralyzed: I could wiggle my fingers and toes, blink my eye, raise my arms and legs. But I could not feel *my skin. It was as if the surface of my flesh, billions and billions of nerve endings, were shot full of Novocaine.*

A young medic noticed I was conscious and approached with a timidity bordering on reverence. "Are you feeling alright?"

"So…thirsty."

"I'll get something," he said. "You're lucky to be alive."

I've heard the refrain so many times it has attained the singsong quality of a show tune: You are lucky to be aaa-live—YES SIR!—

lucky to be drawing breath—OH MY!—a medical miracle for all to see! *The fortuitousness of my survival is, I've come to realize, a wholly subjective matter.*

The medic returned with a glass of water. He was accompanied by an older man who I learned was the surgeon responsible for saving my life.

"You were dead," he told me in the matter-of-fact tone of those inured to death. "When your unit offloaded you from the Huey, your brainwaves were flatlined."

I asked about the others.

"Your unit was disbanded after the mission. Unconditional releases."

He asked how I felt. I told him I could not feel my body.

"That can't be," he said. "We've done reflex-tests and—"

"Not paralyzed. It's just…everything's…numb."

He pinched my arm hard enough to redden the skin. "Nothing?"

I shook my head.

"Well," he shrugged, "side-effects are to be expected. You are lucky to be alive."

"So I've heard."

The left side of my face felt terribly wrong. *I raised my hand to touch it.*

"Don't," the surgeon said. "The wound is still tender. Alex, give him a mirror."

The medic offered me a barber's mirror.

"Oh good Christ…"

"I did the best I could." The surgeon's voice was a million miles away. "There's only so much I could do…"

A chunk of bone and brain and skin roughly the size of a horse's hoof had been carved from my skull. Half my forehead, my left eye, my left nostril and cheek and ear—all gone. A skin-graft—culled, I later realized, from my ass—had been sewn over the gaping wound to prevent the rest of my brain from sloshing out. The transplanted skin was dappled with wiry black hair: my ass *hair. For some reason they continued to grow and I now shave them twice-weekly, pausing occasionally to savor the absurdity.*

I was never exactly a handsome man, but sweet fuck…

The doc said I'd lost one-fifth of my frontal lobe, one-third of my thalamus, nearly all my limbic cortex. If someone were to stab me in the back, I would feel the blade's pressure but there would be no pain whatsoever. It's entirely possible I might bleed to death out of sheer ignorance.

Other complications were expected. I did not disappoint. Apart from the numbness, everything I eat tastes like burnt toast—I ate burnt toast in hopes of it tasting like Lobster Newburg but no such luck. My hearing wavers in and out like a radio on the fritz and I've got no control of my johnson anymore: I pop wood for no earthly reason, sometimes blow my load in public places without a pretty skirt in sight.

"We only use ten percent of our brains," the baby-faced medic told me. "Einstein used eleven and he was a genius."

I said, "Shut up, man."

They sent me to a veteran's sanitarium in Coldwater, Michigan. I wasn't bugshit like the Section-8's they had cooped up there, but the doc felt I'd have difficulty adapting to my "altered physical paradigm."

I met a vet named Eugene there. Eugene was a Major with 7th Recon, spent thirty-three months in Da Nang. It takes a certain type of person to keep their shit wired tight in Recon. Eugene was not that type. At thirty-one years old his hair was snow-drop white, arctic tundra white. He patrolled his room with a squeeze-bottle of Mrs. Butterworth, filling in every crack with syrup to stop the poison gas he thought the Gooks were pumping in. He confided that when he took a dump, the voices of dead Gooks talked to him through his asshole—the shit-voices, telling him to do awful things. Sounds funny, but it wasn't, not really. The poor bastard wore earmuffs to the bathroom.

Eugene killed himself. A lot of vets were doing it back then; bodies left the sanitarium with the regularity of laundry sacks. Nearly cut his head off with a can opener. Tore his jugular open, bled out on the cold tiles of his room. A dull fucking can opener. Vietnam gave us that, at least: the ability to perform the unthinkable…

Twenty years later I'm sitting in room 217 of the *Lucky Sevens* motel in Las Vegas, Nevada. The name is a misnomer: anyone with even a shred of luck wouldn't be reduced to flopping in this shithole. Railcars rattle by outside my window, Sin City washouts hopping boxcars down to California, hoping their luck will turn with a change of scenery. I pity their misplaced optimism.

The telephone is ringing.

The room is a shoebox—cigarette burns in the carpet, mildew in the shitter, mattress smelling like roach powder and stale piss. Outside it's a real skid row district, human wreckage shambling around, last retreat before they die.

The fucking phone ringing, ringing, *ringing.*

"What?"

"It's Len. Getting a game together. You in?"

The oh-so-familiar lightning bolt of anticipation zigzags down my spine.

"Where at?"

"Woodlawn."

"What—the fucking boneyard?"

"Problem?"

"It's creepy. Playing cards in a cemetery—who does that?"

"Archie the Mongoose works there, sweeping up, polishing coffins, stealing gold fillings out of stiffs' mouths—hell, I don't know. Good a place as any. Real ambiance." Len's sun-drenched drawl mangles the word: *aayym-bee-yaance.*

"What are the stakes?"

"Whatever you got."

"I'm tight."

"You're always tight. Regular duck's ass."

"Listen, I'm tight and I got outstanding markers all over town—"

"Cry me a fucking river. Listen, Pokerface: you in, or do I cross you off my list?"

"Don't call me that."

"What?"

"Pokerface. Don't."

"You're right, I shouldn't. You don't *deserve* that name. Why don't you hang up this phone, walk the fifty yards to the railroad, hop the next boxcar? Because you've crapped out, pal. Lost the eye of the tiger."

I tell myself I won't let him get to me, but Len is the consummate psychological acupuncturist, always knowing where to stick the needles.

"You should leave town, Pokerface. You've been busted."

Prick goes the needle.

"Make tracks while you've still got a shred of dignity."

Prick.

"You're so over-the-hill you can't even see the hill you're over anymore."

The guy's such a fucking *prick.*

Finally I say, "What time?"

"An hour."

"See you if I see you."

We both know I'll be there.

The bathroom mirror is smeared with hot-pink nail polish. I use a straight razor to shave the hairs stubbling the gouge in my skull. Once, in a fit of blind depression, I bought a softball to see if it would fit into the divot. It did. My cranial prosthetic rests on the toilet seat. It's non-allergenic ballistic silicone (Sim-Skin™), molded to match the contours of my face. A glass eye stares from between milky folds of rubber. A five-hour operation bolted clips onto my skull which lock the prosthetic in place. I comb my hair forward, black locks descending to the tip of my nose, do my best to pass as a human being.

I've got one-thousand dollars in the back pocket of my Wranglers. A final grub stake. I know what I *should* do: walk to the bus station and catch a Greyhound to somewhere, anywhere, put as many miles between me and Paradise Valley as possible. But I won't. Gambling is a disease, same as malaria or polio or cancer, except the symptoms manifest themselves in your mind instead of your body. I tuck my only real possession—a nickel-plated Cobray M-11—into my waistband before hitting the bricks.

I catch the bus at the corner of Phoebe Drive and Arville Street, heading uptown. The bus threads a meandering path up the Strip. A pack of teens breakdance on the corner of Oakley and Bonita, Converse high-tops beating a tattoo on a flattened cardboard box with Paul Hardcastle's anti-Vietnam anthem "19" pounding from a boom-box: *And the soldier was nineteen, nineteen; ni-ni-ni-ni-ni-ni-nineteen, nineteen...*

An aging showgirl with massive tits boards at the Tropicana. Viet women don't have big tits. Diet and racial tendencies, I guess. Never seen anything bigger than token nubs and I am reminded of a time...

...three months in-country and the unit on a two-day furlough. We spent the night in a village near Quy Nhon, a thatched hut trafficking in Mekong and seasoned whores. The women were hideous, faces like rotted bees nests, but a ground-pounder from 17th Recon named Quillen was horny enough to screw a knothole.

He took one of them out back and fucked her in a pile of drying bamboo. Quillen was so short he could've parachuted off a dime, and Section-8 to boot: when he came, he clamped his teeth over the whore's nipple and chewed it off. She screamed and struggled but Quillen pinned her down and spat the nipple in her face.

"Fucking bitches!" he screamed. "We're here to save you from your miserable existence and you cunts won't even throw some free gash our way!"

A child, maybe eight years old, ran out and started winging punches at Quillen. The whore's son, we figured. The kid's mouth was stuffed with something; he opened his mouth and I saw the blasting cap wedged between his teeth. Then Quillen punched him, an uppercut to the jaw, and the kid's head exploded, fragments of skull and teeth tearing Quillen's face and chest to ribbons.

None of us liked Quillen, but Zippo razed the village on principle…

…I get off the bus at Owens Avenue, two blocks from Woodlawn. To the east is Harte Park, where the bullet-riddled bodies of Bugsy Siegel's rivals are pushing daisies. To the west is Valley Hospital, its wards choked with attempted suicides, strung-out addicts, alkies. I know this city with clinical familiarity. I suspect many prisoners share a similar desire to know the exact dimensions of their cells.

Woodlawn's quiet. I walk between rows of tombstones adorned with wilted flowers and corroded flag holders. Six feet beneath me, the dead are laid out in a matrix as organized as any urban city grid. Boneyard Metropolis, surviving population: zero.

Len greets me at the main entrance. We walk down a red-carpeted hallway, past capsule crypts stacked five-high, skyscrapers of the deceased. I scan brass nameplates for a familiar name, a celebrity or sports hero. Len opens an oak door marked PRIVATE and ushers me inside.

"You got to be shitting me."

In the foreground, four men ring a stainless steel operating table. An Aftercare embalming machine emits a dull mechanic hiss pumping formaldehyde into the carotid artery of a shrouded cadaver. Wiry strands of dead, yellow-streaked hair spill from under the white sheet. The feet are uncovered: gnarled arthritic toes, waxy untrimmed nails. A Plano tackle box sits beside the corpse's head, its shelves unfurled stair-like, stocked with rouge and lipstick, mascara and eyeliner pencils, blush, foundation mask.

I'm somewhat sickened to note this is *not* the strangest place I've played cards.

I scan the table. Two faces I recognize: Archie "Mongoose" Moore, permanent detox case with the loose face of a stroke victim; Ezzard-somebody-or-other, jet-black paintbrush moustache, used to play a doctor on a daytime soap. Neither can play to save their lives:

Archie has so many tells his eyes may as well be mirrors reflecting the cards, while Ezzard blows those soap royalties chasing busted straights and phantom flushes. The other two are unknowns. Sitting directly to my left is a fat-necked, crewcut bulldog. He's wearing an olive-green cableknit sweater with rectangular shoulder patches. His face is thick, with heavy supraorbital ridges canopying small black eyes, and his grey-edged teeth are slightly bucked. The other guy is the bulldog's mirror opposite: a blade-shouldered wisp with features sharp as the creases in a Marine sergeant's dress utilities. The breast pocket of his spotless lab coat is crammed with combs, toothbrushes, and tweezers. His eyes are prune-pits behind thick, square glasses that might resemble ice cubes were it not for the accretion of dust and eye-grit.

"You already know Ezzard and Archie," Len says, taking the seat to my right, "and this is Rocky," nodding at the bulldog, "and George," nod to the rake. "George is the head mortician. Dealer fee's twenty."

I peel a twenty off my wad, which Len palms with the deft sleight-handedness of a sideshow magician. Archie's trembling like a three-toed lady: anticipation or the DT's? I can't tell. The mortician scrapes gunk from beneath his fingernails with a trocar needle.

Len shuffles a deck of Bees and runs down the game: "Straight Five Texas Stud, boys, nothing wild but the players. Bets on the Flop, Turn, and River. Ante's twenty bucks; no max, no min. Rock and roll."

Opening hand: my hole card's an ace and a three, diamonds; the ace is solid if I can find it a date. The Flop is a six, also diamonds. I raise fifty, driving George and Ezzard out. Rocky raises fifty on my fifty. I call. The Turn card is the one-eyed jack of hearts. Fuck. In for one-forty, my flush busted, and unless I pair up I'll be left ace-high and dry. Quick tabulation: three in fifty-two = a 6.98% chance of snagging an ace.

I drop a hundred, hoping to scare Rocky off. The bulldog matches and tosses another hundred. I should fold but instead call. Five-forty in the pot and me holding a handful of scattered shit!

"Down and dirty," Len says.

The River is the ace of clubs. *Fuckin A.* I bet two-hundred, avoiding Rocky's eyes, my body language screaming bluff. Rocky bites hard: two-hundred plus one-fifty, back at me. I goose the pot to twelve-forty and call.

"So what're you packing, kid?" Rocky says.

Spin my ace onto the table.

"Fuck me Frieda," says Rocky. "Rake it." He doesn't show his cards, and doesn't need to: he caught a high face pair, kings or jacks, off the deal. Kept waiting on trips that never materialized and ended up hamstrung with the second-best hand.

I'm up big on my first hand. I should cash in and hightail it. But if I did intelligent things like that, I wouldn't be in this position. I ante up.

Rounds pass, money changing hands only to boomerang back. I watch the other players on the Q.T. Archie's eyes light up brighter than phosphorous flares whenever he snags a sweet holeshot, and Ezzard is plagued by betraying tics: nose scratches, moustache tugs, brow furrows. Rocky plays like a riverboat gambler, bluffing heavy to smokescreen weak cards. The mortician's a tough read: he's lost as many hands as he's won, but his wins are big and he often folds on the Turn if he doesn't get what he needs.

I catch a cold string of rags, mismatched twos and fours, busted straights waiting to happen. I'm folding off the draw, surrendering the ante. My stack's deflating like a tire with a slow leak. I'm down to my initial grubstake when I catch the dream holeshot: red aces, diamonds and hearts.

Betting opens to me. I toss in thirty, Ezzard folds, Rocky gooses to fifty, Archie chases it to seventy-five, George calls. Flop's the king of clubs: no help, no harm. I open with fifty, Rocky ups to seventy, Archie matches with a look that says he's throwing good coin after bad, the mortician calls.

Six-sixty in the pot and the Turn's the king of diamonds. Now everyone's got a high face pair—but I've got two *dynamite* pairs. A brief scan tells me Archie's set to fold but Rocky's still a gamer. I bet a hundred, knowing Archie's tapped but hoping to buffalo Rocky, and maybe George, into throwing down. Rocky, prototypical dick-swinger, chases the ante to one-fifty. Archie folds. The mortician lays his cards face-down and looks ready to follow suit but, with a sideways look at Len, matches at one-fifty.

Len says, "Down and dirty, gentlemen."

The River is the ace of spades. I've caught the strongest possible full house, aces and kings. The lock. The nuts. I pour another shot of C.C.—hands shaking, stop shaking, *stop*—touch my thumbtips together to form a plow with my palms, and push all my chips into the pot.

"What the hell. It's getting late."

Rocky consults his meager stack and must admit his finances are not the equal of his bravado. "I'm out," he says in disgust.

It's me and the mortician. My guess is he's holding the final ace, giving him a knockout double pair, but not enough to sink my full boat. He lifts the edges of his cards, flattened to the table under his left hand, as if expecting them to have changed since the last consultation. Then, with careful, precise movements, he stacks his chips in the pot.

"Yes," he says, "it is getting late."

The mortician's stake outclasses mine by over three-hundred dollars. I fish the pistol from my waistband. "The piece is worth a thou."

"Pokerface—" Len starts.

"Don't call me that."

"Fine, *Neil*. Brand new that gun wasn't worth a thou."

"It's reliable," I counter. "Shoots straight."

"I don't need a gun," the mortician says.

"Who made it," Rocky says, "the Krauts?"

Len says, "It's worth three bills at this table."

"Was it the Ko–*reens*? Liable to shoot your pecker off with one of those."

"I already *have* a gun. A B.B.-gun. It's a Daisy."

"It's settled," Len says. "Gun's worth three bills."

"Fine," I say, flipping my aces and reaching to rake the pot…

…until the mortician turns over his pocket kings.

Archie and Ezzard say "Bad beat" simultaneously. Rocky sucks air through his teeth. I can't draw air into my lungs.

"Four kings beats a full house." Len shrugs expansively, as though to suggest the karmic absurdity of it all. "You can't win every day, Pokerface. Otherwise it'd be no fun when you did."

The chips and cards shimmer out of focus, clean edges disintegrating, colors blurring. I reach for the gun. It's suddenly very important—*crucial*—I hold it.

"What are you doing?" Len says.

I find myself backing out a door. Not the door I entered: this one flimsier, unvarnished pressboard rather than oak. The others follow me into a dimly-lit hallway.

"Hey," the mortician says. "Hey."

The hallway empties into a coffin showroom. In the muddy light I glimpse caskets resting on crushed-velvet catafalques. Pachabel's "Canon in D" pipes in through recessed speakers. Each casket is affixed with a nametag: *Sweet Hereafter*, *Heavenly Chariot*, *Eternal Bliss*.

"Give the man his gun, Neil."

Rocky says, "Nobody likes a sore loser, fella."

I stumble and grab hold of an *Everlasting Salvation* to avoid horizontality. The mortician strides forward, his spindle neck cabled with veins.

"I can't abide welshers."

"You don't need another gun," I remind him.

The mortician removes his glasses. His eyes look like pressed raisins. "It's a matter of principle."

I am fully aware that, if it came down to it, I could kill every man in this room. The gun's got a nine cartridge clip—two slugs for every player, tack on a buckwheat for Len. Not that I'd do it, you understand, but I *could*. These guys see me as a one-eyed washout eaten up by Vegas, and a poor loser to boot...and they're right. But, time was, I ran with the best of the best. Time was, I ran with the Magnificent Seven.

I tuck the pistol into my pants and fix the undertaker with a look meant to freeze the piss in his bladder to ice-cubes. "Here it is," I drawl. "You want it, come get it."

"Terrible sportsmanship." The mortician removes combs, tweezers, and toothbrushes from his pocket, then rolls up his sleeves. "Just...*appalling*."

He comes to get his gun.

The little mortician dances toward me on sneaky feet and loops a tight hook into my bread basket. He feints a right hand and executes the Fitzsimmons' shift, shoes kicking static sparks on the thick scarlet carpeting, popping a short uppercut that catches me on the chinbone. They're not powerful shots but I don't protect myself. I fall flat on my ass. White noise fills my skull. He grabs my shirt, hauls me to my feet, throws me against a *Celestial Conveyance*. I bounce off the heavy wooden coffin and go down. My prosthesis is jarred loose and rolls under a cherrywood casket.

The mortician jumps on me swinging. I get my hands up and catch most of it on my arms and shoulders until he flags. My face, which elicits either disgust or pity in most people, doesn't seem to faze him at all, which I find strangely comforting. I shove him off and stagger away. He finds his second wind and comes at me, lab coat billowing in wings: an albino moth. He grabs me again and drags me to a *Pleasant Slumberer*, pushes me in headfirst. I kick feebly, catching him in the legs and chest, but he's wiry and relentless. He stuffs me down into the innerspring mattress; plush sateen presses against my cheek. He tries to lower the lid but I keep a foot on the edge so it can't be closed and latched.

"Here!" I slip the pistol through the gap. "It's yours!"

The mortician lets up immediately. "Hey, now, that's the spirit." He raises the casket lid but I don't get out. I peek over the coffin lip and watch Len and the others head back to the embalming room. Rocky says, "That was just...*sad*." I cross my arms over my chest and let my head sink into the silk pillow. Well, it's nicer than a lot of places I've flopped.

After awhile I get out. I retrieve my prosthesis and wander around until I find the front doors, knocking over a few urns along the way.

Two hours after entering the mortuary I'm back outside. Nothing seems to have changed—the sun's in the same position, a disc of brimstone pinned to the sky above Bob Stupak's Space Needle. I don't even have bus fare. I trudge southwards.

Three hours later, I'm back in my room at the *Lucky Sevens*. I haven't worn any sunscreen, and my face and arms are sunburned beet-red. I don't feel a thing. Someone once told me the sense of touch was easily the most underrated of the five senses. But, for this brief moment, I'm grateful I can't feel.

A knock on the door.

"Yeah?"

"It's the manager. You Paris?"

"Yeah."

"Letter for you."

"Slide it under the door."

The envelope is stained and smudged, forwarded from the various hotels and motels I've occupied during my slide. It's a miracle I got it—or else someone had a vested interest in making sure I got it.

The first thing to catch my eye is the unsigned check.

One five and four zeroes in a neat little row...

Randy "Answer" Blondeau—Information Extraction
New York, NY.
November 30, 1987. 12:05 p.m.

I rack my first fare of the day at 54th and Lex when two yuppie broads flag me down outside Barney's. They're wearing identical cream silk blouses, tweed skirts—one pleated, one not—and black satin pumps, holding Tab colas in manicured hands. Their hair is shoulder-length and dyed the same retina-searing platinum blonde. Their tits are a surgically-augmented 36C, flashy but not overstated, the size preferred by image-conscious Wall Streeters. Their legs are tanned and toned from personal training sessions, arms baby's-ass smooth from seaweed wraps. They smell like a cosmetics counter: papaya-scented shampoo and sandalwood skin astringent, lemon-grass deep-pore cleanser and Q.T. Instatan bronzing lotion. The scent of them fills the cab, an invisible yet deeply-textured odor.

They give me a fucking headache.

"Where to, ladies?"

One of them gives an address in an upscale section of Greenwich Village. She repeats the address three times, perhaps because she believes I am, or cabbies in general are, retarded.

"Vanessa darling," one of the doppelgangers says once we're moving, "where *are* we going tonight?"

"Brice promised a reservation at Slander—"

"Benjamin Cullen's new restaurant?"

"The very same, Vanessa."

Oh, Christ. They're *both* named Vanessa?

"Have you tried the marlin—the marlin and squab chili?"

"I can't remember." Vanessa plucks a white pill from a Gucci gazelleskin purse and swallows it with a sip of Tab.

"Oh you *must* try it. And the tuna carpaccio? To *die* for."

"People have died for less," Reflecting the red marquee lights of the Winter Garden Theater, the woman's eyes appear to be filled with blood. I unroll my window, beckoning the din of honking horns and squealing tires, jackhammers and surging foot traffic to drown out their voices. It strikes me with a poignancy verging on despair that these women are the end product of our American Dream, the American aristocracy: private schools, Ivy League universities, summer houses in the Hamptons or Martha's Vineyard, vacation villas in Aspen and Monte Carlo. Their husbands are lawyers or stock brokers with seven-figure salaries, their lives a procession of private soirées and exclusive nightclubs and benefit dinners for causes they care nothing about. Their husbands will fuck blonde, big-titted secretaries while they have loveless affairs with tanned masseuses, everyone dining on Waldorf salad and yellowtail sashimi and sun-dried tomatoes. Their existence is that of goldfish in a crystal bowl: the outside world, a world of discount superstores and homeless people and welfare mothers is as remote and unbelievable to them as elves or Chewbacca or Captain Lou Albano or—

"—those panelists on Geraldo Riviera simply *must* be paid performers!" Vanessa squeals. "Yesterday's topic was *Men Living as Women*. You should've *seen*—hairy-knuckled men wearing lavender sundresses, feet stuffed into stiletto heels. Not a designer label in sight!"

It was the American Dream that took me to Vietnam. Uncle Sam wanted Victor Charlie to be just like him, to wear suits and eat cheeseburgers and drive a Chevy. In October 1966, a military Jeep dropped me off at a training facility outside Corpus Christi. It was there my particular…*skills*…were revealed. I was transferred to Duc Phong, fifty miles northeast of Saigon, where I joined the Mobile Guerilla Force, detachment A-303, Blackjack unit. It was my pleasure to serve.

"Ohh, I absolutely *adore* this song," Vanessa says. The dial's tuned to WNYX and "That's All" by Genesis is playing. Vanessa raps on the Plexiglass barrier like a spoiled kid trying to get the attention of a zoo animal. "Turn this up," she commands. To Vanessa: "Phil Collins is *sooo* brilliant. I would have his love child." To me: "High*er*."

I know people in this city. Bad people. I know a man with a drill and an axe and a bottle of acid. I could give this man my passenger's addresses and this man would pay them a visit—maybe not tonight or tomorrow, maybe not for years, but he *would* come. This man would cut their arms off and stab their eyes out and hack a trench down the center of their faces until the pressure forced sections of their brains, dull grey and glistening, through the wounds. The knowledge of this man's existence prevents me from retrieving the silenced .22 Kirikkale pistol from under my seat, jamming it through one of the quarter-sized perforations, and painting the backseat yuppie-red.

That, and the steam-cleaning bill.

"That's All" is followed by "Workin' For a Living" by Huey Lewis and the News. Vanessa holds something in her lap that I mistake for a balled-up Kleenex until it yips and I realize, with dawning sadness, it's a dog: papery, vein-shot ears and black marble eyes that seem on the verge of popping from its skull. My gaze locks with its through the rearview mirror and, in an unprecedented canine-human mindmeld, we simultaneously acknowledge the utter frivolity of its existence. It yips again—token protest?—and Vanessa soothes, "Shhh, Tootsie, shhh." I pity the thing: it's the latest *pet-du-jour* that, like the chinchillas and chows and Shar Peis and Abyssinian cats before it, will be tossed aside in favor of the next treat-of-the-week. I once picked up a lady outside Bloomingdale's who'd slung a live ferret around her shoulders and the sight triggered the memory of…

…*Alex "Slash" Trimball, twenty-three years old, walking away from the blazing village of Bu Von Kon with the flayed corpse of a Viet girl draped around his shoulders. The village was in flames, the air rich with burning bamboo and burning palm leaves and burning…other things. The girl's skinless body shimmered, blood-glazed tissue reflecting firelight the way moon rays reflect off a placid pond's surface. "What do you think?" Trimball asked. He shrugged; the tiny body flapped bonelessly. "Keen… fashion sense," I said. Trimball was a sharecropper from Iowa. Devout Methodist. Father of four. He shaved a ribbon of muscle off the girl's thigh with the detached air of a man whittling wood. The jungle's like that: it gets inside you, under your skin and into your bloodstream, plants roots in your heart and mind and soul. You surrender to its madness as a matter of basic survival…*

…I drop the Vanessas off at a brownstone on the corner of Riverside and Eighty-first. One of them pokes a ten-spot through the window to cover a nine-eighty fare. The two of them perform an intricate farewell ceremony: they clasp hands, bend at the knees, air-kiss, then produce identical daytimers to plan their next excursion. Feels like I'm watching a wildlife documentary: *Inane Rituals of the Manhattan Socialite.*

The CB squelches: "*Need an answer...need an answer man...*"

I switch to a safe band. "Go."

"*Got a hardcase. Real John Dillinger-type.*"

"Sunchasers. Thirty minutes."

I cut up Fifty-Seventh and hang a left on Fifth. Sunchasers is the newest high-society phenomenon: the tanning salon. Some poor yuppie had to cancel a trip to Cancun? No problem. Fifteen minutes on a tanning bed, bombarded with 2,500-watts of ultraviolet light, he's a dead ringer for George Hamilton. Sunchasers is owned by Marco Sorbetti, an old-school Moustache Pete and current Capo of the Westside Outfit. It's a front: drugs, guns, and stolen merchandise are hustled out the back. Half the beds aren't even plugged in. It's the most obvious front I've ever seen—it's in *Harlem.*

Who the fuck needs a tan in Harlem?

How many yups are trekking to the ghetto for a tan?

I park two blocks away and retrieve my black bag from the spare tire well. Stopping at a bodega to buy some heavy-duty trash bags, I spot a bottle of Coppertone oil beside the magazine rack. Eying my purchases, the clerk jerks his head towards the snow-covered sidewalk.

"Bad time of the year to be seeking coloration."

"Taking a trip," I lie. "Milan."

Sunchasers is deserted. A dead Boston fern rests in the window, bookended by two dead cacti. Joe Fresco sits behind the reception desk. Joe is the antithesis of a tanning salon customer: fat and fortyish, pale as mozzarella and hairier than a silverback gorilla.

"Hey, Answer."

"Afternoon, Joe. Phil here?"

"Last door on the left."

I head down the hallway as Joe slouches to the door and, to the utter dismay of the sun-worshipping bag-ladies and winos shuffling around outside, turns the sign from "COME IN, WE'RE OPEN" to "SORRY, CLOSED".

Information and knowledge are two currencies that never go out of style. Those with knowledge excel. But one must know what to look for, how to get it, and its value in a free market economy. Most importantly, one must know the correct questions to ask. And the most effective ways of asking them.

I am in the information business. Information extraction, to put a fine point to it.

The tanning room walls, ceiling, and floor are draped in transparent plastic. The tanning bed is white with the dimensions of a coffin. A decal on the lid reads *TURBOTAN 2000*, and the tagline says: "From Bleached to Bronzed in 10 Minutes Flat!" A man is shackled to a chair in the middle of the room. Behind him stands Phillip Menna. Phil's a bottom-tier Outfit guy, your basic pavement-pounder. He tracks deadbeats and stoolies and anyone else who winds up on the Outfit blacklist—an unhealthy list to be on.

"Afternoon, Phil."

"How they hanging, Answer?"

"Low and lazy."

I set my toolbag next to the captive: early twenties, wearing black-pegged jeans and a torn Judas Priest t-shirt. He's working on some patchy facial hair, it's blooming in dark thatches at his chin and cheek hollows. I've seen him in the line-up at CBGB's, wolf-whistling at chicks outside pool halls and all-nite diners…I haven't seen him *exactly*, you understand, but he looks like a thousand other guys in this city—a *type*.

"Mister Punk Rock here, he and some friends boosted a van last week," Phil tells me. "A cube van full of bathroom fixtures. Now *under* that load, in a false bottom, are the fifty kees of uncut blow that was to be trucked into South Jersey." Phil cuffs the kid upside the head. "Now Mister Punk Rock *knows* where the truck is stashed— isn't that right, shit-for-brains?—but Mister Punk Rock ain't spilling."

I throw a switch on the tanning bed. A faint hum as a slit of purplish light slants between the top and bottom halves. Mister Punk Rock's eyes are a cloudy green. His face is a mask of defiance but around the edges, like a thin lip of light silhouetting a doorframe, I see fear.

"Got a name, kid?"

"Joey."

"Joey who?"

"Joey Ramone."

"Fucking wiseass," says Phil.

"Alright Joey," I say. "Why don't you tell us where the truck is? Then you can go back to shooting stick and chasing underage tail."

"Fuck you, old man."

I'd hoped he might be different. I keep hoping one of them will possess a sense of self-preservation. But no, he's like the rest. Probably been scrapping since childhood, punched and kicked, sliced a few times. Maybe his father used him as a punching bag and he's thinking *I know pain, tasted it, not afraid to taste it again.* He doesn't know pain. None of them do; not really. But I teach them.

I take a straight razor from my toolbag and cut the kid's shirt off. A rockstar body: underfed and sparrow-chested, arms so thin and skin nearly translucent. He wouldn't look out of place at a Nazi internment camp. Some animal, a wolf or fox, is tattooed over his heart. I hook my fingers inside his waistband to get some separation between denim and flesh, carefully slicing through his jeans and boxers.

"You gonna blow me, old man? This give you a thrill, you fucking flamer?"

I say, "Joey look pasty to you, Phil?"

"Fucker looks like he spent the night spooning with Dracula."

"So he could do with some color?"

"I'd say so."

The first Outfit job I pulled was on a sawbones named Dr. Joseph Weinstock. Doc Joe was selling prescription blanks to the Outfit: tablets of one-hundred blanks that runners would forge signatures on and offload at twenty, thirty bucks a pop. The speed freaks and nodders loved it and the scam netted Doc Joe a couple thou a month. But he got greedy and jacked the price. The Outfit balked. Doc Joe threatened to take his business to the Eastside. Bad move. They called me in.

A doctor's hands are his dinner ticket; something happens to his digits and he might as well burn his shingle because his practice is toast. By the time I walked into the soundproofed room, Doc Joe's fingers had been spread and u-clamped to a table. His mouth was duct-taped, nose smeared across half his face; would've looked just like strawberry jam if not for the white humps of cartilage.

"Put him out of business," Marco Sorbetti said.

Using a DeWalt variable-speed drill, I bored pinprick holes through Doc Joe's fingernails, tracing the milky rim of each cuticle. Then I filled an insulin needle with carbolic acid and injected it into the tender flesh under the enamel. There was this violent *fizzling*, like when baking soda and vinegar react, followed by the rank smell of emulsified flesh. Doc Joe's fingers withered, then blackened. It was like watching matchsticks burn down. He broke most of them spasming against the u-clamps. The Outfit was duly impressed. Now I'm their Answer.

I uncap the bottle of Coppertone and slather coconut-scented oil over Joey's chest and arms until his body gleams like a shellacked egg.

"This what you like, you fucking old faggot? Greasing dudes up?"

"Yes," I say softly. "This is how old faggots like me get off."

I crack the tanning bed open. Eight rows of ultraviolet bulbs reflect their heat on my skin. Phil uncuffs Joey and leads him over. The kid's smiling.

"Hey, I could use a tan. Bronze me up and I'll be off to Fantasy Island. *Hey, boss—de plane, de plane!*"

Phil sits Joey on the lip of the tanning bed. I kneel and look into his eyes. I need to make him realize who he is dealing with. I'm not a monster, not exactly, but I do not care about him and he needs to understand this. He needs to know I will hurt him mercilessly until he tells me what I need to know. If he does not, I'll watch him die.

"One more time: where's the truck?"

The kid yawns. "Let me catch some rays, old man."

Sometimes I think that if everyone did what's best for them, my occupation would become redundant. But it is my experience that people rarely act in their own best interests.

I lay Joey down, then close the lid and lock it with a pair of Swedge padlocks. The kid's singing "California Dreaming" by the Mama's & the Papas. Nice voice.

Phil produces a deck of Bikes and we play a few rounds of nickel poker. I'm left holding aces and queens when he trumps me with a full house; then he matches fives on the last card to beat my ace-high. Cards are a great way to kill time; Crosshairs and I used to play in the jungles of Vietnam until he lost his poker face.

Got his poker face *torn off* is more accurate, I suppose.

Ten minutes pass. I check on the kid. He's lobster-red but the pain hasn't registered on his nervous system yet. "Close the lid," he says. "Getting comfy."

I press my finger to his flesh. It leaves a dime-sized spot of whiteness. "Listen to me," I say. "Phil and I are going to lunch. When we get back, I guarantee you'll tell us where the truck is. So why don't you spill now, before I have to scrape you out of this thing with a spatula."

"Bring me back a meatball sub, why don't ya?"

I close and lock the lid.

We choose Honey's, a chicken-and-pizza joint three blocks east.

We sit at a bar strung with winking Christmas lights underneath a banner that reads *HAVE A MERRY HO-HO-HONEY'S CHRISTMAS* and order a jug of Schlitz.

Phil says, "So what's this wiseass gonna look like when we get back?"

I sip my beer, considering. "Well, once I put a hotdog into one of those turbo-model tanning beds. One hour cooked it. Two hours and it looked like beefy jerky. Three, shoe leather. After four it was pretty much ashes."

"Je-*sus*," Phil says. "Kid gonna be *able* to spill?"

"He'll talk."

By the time we finish our drinks and walk back to Sunchasers, nearly two hours have passed. Joe waves his hand in front of his face as we enter.

"Roasting a pig back there, Answer?"

"Something like that."

The odor intensifies as we get closer: a sickly-sweet mingling of cooked meat, blood, coconut. Phil covers his nose and mouth with an embroidered handkerchief.

"Smells like a fucking glue factory."

Blood seeps between the seams of the tanning bed, thin runners that look a little like warm tar. Feeble scratching noises coming from inside.

I unlock the lid and open it. The kid is in rough shape.

His body is stoplight red, except for the odd patch charred black. Joey is…*steaming*. It rises off him in savory plumes, as from the surface of a hot bath.

In his agony he opened his eyes. The ultraviolet light has blinded him: his eyes are completely bloodshot, the eyes of an albino. He thrashes mindlessly as I unplug the unit. His flesh is loose, more of a sheath than a part of him. It jiggles like the membrane that forms on unstirred soup.

"Christ," Phil says, staring at the writhing thing. "They sell these things? People lie in them…*willingly*?"

The kid holds his hand out to me like a frightened boy who's lost his mother. He is trying to say something but his lips are melted black, tongue a swollen bulb in his mouth. I take his hand and there is a moist tearing sound as the flesh of his fingers and wrist comes off, all in one piece, like a wash-glove. Underneath are long ropes of muscle and knobs of whiteness where his knuckles are exposed, the yellow half-moons of his fingernails. The shed skin is warm in my hand, slack and slippery.

"Oh, this is too much." Phil unbuttons his Soprani blazer and reaches for his piece, thinking about a mercy-killing. "This cannot *be*."

"No," I say quietly. "In a minute."

I kneel beside the kid. His face, what remains of it, is bloated and pocked with suppurating boils leaking pus of a shade I'd previously regarded as impossible for a human body to produce. I ask the same question I asked two hours ago, when there was still a chance the kid might've walked away breathing.

"Where is the truck.?"

"Ungh…ungh…uhhh…"

"Just tell me, kid. I'll make the whole world go away."

"U…u…u…sto…Storage…"

I turn to Phil. "U-Storage?"

"Yeah." Phil's skin is the color of unripe bananas. "Long-term storage joint down on the Hudson."

"We need anything else?"

"No. Christ, no."

With a strength I didn't think he possessed, the kid heaves himself up. A noise like wet leather tearing as the skin of his back and arms, which has melted to the glass, disconnects from his body. He makes a mewling noise, a strangled kitten, and I'm now staring at the flayed panorama of his back, these long red highways of sinew, glistening pockets of fat, a steaming landscape of tendon-knitted muscle that looks a little like rolled roast beef with the stark-white constellation of his vertebrae poking through at even intervals. He squawks and topples out of the unit. The flesh of his chest and legs and feet and head *stays* in the bed and now I'm staring at this mass of bloody meat squirming on the clear plastic tarp, this thrashing creature that was recently an arrogant boy. The veins of his throat resemble bluish tubes and strands of hair are plastered to the gummy redness of his face but there is only blackness, pitch blackness, at his pupils and mouth.

Phil moans and staggers back until his ass hits the doorknob. This he takes as an omen and clears out. Now it's just me and the flayed red thing on the floor.

And for some reason I wonder what might happen if I were to take this new, stripped-down version of Joey, and place him back in the tanning bed. Would he give birth to yet another, slightly smaller, slightly more agonized, slightly less human version of himself? How many layers does he possess? I think of a Russian doll, one inside another, smaller and smaller, until you reach the true center. And it bothers me, on a remote level, that only a nagging sense of professionalism prevents me from peeling Joey down to his very core.

Instead, I produce a silenced .22 Kirikkale from my toolbag. The desperate skinless thing struggles as I wrap a trash bag around its head and drill two slugs through the black plastic. The body spasms. Soupy red matter spills from the bag-holes. I roll the body up in the tarp. The plastic turns opaque with steam.

Phil waits with Joe in the reception area.

"You leave a mess?" Joe asks.

"A little bit. It's rolled up in the tarp."

Joe cocks a thumb at his partner. "What happened to my man here? Looks like he ate a boatload of bad clams."

"You okay?" I ask.

"Sure," Phil says, nodding a little too emphatically. "I—I seen worse."

Joe cocks an eyebrow. "Yeah?"

"Yeah," he says, but quietly and staring out at the street. "Yeah, sure."

Joe pulls an envelope from the desk drawer and hands it over. "Want to count it?"

"No need."

Joe smiles. "Be seeing you, Answer."

"Catch you on the flipside, Joe. Take care, Phil."

Phil doesn't say goodbye. His eyes don't leave the street.

I drive back to the hack rack. The dispatcher gives me a sour look—only ten bucks to show for a five-hour shift—but it only takes a sawbuck to turn his frown upside-down. My apartment's two blocks away. Walking home, I buy a warm pretzel from a street vendor, enjoying the salt and hot mustard. The sky is darkening and it looks like snow on the horizon. The slate-gray cloudbanks remind me of a recurring dream in which skulls rain down from the sky like hailstones, millions of gleaming skulls covering me in a clattering drift of smooth bone and teeth. What's most puzzling is that the dream does not disturb me, as I imagine it would most people. I often close my eyes hoping, with a sort of desperate longing, that it will come to me as I sleep.

There's an envelope in my mailbox with no return address.

A brief letter. A first-class airline ticket to Toronto, Canada.

An unsigned check for fifty thousand dollars.

Jerome "Oddy" Grant—Tragic Hero
Washington, DC.
November 30th, 1987. 12:05 p.m.

I haven't really slept for twenty years. I lie down, yes, but I don't sleep. I'm watching the door, the window, then back to the door. There's always something within reach: maybe a baseball bat, or a knife. I sleep with a gun under my pillow, another under my mattress, another in the drawer next to the bed. I get up at half-hour intervals to walk my perimeter. Every half hour on the *dot*. It's like that until the sun comes up. Then I can sleep for an hour or two.

"Got your walking sticks, son?"

My man Deacon hefts a pair of Webley Mark 6 hand-cannons capable of coldcocking a rhino. "Cocked, locked, and ready to rock, boss."

The Chevy van is faded kelly green, the sides painted with red letters spelling out *FLOWERS BY ALGERNON*. It idles across the street from a building with the words KEYBANK WASHINGTON spelled out in two-foot-high brass letters. The van is not filled with flowers, by Algernon or anyone else. It's jam-packed with five gun-toting brothers who've robbed close to thirty banks in fifteen states over the past five years.

We got my man Tiny, but that name's a misnomer because he's three-hundred pounds of chocolate thunder toting a Mossburg pump. We got Deacon, ex-Marine Corps demolitions expert. We got Dade, a solid soldier and strong-arm expert who's gotten a bit squirrely these last few jobs. We got Malik the wheelman, a cat who makes this

Chevy walk and talk. Last we got yours truly, Oddy, old hand and unquestioned leader.

I say, "Suit up."

We don masks. Tiny, Deacon, Dade, Malik, and Oddy become Michael, Jermaine, Tito, Jackie, and Marlon: The Jackson Five. The latex mask reeks of stale sweat and adrenaline. The smell is narcotic, the only thing reminding me I'm alive.

"In and out in two," I say. "Any more and we'll be rubbing elbows with Dirty City's finest."

"Maybe I want to bag a few piggies," Dade says, oinking. "Soo-wee! Soo-wee!"

Squeezed around the cherrywood stock of a Kalashnikov assault rifle, I notice Dade's hands are trembling. Is it fear or anticipation or plain old batshit-craziness? Can't tell. Not an encouraging sign.

"In and out in two," I repeat. "No fuss, no muss."

Malik pulls a smooth U-turn across the boulevard and stops ten feet from the bank entrance. I pop the rear doors and we fan out, walking four abreast, a bad-ass chorus line waiting for the music to start. And the music *does* start, somewhere inside my head, and the song is "Rock Around the Clock" by Bill Haley and the Comets.

One-two-three o'clock, four o'clock ROCK…

I lead them through the revolving doors, Deacon and Tiny flanking, Dade pulling up the rear. The bank foyer is warm and faintly pine-scented, either from the disinfectant the cleaning staff uses or the massive Christmas tree erected beside the teller wickets.

A pair of pasty rent-a-cops lean against alabaster pillars, half-asleep. Five customers wait in line and three are being served; they're either old or female or both, not a cowboy amongst them. Three tellers, young and WASPish, two chicks and a fellow. Mr. Branch Manager sits off to the side, his office hemmed by red velvet ropes.

Tiny taps one of the rent-a-cops with the barrel of his shotgun. The drowsy son of a bitch stares up at one towering mountain of Tito Jackson and hands over his revolver rickety-tick. Dade disarms the second guard.

Five-six-seven o'clock, eight o'clock ROCK…

Tiny hustles the first guard over to join the second and withdraws to cover the entrance. Twenty-five seconds gone. So far everything's clockwork. Deacon springboards the counter, Webley drawn. The customers scream and the tellers pale. Deacon hands one of them a pillowcase and points to the cash drawers.

"Everybody be cool," I say. "Zip your lips and sit your asses down and everything's gonna be everything."

Twenty-four ass-cheeks hit the floor. I come around Mr. Branch Manager's desk, grab him by his tie—a Goofy-playing-golf motif—and jerk him to his feet.

"What's your name?"

"P-Puh-Paul."

"Okay, Paul, let me shake it down: you're going to take me back to the vault and fill this bag with twenties and fifties. You tuned in on my wavelength, cupcake?"

"Y-y-yes."

Paul is young and handsome, early thirties. Probably got a wall full of diplomas in a suburban brownstone, drives a Lincoln or a low-end Beamer, trophy wife and a kid away at boarding school. And now he's face-to-face with a posse of heavily-armed, highly-skilled Soultrain motherfuckers; poor Paul's living out every WASP's worst nightmare, live and in blinding Technicolor.

We're gonna ROCK...

Paul is working on the vault combination when I hear this awful *cracking* sound. I poke my head into the lobby to see one of the rent-a-cops clutching his hands to his face, blood geysering between his fingers. Dade stands over him, rifle butt dripping red.

"The fuck you doing?" Tiny says.

"Uncle salty here called me a nigger," says Dade.

Dade's lying. Guard's so piss-scared he wouldn't say shit if he had a mouthful.

"I don't give a diddlyfuck what he's jawing," I yell over. "Square your shit away."

AROUND...

Meanwhile Deacon's emptied the cash drawers. He conducts the tellers and customers over to the vault, where they will remain locked while we make our getaway. Paul forks stacks of twenties into a Hefty Bag as fast as his trembling fingers can manage.

"Bring the guards in," I say.

"You heard the man," Dade hollers at the guards. "Move your asses!"

The unharmed guard complies but the other one, he of the busted face, doesn't move. So Dade seizes a handful of hair and drags the man, thrashing and wailing, across the tiles. Tiny breaks from position to intercept.

"The *fuck* you doing?"

"Following orders," Dade says. His eyes read like a grim weather forecast: storm clouds gathering.

Tiny says, "Gonna kill him."

"Fucker called me a nigger! The fuck would you do?"

THE CLOCK...

They're chest-to-chest, Dade glaring up at Tiny. Forgotten behind them, the injured guard raises his pantleg and grabs something black and snub-nosed from a cheater holster. He has the hammer cocked and a bead drawn before I holler:

"*Gun!*"

KRA-THACK is the sound the pistol makes and *ka-chunk* is the sound the bullet makes flattening against Tiny's forehead. The peak of his skull shears off and his eyes roll back in their sockets. His finger spasms on the shotgun's trigger and the sound is deafening as buckshot tears his feet to shreds but it doesn't matter because he's dead, dead on his feet, dead on his stumps, fucking *dead*.

Dade swivels, AK riding his hip, and opens fire. The Kalishnakov kicks and the rent-a-cop's face disintegrates in a cloud of red.

...TONIGHT!

Screams fill the vault. Most of these folks have never heard gun-shots before and they're thinking WWIII has broken out in the foyer. I grab the Hefty Bag from Paul. Deacon smashes the emergency phone and slams the vault's door on thirteen very relieved faces.

Dade inserts another banana clip and racks the AK's bolt. His Converse hightops are coated in blood and chunks of someone, Tiny, rent-a-cop, I don't know who the fuck. He's Section-8, and maybe he's been that way for a while now. I should've seen he wasn't wired tight but I didn't and now we're wading through a bloodbath.

"Time to go," I say through gritted teeth.

The sidewalk is mercifully deserted. Maybe, just maybe, we're going to clear this tits-up. But no: we're halfway between the bank and the van when a police cruiser fishtails around the corner at Elm and Prescott.

Deacon drops into a shooter's stance and snaps off six shots. The first flattens the cruiser's front right tire, the third flattens the left, four, five and six punch through the grille. The cruiser skids to a standstill, steam boiling up from under the hood.

Perfect. The cruiser's disabled and nobody's hurt.

Dade erases all that.

He opens up with the Kalishnikov, sweeping the barrel side-to-side like a kid pissing in a snow bank. The cruiser's windshield implodes and the frame rocks—actually *rocks* back and forth, like a ragtop on Lover's Lane—as copperjackets tear through it. And I can make out two bodies jitterbugging in the front seat: maybe young cops, maybe old cops, maybe single cops, maybe married cops, but the only certainty is that they're *dead* cops, dead as disco, and the mindlessness of their deaths sickens me. Then the cruiser explodes, erupting into a furious flaming scrapheap that rains charred metal and smoking flesh onto the cold November tarmac.

I slam my hand down on the AK's barrel. Dade stares at me with empty eyes.

"Take me home, Oddy," he whispers. "Take me home."

"Yeah, Dade," I say. "Yeah, okay."

We pile into the van and pull away, leaving four funerals in our wake. I stare out the window at the flaming scalps of radial tire and charred metal and remember...

...The Magnificent Seven on Long Range Reconnaissance Patrol eighty klicks east of Saigon, walking a trail overlooking the South China Sea. Intel had reported the NVA was offloading three boatloads of weapons in a Mekong bay. Zippo scouted ahead and found the drop point as night fell.

We moved in. It was about ten o'clock at night. We saw people unloading long boxes we assumed were rifles. I gave the order to open up on them.

I remember the sound of wood splintering and things exploding and, like a deep-space transmission, screaming. People were running around the decks like headless chickens. A man was on fire, body an oily tower of red and black flame, and he grabbed someone else and soon they were both ablaze, fire pouring out of their mouths like flame-swallowers at the circus. I remember a man raising what could have been a rifle or a fishing pole, remember pulling the trigger and watching his face collapse into itself in a red spray, remember his features the split-second before the slug destroyed them, their flatly elegant symmetry.

Swift, silent, deadly.

Daylight came, and we discovered that we had killed a lot of fishermen and children. Intel had fucked up. I got on the blower to command. I was screaming into the handset while Tripwire knelt with this kid's body in his lap, a body with no head, and I was saying: "We got a royal fuck-up here, Colonel. Dead kids and dead fishermen and not one gun on board."

The Colonel said: "Don't worry. It'll spin, Sergeant. We got body count."

So I turned to my unit and said, "Don't worry about it. Everything's fine," because that's what I was getting from upstairs. But we had dead bodies draining over bullet-riddled gunnels, bodies of children and eels and monkfish baking together in the bank's red sands so everything was most definitely not fine, top brass could spin that motherfucker to the moon but the stink was going to linger.

They gave us all the Combat Infantry Badge for that action. There was an award ceremony, the seven of us standing on a makeshift platform with medals stuck on our chests for killing innocent civilians. I knew in my heart it was wrong. But we were at war and different rules applied...

...Malik cuts onto the freeway before turning back on us like an exasperated parent and asking, "What the fuck happened in there?"

"Dade happened," Deacon says. "Dade happened *all over* that motherfucker."

"Where's Tiny?"

"Dead," I say. "Got his shit scattered by some rent-a-cop packing a pistol should've been taken off him three seconds after we cleared the front doors—"

"Don't you fucking pin Tiny's death on me—"

"That guard was your cover!" Deacon shouts at Dade. "Why the hell didn't you pat him down? Armed robbery 101, mother*fuck*!"

Malik pulls into the fast lane. Five or six squad cars, sirens wailing, speed by in the opposite lane. Between us, spilled across the van's floor panels, are stacks and stacks of bills.

"And what about the cops?" Deacon continues. "Why'd you kill *them*?"

"Shitcan the questions," I say. "Not here, not now. People are dead, Tiny is dead, and all we can do is deal." To Dade: "This is the end of the line for you. No more jobs. Take your cut and run, son. Find some sunny somewhere and square your shit away."

"I'm okay, boss," Dade says.

"No, Dade," I say, placing a hand on his shoulder, feeling him shiver. "You're not okay. You need help. I wish I could help you myself, but I can't."

"My shit's hardwired, Oddy. I'm watertight."

"You're fucking bugshit," Deacon spits. "Killing people for no goddamn reason."

"Say that again." Dade's voice is barely audible above the wind whistling through the van's seams. "Just one…more…time."

"What the fuck's going on back there?" Malik asks.

"Not a goddamn thing," I say. "Everything's cool and the gang, isn't that right?"

But Deacon blows any good vibes out of the water when he says, "You heard me: you're bugshit. Section-*fucking*-8."

"Take that back," Dade whispers. "Take it back or I'll shoot you in the face."

Deacon leans forward until his face is inches from Dade's. "Go…*fuck*."

And now I know, now I am absolutely certain, call me Kreskin because I am fucking positive this is going to end badly.

Everything happens with the rapidity of fireworks going off. Dade reaches inside his jacket for the .38 we all know is there. Deacon claws at his waistband to free a Webley but it's jammed, the cylinder won't clear, and now Dade's got the drop.

These are the decisions you've got to make as a leader. Who stays and who goes. I don't relish them. I wish it didn't have to be like this. But it is, and all I can do is make the decision, who lives and who dies, and live with it.

These are the choices that made me old when I was young.

I pull my .45 Chief's Special from a Bianchi shoulder holster and extend to Dade the same mercy I'd offer a rabid dog.

BOOM.

The middle of Dade's face explodes inward, the bullet blowing Dade's teeth out the back of his skull, molars and canines pinging off sheet metal and there's just this hole, this stark emptiness where Dade's face used to be and the blowback throws his body against the rear doors which buckle outwards like a bomb-bay and then Dade's body is tumbling across the highway, a dead dusky tumbleweed.

"Jesus!" Malik screams, cupping a hand over his ear. "Oddy, what the hell—?"

"Just drive, son," I say. "Get us to that parking lot."

Nobody says much as we pull into a *Pay-n-Park* lot and transfer the cash to a VW Minibus we've stashed there for days. Deacon sets an incendiary charge that'll gut the Chevy van, torching any evidence. We drive in silence to a motel on DC's outskirts.

The total haul, tills and vault, is $310,580. Nearly eighty grand a head, split four ways. Tiny's got a wife and kid in Sioux Falls; Malik promises to get Tiny's cut to his widow.

"This wasn't the way it was supposed to end," Malik says as I hand him his split.

"No, it wasn't. But we don't have script approval, son. Sometimes things just end the way they end."

Malik opens the door. We shake hands, clap one another on the back, and fall into a half-embrace that is the closest thing to tenderness men like us can achieve. He stares towards the shrouded DC skyline, then at the unbroken stretch of blacktop leading in the opposite direction. He knows, as I know, there is nothing for us in either direction.

"I'd go over the top with you anytime, Oddy," he says. "My life in your hands."

He leaves. Deacon is sitting on the bed.

"I shouldn't have said those things to Dade," he says. "Called him Section-8. Shouldn't have done that."

"Not really your fault," I say. "A man turns that way, well, there's not much any of us can do to save him."

"What happened?" Deacon asked. "How did he end up like that?"

I shrug. "As to Dade's particular story, I really don't know. All I know is that in Vietnam, soldiers were told to take all their pity, their mercy, their compassion and lock it away until it was no longer part of them. They were taught to fill that void with the emotions they needed to make it out alive: cruelty and hatred and rage. A soldier who did enough Tours became emotionless, you know? Became a creature of drives: eat, sleep, kill. Just a cog in The Big Green Machine. I've seen men like that, Deacon. They existed, and they weren't exactly human."

An early twilight hung suspended over the undeveloped land across the road, patches of dull orange burning between the trees. "I once read about something called an Act of Erasure. It's common in soldiers; they lose touch with reality, stop caring about living or dying. So a guy starts acting crazy, taking stupid risks, putting himself in harm's way when there's no need, even hurting the people he cares for. Trying to kill himself, in a roundabout way. That's what happened to Dade, I think. Same thing happened to my father in Big Two. They were good men. Weak maybe, but good men. It happens."

Deacon nods. "It's just, when he shot those cops…they were

harmless and he had to go fucking murder them? I mean, there's no…" he shakes his head violently. "Where's the fucking *sense* in that?"

I wrap a rubber band around a thick stack of bills and drop it on the bed.

"We're only human, Deke. We all got our breaking point. Why did Dade become like that? I honestly don't know. But humans are half-devil. Three-quarters, even."

We sit in silence for awhile. Then Deacon says, "You saved my life." He states it as a simple fact. "Saved my life and there's no way I can pay you back."

"Saved your life, took Dade's: all one and the same, son." I stare out the window, where a fine layer of snow blankets the landscape. "It's a hell of a thing."

"He had it coming."

"We all have it coming."

I shake Deacon's hand. "You're a good kid. That thing with Dade, don't let it eat at you. Nothing you or I or anyone could've done. Get out of here, now."

Back in A-303 Blackjack, my man Tripwire hung the nickname "Oddy" on me, short for Odysseus. And it's stupid, but over the years I began to see myself as the ancient Greek hero: *put your faith in me and I will lead you through the clashing rocks, deflect the Siren's song, lead you to a safe harbor. Give me your hand, trust in me, and I will take you home.* And up until today, I had.

Except that one time. That one time deep in the jungle, in the tiny village where skinned bodies hung and we fought a monster who killed two of my men and might have killed us all…

Stop. Best not to think of those times.

I take a cab to the Dale City bus terminal and catch a Greyhound to Pittsburgh. The miles peel away and I try to sleep but every time I close my eyes I see Dade as he looked after I shot him, Dade with a gaping pit where his face should've been. At a P.O. box in Pittsburgh, the closest thing to an address I lay claim to, I find an envelope containing a plane ticket, an unsigned check for fifty grand, and a letter:

Mr. Grant,

I have a business proposition for you. If you are interested, meet me at the bar of the Sheraton Hotel, downtown Toronto, on December 8th, at 5 o'clock. If and when you arrive, I will sign the check. Fifty-thousand dollars for a no-strings-attached meeting—interested?

Sincerely,
Anton Grosevoir

Tony "Tripwire" Walker—Auteur
Los Angeles, California.
November 30, 1987. 12:05 p.m.

We're filming in a beachfront bungalow in Malibu owned by a B-movie producer who's a fan of my stuff. This producer—a rickety old potbellied perv wearing a silk robe and yellow-lensed sunglasses—has spent the morning in a wicker chair overlooking the set, sipping Glenlivet and kneading his crotch like an infant who's recently discovered the pleasure principle.

The dick I hired for this flick—working title: *Butt-Blasted Nymphos*—is a midwestern bohunk named Chad or Thad or Brad. His screen credit will read "Rock Hardson" so his name's a moot point. He's twenty-two years old, six-foot-one, two-hundred pounds of grain-fed Nebraska farm muscle with defined delts, ripped pecs, absolutely *shredded* abs and, most importantly, a cock of equine proportion that seems to embarrass him.

The chick's name is Charity Chest but she sure isn't giving herself away: it took three grand to secure her platinum ringlets, collagen-pumped lips, and Hindenburg tits. She could be anywhere between thirty-five and fifty, nipped and tucked and smoothed out of all proportion by Hollywood's most persistent carrion crow, the plastic surgeon. Her "handler," a fey Latino whose only job appears to be keeping her stoned, is doing his duty: Charity's nostrils are frosted whiter than the rims of margarita glasses.

"We cued, Freddy?"

Frederico Achebe, my steadycam man, nods. Freddy's been with me since my first feature, *The Butt-Ripping Cocksman*. He stayed on through my sophomore efforts (*Snatches in Batches, Buttplug Blastoff, The Grapple Humping Gangbang*), my European (*Hirsute Hoes*), artsy (*Pygmalion Pussy*) and experimental (*Barnyard Follies*) periods. Frederico's gay as a French horn and I think the sexual detachment allows him to maintain a calm hand.

"Ready, Thad?"

"It's Chad, sir."

"Right. Ready?"

Chad's wearing a T-shirt that hugs every ridge of his torso, Levis so tight they make poetry of his ass and leave no doubt as to his religious convictions.

"Action."

He mounts the front steps and knocks on the heavy oak door. Charity answers wearing red silk panties and a push-up bra on the verge of collapsing under its unfair burden.

"Are you the handyman?"

"I am," Chad says, "and I hear you have a crack that needs to be…um, filled."

"Why yes, I do. Come in."

Charity leads Chad into the living room. It's an ivory oasis: white shag carpet, bleached calfskin sofa and loveseat, walls painted eggshell white and hung with paintings of snow-covered vistas. I'm concerned that Charity—whose skin tone roughly approximates meringue—will be invisible.

"So where's this crack?"

Charity doffs her panties with the practiced air of a magician performing an oft-repeated trick. Her pussy is outfitted with a racing stripe of downy blonde fuzz, the pornstar hairdo *du jour*.

"Can you plug it?"

"Lady, I've got just the right tool."

Cue bass guitar riff: *oom-chaka, oom-chaka, oom-chaka-lacka…*

What's that old wheeze about sons either becoming their fathers or the exact opposite of their fathers? Well, it holds true for me. My father was a Baptist minister who plied his faith in the remote reaches of Devil's Lake, North Dakota. *By the time I'm finished, they will change the name to Savior's Lake*, he'd say without a trace of irony. My father possessed a body naturally predisposed to fire and brimstone: tall and lean and angular, thin nose hooked like a raven's beak, blue eyes like crosshairs and a disturbing solidity, a sense he could weather any storm, continue on while others fell and died.

Thank God perserverance is about the only trait to clear the generation gap.

The human body disgusted my father. The muscle and sinew and tissue so prone to desiccation, the blood and bile and semen and other dreadful liquids that eventually soured or coagulated, bones that warped, skin that yellowed and wrinkled and lost elasticity...these natural changes revolted him. I'd catch him looking into the bathroom mirror, stretching the skin of his jowls taut and grimacing at the way it slackened around his long, bird-like neck. Sometimes he'd just sat and stared silently at his hands, the fingers twitching slightly, the hairs on the back of his wrist grey and hoary. My mother and I knew to avoid him at those times. This delirium carried over into the bedroom. In many ways it's a miracle I'm alive, since my father's distaste for sex was all-encompassing. I imagine he viewed my mother's privates with the same foreboding he'd accord a pagan ritual site: one wrong move and vengeful demons would swoop from the folds of her labia, roasting his eyes in their sockets.

One afternoon he'd returned early from a spiritual retreat to find my mother masturbating in her bedroom. He proceeded to lash her with an extension cord until her flesh was a roadmap of ugly purple and black welts that split open and bled onto the floorboards. When I came home after school she was huddled on the porch swing in a white sheet. The sheet was crisscrossed with bloodstains. I remember a gash running from her neck down beneath the sheet, the skin split open, puffed red at the edges. She stared at me—stared *through* me, it seemed—at the hilltop marking the perimeter of our property, as if she expected someone to come walking over the rise. When she spoke her voice was distant and toneless, like the automated telephone voice telling you you've dialed an out-of-service number.

"Go," she said. "As soon as you can. As soon as you're able. Just...*go*."

I wanted to rescue her. But all I could hope was to save myself.

I enlisted on October 7th, 1966. I was seventeen.

At a training compound near Corpus Christi, I discovered an ability that had long lain dormant: I was good at blowing shit up. Dynamite, C-4, cordite, gunpowder: these substances fascinated me. Feeling it in my hands, the destructive power contained within a few slender red sticks or a fist-sized lump of gray, oily plastique...mesmerizing. I even loved the names: Toe-Poppers, Bouncing Betties, M-40s, Willie Peters, Claymores. I was the fuckin' Albert Einstein of demolitions; an idiot savant. Top Brass transferred me to Camp Pendleton, where I underwent an intensive medic aide's course, and then to Duc Phong, a training compound fifty miles north of Saigon. There I became a member of A-303 Blackjack, a seven-man Black Ops unit.

After the madness of the Green Hell, I had no desire to return to Cold Lake. I wasn't sure I wanted to return stateside at all: there were rumors of vets being spat on by scraggly-haired, pot-smoking, guitar-strumming, flower-picking hippies—I was afraid I'd lose my cool, firebomb a Wavy Gravy concert. Instead I boozed myself from one Far-Eastern country to the next, crossing borders in a fogged-out haze, until I washed up, down and out, in a flophouse on Kho Phet road, Bangkok. One night, staggering back to my room drunk on Mekong, I found a pamphlet jammed under my door. *BIZZARRE SEX ACTS*, it promised. Intrigued, I went the very next night.

The venue's entrance was a scarred black door at the end of an alley smelling of piss and rotting vegetables. Behind the door was a low-ceilinged room with a stage in its center. Chairs lined the walls on all sides. Seated on those chairs were a parade of button-down executive types, all male, who wouldn't be caught dead in a place like this back home. But this was Thailand, a carnal candyland where any pleasure or depravity could be bought with cold, hard green. Thai women in sequined underwear circulated with trays of ice-cold Singha beer, lithe bodies weaving through a throng of desperate male flesh, contours molded lovingly in blacklight.

A young woman took the stage. Tall and slender and shockingly pale with crooked white teeth. A bullseye was painted on her pussy and thighs and lower abs and I was momentarily rocked by the memory of…

…Neil "Crosshairs" Paris, Blackjack's sniper, drawing a bead on the thing we'd found snarling and gibbering amidst a hanging garden of skinless Vietnamese bodies. Silhouetted by the glare of burning huts, the bullet-riddled corpses—glistening red, tendons and ligaments running in long twisting ribbons, large bluish veins threaded like nightcrawlers through a bed of soft tissue—spun lazily on copper-wire garrotes. Their shed skins pooled in dusky yellow puddles beneath blood-glazed feet. Then the thing turned to face us and its eyes, oh Christ those eyes, and its head bluntly misshapen, snouted, with the features of a boar or a horse or…

...a donkey was led onstage by a dwarf wearing a white satin codpiece. The donkey's head swayed side to side and its hooves clipclopped the floor. The woman cooed as her bestial suitor approached, fingering her bullseyed cunt which was, somewhat surprisingly, very wet.

The dwarf yoked the animal to a ring bolted onstage. It brayed sonorously, nostrils flared, eyes focused on the woman caressing its flanks.

I scanned the crowd. A man in a thousand-dollar Armani suit stroked his cock, a stain already darkening his slacks. Another guy straddled his chair, thrusting his crotch against the molded plastic seatback. They had the powerbroker look of men who wheeled and dealed with sums of money vaster than most would ever earn in a lifetime. Yet here they were, united in their desire to see a beautiful woman shagged by a donkey.

The gears started to mesh.

Two days after the show, I bartered my Silver Star for an Edelweiss 8mm film camera. I returned to the club and asked the owner if I could film the night's performance. He told me to fuck off. I offered him my Combat Infantry Badge. We had a deal.

The performance was a good one—the donkey blew a load that nearly tore the chick's head off. I placed ads in *Screw*, *Hustler*, a couple European sex rags, advertising:

BESTIAL SEX FILM
FROM THE FORBIDDEN EAST!

The response was overwhelming. Money orders flooded my P.O. box. I shipped the film—titled, appropriately but apathetically, *Woman Fucked by Donkey*—in plain paper packaging—which, as far as I'm concerned, is every bit as conspicuous as a package stamped "Deviant Pornography."

Soon afterward, I received my first request. It was written in a jittery hand on business letterhead with the company name scratched out:

> *Dear Sir,*
> *I am very much impressed with your film, "Woman Fucked by Donkey." It has provided me many moments of pleasure. I understand Thailand*

has many transsexuals—I believe you call them lady-boys? Could you film a beautiful ladyboy—blonde, elegant, big-breasted—being sodomized by a dog? A collie, preferably?

A price was quoted. Either the nutjob was filthy rich or held his fetish dear enough to drop his life savings on the thrill! I found a broken-down ladyboy named Keith who agreed to be buggered by a stray pooch for five-hundred baht and a bowl of sharkfin soup. I cleared a cool five grand on the deal.

Business boomed. I changed my ad to read:

FREELANCE ADULT FILMMAKER
WORKING OUT OF THAILAND.
NO PERVERSION TOO PERVERSE!
ALL FETISHES EXPLORED!

The proposals poured in:
Dear Sir,
...could you film two pregnant woman rubbing themselves with spawning carp?...
...men dressed as SS stormtroopers shitting into diapers?...
...a women dressed as Shirley Temple getting reamed with a broomstick?...
...a chorusline of men in shower shoes and bathing caps bug-gering each other?...
My answer was invariably the same:
Yessir, I can do that.
No problem, bucko.
You got it, Pontiac.
The money was great and the work steady, but I was beginning to suffer the Far East jitters: an overload of yellow skin, jabberwocky dialect, flayed cocker spaniels hanging in restaurant windows, the irrational fear that the next pussy I saw would run horizontally instead of vertically. I had to get back to the States. But I needed to go someplace where a man in my line of work could operate free of restrictions, somewhere I could blend among a colorful parade of freaks and weirdos and sycophants, a place so self-absorbed that my own down-and-dirty ventures wouldn't merit a second glance.
Only one city fit the bill: Tinseltown.

I returned in the Fall of 1975 and rented a bungalow off Encida Boulevard. I purchased time at a Burbank studio, adopted the director's name of "Cyril St. Cyr," and hung out my shingle as an adult film producer.

You reach a saturation point, of course. I've seen more cumshots than a veteran glory hole guzzler, heard more faked orgasms than an octogenarian billionaire with a trophy wife, smelled so much sex it's permeated my nostrils the way smoke will permeate a wool sweater. About the only thing that gives me a boner anymore is a hot shower, good Szechuan takeout, and a Lakers game on NBC. My job has become just that, with all the tedium, self-doubt, and borderline loathing felt by any beancounter trapped in any dead-end occupation.

"Give us the money shot, big guy!" I shout now, moments before Chad blows his load on Charity's jutting chest with a heifer-like grunt. I'm astonished—not pleasantly—when Chad's cock burps out a weak, thin, dismal stream of jizz. Semen does not so much spurt as stagger out of his heroically-proportioned cock, as if the long march has left his little soldiers exhausted. An eighty-year-old eunuch could've done better.

"Poor guy's a dribbler," Frederico whispers to me.

"Uhhh…that's a wrap, I guess."

The crew starts taking down the klieg lights, tripods, and tinting screens. Charity's pusher hands her a clean towel and she wipes Chad's deposit off her tits with a brisk swipe. The pervy old producer had freed his cock from his robe—it resembled a baby mouse, or, charitably, a shaved vole—and had been flogging it desperately up until Chad's less than stellar finale. Now he tucks the poor shriveled thing away and heads onto the balcony, shaking his head in dismay.

I congratulate everybody on a job well done, even Chad. Who am I to break his heart? As I'm climbing into my Jeep Cherokee, Charity sidles alongside and cadges a lift.

I drive down Mulhulland's twisting slope, aiming for Sunset Boulevard. The sky is darkening, only a few blue ashes of light to the west, over the Pacific. Charity's wired out of her mind, chirping on about the outrageous price of liposuction. Cyndi Lauper's "Time After Time" lilts out of the speakers.

I stare at the man who stares back at me in the rearview mirror. The man is thirty-nine years old, teetering on the verge of true middle age, buttery from years of liquid lunches. His hair is pinned back in a gray-streaked ponytail that he knows looks faggy but is a necessary evil in the industry. This man has spent so many years just happy to be alive, passed two decades trying to forget what he has seen in the dark jungles of Vietnam, spent half a lifetime struggling with the concrete knowledge that, no matter what filth fills his camera lens, he can always say, with terrifying sincerity: *I have seen worse.*

No family. No children. No ties. The man wonders how his life might have unfolded had he not enlisted. Would he have saved his mother from his father's tyranny? Enrolled in college? Earned a degree? Met a pretty young freshman, married her, house in the suburbs, two-and-a-half children, the prototypical American family? Was there ever a chance, however remote, that he might not be haunted by dreams in which the skinned limbs of faceless Vietnamese children burst through the black jungle soil, a million legs and fingers and toes swaying like wheat in a wind-whipped field?

Did that possibility even *exist*?

Charity's condo is off Sepulveda. By the time I drop her off she's gone through one vial of coke and is itching for another.

"Call me," she says, leaning over for a cheek-peck and crotch-squeeze, the traditional porn biz adieu. "I love fucking for you, Cyril."

It strikes me that, despite working on-and-off for nearly five years, we don't know each other's real names. Ten feet from her door, she pukes. Illuminated under the glare of arc-sodium security lights, she appears to have vomited white-flecked blood.

I drive up Mulholland into the Hollywood foothills, stopping near the summit of Mount Lee, a stone's throw from the Hollywood sign that Peg Entwhistle, a fading starlet, made infamous by jumping to her death off the fifty-foot high "H." This city will do that to you. Chew you up, spit you out. It's nothing personal. The town was here before you arrived and will remain long after you've gone. Its highways and byways, thoroughfares and side-streets, mansions and flop-houses are all part of a great, glittering illusion, an illusion that always promises but seldom delivers. The town does not care about you, whether you live or die. It is a dream factory.

And dreams—like nightmares—never die.

A Smith and Wesson .38 rests in my glove compartment, loaded with hollowpoint slugs. If anyone ever asked, I would tell them it is a precaution against the road-ragers plaguing the freeways.

Of course, that would be a lie.

The truth?

It's my fifty-foot high "H."

By the time I arrive home, early morning sunlight is throwing long embers over the horizon. I empty my mailbox and leaf through the envelopes.

Bill. Bill. Invoice.

Now what the hell's this?

War Zone D, South Vietnam
July 15th, 1967. 18:30 hours.

A-303 Blackjack had been on the hump for six hours. They carved a zigzagging path through the jungle, Oddy walking point. The landscape was post-apocalyptic: copses of trees shattered by Stinger missiles, hilltops blackened with napalm scars, the sickly-ripe smell of corpses left to rot on the jungle floor.

They waded across a fast-moving stream, firearms held at port arms. On the far shore, Tripwire shook a canister of chili powder along the banks to throw off the dogs. Zippo pulled a bottle of bug juice and squirted it on a plump leech stuck to the side of Crosshairs's throat. When he showed it to the sniper, Crosshairs recoiled in disgust. Zippo pulped the blood-fattened leech between his fingers and grinned.

About a klick past the stream, the unit came across a tiny hamlet. Most of it had burned down, the bamboo huts reduced to smoldering ash and char. The smoke from the burning hootches smelled like straw; it moved in patches across the village square, not thick, just a light, foggy rippling. The ground was stitched with bullet holes, small deep craters where the Cobra gunships had laid down long lines of fire.

An old man lay dead in the middle of the square. It looked as if he'd been carrying water: a length of bamboo with large pails on either side still hung around his shoulders. He lay on his back in the square, a ragged hole in his chest where the gunship's .50-caliber bullet ripped through. Flaming straw fell on his face, igniting his hair, scorching his face beyond recognition. The only noise came from the pig pen, where three or four piglets ran in mad, squealing circles. Slash went over and opened the pen's gate. The piglets tore off into the jungle.

The boy could've been thirteen, though maybe younger. He sat in front of a burned hut. He had black hair and brown skin. He was drawing strange patterns in the dirt: intersecting lines, concentric circles, odd looping scrolls.

"The hell's he doing?" Gunner said.

The boy didn't look at the men. His fingers continued to describe weird shapes and configurations in the loose red earth. The men searched the wreckage but there wasn't much to find. Zippo and Crosshairs dragged the burned man into some bushes and wrapped him in an old blanket. The boy drew more, his canvas spreading and growing; sometimes he smiled to himself, sometimes frowned.

"Why's he doing that?" Gunner said.

"It doesn't matter why, son," Oddy said. "He just is."

Answer stepped past the boy, into the burned hut. "In here," he said. The men went in and saw the bodies. An infant and an older woman and a younger woman. They were all badly burned and there must've been something wrong with the old woman's legs because she was still sitting. She must've sat all the while, even as the flames consumed her.

When the men dragged the bodies out, the boy kept drawing. In fact, he drew a bit quicker. He placed the palms of his hands against his ears, then over his eyes, then his mouth, each one in time, then went back to his odd task. His limbs were very graceful, his body tight and limber. What was he drawing; what was he trying to say?

"The *fuck's* he doing?" Gunner said.

Tripwire offered the boy some M&Ms, which he usually saved for badly injured soldiers. The boy wouldn't look at him. Tripwire scattered some candy on the ground near his legs, over the strange things he'd drawn. They looked very colorful against the brown earth and black soot. "C'mon," he said softly. "Try them." The boy traced circles around each M&M: a dozen multicolored eyes peering up from the ground.

The men wrapped the burned bodies in blankets and fronds. There was nothing more they could do. "Let's diddlybop," Oddy said. The unit moved out. Zippo looked over his shoulder. The boy was still drawing, grinning, alone in the still-smoking hamlet.

They marched for another hour and reached a bamboo thicket.

Slash removed a machete from his utility belt and set to work cutting through it. The thicket terminated on the ridge of a deep, wide valley spread with breadfruit and other dark-leafed trees.

"Hunker down," Oddy said. "Chow."

The men unshouldered their packs. Zippo cleared a spot in the wet earth, lit a cube of incendiary C4, and set a pot of water atop the smokeless flames. They boiled rice and mixed it with tinned beef, Spam, or whatever c-rations they had. None of them could cook worth a shit and their dishes possessed all the flavor of wet napkins.

"Tastes like ripe ass," Gunner said.

"What would you know?" Crosshairs said. "All the amphetamines you been jamming, I'd be surprised you got a tastebud left in your head."

"Gotta stay sharp."

Oddy slapped Gunner on the shoulder and said, "Keep jamming on those little pink pills and you're gonna wind up sharp as a balloon."

The soldiers ate in defiance of the food's flavor, needing the nourishment. Nobody talked about the dancing boy. Best to forget and move on. Memories like that didn't do anyone any good.

Afterwards, Crosshairs produced a deck of cards from his helmet's webbing and he and Slash played poker by the light of the dying sun. Gunner and Zippo leaned together against a shattered tree trunk and talked of the haunts they would frequent on their next visit to Ho Chi Minh City, which whores they intended to fuck, and in which orifices. Answer sat on a decomposing stump far from the others. Oddy and Tripwire crouched near the valley ridge, smoking Luckies.

"How far you think we got to go before hitting this village, Sarge?"

"The Viet told Answer what—ten, twelve klicks?" Oddy said. "Getting close."

Tripwire said, "You think he might've been lying?"

"You remember anyone feeding Answer a lie?"

Tripwire chewed on it for a moment before saying, "I guess not, no."

"Boy could make Satan himself roll over."

Oddy lit a fresh Lucky off the butt of the last and passed the pack to Tripwire.

"Does it make sense to you?" Tripwire said. "VC stockpiling arms in a pissant village miles from the hot zones?"

Oddy rubbed the bridge of his nose between thumb and fore-finger. "Not to get overly philosophical, son, but nothing about this conflict has ever made much sense."

Tripwire nodded. It was all he could do when Oddy got in this frame of mind. "Logistically, though, it's a mindfuck. Transporting the weapons alone..."

"I know what you're saying," Oddy said. "Very un-Charlie. Then again, he's always doing what's least anticipated, uh?"

They sat in silence, staring out over the Vietnamese landscape. Lush and vibrant, the valley's green canopy etched in ebbing sunlight, the sky now a dull orange, a lingering band of copper tracing the Earth's curve. The knowledge that he could call an airstrike and destroy acre upon acre of this beautiful countryside filled Oddy with a gnawing melancholy.

Then, deep in the valley heart, a flash of light.

"Gunner," Oddy said. "Toss me your specs."

Gunner retrieved a pair of Bushnell high-powered binoculars and handed them to Oddy. "See something, Sarge?"

Oddy put the binoculars to his eyes. The rest of the unit made their way over to the ridge. They squinted down into the valley, trying to spot what had twigged their Sergeant.

"The village is down there," Oddy said. "Almost missed it."

He handed the binoculars to Tripwire and pointed out the village's location. It was about one-thousand yards down-slope, in the base of the valley. A small circle of thatched huts, two outlying long-houses, a central fire pit. It seemed to be deserted: the fire remained unlit despite the evening's chill, no smoke rose through the vents in the huts, nobody congregated in the village proper.

"Where is everyone?" Tripwire asked.

Oddy shrugged. "Could they be in one of the longhouses?"

"Doesn't look like it."

"Crosshairs, give it a boo."

Crosshairs retrieved his sniper rifle, its Gewher scope much more powerful than the binoculars. "Nothing," he said, scanning the village. "They could be inside, but...sitting in the dark?"

"Doesn't make any sense," Zippo said.

"Maybe they got their wind up," Answer said. "They know we're coming."

They retreated from the ridge. The soldiers took a knee, waiting on Oddy's decision. Whatever choice he made, they would obey. Not out of fear or responsibility, but out of a deep and enduring respect. Even Zippo and Gunner, who hailed from states in which people of Oddy's complexion were once lynched and still treated as second-class citizens, accorded Oddy their undying loyalty.

"We could wait for daylight," Oddy said. "But we operate best at night. Up to it?"

Six heads nodded steadily.

"Okay." Oddy sketched a diagram in the dirt. "Zippo, Slash, Answer, I want you to flank around the village and set up on the far side. Gunner, Tripwire, Crosshairs, and I will move down the valley and string out along the near side. You boys on the far side, position yourselves to the left of the longhouses, we'll take the right. That'll prevent any crossfire. Wait for my signal before moving in." He removed a Mossberg pump-action shotgun from his pack and said, "Gear up."

Crosshairs loaded a fresh clip into his G3SG/1 sniper rifle while Zippo checked the jellied-fuel in his flame-thrower's dual tanks. Slash strapped a bandolier of fragmentation grenades across his chest. Tripwire filled the pockets of his combat jacket with explosives, blasting caps, insulated wire, and a detonating plunger. He sang his standard pre-combat melody: "My Boyfriend's Back," by The Angels.

"That's a fag-song," Gunner said, rolling a lambskin condom over the barrel of his Stoner M63A1 light machine-gun.

"*Hey-la, hey-la, my boyfriend's back,*" Tripwire sang, blowing Gunner a kiss. The burly Iowa native flipped him the bird.

Answer smeared black Kiwi shoe polish on his face and hands and slammed a clip into his M16. The Magnificent Seven were ready to rock and roll.

"Flanking team," Oddy said, "take as wide a berth around the village as you can. I'd like to be in position while there's some daylight left. You dig?"

"We dig," Zippo said.

"So let's do it to it."

Zippo, Answer, and Slash disappeared down the slope. Oddy gave them fifteen minutes before leading the remaining team members down a winding speed trail into the valley basin. Underneath the jungle canopy, everything was tinted chlorophyll-green. To his left, perhaps three-hundred meters, Oddy heard swift-running water. He asked Gunner for the acetate-covered map and unfolded it across the machine-gunner's broad back.

"That's a major waterway," he said. "A tributary of the Song-Hu river, wide and deep enough to support boat traffic."

"Think that's how the weapons are being transported?" Gunner asked.

"Could be," Oddy said. "I thought they'd be air-dropped or slogged in on foot but—"

"Charlie's always doing what's least expected," Tripwire said.

It was a sketchy situation, an ambush waiting to happen. *Charlie, you fucking snake*, Oddy thought, *What are you up to?* A B-52 Bomber passed low overhead, the force generated from its six engines vibrating the soldier's bodies. Something in the Sergeant, a subconscious twinge, told him to pull back and assess the situation. But his conscious mind assured him the men were amped-up and raring to engage. He folded the map and tucked it into Gunner's pack.

"Can't be far now."

The village appeared through a gap in the foliage. In the gathering dusk, the huts cast long shadows, their outer walls stained with dark slashes that could have been oil, or river mud, or blood. Embers shimmered in the firepit and pots were ranged on the hot rocks. The longhouses stood in darkness, not a hint of movement from within. It was as if the villagers had grown weary of their location and elected to abandon their homes, a mass exodus, leaving their possessions behind.

Either that, or someone—some*thing*—had beaten them to the punch.

"Where the hell is everybody?" Crosshairs said.

"On a nature hike?" Gunner said. He wasn't smiling.

Tripwire whispered, "Bad mojo, Mogumbo."

Oddy set the binoculars on the bridge of his nose and surveyed the left flank of the far longhouse. He whistled shrilly, the sound a fair replication of a jungle bird's call. A reply came from the tree line behind the far longhouse. "They're in position."

"Something's righteously fucked here, Sarge." The note of apprehension in Tripwire's voice was jarring. "You think they're waiting inside the huts—armed?"

They'd all heard horror stories of headstrong units charging into seemingly safe situations only to be surrounded and torn to shreds by disguised enemy troops, or sometimes even villagers with single-shot Chinese rifles and pitchforks.

"Give it a few minutes," Oddy said. "We got nothing but time."

A massive raven settled to roost on the peaked roof of the central hut. It preened itself with a hooked beak, digging ticks and other parasites from its molting plumage. The walls of the hut rattled. The startled raven took flight, leaving a drift of black feathers on the thatched roof. A smell wafted across the village grounds to where the soldiers were hunkered.

"Jesus," Crosshairs gagged. "The fuck is that?"

Nobody could liken it to anything they had ever smelled before—except Gunner, who, as a teen, had worked in his uncle's hog-butchering pen. The smell reminded him of standing above a vat of rendering hog fat, the fumes thick enough to achieve a nauseating, buttery physicality beyond mere scent, forcing itself to be felt and tasted.

"Something's not kosher here." Oddy's extremities had gone numb for some unexplained reason. "So we'll sit tight and see what happens."

The sound of a choppy motor in the distance. It was near dark, and Oddy had to squint through the binoculars as he focused on the waterline. A pair of NVA gunboats beached on the sandy shore. Soldiers offloaded long wooden crates.

"We got company," Oddy said. "Ten-twelve NVA with a shitload of crated firepower."

The Viet soldiers made their way up the gradual grade leading from the shore to the village. Two-man teams carried crates on their shoulders, or by the hemp handles hung on each side. Their cigarette tips bobbed in the darkness, easy targets for Crosshairs or any member of Team Blackjack, all competent marksmen. Their officer, identified by his yellow armband, called out. When nobody answered, he ordered his men to search the huts. Soldiers entered and exited two huts without incident. Then they entered the third, central hut.

And all hell broke loose.

The soldier's screams were unlike anything Team Blackjack had ever heard: high and blood-curdling, the screams of small children caught in savage traps. Pieces of meat spewed out of the hut's tombstone-shaped entryway, resembling wet rags or scraps of fat.

More screams. This time they were worse. Much worse. They wailed out and out, as if the soldiers' lungs had been soaked in napalm and lit.

The remaining Viet soldiers were of two minds: some of them drew their weapons and stood firm, while others fled towards the boats. Another sound emanated from the darkened hut: the sound of giant, clattering teeth, or threshing steel gears.

The NVA officer detonated a percussion grenade and rolled it through the entryway. It exploded in a starburst of white light and Oddy saw, for the briefest second, shapes hanging from the hut ceiling.

Long slack shapes. Muscle-corded and tendon-strung shapes. Bright red shapes.

A soldier was thrust from the doorway. He appeared uninjured until he spun in a drunken circle to reveal the flayed tableau of his back, spine torn down to the hipbone, hanging between his legs like a freakish segmented tail. He toppled forward into the fire pit, dead before the embers began to sear his flesh.

Oddy wasn't sure who the enemy was anymore.

Charlie was a savage motherfucker.

But at least he was *human*.

The NVA officer pulled his .38 service revolver and aimed it at the entryway. He squeezed off a shot, knowing his men were dead, not knowing who or what had killed them. The gunshot echoed into silence. Oddy waited, poised, listening.

A pair of eyes, blood-red, stared from the blackened hut.

There was nothing human in those eyes. Nothing at all.

For the first time ever, The Magnificent Seven were in way, way over their heads.

**Excerpted from the *Slave River Journal*,
April 12th, 1986:**

SEARCH AND RESCUE TEAM SENT TO FIND
DNR RESEARCHERS NOW MISSING

"Nothing to Worry About,"
—RCMP's Spokesman Says

By Michael Fulton

Fort Simpson, NWT: A ten-man search and rescue team headed by Ed "Mad Dog" Rabidowski, the elite RCMP tracker, have gone missing in the area surrounding Great Bear Lake. Communication between the search and rescue team and their base of operations ceased on April 10th at 3:30 a.m., and no further contact has passed. The team, sent to find three-member Department of Natural Resources research crew of Carl Rosenberg, Bill Myers, and Lillian Hapley, had been checking in at three-hour intervals.

"There is nothing to worry about," cautioned RCMP spokesman Sid Grimes at a hastily-held news conference. "The magnetic pull of the poles is strong up there, and has probably fouled up their communication link. I have the utmost confidence that Mr. Rabidowski's team is safe, and will be in contact soon."

In the meantime, another ten-man team is being put together to search out Rabidowski's missing crew. The new team, headed by Earl Triggers, will follow in the missing team's footsteps, and hopefully find clues as to...

III.

RECONNOITER

Toronto, Ontario, Canada.
December 5th, 1987. 4:05 p.m.

Oddy Grant acknowledged the stewardess's chirpy "Enjoy your stay in Toronto," with a sober nod, then moved down the tube connecting the Douglas DC-9 to the main concourse. Snow pelted the tube's shell, which swayed slightly with the wind. An overweight Canada Customs agent with a beery face and shellacked hair gave his passport a cursory glance while an equally obese agent inspected the contents of his duffel bag.

"Have a nice stay, Mr. Grant."

"Do my best."

Pearson International Airport was an architectural nightmare: Roman-style granite columns lacking any practical purpose rose to an arched ceiling adorned with a nationalist mural—fir trees blending into buck-toothed beavers melting into the cascading waters of Niagara Falls ceding to the shimmering glow of the Northern Lights. The structural schizophrenia continued in the Arrivals area, where steel pillars were again employed to no functional purpose, except perhaps to divert attention from a sculpture of what may have been a killer whale, a crushed '67 Dodge Dart, or anything in between.

Oddy bypassed the baggage carousel and made his way through a pair of frosted-glass sliding doors onto the main concourse. He walked to the outdoor taxi stand, buttoning his buckskin jacket against the cold.

"Chilly oot there, eh?" The taxi driver was stereotypically-attired: floppy cabbie hat and checkered lumberjack shirt. "Where to?"

"The Sheraton," Oddy said, mildly surprised the cabbie hadn't tacked on "Mac."

"You got it, Mac."

Oddy leaned back. The cabbie stole furtive glances at him through the rearview mirror: black and bumpy and bald, broad as a meat locker with a neatly-trimmed goatee, whiskers shockingly white. Thick lips, large white teeth. Eyes close-set, but their closeness did not accord him the look of dopeyness that characterized a high-profile athlete the cabbie had once driven. Wearing khakis and a pearl-snap shirt, a buckskin jacket the Toronto winter would slice through like razor blades.

"In town on business or pleasure?"

"Not sure," Oddy answered honestly.

The cabbie drummed his fingers on the steering wheel. "First time in the city?"

Oddy nodded, staring out over the bleak cityscape. Grey clouds hung so low Oddy was half-convinced he could roll down the window and grab a thickened handful.

"Lots to see, lots to do," the cabbie continued. "You like plays? *The Phantom of the Opera* just opened." The cab hit a pothole. The bobble-headed Dalmatian on the dashboard bobbed accordingly. "The fucking *Phantom*. City's getting some class."

"Huh," Oddy said noncommittally. His mind was occupied with other thoughts, specifically, what he might expect over the next few hours.

He didn't need to be told it was a scenario out of a schlocky B-movie: a mysterious stranger with a queer name—Anton Grosevoir? Come *on*—requesting an opportunity to discuss—what? But Oddy didn't have any enemies (at least not any *Canadian* ones), and the location was safe: nobody was going to get whacked in a witness-packed bar in a busy downtown area. Fifty grand for an afternoon's work, work that didn't involve wearing a mask or shoving a gun up someone's nose. Easy money. Ludicrously easy.

"Some nice museums, too," the cabbie droned on. Oddy exhaled loudly through his nostrils in an attempt to convey his utter disinterest. If the cabbie noticed, he was unfazed. "The Royal Ontario Museum is a good one. Lots of pretty paintings. And there's an indoor botanical garden, if you're keen on flowers'n such…"

Ten interminable minutes later the cab pulled into the Sheraton's horseshoe-shaped drive. A bellhop opened the hotel's thick glass door, ushering Oddy into the opulent lobby. The clerks, two girls with cute prairie faces wearing pinstriped gray uniforms, regarded him with pasted-on smiles. He winked. They averted their eyes, giggling. The bar was called *Canary Isle*, a name Oddy felt would attract homosexuals like mosquitoes to a bug-zapper. The décor was neo-something, very trendy, clear Plexiglas bar threaded with colored neon lights—green, purple, and hot pink running through lengths of flexible PVC tubing. The stools were also Plexiglas, seats stenciled with the initials *CI* in gold lettering. A Muzak version of Belinda Carlisle's "Heaven is a Place on Earth" filtered through recessed speakers. It seemed to Oddy an environment catering to gold-diggers, fledgling adulterers, and poseurs of every stripe.

The bartender was a blonde beefcake in a vanilla silk suit. "What can I get you?"

"Beer you got on tap?"

"Molson Canadian, Labatt's Blue, Coors, Coors Light, Budweiser, Connors Best Bitter, Kilkenny Red, Rickard's Red, Clancy's Red, Propeller, Garrison's—"

"Canadian's fine," Oddy said to ensure he got a drink before nightfall.

The beer arrived in a tapered glass with a tiny and utterly useless handle, like on a teacup. Oddy was somewhat relieved he hadn't smuggled a firearm: the urge to shoot up *Canary Isle* was over-whelming. Who knew Canadians could be so pretentious?

Oddy scanned the room. A man sat in a plush booth, his back turned away from the bar. A woman and a man, the woman dazzling, the man hideously ugly but wearing a platinum Rolex, talked in hushed tones at a corner table. Another man sat on the far side of the oval-shaped bar, everything except his Blue Jays cap obscured by a central display of liquor bottles.

Oddy sipped his beer and imagined what Mr. Anton Grosevoir might look like: he pictured a remarkably tall and spindly man with watery joints, a marionette cut loose of its strings. Oddy figured he'd slap the check down, get it signed, listen to Grosevoir for as long as he cared to, then hit the bricks.

A guy sat down a few stools away. Oddy cut a look at him: same age or perhaps a few years younger, a paunch he carried well, tanned, a gray-streaked ponytail and a t-shirt reading "*HERE'S* THE BEEF" with an arrow pointing down. He ordered a double Stolichnaya and tonic, then told the bartender to fuck the tonic. The beefcake barman copped perplexity.

"Don't want you to stick your pecker in the seltzer spritzer," the guy said. "Just deep-six the tonic, okay?"

The guy had an accent in conflict with his tan: Upper Plain States, Nebraska or Minnesota. Oddy squinted at him; he seemed recognizable in a distant, unreal way, as if Oddy had once dreamt him.

A woman with blood-red lipstick, gold hoop earrings, a white miniskirt, and fuck-me pumps strutted into the bar, seating herself at the ugly man's table. She nodded and smiled at the other woman and soon their hands were playing over the man's vulturish shoulders and wet-noodle arms as if he were Adonis himself.

"There anything money *can't* buy?" The ponytailed man said, eyeing the display.

"What it can't buy I don't need." Oddy found himself smiling for reasons he couldn't explain. "Real pretty ladies, though."

Ponytail shrugged, as though he'd seen so many beautiful women the gender itself now bored him. He pulled a soft pack of Lucky Strikes from his jacket and asked the bartender for a matchbook. "Filthy habit," he said.

"We all got our vices, son."

Ponytail looked at him funny. He offered the pack.

"I quit," Oddy said. "But that was my brand."

"Name's a mislabeling," Ponytail said. "Nothing lucky about these fuckers. Been smoking them since…" Ponytail rolled the cigarette from one side of his mouth to the other and said, "Since too long." A disgusted snort. "Lost my willpower somewhere."

Another man entered the bar. Short and thickly-muscled, dressed in a charcoal suit by Brooks Brothers, right arm in a paisley-patterned sling. His eyes locked with Oddy's for a moment. He frowned, opened his mouth, closed it, then seated himself in one of the booths.

"My boyfriend's back and there's gonna be trouble…"

Oddy swiveled on his stool to look at the singer. Ponytail was looking back at him, smiling slightly.

"Hey-la, hey-la, my boyfriend's back…" sang Ponytail.

It slammed together in Oddy's head with all the snap and flicker of billiard balls following a crisp break. He stared at Ponytail, at the crow's feet and wrinkles, searching out the young, recognizable face beneath the accumulated years. "Tony… Jesus… *Tripwire?*"

Tripwire slammed his palm on the bar. "I can't believe it—Oddy, Christ! I never would've figured except you calling me 'son.' So I thought—"

"You'd sing that trademark tune of yours—"

"And if it was you, you'd understand, and if it wasn't—"

"I'd just think you were some nutjob who got off singing in bars!" They shook hands, then, needing something more, chucked each other on the shoulder. He took the stool next to Oddy, his head shaking, a goofy grin on his face.

"This is too much. It's been, what…?"

"Twenty years."

"Twenty?" Tripwire's shoulders slumped. "Jesus. Half a lifetime."

"You look good," Oddy said. "A bronzed god."

Tripwire looked relieved. "You think? Man, it's a miracle, then— haven't exercised in a decade. You, though—what'd you do, swallow a goddamn refrigerator?"

Oddy smiled. "Clean living, son."

"And steroids?"

"Clean living."

They ordered another round. At the corner table, the ugly rich man swore loudly and kneaded the women's thighs under the table.

"So," Oddy said, "what you been up to?"

"Pretty broad question, Sarge," Tripwire said, slipping effortlessly into their old dynamic. "Job-wise…" He coughed into a cupped palm. "I direct adult features."

Oddy cocked an eyebrow.

"Ah, fuck it," Tripwire said. "I make pornos."

"Ah," Oddy said, considering. "Well, are they good? I mean… *artistic*?"

"Well, we're not talking Fellini or anything, but…sure, they've got merit."

"Anything I might have seen?"

"Ever watch *Dirty Sanchez Versus the Anal Virgins of the Sierra Madré*?"

"Must've missed that one. Sure sounds artistic."

"Oh, it was." Tripwire rolled his eyes. "And you?"

"Been robbing banks the past five years."

It was Tripwire's turn to cock an eyebrow. "Yeah?"

"Last one was a balls-up. I shut it down."

"Wait a sec." Tripwire covered his mouth with his hand, eyes staring down in concentration, as if consulting an internal Rolodex. "I read about a botched job in, where was it…Washington, I think. Was that *you*?"

Oddy shrugged.

"Holy shit. There were, what, four bodies or something? A security guard, a couple cops—"

"Yeah," Oddy said. "A guy on the crew went Section-8. Total apeshit."

"*Fuuuuck,*" Tripwire said. "So, you up here 'till the heat dies down?"

Oddy shifted on his stool and said, "Not really sure *why* I'm here, son."

"Makes two of us."

At the corner table, one of the women stood abruptly. She shouted something at the hideous rich man and threw a vodka gimlet in his face. The man cackled and grabbed at her ass, greasy black hair plastered to his scalp in three long ropes. The woman took a step back and kicked at him. Displaying perhaps the most grace he ever had or ever would, the man caught her foot deftly, doffed her satin pump, and tried to suck her toes off. The woman squealed as his thick pink lips engulfed her big toe.

The man in the Brooks Brothers suit exited his booth, crossed to the corner table, grabbed the toe-sucker by his collar, spun him around, and punched him in the face, all with one hand. Mr. Toe-sucker folded like a Mongolian lawn chair and went down under the Plexiglas table. The woman frantically swabbed her toes with cocktail napkins. Mr. Toe-sucker struggled to sit up but the other woman kicked him in the nose. He went down again, head hitting a table leg with a hollow sound. The white knight laughed. Oddy and Tripwire exchanged glances.

"Couldn't be—"

"No fucking way," Tripwire said. "Danny? Hey!"

Zippo turned and saw the huge black man he'd noticed on the way in sitting beside a Coppertoned longhair wearing an obscene t-shirt. Both of them were grinning like goons.

"Get your ass over here," the black dude said.

"You got a problem?" Danny pointed at Mr. Toe-sucker. "Want some of what he got?"

The beatnik leaned forward, feet hooked around the stool legs, arms outstretched.

"Danny," he said in a chiding tone. "*Zippo.* Don't leave us hanging, baby."

Zippo's mouth fell open. "Tripwire? Get the *fuck* out of here." He took a step back, squinting at the black guy like he was staring directly at the sun. "Od...*Oddy?*"

"The one and only, son."

"I can't believe...how *long?*" Zippo brushed off the woman's grateful half-embrace and muttered, "No problem, toots," before making a beeline for his long-lost unit members.

Oddy pulled him into a rough embrace; Zippo sucked air through his teeth as Oddy's shoulder pressed against his injured arm. When Tripwire hugged him, Zippo felt the ex-demo-man's beefy paunch pressing against his own toned abs.

They relocated to a booth. When asked what he did for a living, Zippo ran a finger across his upper lip and said: "I clean up messes." Oddy said he didn't know many janitors who wore thousand-dollar suits. They ordered another round, Zippo taking a double-shot of Dewars.

"This is some coincidence," Tripwire said after awhile. The question hung.

"Anton Grosevoir," Oddy said.

"Think I heard that name before," said Zippo.

Tripwire nodded. "Fifty G's to meet in a certain upscale bar got a familiar ring to it?"

Oddy patted his breast pocket. "Check's right here."

Their drinks arrived. Each man took a long swallow. Their minds were abuzz with questions: Who knew of the connection between them? Why, knowing this connection, would someone seek a reunion? What would they have to do to earn fifty-thousand dollars? And who the hell was Anton Grosevoir?

Tripwire's over-stimulated mind concocted a ludicrous revenge-fantasy: a dirt-poor Vietnamese village boy had witnessed an atrocity the unit committed in the heat of battle, killing his father or mother perhaps. Later, the boy flees to North America, becomes fantastically wealthy, and concocts an elaborate scheme to avenge himself on the men who'd ruined his life. Ridiculous, yes. Paranoid, definitely. But beyond the realm of possibility...?

"So," Oddy said, "Anyone got the slightest idea of how this might play out?"

Zippo took a Cuban cigar from his inside pocket. He snipped the tip off between his teeth and said, "Plan A: This Grosevoir cat signs our checks." He spat the nub into an crystal ashtray. "Plan B: He refuses and I floss my teeth with his guts." Zippo's tone suggested Plan A and Plan B possessed equal appeal.

"Some things never change," Oddy said.

"Fair's fair, Sarge." Zippo exhaled a quivering smoke ring. "Some guy's going to drag our asses out here, we better get paid."

"He isn't just going to hand over fifty large for nothing," Tripwire said. "Cough up that kind of green for a *meeting*?"

Oddy said, "A deal's a deal. Letter doesn't mention anything beyond a meeting."

"And woe betide the fuck who welshes on me," said the hitman.

Tripwire slugged back the last of his Stoli and said, "Just us, though?"

"What do you mean?"

"I mean, our unit. Only us three? What about Crosshairs—"

"Last time I saw Crosshairs, he wasn't looking so shit-hot," Zippo said quietly.

"But he survived," Tripwire said. "I got a letter from him, way back. And Answer—"

"It's been twenty years," Oddy said. "People go missing. People die."

"I'm not sure Answer will ever die," Zippo said, "because I'm not positive that fucker was ever *alive*."

Oddy smiled. "I used to say that boy could make Satan himself roll over."

"Ice water pumping through those veins," Tripwire agreed.

Oddy said, "Or brimstone."

Another man entered the bar. Six-feet but a stooped posture made him look shorter, wearing tattered corduroys, Asics tennis shoes, a dirty sweatshirt with a picture of an overflowing slot machine above the caption "*Everybody* scores in Vegas!" His features were draped by black bangs grown long and combed down. Despite this attempted camouflage, Oddy could tell there was something wrong: the man's face looked unnatural, like a burn victim's.

"The last time I saw Crosshairs—" Tripwire started.

"He was missing half his face—" Zippo continued.

"And you don't have to be Perry Mason to tell—"

"That guy there—"

"Is hiding something," Tripwire finished.

Zippo dragged deeply on his Cuban, hissed bluish smoke through his teeth, and said, "Hey, Neil. *Crosshairs*. Over here."

The man turned. His eyes—or so it then appeared—stared through the fringe of his hair with dawning awareness. His lips split in a huge grin as he ambled over.

"Is this a mirage?" He mimed rubbing his eyes, sitting down and shaking hands with the others. Then he frowned and said, "One of you guys didn't send that letter, did you? This isn't some kind of surprise reunion—"

"No, son," Oddy assured him.

"Good." The look of relief was unmistakable. "Not that it's not great to see you guys, but…I need that fucking money."

Nobody needed to be told this: it looked as if Crosshairs had recently crawled out of a dumpster, ditched the bottle of T-bird, waved goodbye to his fellow winos, and hopped a plane to Toronto.

"You look…good," Tripwire managed.

"And you were always a piss-poor liar," Crosshairs said. "Zippo, how do I look?"

"Like twice-pounded shit, my friend."

"Same old Zippo." Crosshairs laughed. It felt so good to laugh. "What about you, Sarge—ever seen such a specimen?"

"You're looking better than last time I saw you," Oddy said. "But barely, son."

They were peering at his face with curiosity normally reserved for a Rubik's Cube. Crosshairs said, "Might as well get this over with," and lifted his bangs.

Nobody turned away, or grimaced, or stared with leering intensity. Oddy furrowed his brow and said, "Not a bad job." Zippo agreed while noting the color was slightly off. Then Crosshairs sprung the clips that secured the prosthesis to his skull, detaching a portion of his face. Tripwire slitted his eyes and looked at the dark hairs dappling the divot. Crosshairs told him about the transplanted ass-skin. Tripwire asked to see his ass. Crosshairs shot him the bird. Zippo sniffed the prosthesis, declared it "rank," and told Crosshairs he ought to wash it once in a goddamn while. Oddy asked him how the injury had affected him, and they all agreed it sucked to have everything taste like burnt toast.

"Even pussy?" Zippo asked.

"Even pussy."

"That fucking war," Zippo said.

Another round arrived, then another. Oddy regarded his old unit members. Perhaps it was the potent Canadian beer, or simply the dimness of the bar, but for the briefest moment Oddy saw them as they had been in 1967: Crosshairs was leaning back in his seat, arm thrown over the seatback above Tripwire's head; he'd swept his bangs back, not caring who saw his face, comfortable, laughing at something Zippo had said. Tripwire was sitting to Crosshairs' right, and the creases of his face, creases that had prevented Oddy from recognizing him, seemed to be melting away like ice during a spring thaw. Sitting next to him, steepled fingers pressed to his lips, Zippo waited for the other two to quit talking nonsense so he could tell them *the way it was*.

It was as if the twenty-year interval was nothing, as if it had only been a week, a day, since they'd last met, drank, laughed. Oddy watched this almost unconscious knitting-together, this sort of easy falling-back into old roles, with intermixed fascination and unease. It was like watching puzzle pieces being slotted together by invisible hands. This was not an overly comforting image. It made him feel like a man strapped to the nose cone of a heat-seeking missile.

"And then there were four," Oddy said during a lull in conversation.

"Yeah," Crosshairs said. "Just missing—"

"Afternoon, fellows."

Answer appeared in the manner he always did: as if from thin air. One moment he was nonexistent and the next he was standing at the booth's mouth, lips curled at the edges like charring paper. His hair was long, the fiery red had faded to strawberry-blonde and receding into a widow's peak. He didn't appear to have matured physically at all: his shoulders were still jagged peaks, his reedy arms and legs free-floating within flared jeans and chambray shirt. Oddy noticed the Blue Jays cap in his hand and realized Answer had been in the bar all along, sitting alone on the far side. Oddy knew then he'd observed everything—his and Tripwire's meeting, Zippo punching Mr. Toesucker, Crosshairs's appearance—waiting and appraising until he'd decided to make his presence known. Oddy wasn't angry at Answer, exactly. He might as well be angry at a wolf for slaughtering sheep, a preying mantis for consuming its mate, or any other creature of instinct for doing what came naturally.

"Well, well," Zippo said as Answer sat down with the unnerving sinuosity that characterized all his movements. "If it isn't the wraith hisowndamnself."

Answer shook hands with everyone. His grip was loose and cold, his skin dry. He looked at Crosshairs's new face and cocked his head to one side, a gesture they were all familiar with. "So," he said. "Who'd've figured Crosshairs would turn out to be the handsomest one of the bunch?"

Every once in a while Answer could fire off a zinger. The other four cracked up.

"What about you," Crosshairs said. "Looking like a strung-out Opie."

Zippo whistled the opening bars of *The Andy Griffith Show*.

"You weren't the one who sent the letter, were you?" Oddy asked. "Seeing as it's the type of thing you'd find amusing."

Answer shook his head. "Just looked like a way to score some easy dough."

"*Too* easy," Tripwire said.

"You sound like a character in a bad slasher movie," Zippo said. "It may surprise you, but there are many wealthy, harmless, and utterly batshit people in this world. We just hit the motherlode."

Nobody heard the approaching footsteps. Nobody saw a shadow cast across the table's surface, perhaps because the bar was too dark.

Or perhaps no shadow was cast.

"Good afternoon, gentlemen." The voice was buttery and fluid. "So nice to see you've been reacquainted."

«««—»»»

The speaker looked as though he'd stepped off the stage of a freakshow: roughly the height of an eight-year-old boy, stubby digits, arms projecting like flippers. Thin wormish lips, like a pair of parallel nightcrawlers. He was radish-eyed with one red iris, but whether he was a true albino or if this was an affectation, a tinted contact lens, was uncertain. Only one eye was visible, the other covered by an embroidered eyepatch. A pungent odor wafted off him, an unsavory blend of tannic and Old World spices. His sharply-tailored suit, gleaming gold cufflinks, and crocodile loafers couldn't disguise the stone-cold fact the man seemed preternaturally suited to carnival geekdom, biting the heads off chickens or pounding a railroad spike up his nostril.

He advanced to the head of the table, which reached his nipples, placing his hands on the transparent Plexiglas. They did not jibe with the rest of his appearance: mechanics' hands, creases rimed with dark filth, grease or crankcase oil.

"It's wonderful you all came," he said. "I thought some of you might've viewed my letter as a hoax." He tipped Tripwire a wink. "Or thought someone had a mind to set you up."

Oddy shot a hard look at the midget. "Anton Grosevoir, I'm figuring?"

The dwarf beamed. "Excellent pronunciation, Mr. Grant! Most people mangle my name so horribly it makes me wince to hear it."

Oddy was confident that wincing would only improve Grosevoir's appearance. *That*, he thought, *or a total body transplant*.

"Yes, I'm Grosevoir," the man continued. "And I'm just overjoyed, I mean positively *elated*, you all came." He clapped his hands together, producing a sound like gutted trout colliding. "Now, if you'd all be so kind as to follow me—"

"Hold the phone, stumpy." Zippo produced the unsigned check and slapped it on the table. "I'll be needing your John Hancock before I go any further."

Grosevoir appeared miffed. Zippo inspired this basic reaction in all carbon-based life forms. "If you'd rather," Grosevoir said, uncapping a platinum Mont Blanc. "But, as I said in the letter, the fifty thousand is only a, what do you call it, appearance fee?" He pulled the check to him, fingertips leaving gelid snail-trails on the Plexiglas. "My proposal—which, I take it, you have no desire to entertain—is much more lucrative."

Grosevoir's pen hovered above the check. Zippo drew it back, folded it neatly into his pocket, and said, "What the hell. I came all this way."

"Splendid!" Grosevoir's tongue, pink as a baby's ass, darted out to slick his lips. "Please follow me. I have a room where we can discuss my proposition in privacy."

"Just a minute, Mr. Grosevoir." Oddy appraised the diminutive man in the way one might appraise a small but possibly vicious dog. "How do you know about our connection?"

"Your...*connection*?"

Oddy stared at him, fingers drumming the tabletop.

"Okay, okay," Grosevoir buckled. "What can I say? All information is available for a price." He rubbed his thumb and forefinger together. "The American military maintains records of its soldiery, the elite units and so on. I was able to access the information on yours. I liked what I saw."

"But why us?" Crosshairs said. "Whatever the job is, why choose—?"

"I can answer all your questions." Grosevoir spread his arms, palms open. "But please, let us conduct ourselves in private."

He stood aside as the men filed out of the booth. He led them across the lobby, walking with an awkward capering gait that struck the men as undignified and schoolgirlish. Tripwire whispered to Crosshairs, "Guy looks like he should be standing next to Ricardo Montalban on *Fantasy Island*." Crosshairs whispered back: "Yeah, or leaping out of a box of Lucky Charms."

Grosevoir instructed the elevator attendant to direct them to the penthouse. Oddy was apprehensive: the suite could be jam-packed with assassins, black market organ farmers, a snuff film-making crew. He felt utterly unprepared and exposed, lashed to the train tracks with the 5:05 Amtrak bearing down.

Zippo, on the other hand, adhered to the Boy Scout credo of "Always Be Prepared." He'd stopped at a local hardware store and purchased a twist-lock box-cutter, two screwdrivers—one Phillips, one Slot—and a 16-oz. Hammertooth antivibe hammer, the tools currently strapped to various parts of his body. Answer cashed in his plane ticket in favor of a Greyhound pass; this allowed him to smuggle his Kirikkale pistols across the border, one of which was now secured under each armpit.

The elevator ascended rapidly. This was a blessing, as in close quarters Grosevoir's repellant aroma burned in their nostrils and behind their eyeballs like battery acid. The polished brass doors slid open with a merciful in-rush of fresh air.

Grosevoir led them down a hallway lit by frosted-glass coach lamps, stopping in front of a pair of mahogany double doors. He fumbled with the oversize key.

Oddy placed a hand the size of a shovel blade over the smaller man's, enveloping it like a pitcher plant swallowing a gnat. "If it's all the same, I'll go first."

Oddy shot a quick look at Zippo, who grabbed Grosevoir by the collar and yanked him back. Grosevoir issued an indignant squawk as the tip of a Phillips-head screwdriver feathered his ear canal.

Oddy inserted key into lock. "Now if anyone's waiting on the other side of this door packing heat and bad intentions, my man Zippo's going to be performing some impromptu neurosurgery."

Grosevoir gulped like a boated mackerel. "This is foolish. I mean you no harm."

Tripwire was skeptical of Grosevoir's lame-duck performance: this was a man who felt no fear doing his best to impersonate someone who did. Tripwire got the impression Grosevoir was conversant with the mannerisms of fear in a role of one who inspired terror in others, rather than one who'd experienced the emotion first-hand.

Lock tumblers engaged with a soft *click*. Oddy threw the doors open and stepped into the lip of darkness. He searched the near wall for a light switch, keenly aware of his exposure, his only comfort the knowledge that Zippo'd plunge the screwdriver hilt-deep into the midget's melon at the first hint of trouble. His fingers brushed a dimmer switch. Stark white light flooded the room, revealing...

A regally-appointed hotel suite. Plush cream carpet gave way to a flight of marble stairs terminating in a circular salon. A massive bay window offered a sweeping view of the Toronto skyline. To the left: an executive bathroom complete with jet tub. To the right: a bedroom with king size bed and satin sheets.

Oddy felt more than slightly foolish.

No pajama-clad ninjas. No swarthy organ farmers.

Nobody except one offended little man requesting a screwdriver be removed from his ear. Zippo shrugged, indifferent, but did as asked.

"Come, come," Grosevoir said, high spirits returning. Either the man possessed the short-term memory of a fruitfly or the preceding hostilities had caused no real discomfort. He gestured to a stocked minibar. "Help yourselves and take a seat."

The men selected bottles of Moosehead beer and ranged themselves on plush leather chairs while Grosevoir busied himself in the bedroom. An overhead projector was set up on a cut-glass coffee table.

"What do you think that's for?" Crosshairs whispered to Zippo.

Zippo jabbed him in the ribs and said, "Who am I, Uri Geller?"

Grosevoir exited the bedroom with a roll of transparencies.

"May I dim the lights?" A deferential bow to Oddy. "I promise there are no guerilla troops hidden in the closets."

Grosevoir smiled. Every tooth was a dead, nerveless gray. Oddy's hackles rose, short hairs on the nape of his neck stiffening like hog bristles.

Grosevoir switched on the projector and centered a transparency on the glass plate. A topographical map of the Northwest Territories was projected onto the wall.

"This," he pointed to a spot near Great Bear Lake, "is the location of the Saugeen Valley Penitentiary. Of course, I'm sure none of you have ever experienced incarceration." Another smile touched his mulberry-colored lips, exposing a cobalt slit of teeth. "But this institution is the first Canadian 'Super-Max' facility, an idea conceived by and borrowed from their neighbors to the south." Crosshairs recalled an article in *Newsweek* about the Red Onion State Prison in Virginia, the original Super-Max. The brainchild of Governor Edward "Lee" Barnett, Super-Max prisons were designed to break inmates down to the level of infants in order to rebuild them as functional members of society. Conditions resembled a gulag: prisoners spent twenty-three hours a day in solitary, their lone hour of recreation taking place in a sunless twelve-by-twelve concrete chamber. Even the shower stalls had bars.

"It was built to house the worst of the worst," Grosevoir continued. "Serial killers and rapists, degenerates and recidivist felons; the scum of the scum. It is Hell on earth, and such prisoners deserve no less."

Tripwire was bemused: Canada, a country populated by infuriatingly polite bumpkins, required a Super-Max? He couldn't quite grasp the concept of a Canadian serial killer. How would he approach a potential victim: "Pardon me, eh, but I was thinking a-*boot* cutting your head off and skewering it on a pike. Okay by you?" Perhaps the victims were unusually accommodating: "Alright, eh. Just don't go making lampshades out of my skin, you hoser."

"The Penitentiary is supposedly water-tight," Grosevoir continued. "The theory goes that, even if someone managed to escape, the surrounding wilderness and sub-zero temperatures would make short work of even the most rugged escapee." His face, illuminated by the funneled light cast by the projector, bore an expression of wry amusement. "But it seems that humankind has been put on this planet to show how any theory, no matter how vigorously asserted, can be disproved."

Grosevoir removed the map and centered another transparency. His hands moved with swift assurance, out of all context with the rest of his body: it was like watching a baboon play a concerto.

"This man," he indicated the projected mugshot, "is the proverbial exception to the rule. Marcus Overton was the leader of a group of drug-addicts-turned-murderers who massacred twelve people during the summer of 1981. Self-styled champions of the underprivileged, their twisted *modus operandi* was the slaughter of upper-class families, the idea being anyone who had attained wealth had attained it at the expense of the working-class. Their eldest victim was Muriel Conway, an eighty-three-year-old grandmother; the youngest Elliot Conway, her six-year-old great-grandson."

Zippo was, unsurprisingly, something of a serial killer buff. He'd recently read *Buried Dreams: The John Wayne Gacy Case*, and *Unnatural Acts: The Ted Bundy Story*. For this reason he was more than a little surprised to have never heard of Marcus Overton: twelve stiffs, by serial killer standards, was a gold medal performance. Manson & Co. had secured an immortal legacy with less than ten— which was far fewer than Zippo himself had dispatched on the job, the fact of which swelled his chest with professional pride.

"Overton and the surviving members of his gang were sentenced to forty consecutive life sentences and remanded to the Saugeen Valley Penitentiary in the fall of 1982. Two weeks ago, Overton and three of his disciples escaped. From what's been pieced together in the aftermath, the break was planned over several years. Since the men rarely had personal contact, they communicated via a code-system tapped out on the walls of their adjoining cells. Neither the prison guards nor the warden believed them capable of such cunning." A rueful smile. "Obviously they were mistaken."

The men appraised Marcus Overton's mugshot. But they did not see the same image. Overton's facial features varied wildly according to each man:

To Tripwire, Overton's hooked nose, angular bone structure, and ice-pick eyes reminded him, jarringly, of his father.

To Crosshairs, Overton's switchblade sneer, sunkissed skin, and ironically-cocked eyebrow made him a dead ringer for Len the cardshark.

To Oddy, Overton appeared as a black man whose features were a fusion of his father and Dade, men he loved and hated in equal measure.

To Zippo, Overton's ghostly-pale skin, immaculately-coiffed hair, and pouty, come-hither expression made him the ultimate GLAAD poster boy. *Fucking gift-giving ass bandit*, he seethed inwardly. *Shitstains like you give serial killers a bad name!*

Only Answer saw the mugshot as it truly appeared: a grainy, out-of-focus photograph of a man who resembled, and quite possibly was, ex-president Richard M. Nixon. Answer kept this to himself.

"After stabbing a guard to death with a sharpened toothbrush, Overton successfully freed five of his fellow inmates. They caught the control room guards unawares and massacred them all, losing two of their own in the process. The remaining three, led by Overton, stole weapons and winter clothing before clearing the prison's perimeter. They are currently at large somewhere in the four-thousand square miles of forest ringing the penitentiary."

Grosevoir switched off the projector and sat on the edge of the coffee table. With knees drawn up and fists balled at his hips he resembled a gargoyle perched on the ledge of a crumbling gothic manor. "My request is a simple one," he said. "Locate Overton. Kill him."

The pendulum on an ivory wall clock produced a steady tick-tock, the only noise to impinge on an otherwise pervasive silence.

Crosshairs crossed his legs and sipped his beer nervously, thinking, *I need money—but do I need it that bad?*

"Why?" Oddy said.

"Why what?" Grosevoir said.

"Why us, for starters? The youngest of us is, how old are you Answer, late thirties? Me, I'm mid-forties. It's been years since any of us went out on recon."

"None of you are old, all of you are seasoned, some of you," Grosevoir nodded at Answer, Zippo, Oddy, "work in fields that will be helpful on this assignment. I have no need for youthful bravado; I'm seeking competence and an ability to execute."

Zippo hated the way Grosevoir looked at him: the man's gaze felt like cockroaches scuttling up his neckline. "Why go through the trouble?" he said. "Tracking us down, firing off letters, no guarantee we're going to show? Hell, I know crews—professional, ruthless mercs—who'd've taken the contract for less than you're paying us for a meeting. These guys aren't advertising in *Soldier of Fortune*, but they don't take much legwork to track down. Besides, we haven't worked together in twenty-odd years. One of us," pointing at Tripwire, "looks like he stepped out of the potato patch at a kibbutz, and our sniper is missing half his fucking face, in case you didn't notice. No offence, guys."

Crosshairs flicked a bottle cap at him. "None taken, shitbird."

"I'm a neophyte in the business of hiring contract killers," Grosevoir said. "I have a connection in the U.S. Armed Forces who told me your unit was the most highly-decorated in the Vietnam conflict."

Something tightened inside Tripwire like a wet rag being wrung out by hand: an image of them all receiving the combat infantry badge for slaughtering a boatload of children.

Grosevoir continued, "This friend of mine was able to secure your most recent mailing addresses. All I did was send the letters."

"I still don't get why you need us," Crosshairs said. "I mean, the woods have got to be crawling with task forces, Mounties or whatever tracking Overton down—"

"And besides," Tripwire added, "wouldn't those woods be full of animals—wolves and bears, maybe...badgers?"

"Yeah," Zippo snorted. "Gotta watch out for those rabid badgers."

"Oh, yes, there are some terribly vicious creatures in those woods," Grosevoir said. "But, as I said, the escapees are armed and cunning. I have no doubt they're alive. Excusing the cliché, I feel it in my bones."

Crosshairs was highly dubious of Grosevoir feeling *anything*, be it in his bones, his heart, his soul, or elsewhere.

"As for the Mounties," Grosevoir continued, "I'm sure they'll eventually track Overton down. Then what? Another trial, more media exposure, another book deal inked, panties and marriage proposals from adoring fans? Back to prison with nothing to lose, the opportunity to kill again? No. I can't have it. I want the Mounties to find bodies—stiff, lifeless, headless bodies."

Tripwire was reminded of a movie he'd shot in southern California. An homage of sorts to Disney's *The Apple Dumpling Gang*, he'd titled it: *The Grapple Humping Gangbang*. The plot, such as it was, involved a gang of female desperadoes, led by Charity Chest as "Bitch Chas-titty," escaping jail on the day they were to be hanged for wanton promiscuity. The sheriff, a young Johnny Wadd, assembled a posse of sexual lawmen—including two full-blooded Navajos skilled in ancient "Grapple Humping" techniques—and eventually shanghaied the lasses frolicking, stark naked, in a babbling brook. The posse, unhinged by lust, descended upon the helpless nymphs. A massive gangbang ensued.

Tripwire doubted the assignment Grosevoir had tabled would end so agreeably.

"You still haven't answered my question," Oddy said. "Why do you want this guy dead? Don't play it off as some kind of samaritanism, 'cause I'm not buying it."

Grosevoir gave Oddy a look. It was the look a top-rank boxer might give his sparring partner after being tagged with a hard shot: a look of stunned surprise. Perhaps Grosevoir assumed he'd known these men, their financial difficulties and moral shortcomings, and hadn't expected this level of questioning. He applied to his face an expression of soul-wrenching sadness and removed a picture from his pocket.

"This was my family," he said quietly. "June and Allison Grosevoir. Do I need to tell you who slaughtered them?" The photo was passed around. As had been the case with Overton's picture, no two men saw the same image. Each of them saw two women who resembled, in some way, their mothers, or sisters, or girlfriends loved and lost. Again, only Answer saw the photo for what it truly was: a stock picture frame insert featuring a tow-headed boy and a golden retriever, with the frame size—*8 in. x 10 in.*—stamped prominently in the left-hand corner. He looked up from the photo to see Grosevoir eyeing him impassively.

"So that's what this is?" Crosshairs asked. "A mission of revenge?"

"Revenge" Grosevoir challenged, "or social obligation? When a vicious animal escapes its cage, what's a responsible human being to do?" A weary shrug suggested the answer was too self-evident to bother vocalizing. "Overton should be dead already. If he'd committed his crimes in Texas, he and his sadistic cronies would be ashes. But bleeding-heart Canadians outlawed capital punishment, so he lives. And the thought of that monster drawing breath while my wife and daughter lie entombed, the thought he might outlive *me*…no, it's intolerable. Plain and simple, I want them dead."

"You want him iced, fine. He offed your family; must eat at your guts. I can sympathize." Zippo ran his tongue across his teeth. "But the question remains: how *badly* do you want him dead?"

"Down to brass tacks, are we?" Grosevoir rubbed his hands together. "As you've no doubt surmised, I am a wealthy man. I leave my net worth to my accountants, but the simple fact is I have more money than I could possibly spend should I live to be a thousand years old." The little man chuckled, as if the thought of such longevity was amusing. "I've never put a price on my peace of mind before, but in this case I'd say my peace of mind is worth exactly one million dollars…for each of you."

Tripwire's jaw couldn't have dropped any lower had Hulk Hogan wedged a crowbar between his teeth and pried with all his might. Crosshairs looked like Iron Mike Tyson had just busted him one in the chops. Even Oddy had a tough time keeping a straight face.

One million dollars *each*?

"Wait a sec," Zippo said, blinking away the dollar signs that flashed before his eyes. "You're going to pony up a million bucks if we—"

"Five million dollars, one million each, if you track down and kill the men who slaughtered my wife and daughter, yes," Grosevoir said. "Does that sound fair?"

Does it sound fair? Crosshairs's mind boggled at the concept. *A cool mil' to rub out some degenerate rat-fucks who murdered kids and old ladies?* He'd have had a more profound crisis of conscience had he been asked to stomp a cockroach! Fifty grand would clear his debts, but a million would rocket him to the top of the high-roller list. He pictured himself at World Series of Poker, Binion's Horseshoe Casino in Vegas, sitting at the final table behind multicolored stacks of chips, staring across the felt at Stu Ungar and T.J. Cloutier and Johnny Chan, matching wits with those leather-assed road gamblers. The other men entertained fantasies of their own. A *million* dollars. That kind of cashola could change anyone's life.

"How do we know you're gonna pay?" Oddy said. "We don't know you from Adam."

"Because I am neither bored enough to plan all of this as a hoax, nor foolish enough to believe you'd react charitably if I did," Grosevoir said. "This venture requires trust on both sides. I trust you to kill Overton. You trust me to pay." He removed an alligator-skin checkbook from his blazer. "Perhaps I should cut a check for, say, two-hundred thousand dollars to each of you—a good faith gesture?"

"Before you do, we'll need to discuss your offer," Oddy said. "In private."

"Of course. I'll wait in the bedroom."

A strained silence followed Grosevoir's departure. Zippo reached another bottle of Moosehead from the minibar, cracked the cap, drank deeply. "What's to discuss? You want in, get in. If not, don't let the doorknob hit you where the good lord split you."

"Not arguing that," Oddy said. "We're grown men, each of us will make his own choice. But he contacted *all* of us. He wanted Blackjack. He wanted the Magnificent Seven."

"No chance of that, is there, Sarge?" Answer said. "I mean, barring a séance."

It was the first time anyone had invoked the deaths of Slash and Gunner. "You're right on that, son," Oddy said, biting back a caustic rejoinder. "But what I'm saying is, he didn't want one of us, or two, but everyone."

"I don't know how you guys've spent the last twenty years," Tripwire said. "But me, I've been sitting on my rapidly-expanding ass. The only explosions I've witnessed recently are Peter North cumshots. Any recruit fresh out of munitions training could run circles around me."

"And I haven't fired a rifle in years," Crosshairs said, rapping his knuckles on the prosthesis. "My peripherals are all fucked. Doesn't mean I don't want in on the deal...but it *is* odd."

"Ninety-nine percent of these deals *are* odd," Zippo said. "Trust me. And at least this fruitcake has a decent reason for wanting someone dead." Zippo's tone suggested Grosevoir's motivation was, in his experience, rare. "Hell, I'd cold-cock Jesus H. Christ himself for a million bucks, but this Overton fuck truly deserves to get smoked."

Oddy said, "So you're decided?"

Zippo nodded. "Hell, it'd be swell to have you boys along for old times' sake, but I'm set to go this solo."

"What about the rest of you?"

Crosshairs nodded. Answer nodded. Tripwire said, "Depends. Are you going?"

Oddy felt like a man trying to hold his ground against a tornado or a tidal wave. It was hopeless. You could only go limp, give yourself over to the gathering momentum, and pray you'd be left relatively unscathed.

"Yeah, okay. I'm in."

Tripwire said, "Then so am I."

"So it's settled!" Grosevoir said, exiting the bedroom. He brought his stench with him; Zippo momentarily envied Crosshairs's immunity to odors. "This is simply marvelous! Everything's ready; I'll have a limo take you to the airport, where a Learjet is waiting to—"

"Hold on," Oddy interrupted. "We're going to need warm clothes, maps, guns—"

"Yes, yes," Grosevoir said. "All under control. But time is of the essence!"

The men rose. Grosevoir made a show of patting their backs, "It's a noble thing you're doing, terribly noble." Crosshairs didn't see anything noble about hunting down other human beings, even cold blooded killers, in exchange for a bagful of money. The gaudy specter of cash rendered any notions of nobility hollow as a termite-ridden elm.

Tripwire stared out over the blackened cityscape, even squares of darkness and light laid out in a patchwork grid. He had no idea it would be the last time he'd see Toronto's, or any city's, skyline. For a few of them, the following hours would comprise a series of lasts: their last car ride, their last decent meal, their last casual and thoughtless interaction with people other than the men they would fight and die beside.

Answer was the last to exit. Grosevoir grabbed his shirtsleeve. Answer stared down into Grosevoir's wet-ruby eye, seeing his own image reflected in it, swelled and monstrous. The way Grosevoir appraised him was disconcerting: as if Answer was a suit coat that, with the proper alterations, would make a perfect fit. Answer tried to pull free. Grosevoir held him for a moment before releasing his grip. His gray teeth resembled weather-beaten tombstones.

"Run along now," he whispered.

Answer did as he was told.

**Excerpted from the *Slave River Journal*,
April 16th, 1986:**

INTREPID REPORTER NEWEST MEMBER
OF THE MISSING

"A Good Boy, But Always So Curious,"
—Says Tearful Mother

By Adriana Fellows

Fort Simpson, NWT: Michael Fulton, intrepid cub reporter for
this newspaper, has gone missing somewhere around Great Bear
Lake. Unbeknownst to family, friends, or his editor, Fulton hired
famed backwoodsman Herman Kint and set off into the wilderness, following "The Path of the Missing," as it is now called.
This same path was set down by search and rescue parties headed
by Ed "Mad Dog" Rabidowski and Earl Triggers—twenty men in
total, all now missing. RCMP Spokesman Sid Grimes, fielding
questions about an area that seems to be Canada's equivalent of
the Bermuda Triangle, had this to say: "The urge in cases such as
this is to rush to conclusions. Well, I'm not a rusher. Never have
been. We have assembled another search and rescue crew, and
will continue with due vigilance."

Stella Fulton, the missing reporter's mother, said, "The boy
would do anything for a story–for a 'scoop,' as he was forever
calling them. Even as a boy he was curious, always searching,
never satisfied."

Aerial photography of the terrain indicates…

IV.
DREAM OF A
NORTHERN LAND

Northwest Territories
December 6th, 1987. 2:17 p.m.

The thrum of CH-113 Labrador helicopter blades filled the cabin. Five-hundred feet below, the snow-crusted scrubland of the Canadian Shield was a white-and-green blur at 350 mph. Out the west-facing porthole, the Rocky Mountains rose in sheer spires of schist and granite. Five middle-aged men sat in canvas web-seats, feet shod in ballistic nylon combat boots. Five Jack Wolfskin backpacks rested in the cargo hold, pockets crammed with camping gear and dehydrated food packets.

The pilot's face was obscured by a smoked-plastic visor. He said, "Five minutes to drop-off."

Oddy recounted the events of the past twelve hours. From the hotel, they took a limousine to Pearson International. On the way, Grosevoir made telephone arrangements to transfer a quarter of a million dollars into five Swiss bank accounts. They taxied to a private runway and boarded a Learjet, arriving five hours later at an airstrip near Fort Nelson, British Columbia. Waiting in a supply shed was an arsenal to rival a small war-mongering nation. Some of the weaponry was so cutting-edge that nobody had even *heard* of it.

"Gear up," Oddy said.

Crosshairs selected a silenced Remington Model 700 sniper rifle outfitted with an Ajack telescopic sight. Tripwire took a DeLisle Carbine—a self-silenced machinegun used by elite commando forces—and strapped a bandolier of M14's, PBX explosives, and white phosphorus grenades across his chest. Answer kept his

Kirikkales and added a Sig Sauer SG540 light-assault rifle. Oddy choose a fifty-pound Heckler and Koch HK23 heavy machine gun and tucked a pair of Webley Mark 6 pistols into his waistband, remembering how well they'd served Deacon. Zippo loaded a pair of Llamas—the exact model he'd been using for years—and was leaning towards a Galil SAR assault carbine when Grosevoir motioned to a canvas-draped object in the far corner.

"Why not go for what's behind door number three?" he said.

Zippo grunted and pulled the canvas clear. His eyes widened. "Is that—?"

"The M2A1-7," Grosevoir said.

The M2A1-7 flame-thrower was developed in the early eighties by the U.S. military. Two lightweight alloy canisters held six gallons of jellied gasoline which, when drawn through an asbestos-coated tube into a pressurized mixing chamber, produced a forty-foot stream of liquid fire capable of melting flesh off bones in the time it takes to spark a cigarette. Zippo hefted it. The unit was much lighter than the LPO-50 he used in 'Nam. He shouldered it, snapping the buckles over his chest and stomach. He looked kind of foolish: a squat man in Brooks Brothers suit with a Buck-Rogersish jetpack contraption strapped to his back.

Then he thumbed the pilot light and stepped outside and unleashed a sizzling rope of flame that turned a nearby pine into a towering cone of fire. Everyone agreed he didn't look so foolish anymore.

"I'll take it."

Crosshairs wondered if such massive firepower was really necessary to take down three poorly armed prisoners. Kind of like using a bazooka to kill a doodlebug.

Grosevoir outfitted them with tents, parkas, snow pants, boots, toques and gloves, all top-quality. They were also provided a set of collapsible snowshoes, fishing line and hooks, and an M-5 medical kit.

The Labrador helicopter idled on a nearby pad. Grosevoir clapped each man on the back as they boarded, face set in a mask of solemnity.

"Do it for Judy," he told Oddy, the last to board. "Do it for Allison. Just do it."

"Like the shoe commercial," Oddy said, deadpan.

Grosevoir watched the Labrador lift off, carrying the men up and off into the night. The flashing red lights on the helicopter's hull were only slightly more brilliant than his own crimson eye.

"See you soon," he whispered.

The Labrador pitched side-to-side with turbulence. The men swayed with the familiar movement. Tripwire checked his watch: 3:00 p.m. Twenty-two hours since he'd met Oddy in *Canary Isle*. Now here they were, miles away from civilization on a fool's errand for a lunatic millionaire. What the hell was he *doing* here? Had someone slipped an idiot pill into his vodka, making him submissive to this lunacy?

Oddy stared out the window. Although daytime, the landscape was draped in permanent twilight. He tapped the pilot's shoulder. "Will it be like this the whole time?"

"This time of year, yeah," the pilot said. "Be a little lighter in the morning and a little darker come nightfall, but otherwise it's this endless dusk."

The helicopter's nose dipped as it made its descent. Cold air hissed through seams in the airframe. The pilot set them down on a flat-hatted hilltop. The bay-hatch lowered.

"Everyone out." The pilot's visor-shielded eyes swept the barren terrain as if expecting a sudden attack.

From who? Or what?

They shouldered their packs and weapons and moved down the gangway. Oddy paused at the lip. "This is the rendezvous point?" he asked the pilot.

"Back in three days."

"See you then."

"If you say so," the pilot said grimly.

The gangway rose and the Labrador lifted off, quickly disappearing from sight.

The men looked around. They stood on a rocky, rubble-strewn plate which slid out of the thin earth directly ahead like a dark slate tongue. There was a vastness to the landscape, an unpeopled rawness, just the trees and the sky and the land reaching out towards nowhere. Down the rise and all around, fir trees grew where they could, jutting up between and around huge boulders left by receding glaciers and crumbling rock piles. The color of the rocks varied: some were black as obsidian, others so white as to blend in with the snow, others carpeted in sickly yellow moss the hue of calluses, others dappled with light brown splotches resembling rust.

A steady wind blew coldly in their faces, carrying with it the scent of…nothing. The air was completely sterile, scentless. Staring down the hill, Crosshairs thought he saw shapes moving beyond the gloom cast by the trees—the oldest, tallest firs he'd ever seen. The whole effect of this high, empty place was emptiness, though an emptiness that somehow resonated with something feathery and alive. The cold was shocking. A dry, arid cold; the men were forced to breathe through their mouths when the mucous in their noses froze, pinching their airways shut. Answer had only felt this cold once before, when he'd interrogated a Castiglio snitch in a sub-zero meat locker. It was a mind-deadening coldness that crawled around the base of their skulls and seeped up their brainstems, wrapping their thoughts in layers of numbness.

"No wonder the people up here live in igloos," Zippo said. "Goddamn brain freeze must keep them from coming up with a better idea."

"We've got to find low ground," Oddy said, "set up camp."

They found a path zigzagging down the hillside and followed it, soles skittering across patches of bare ice. Crosshairs was surprised at the lack of forest sounds. The jungles of 'Nam were full of them, sly and furtive and skulking. But it now felt as if they were moving through a noiseless vacuum sucked clean of life. No birds chirping. No forest animals scuttling beneath the underbrush. Nothing.

As they moved deeper into the forest, Tripwire experienced the sensation of the trees closing in behind him, blocking the way out. He could almost hear the firs stealthily disentangling themselves from the ground, dragging their ages-old root systems and empty birds' nests, settling down over the path to bar any escape. Tripwire was seized by the momentary fear he'd developed an early case of north-woods *delirium tremens*, and that he'd soon be seeing two-headed snakes darting between the rocks, flying eels arcing through the dark-ened sky, perhaps a massive asthmatic toad croaking at the foot of his sleeping bag. *Fuck.* He'd rather die than end up like those shell-shocked vets who dove under the table every time someone banged the kitchen pots. He shook his head violently, slapped his face a few times, and walked on.

Answer located a circle of scrubland ringed by tall trees. "It'll do," Oddy said.

Zippo and Crosshairs were elected wood-gatherers. Searching beneath the canopy of firs, Crosshairs stumbled across the gutted car-cass of a fawn. Its belly was slashed open and its guts torn out. Viscera lay in haphazard piles around the body like moons surrounding a dead planet. Its large black eyes and unhinged mouth were set in a rictus of animal terror, pink tongue lolling between teeth the color of old bone.

"Don't worry, little boy." Zippo patted Crosshairs on the shoulder. "It's just sleeping."

"What the hell did this?"

"Some mean motherfucker for sure—bear?"

"Yeah, but nothing's been eaten. And aren't bears hibernating this time of year?"

"Listen to Mister-*fucking*-Wizard," Zippo said. "So maybe it wasn't a bear."

"Not one bite taken. Like whatever did it...did it purely for *mean*."

"Circle of life." Zippo was unfazed. "Use that one good eye to scope some kindling."

"Take a break," Crosshairs told him. "You don't have to be a bastard every day of your life, you know."

By the time they returned, the other three had set up camp. The tents Grosevoir had provided were, although expensive, utterly useless against the bitter cold. Instead, Answer and Oddy had constructed a makeshift lean-to, and Tripwire was busy tacking tent shells to the roof and sides. Thanks to a liberal dousing of lighter fluid, they soon had a blazing fire. They sat in a tight circle around the flames, unzipping their parkas to let the warmth in. All of them were silently astounded at their cohesion: in the half-hour since the heli dropped them, they had located a sheltered area with good sight lines, bivouacked, and got a fire going. It had been done in the same methodically urgent manner their Special Ops training had imparted years ago, four fingers and a thumb working in perfect sync.

"So," Tripwire said, jimmying a tin of peaches open with his knife, "this is the Canadian wilderness I've heard so much about."

"Who the hell would live in this?" Zippo wanted to know.

"You got nomads living in the Sahara," Crosshairs said. "This is the other extreme."

"I think it's beautiful," Answer said.

And, in the way unsullied nature often can be, it *was* beautiful. The landscape was an exercise in minimalism: windswept scrubland extended in every direction, the majority of it stony, snow-covered ground in which sickly shrubs struggled for survival. Jack pines and black spruces took root in the inhospitable soil, many of them so wind-twisted they did not look so much like trees as they did a madman's conception of the same. The beauty was harsh but unspoiled: no candy bar wrappers or open sewer grates issuing noxious fumes, no gutter rats scurrying beneath the trees or pigeons roosting on shit-spattered boughs.

Oddy speared a peach half from the passing tin and said, "Beautiful, maybe. But we got a job to do." He unfolded an acetate-covered map. "This is the penitentiary," he pointed to a red dot, "and this is our location," pointing to a location twenty miles south. "Overton and company have been on the lam for two weeks, so our search radius is pretty damn broad."

"Who's to say they're even up here anymore?" Crosshairs asked. "They could've hiked to a side road, flagged down a truck, and be a thousand miles south by now—"

"I don't think so," Answer said. "There would've been an APB put on some extremely dangerous escapees, probably radio broadcasts warning motorists to report any hitchers in the pen's vicinity—"

"And don't forget that Overton's crew only stole warm clothes and weapons," Tripwire added. "No food. They must be half-starved by now, living on nuts and berries and melted snow."

"Easy meat," Zippo said around a mouthful of peach.

"Maybe," Oddy said. "But these guys are killers, and killers are like animals: both are dangerous when cornered."

A feral howl arose somewhere in the forest primeval. There was something intensely unsettling about the sound: like a human being screaming through the vocal cords of a wolf.

"Jesus," Crosshairs said. "Well, at least there's *something* living out here."

"Don't be afraid, little guy," Zippo said. "I brought clean diapers in case you shit the ones you're wearing."

"Screw a shoe, Zip."

"Hey, maybe I'll save my loot and screw a boot."

Oddy folded the map and shoved it in his pocket. "I say we make a circuit around Great Bear Lake," he said. "It's the only fresh water source for miles, so they're probably hunkered nearby."

"How long is that going to take?" Answer asked.

"Twenty years back, we hoof doubletime, circuit it in two days. But now, in these conditions? Say three, three-and-a-half."

"Goddamn, Trip," Zippo said, shooting the doughy porn director a dirty look. "Would it have killed you to hit the gym once in a goddamn while—some jazzercize, for fuck's sake?"

"You set the pace, trashmouth," Tripwire said. "I'll match it."

"On what—a Ski Doo?"

"You're about as funny as a kick in the teeth."

Oddy checked his watch: 4:00 p.m. Twenty-three hours had passed since their meeting with Grosevoir and, apart from a few fitful hours on the Learjet, none of them had slept.

"I'm going to get some shut-eye," he said. "Head out at first light."

"Who's taking first watch?" Crosshairs said.

Zippo said, "Aren't any Gooks waiting in ambush out there."

"I know," Crosshairs said defensively. "But there could be…other things."

"I'll take it," Answer said.

Oddy nodded. "Tell when you want to switch off."

The men shucked their boots and zipped into their bags. Despite the ground's total lack of lumbar support they were soon deep in exhausted slumber. Their dreams, mercifully unremembered, were the dreams of combat vets: burning villages and burning farmland and burning children, brutally disfigured but oh-so-familiar faces screaming up through the haze of memory.

They were as yet unaware that there never was, and never would be, a Saugeen Valley Penitentiary. They were unaware that Marcus Overton did not exist; his name was selected from a phone book, his crimes fabricated. They were unaware of what waited for them in the surrounding wilderness, waiting with sharp claws and sharp teeth and ageless cunning. They were unaware of why a creature masquerading as a man had drawn them there, alone, together.

But they would. Soon.

《《—》》

At midnight, the man came.

Stumbling blindly through the trees he came, parka torn and bloodstained. Mouth open in a silent scream he came, hands clutching a pair of silenced Berettas, hammers cocked, clips empty. Terror-stricken he came, casting quick glances over his shoulder as if the Furies themselves were in pursuit. Half-dead he came, arms and chest scored with long bloody scratches, chunks of flesh missing from his shoulders and calves.

Answer watched him blunder into the clearing. The man was oblivious to the guttering fire and the sleeping men. His eyes were focused on a distant hilltop—the same hilltop upon which the helicopter had dropped Answer hours before—with an intensity suggestive of emancipation.

The man ran recklessly, as though blind. Not knowing whether he was one of the men they were hunting, Answer tackled him around the ankles. The man fell on his face and the pistols skittered out of reach. Answer shimmied up his body like it was a pole, pinning the man's arms to his sides. The man offered little resistance. He made feeble whimpering noises, like a frightened animal.

The commotion roused the others, who zipped out of their sleeping bags and joined Answer.

"Lookee, lookee," Zippo said, ever the optimist. "Could this be one of the dogfuckers, served up on a silver platter?" He envisioned a brisk wrap-up, Overton and Co. dead, their heads in a backpack, and him free for a week of R&R. Maybe he'd take a nature hike, cataloguing the native flora and fauna. Or maybe he'd use the M2A1-7 to flash-fry a moose. The possibilities were endless.

"Doesn't look like Overton," Tripwire said, rubbing sleep-crust from his eyes.

The man's face was a death mask: the haggard features were engraved with shock and, nibbling at the edges like hungry mice, dawning insanity. He bore the unmistakable marks of the hunted: eyes darting like flies trapped in walnut husks, limbs twitching with the instinctive urge to flee, chest expanding and contracting in an attempt to oxygenate an overtaxed nervous system. Crosshairs noted, with more than a little unease, the man was dressed as they were. "Let me go! Goddamnit, they're coming!"

Who's coming? Oddy thought. *Unless this guy is one of Overton's crew, on the run from the Mounties or some other task force.* He didn't relish the prospect of wrangling with the Canadian authorities to claim him, especially with hair-triggers like Zippo and Answer in the mix. Situation had "international incident" written all over it.

The man's head was shaven, the lines of his skull visible. Through a tear in his parka, Answer saw a tattoo stamped across his biceps: a pair of interlocking wings with the words CANADIAN AIRBORNE REGIMENT underneath. Evidently the man had once been part of a military unit. The name "Edwards" was stitched on the parka's breast.

"You are all going to die," his voice eerily calm, "if you don't let me up."

"Who's gonna kill us, shitbird?" Zippo said. "You?"

"Not me. They're out there. In the woods. Getting closer."

"Edwards? That your name?" Oddy asked. The man bobbled his head like a pigeon. "Edwards, what are *you* doing out here?"

Edwards shook his head, as if to reply would be redundant, a waste of precious time. Deep in the forest, the snap of branches.

"Do you know anything about Marcus Overton?" Oddy asked. The man's mouth unhinged like a ventriloquist's dummy. "Oh, Jesus..."

"What?" Tripwire asked. "What's wrong?"

Sounds drawing nearer. All around the clearing. Low, choked moans.

"He sent you, didn't he?" Edwards said. "You landed on that hill, didn't you?"

"*Who* sent us?" Oddy said.

"That fucking monster. Anton Grosevoir."

A spikewave of dread hammered down Oddy's spine.

"Do you have guns?" Edwards asked. "Get them."

Crosshairs asked why.

"You wouldn't believe me if I told you."

"Listen." Oddy squinted at the tree line. "We've been sent to find Marcus Overton, an escapee from the Saugeen Valley Supermax. If you know anything, can help in any way, I'll make sure—"

"There is no Saugeen Valley Supermax. Never was. No Marcus Overton. There is nobody left. My team is dead. Just me...and you... and *them*."

"Them *who?*" Unnerved by Edwards's warnings, Tripwire slammed a clip into the DeLisle Carbine. "Who the fuck are you running from?"

As if in preemptive reply, the first one emerged from the sheltering firs. Initially it was as indistinct as the bushes and trees near its sides; then it stepped forward, limping towards the fire's glow. It shuffled stiffly, as if it had steel rods inserted into its limbs preventing smooth motion.

"What the fuck—?" Zippo said.

"Just shoot it. Now," Edwards moaned.

It looked human—at least, it walked upright, and possessed the basic appendages of one. But something was fundamentally *wrong* with its face: it was red and glistening, as if the flesh had been stripped away. It staggered closer. There was a black pit where its right eye used to be. Knotted strands of black hair stuck with cockleburs hung from its skull in rotting ropes. It stumbled on a tree stump and spun like a drunkard. It had, at some distant time, been a woman. One breast hung to her navel, patches of decay blooming across the seam joining it to her chest. The other one was missing entirely, a pulpy round disc where it should've been, black and squirming with maggots. Most disturbing were the guts hanging out of her stomach, swaying between her festering legs like a hula dancer's grass skirt.

"Shoot it," Edwards pleaded. "*Shoooot* it."

Behind the woman was another one, this one male. Tall and once-muscular, his chest draped in the remains of an ice-crusted tee-shirt that read: "WORLD'S GREATEST LOVER." His flesh was black and bloated and shiny, like a wet innertube. One arm was missing entirely; a bleached shoulder socket peeked through a vent in the fabric. The other arm was stripped of flesh, bones clicking and clattering skeletally. At some point his putrefied neck muscles had been unable to support the weight of his skull; his head hung halfway down his chest on a few strands of tendon, the rest having pulled apart like taffy in the hands of hungry children. Despite the troublesome handicap, his jaws continued to snap fitfully.

Zombies? Tripwire's mind reeled. *Was it possible?*

It was Crosshairs who acted first. Raising the rifle and centering the lead zombie in the crosshairs, he exhaled completely, and fired. The Remington kicked solidly against his shoulder and the muzzle spat flame. The back of the dead woman's head exploded outward, the spray of blood and bone and tissue splattering the bark of a nearby tree. Her body continued forward for a few steps before her atrophied nervous system got the message she was officially dead.

More of them appeared. Inconceivably, they were in worse shape than the first two. Heading the second wave was something that appeared to be female, but, this was at best an educated guess. Its flesh was coal-black, whether from rot or flame was uncertain, and its eyes had been punched from their sockets; they hung pendant on red stalks, bump-bumping against its blackened cheeks in time with its shuffling footsteps. Some of its torso was intact, but much of it was hollowed out. Its ribcage was burst open from the gaseous rot of its internal organs, tatters of flesh hanging in rips and rags; the hollowed cavity had been stuffed with weeds and dead fescue, as though the creature still felt a need its body should be filled with something, anything.

"Shoot them in the head!" Edwards screamed. "Don't let them touch you!"

Zippo secured the flame-thrower on his back and thumbed the pilot light. Answer cocked his Kirikkales and grabbed a hatchet. Tripwire leveled the DeLisle and fired a burst through the nearest zombie. The bullets punched through its chest, ripping away chunks of flesh, but it continued to advance, moaning, a sound like an old man dying in his sleep.

On the heels of the peeled zombie came a half-man: somewhere along the way he'd misplaced his legs. But, with a determination borne of extreme hunger, he dragged himself along using his hands. Due to the gaping hole where his legs were once attached, and the combination of rocks, weeds, and bushes, much of his insides had been tugged from his body cavity and now trailed behind him, a rotting anatomical smorgasbord. A silver fox tore at a long gray-green rope of intestine that played out behind the zombie like a grisly umbilical cord. He neither noticed nor cared, focusing on Zippo with eyes that leaked gummy fluid like those of a sickly animal.

More appeared every second, pouring out of the trees like rats from a burning building. One was dressed in a red Mountie uniform, the brass buttons tarnished brown, the icy fabric crackling like dull metal as it advanced. Another looked young and recently dead; a Nikon camera with a spiderwebbed lens hung on a strap around its neck, cutting deep into the curdled flesh.

"Jesus," Zippo muttered. "Look at all the dead fucks."

Oddy nocked the HK21 heavy-machinegun on his right hip and let it rip. .223-inch belt-fed rounds passed through the firing chamber at the rate of ten-per-second, exiting the muzzle at 3,250 feet-per-second. The results were spectacular: bullets slammed into trees like a buzzsaw, wet splinters exploding in all directions. Oddy trained the barrel on the self-proclaimed World's Greatest Lover and watched as the lothario's body was ripped to shreds, yellow pus and clotted innards spewing from the bullet holes in foul-smelling rivulets. The force of the slugs knocked Romeo on his back and his free-floating head split open on a sharp rock. Curds of blood-dappled brain spurted wildly. Oddy let out a war-whoop and blew at wisps of smoke curling from the gun barrel.

Answer approached the peeled one. It tracked him blindly, as an earthworm might, rotting arms outstretched. Answer methodically placed bullets through each of its legs. Kneecaps shattered like china plates and the zombie plopped down in the snow but continued forward. Answer stepped back, shielding his eyes, and brought the hatchet down into its face, blade hacking at an angle into its open mouth. Its eyes stayed open. Not even a flinch. A thin stream of dark blood pissed around the blade. It grabbed at the handle, and Answer's attached hand.

Answer pulled the hatchet out of the zombie's face, shearing the remains of its nose off in the process, and struck again, but higher up this time, splitting the charred dome of its forehead. He wiggled the blade back and forth, like a woodsman trying to extricate his axe from a knotty bit of wood. A fissure transected the zombie's skull down the center and then both halves fell away. It looked like a ladybug opening its wings. Its brain was alive with maggots and red winged insects, some of which were crawling the hatchet blade. With the detachment of a surgeon, Answer inserted the gun between its remaining teeth and, angling the barrel slightly upwards, blew its head into sticky red confetti. "Huh," he said.

"More coming out of the woodwork over here!" Crosshairs hollered.

A third line advanced sluggishly. Their sloth was due in great part to their degree of decomposition. The few that could walk did so haltingly, their muscles having reached a level of decay so as to render locomotion a speculative endeavor. One of them, perhaps a woman, perhaps once beautiful, lurched forward jerkily, as though she were a marionette controlled by a Parkinson's-afflicted puppeteer; her liver, a black-grey sack dimpled with milky lesions, slipped through a deep gash in her side, which she ground into mush underfoot. Another—legless, armless, sexless, rotted to the bones—pulled itself through the snow using its mostly toothless mouth.

"Let me do you a favor," Zippo said, training his flame-thrower on the nearest crawler. The weapon hissed a lance of flame that consumed the zombie from head to hips. Zippo traced its limbs with fire, watching flesh transform into crusted ash. The zombie continued to press forward until it reached Zippo's feet. It stared up at him, fire pouring out of its eye sockets like two flaming sambuca shots, and began to gnaw on his boot. Zippo grimaced with something close to pity before bringing his other boot down on its skull, the force of which caused broiled gray matter to spurt in black, pus-threaded jets from its ears and nostrils and eye sockets.

Crosshairs took a knee and racked the bolt smoothly before picking off three zombies with explosive head shots. His final shot sheared off a deadhead's skull to reveal a brain half-consumed by a family of mice who'd chewed their way in through an ear.

"Damn you, go *down!*" Tripwire screamed at a particularly tenacious zombie. He'd torn its arms off with the DeLisle and punched a softball-sized hole through its neck. Still it came. Tripwire pulled the trigger to hear a dry *click*: out of ammo. The dead thing reached for him. Skeletal fingers hung with strips of rotting meat brushed his parka, yellow nails ripping the fabric with terrifying strength. It smelled of a slaughterhouse sluice-grate.

Tripwire pulled out his K-Bar. Stepping back, he slashed across the thing's pendant belly. It opened up like someone had jerked the seam on a Ziploc bag full of medical waste. Decayed viscera splashed across the snow. The zombie, spurred by some vestigial instinct, bowed and attempted to gather up its truant intestines. Tripwire brought the knife up into its face, burying five inches of tempered steel into its left eye. He stepped back and kicked the hilt in the manner of a football punter. The blade passed through the zombie's diseased brain-pan to exit, in a little gout of gore, at the tip of its spinal column.

Unnoticed amidst the carnage, a single deadhead slipped under the radar: an infant, or something that had once been one. Its skin was glistening and slick with a coating of mucous-like slime. A shred of placenta, rotting black, was perched atop its bulbous bald skull in a travesty of a baby's bonnet. A great deal of undeveloped intestine drooled out of its anus in soupy loops, riddled with holes pecked by hungry ravens. The infant deadhead pulled itself along by its hands, as its feet had been hacked or eaten away.

Oddy drew a Webley as one of the fleeter zombies made a stumblebum lunge for him. Oddy dodged left, cat-quick for his size, grabbed the thing's outstretched arm—like grabbing a sausage casing filled with cold jelly—and tore it from its socket. As the zombie lacked eyebrows, eyelids, or a jaw, Oddy was unable to tell if the loss of its limb left it feeling surprised, or outraged, or blasé. He rendered all conjecture a moot point by jamming the Webley's muzzle into its pus-slobbering nasal cavity and pulling the trigger.

When the gunshot died away, he heard shrill, horror-struck screaming.

Edwards.

Who was being eaten by the very small but very persistent deadhead. He writhed on the ground, kicking up puffs of powdery snow. The tiny zombie had clamped itself onto Edwards' right eyelid; his skin stretched like salt taffy before tearing loose. Edwards' lidless eye was horridly round and wide, cornea threaded with bright stitches of blood. The man's screams felt like ice picks sliding into Crosshairs' ears. *It's the ultimate dead baby joke,* he thought wildly. *Except the joke's on that poor fuck.*

"Jesus—Jesu!" Edwards blubbered, swaying to his feet. "Get it off...get it *aaaawwwff!*"

The dead baby grasped Edwards' ears as he flailed in a shrieking circle. Its toothless mouth was battened over Edwards' eye socket like a leech. A sickening *pop* as it sucked Edwards' eye from its cup. Edwards' screams intensified, boots mashing the infant's trailing innards into paste.

Its grip on Edwards' ears slipped and it fell. But its descent was checked by Edwards' ocular stalk, still attached to his eye, which resided in the dead baby's mouth. Edwards spun in a pain-frenzied dervish. Blood gushed from his socket. "Ag!" he screamed. "Ag! Ag! Ag!"

The baby clung resolutely to its prize until the stalk broke, gummy red cord snapping back into Edwards' socket like an over-taxed elastic band, the baby tumbling into the snow. Moments later, Answer's booted foot came down on its head. Crunch.

Zippo looked around: bullet-riddled and blade-reamed bodies lay around the campsite. Arms and legs and heads were scattered akimbo, mouths still opening and closing. The syrupy-sickly smell of rotting and burning flesh. Organs dappling the ground like misshapen gemstones...

And a half-blind man clutching both hands over an empty, blood-jetting socket, screaming, "It ate my eye! The fucking thing *ate* my fucking *eye!*"

Tripwire retrieved the First Aid kit and knelt beside Edwards. "Take it easy," he said. "Lay still."

"Take it *easy?* A fucking dead baby just ate my fucking—"

"Chill, son," Oddy soothed. "Gonna be fine."

"Boy doesn't look so hot to me, Sarge," Zippo said.

"Shitcan that lip."

Tripwire pumped a syrette of morphine sulfate into Edwards's chest. That quieted him down. Then he soaked a wad of gauze in Dextram and poked it into the empty socket. Edwards lay back, semi-comatose with morphine and shock.

Crosshairs summed up the group's feeling: "No...fucking...*way.* That did not just happen."

But the bodies and parts of bodies surrounding them stood as undeniable proof it *had* happened. As if to hammer the point home, a decapitated head near Zippo's feet began to make gluttonous sounds through a mouthful of brown bile.

"Tell this one here nothing happened," Zippo said, smashing at the head with the flame-thrower's butt.

"But these people are *dead*," Crosshairs said, steadfastly refusing belief. "The dead do not get up and walk."

"Or crawl," Oddy said.

"Or eat." Tripwire.

"Yet here they are, defying all reason." Answer.

Edwards moaned fitfully. Bloody petals bloomed through the gauze.

"You think it's true, what he said?" Zippo hooked a thumb at Edwards. "No Overton, no prison? Then what the fuck are we doing here?"

"Perhaps I can shed some light on that, gentlemen."

The voice came from behind them.

A smooth, buttery voice that turned their collective bone-marrow to jelly.

They turned to face the speaker.

Who was, of course, Anton Grosevoir.

War Zone "D," South Vietnam
July 15th, 1967. 20:49 hours.

The central hut.

Wet ripping noises came from inside. A sound like waterlogged canvas splitting down the seams. Then a wretched scream, choked off in mid-stream. More noises: moist and sucking.

"Jesus Christ, Sarge." Tripwire's breath hot and ragged in Oddy's ear. "What could it be—some kind of animal?"

"Not like any animal I've ever seen," Gunner's knotty, farm-strong hands trembled around the Stoner's molded handgrips.

Oddy, who'd seen the hanging shapes inside the hut, shapes resembling flayed human corpses, was, for the first time as unit leader, unsure of how to proceed. On one hand, they had a clear objective: destroy the weapons shipment, kill every VC they encountered. On the other hand, he was possessed by a primitive and instinctive urge to flee, an impulse stirred by whoever or whatever was in that hut. He glanced across the clearing where the flanking team was hunkered. The pinprick glow of Zippo's pilot light indicated they were ready to engage on his signal.

The VC officer arranged his remaining troops in a rough firing line. Eight AK-47's were nocked on eight shoulders, eight barrels trained on the hut. Autofire and muzzle flash lit the night. Bamboo stalks shattered like brittle bones. Black blood, the blood of the dead, spattered from the hut's mouth. Hut supports snapped. The soldiers paused to reload.

It was the last thing they'd ever do.

The moment before the creature emerged, Oddy was rocked by a feeling of complete and utter helplessness. He felt like a small child being pulled, kicking and screaming, to the dentist's chair, or a puppy dragged by an incensed owner to have its snout smeared in its own shit. There was nothing he could do to stop what he was about to see. His limbs felt shackled, his eyelids pierced with fishhooks and tugged wide, his heart and mind forced to confront the dawning reality.

A form took shape, melting out of the darkened hut, revealing itself with aching slowness, inch by inch, limb by nightmare limb.

"Dear God," Crosshairs whispered as every monstrous appendage, every unfathomable proportion, every heart-stopping dimension flayed themselves into his cortex with hellish clarity.

In its totality it was unlike anything they had ever seen, although portions of its anatomy were dimly recognizable. It was short and squat, capable of walking on two limbs, or four, or six. Some of these limbs terminated in cloven hooves, others webbed digits, or suction-cup discs, or nail-tipped claws.

The body was skinless, thick cables of muscle knitting together an alien skeletal structure. Bristly hairs grew through raw tendons crawling with black flies. The head was scooped inwards like a shovel's blade; two flaps of skin rose from its shoulder blades to encompass the skull in the manner of a cobra's hood. The eyes were huge and multifaceted, like a dragonfly's, mouth spanning half its face, studded with row upon row of needle-sharp teeth. A pair of tarantula-like fangs, long and black, curved below the creature's jaw-bone, dripping venom that sizzled the moist earth. It regarded the VC soldiers with horrible understanding: like a malicious child peering at bottled insects.

I don't believe this, Oddy thought. *I'm not seeing this. Maybe I'm asleep and this is just a very intense dream. Maybe I'm dead and unaware of it. Could this be hell?*

And yet he knew he was not dead, not dreaming, and this was as real as any event in his life had been. As a soldier, you had to trust your senses: sight, smell, touch, memory. If you could not trust them, you could not trust anyone or anything. And if you couldn't trust, you would not survive. So Oddy was forced to believe what he saw, even if it meant questioning every truth of the world he existed in.

The VC soldiers fumbled to insert fresh clips into their AK's.

Too slow. Eons too slow.

With a quickness defying the laws of physics and locomotion, the skinless creature advanced. Limbs whirling, it moved down the line of soldiers. None of them moved. None of them screamed. The telltale sound of cleaved flesh carried across the clearing.

The creature paused, a magician preparing to reveal a most bewildering sleight of hand. One by one, like deadheaded dandelions, the soldier's heads fell to the ground. The killing slices were surgically straight: it would've been possible to center the bubble on a carpenter's level by laying it across the severed necks. Solid columns of blood gushed from the stumps, high into the air, a horrific water ballet.

Eight men dead. That fast. A heartbeat. A *blink.*

The creature pounced on the terrified officer.

Tripwire, Gunner, and Crosshairs stared at their Sergeant. Zippo, Answer, and Slash waited for a signal.

Oddy was on the bubble. He thought back to officer's training, the five cardinal questions an officer must address before engaging. Yet he knew this decision could not be made by following institutionalized guidelines. It had to be a gut reaction. And his gut said:

DO IT. FAST AND HARD.

DO IT *NOW.*

The creature slashed at the VC officer's face and chest in the manner of a hen scratching the dirt of its coop. The smell of blood overhung the village like a cowl.

We have to kill it, Oddy thought. *Kill it now or die trying.*

"Follow me if you want," Oddy said. "No shame if you don't."

Then he stepped into the clearing.

Every heartbeat thundered in Oddy's chest like a cathedral bell. He was hyperaware, moving quickly but silently. Out of the corner of his eye he saw Zippo and Slash cutting across to rendezvous. Their eyes were wide and terror-filled. But they came.

Anytime. Anywhere. Anyhow.

I will die for you.

Oddy racked the Mossberg scattergun. He'd picked up the nasty habit of soaking the buckshot in rat poison and repacking the shells. It was a dirty trick, but he'd seen Charlie pull some doozies over the course of his three Tours. Factoring in the creature's speed, the best he could hope was to get off two, maybe three good shots.

He felt something whiz past his right ear and, a fraction of a second later, a hunk of the creature's cobra-like hood vaporized in a cloud of red. Oddy craned his neck to see Crosshairs reloading his sniper rifle. The bullet missed Oddy's head by two inches, maybe less.

The creature let loose an ear-piercing shriek. Beneath it, the VC officer was a scattering of skin-rags that only a seasoned forensic pathologist could've identified as of human origin. Its jaws snapped. Oddy saw tiny white worms crawling between its teeth. He raised the shotgun and unloaded buckshot into those teeth. Zippo charged hard. The creature was flat on its back, its face buckshot-torn. Zippo pulled up at twenty feet and trained the nozzle. *Whoooosh.* A spiraling funnel of fire ripped across the night to engulf the creature's thrashing form. Zippo swept the nozzle side-to-side, screaming, "Eat it! A–hooo–*yeah!* Eat it and *die!*"

The creature stood in the bath of flame. One of its eyes drooped like a half-inflated balloon, the membrane withered like an apple gone to rot. Its mouth and surrounding flesh were pocked with blackened perforations where double-aught buckshot burrowed home, streams of greenish fluid trickling from the holes. Fire lived on its shoulders and limbs, swirling eddies and flaming dust-devils pouring out of its mouth and rising from its back in fiery wings.

And yet, if its remaining eye could've been said to reflect any emotion, that emotion would be wry amusement.

It's been so long, young one, a faraway voice chimed in Oddy's head. *So long since I've been tested.*

Perhaps it was a need for cover that made Slash duck into the central hut. Perhaps it was simple curiosity. Inside it smelled primal and hostile: if it were possible to breathe blood, Slash felt he was now doing so. Sarge's shotgun barked outside, then Zippo screamed something over the gale of his flame-thrower. The ground beneath Slash's feet was uneven and slippery. Felt like standing on a pile of wet latex. He lit a flare, illuminating the hut in stark orange light.

Skinned bodies—ten, fifteen, more—hung suspended from bamboo poles. Robbed of their flesh, the bodies were sickeningly skinny. On the floor beneath them, their skins lay in yellow pools. It filled every one of his senses: the stench of opened entrails, the sight of the bodies, the feel of their flesh under his boots, the creaking sound as they spun on copper-wire garrotes, the air salty with blood. The majority were children. Their underdeveloped penises were flaccid red knobs, skinned vaginas the petals of scarlet flowers slicked with dew. Slash reeled. His face brushed a flank of tacky meat. He could remember nothing of his life before this moment: he'd been born into this horror, reared in it, knew nothing but.

He unhooked a body, a young girl, from the garrote…

Tssst, Crosshairs' rifle whispered. *Thuup*: a flaming wedge disappeared from the creature's scalp. But it would not go down. Was this something that could be killed using the customary tools of warfare, bullets and fire and black rage? Or was something greater required: faith, holy water, a sacrificial virgin? Crosshairs ejected the spent shell from the rifle breech, jacked a new round, exhaled. *Tssst*.

Zippo jettisoned the LPO-50 in favor of a pair of Magnums. He held one in each hand, firing them one at a time, right hand, left hand, right, left. His eyes were huge and he was thinking, *What the fuck's it gonna take?*

"Duck, Sarge!"

Oddy hit the dirt as Gunner opened up with the Stoner. Set on full autofire, the gun sounded like a jackhammer. Bullets slammed into the creature, stitching its torso and ripping gobbets of melting flesh from its sides. Oddy saw, for the first time, an expression cross those nightmare features to give him hope.

Ouch, the expression said. *That fucking hurts.*

So it did something about it.

One second the creature wasn't there and the next it was on top of Oddy. He thrashed against its seething strength, but his arms were quickly pinned to his sides with the ease of a mother restraining a fretting infant. The creature's smell—wet rawhide burning in a campfire—filled his nostrils. Up close, its features were a lunatic mishmash of animal, human, monster. One insectoid eye was now completely deflated, corneal jam sizzling down a flaming cheek. Its teeth were those of an extinct species, some giant carnivorous lizard. Its skinned nose was pert and upturned, a schoolgirl's nose. Oddy was suddenly aware of how full his bowels were.

A claw-tipped limb ripped through his fatigues, shredding his flak jacket like it were tissue paper. Oddy sucked his stomach in, but one of the claws pulled a sizzling line of pain across his chest. Blood gushed out of him to spatter his pants, his boots, the dirt. It hoisted Oddy as if he were no more substantial than a seamstress's dummy and hurled him toward the fire pit. Oddy hit the ground hard, saw stars, struggled to a sitting position, and saw his thighs were coated in blood.

For the past forty-seven seconds—the time that had passed since Oddy stepped into the clearing—Crosshairs had been in "the zone." A preternatural calm had settled over him. The world receded until all that remained was the pinprick of existence seen through his Gewher scope. His hands did not shake, and he fired as smoothly and easily as he had at the firing range in Duc Phong. His fingers worked the bolt crisply and his shots, give or take an inch, hit their mark. He chambered another round and squeezed the trigger as Oddy sailed through the air. The slug struck the creature's flank, tearing loose a knotted network of muscle. The creature turned sharply, clawing at the spot where the slug had tore through, slitting its remaining eye at the sniper hunkered behind a copse of mangroves.

Then it came for him.

When Crosshairs was a small boy, he'd once rolled a flaming, kerosene-soaked tire down a hill. It was night, the hill steep. The tire wobbled as it rolled downhill, picking up speed, flames spun by centrifugal force to resemble a glowing buzz saw, wild and uncontrolled and unstoppable, strangely beautiful, strangely terrifying.

This is what the creature reminded him of as it closed in on him: a flaming dervish rushing headlong at top speed. He squeezed off a final shot. Then it was on him.

This is how a gym rope must feel, he though crazily as the creature shimmied up his body. Fire-tipped claws ripped into his flesh; octopus-like suction discs, blazing hot, leeched to his skin leaving blistering circles. A wall of gnashing, blood-stained teeth reared. A brittle *crunch*. Crosshairs crumpled to the ground, the top-left portion of his head gone.

The creature turned to Gunner, who was slamming another clip into the Stoner. Zippo continued to fire the Magnums: flaming plugs of tissue leapt off the creature's body, dotting the ground like glowing coals. The creature moved slower, badly wounded, less assured but more enraged.

Oddy's pants and underwear were soaked against his skin with blood. He had no idea how badly he was hurt. He heaved himself up and stumbled towards Crosshairs.

"Come on!" Gunner screamed at the thing. "Come get some!"

The hydrostatic shock of the Stoner's .223-inch rounds were capable of killing a bull moose. In the three seconds it took to cover the distance between Crosshairs' body, Gunner plugged no less than eighteen rounds into the creature, many at point-blank range.

He might as well have been armed with a pea shooter.

The creature lashed out. Gunner's weapon fell to the ground. Unfortunately for Gunner, his arms were still attached to it. "Oh god," Gunner mumbled.

Darkness prevented the others from seeing Gunner backing into the jungle. They could only hear screaming, and the spraylike sound of blood. Then, for a heart-wrenching moment, Tripwire saw Gunner illuminated by the flickering flames that rose off the creature's body. The armless machine-gunner's face was ghost-white, his eyes wide and terror-filled, like a child face-to-face with the monster lurking beneath his bed.

"TobyNancyHollyBradTobyNancyHollyBrad," Gunner said, retreating further into the jungle. The names were those of his children. He'd been a poor husband and a poorer father, disrespectful of his marriage vows and neglectful of his children. Yet he had hoped, with the sincerity of feeling not unusual in those who'd faced death, to turn over a new leaf upon his return. There would be little league games and soapbox racers, school plays and piano recitals. Now, the blood from his madly-jetting stumps plastering his face, he knew this would never be. This certainty, the bitter clarity of it, filled him with a depth of regret so profound it was as if his heart had been seized in a cold fist and compressed into a tiny red agate. He thought, senselessly, that if he continued backing away he might somehow retreat in time—return to yesterday, last week, last year. Perhaps, were he to retreat far enough, he could return to the exact moment of decision and choose differently, make a choice that ensured he wouldn't die here, like this, half a world removed from everything he knew and loved.

The creature lashed again. Gunner's perspective suddenly dropped two feet as his legs were cut from under him. He turned, this armless, legless thing, running clumsily, running on shredded stumps, running until equilibrium deserted and he fell face-first into the dirt, leg-stubs kicking feebly.

"TobNantyHoddyBlad," he whimpered, mouth filling with dark jungle soil.

Something slashed the back of his neck. Then nothing.

By the time Oddy reached him, Crosshairs had two morphine syrettes jutting from his chest. He was uncapping another. Oddy eased it from his fingers. "Pacify, son," he said. "You're gonna be fine. Fine as cherry wine."

He removed his shredded flak jacket and propped it under Crosshairs's head. Then he covered his face with his fatigue vest. The damage was too gruesome to contemplate. Huts blazed all around them, bright orange shafts holding the night at bay.

"We need a med evac now!" Oddy shouted into the PRC's mouthpiece.

"*What's your twenty?*" dispatch asked.

Oddy fed the rough coordinates. Dispatch spat out a landing area one klick east.

"How soon?" Oddy asked.

"*Give it twenty.*"

"Better make it faster. We got some KIA's, another one on death's door."

"*Give it twenty,*" came dispatch's impersonal reply.

Answer had not moved when Oddy stepped into the clearing. It had nothing to do with fear, or apprehension, or panic. If Answer felt these emotions at all, it was on a remote and rudimentary level, the level upon which lesser gods and demons experience emotion. He didn't engage because he was certain the creature they sought to kill was intrinsically unkillable. But, more importantly, he suspected that on some level, possibly cellular, he and it were identical. It would be as counterproductive as attempting to destroy one's mirrored image.

Slash stepped from the hut. Blood ringed his neck like a sunburn. Something was draped around his shoulders, something slack and greasy resembling a small animal turned inside-out. Answer realized it was a child's body. Slash began walking into the jungle.

Answer stepped into his path. He recognized, with perfect clarity, that Slash had gone insane. Something about the set of his mouth and the way he'd wrapped the child's arm around his neck like a scarf.

"What do you think?" Slash shrugged. The tiny body flapped.

Answer said, "Keen...fashion sense."

Slash unsheathed his knife. He shaved a ribbon of flesh off the dead girl's thigh with slow deliberation. It landed in the dirt, stuck with pebbly soil the color and texture of coffee grounds. "There's more inside," he said. "Hanging. Some kind of altar."

"I don't know what you're talking about," Answer said.

"Why didn't you help?" Slash pushed the knife-tip into one of the girl's eyes. "Why are you still *here?*"

Answer said, "Why aren't you helping?"

"I got...sidetracked," Slash said. "We needed you. I think Gunner's dead, and Crosshairs...where the fuck *were* you?" Slash jabbed the knife in Answer's direction. "We got to stick together, man. We don't, what are we? Animals, man. Fuckin' animals."

"Put the knife away."

"You ain't my C.O., man." The knife weaved in front of Slash's face like a hypnotized cobra. "You don't tell me what to do."

"I'm not telling you anything." Answer flicked his wrist and the carving chisel he'd loaded up his shirtsleeve dropped into his waiting palm. "I'm asking you. Nicely."

Slash sneered. "You little prick. So young, so righteously fucked up." Jab-jab went the knife. "I'd be doing the world a favor."

"I'm sorry you feel that way."

"Not as sorry as you're going to be."

Slash chopped sideways with the knife, but clumsily, the flayed corpse screwing with his balance. Answer deflected the blade, taking a deep gash across his fingers, and brought the chisel up in a tight arc, stabbing it into the flesh between Slash's second and third ribs. Slash made a barfing noise—*braaak!*—dropping the knife. Answer pulled the chisel out. Very little blood.

Wrapping his right leg behind Slash's left and pushing his head back forcefully, Answer tripped him. As they fell, he positioned the chisel beneath Slash's breastbone. They hit the ground hard and the force of impact drove the chisel into Slash's chest, puncturing a lung. Blood burbled around the handle, flecking their chins and throats. Slash was not screaming. Answer covered his mouth anyway. Slash bit his fingers. The noises he was making were, for the most part, incomprehensible.

"Shshsh," Answer soothed. "Shshsh."

Slash spasmed once, twice, three times in all. Answer rolled off him and tossed the chisel into the bushes. The flayed child remained wound around Slash's shoulders, a gruesome boa. It was the first time Answer had killed an ally. Characteristically, he felt nothing. Perhaps it was this lack of regret, this utter absence of emotion, that drew the creature to him.

Answer heard rustling in the palms behind him and knew instinctively who, or what, had sought him out.

The creature presented itself slowly, with obvious pleasure: a peacock fanning its plumage. It was injured, and badly: one eye hung down its cheek like a lanced condom, its limbs riddled with leaking holes. Yet it seemed well-pleased, as if the village, with its flayed children and decapitated bodies, dying and dead men, fire and blood, was an element it took to as naturally as a fish to water.

Answer looked at the thing. Close up, it seemed older than he'd imagined possible. Its raw flesh was lined with tiny wrinkles and cracks, like those in granite. It seemed to be smiling, or baring its teeth, both at once.

Hovering above Slash's corpse, it hooked a pair of talon-tipped appendages on either side of his skull, under the jawbone. Answer watched it tug at Slash's head, pulling it away from the body, cracking the spine, ripping it off. It hurled the head into the clearing as if it were an emptied peanut shell.

The creature's voice grated like glass shards over exposed bone. "Sit," it told Answer. "Listen."

Northwest Territories
December 7th, 1987. 1:14 a.m.

"Sit," Anton Grosevoir said. "Listen."

Zippo leveled a Llama at the little man's head. "Why don't I just whisper a little breeze through your skull instead, you lying, creepy little weasel."

"Then there's a zero-percent chance you'll get out of this alive," Grosevoir said evenly. "And, much worse, you run the risk of meeting death without the foggiest idea of what this place is, the creatures who inhabit it, and how you *might*—" a sharkish smile, "—survive."

Fingers of light crawled over the eastern horizon, long dim corridors offering no heat whatsoever. What the light did was brighten the campsite, etching the bodies of the twice-dead strewn across the uneven ground. The fact they were now officially dead had somehow accelerated the decay process: the bodies rotted before the men's eyes, skin and bones and even teeth melting into puddles of putrescence with the rapidity of Popsicles on a summer sidewalk. The frigid temperatures did nothing to deaden the smell of rot, which cold-cocked them like a closed fist.

Edwards moaned. Oddy glanced at Grosevoir, unable to ignore the fact he'd appeared out of nowhere (thinking, *He's taken a page from Answer's book*), and said, "Edwards—you hired him?"

"Yes." Grosevoir perched himself on a rock. "Edwards and many others like him, for several years now." He regarded the rotting zombies as if they'd been amusing, if hideous, pets who'd unexpectedly kicked the bucket.

"What kind of sick game are you playing?" Crosshairs wanted to know. "Is it true, what Edwards said—no prison?"

Grosevoir cocked his head to one side. "None of you are fools. Do I have to answer?"

"What are we doing here, then?" Tripwire said. "We do something to you?"

"Not exactly," Grosevoir said, after a moment. "Your role is that of, how should I put it…stimulant."

"What are you talking about?" Oddy said.

Grosevoir flicked a cocklebur off his jacket lapel and said, "You might think keeping captive creatures alive is an easy task. Lock them up, feed them regularly, clean their cages of piss and shit and they should live long and healthy lives, yes? Not so. Captive animals rarely live as long as their wild brethren, despite a steady diet and absence of natural predators. Why? The reason is simple: they die of loneliness, or apathy, or sheer boredom.

"You see, life in captivity is a most unnatural state of being. No matter how diligently you imitate their natural environment, no matter if you regulate the temperature of their pens to a fraction of a degree, no matter if you feed them exactly what they'd eat in the wild, all captive creatures eventually realize the elemental truth of their situation: their existence is delineated by four square walls, their lives subject to the whims of another. Nobody, beast or man, wants to live that way. Many choose death as an alternative."

Grosevoir produced a cigarillo from his pocket and lit it with a wooden matchstick. He scanned the men's faces for signs of dawning awareness. "So how does a zookeeper ensure his charges choose life over death?" he continued. "In some cases, finding a compatible mate does the trick. Other times, human interaction in the form of grooming, hand-feeding, and so on. But, most often, exercises that engage the body, mind, and soul are most effective. The most elementary methods often prove most effective. Instead of scattering fruits and nuts, which requires an animal do nothing more than collect, a keeper might hide them in sealed boxes, forcing the animal to employ its cognitive and instinctive skills—make it sing for its supper, as it were. Other methods can be used—freezing herring in ice-blocks for polar bears, or constructing challenging maze-systems for rodents. The same principal applies in prisons. Inmates aren't stamping license plates to make money for themselves or the state. It is simply a means of keeping them occupied, and somewhat pacific. Idle hands seek the devil's work, hmm?"

Grosevoir tapped ash onto the snow. A picture was developing in the back of Oddy's mind, becoming clearer with every word Grosevoir spoke. Its likeness was that of a Bosch or Dali painting: ludicrous, unbelievable, horrific.

"So you know a lot about animal care," Zippo said. "Open a fucking pet store."

"I have, of a sort."

"What does any of this have to do with *us*?" Tripwire asked.

"Don't you see?" Grosevoir replied. "You are the fruit slice in the box. You are the herring encased in ice. You are…" a slowly-dawning grin, "…the mice in the maze."

The words, the manner in which they had been spoken, exploded at the base of Crosshairs's spine, shooting shards of dread off in every direction. "You're not making any sense…"

"Am I not? Or is it that you refuse understanding? Look at the ground. What are those things? Don't answer with your minds, which have been conditioned to reject such realities, but with what your senses show you."

"They're zombies," Answer said.

Grosevoir chuckled. "They are that exactly. The walking undead. That Romero fellow got it right."

"H-h-how," Tripwire stammered, "did they get here?"

"I collected them. Four in Haiti, two in Africa, one in an old-folks home in Peterborough, seven in a run-down trailer park in Arkansas. As you can imagine, transportation was a problem: the undead do not take kindly to moving, and many parts were lost along the way. Their numbers were growing steadily until this little fracas." Grosevoir clapped his hands together briskly. "No matter! Darwinism, survival of the fittest, and all that…*ahem*…rot."

Edwards groaned. His face had paled several shades.

"Allow me to detail the situation," Grosevoir continued. "The territory surrounding Great Bear Lake is a preserve. A preserve, as you all know, is a safe haven where endangered species are allowed to exist free from the distresses—poachers, hostile predators, and so on—responsible for dwindling their numbers. But this is not a preserve for the Snowy Egret, or the Duck-billed Platypus, or the Arctic Fox. It is a preserve for monsters.

"I only use the term *monster* because it is the term your society has pinned on creatures of myth and superstition. They are far from monstrous to me. In addition to the undead, other species include lycanthropes, or werewolves in the popular vernacular, and wampyrii. There are others, both large and small, you may also encounter."

The setup struck Oddy as queer. Vampires were creatures of gothic mystery who dressed in crushed velvet robes and inhabited crumbling New Orleans manors. He couldn't envision one of them running around in the woods, sucking blood out of squirrels and field mice—it was *undignified*. "Why would they stay here?" he asked. "Must be places they'd rather be."

"Of course," Grosevoir agreed. "But the fact of the matter is they're dying out. Otherwise all of this would be unnecessary."

"Why are they dying?"

Perhaps it was a trick of the light, but for a moment Grosevoir looked wistful. "I'd like to tell you it has something to do with lack of faith, that modern society's cynicism and disbelief is slowly killing the creatures that once terrified it. The truth is much more colorless: like the dinosaurs and Dodo bird before them, they are unable to adapt. Their world changes, they do not. They are old and stupid, or stubborn."

"I don't get it," Zippo said. "These things are supposed to be smarter, stronger, quicker than us. How is it possible they're gonna go extinct?"

"Some, like the undead, lack the awareness to keep themselves from extinction. Others, like the wampyrii, have become arrogant, which has led to carelessness, which in turn has led to death at the hands of those thought too weak or ignorant to pose a threat. Still others, like the werewolves, have diluted their pure bloodlines through mongrel mating habits. Predator has become prey. Or, if not prey, then certainly in need of protection."

"But how do you keep them here?" Tripwire said. "I don't see any cages, and how could you cage a vampire, anyway? Why don't they leave?"

"They could," Grosevoir admitted. "I've set up perimeters, employing certain spiritual totems to discourage escape. But the creatures living here are quite powerful and could leave at any time. Most stay because they realize I am trying to help them." Grosevoir tipped a knowing wink. "Plus, they enjoy the sport I provide."

The picture was becoming painfully clear. Oddy shut his eyes against the developing image. Some masochistic impulse prompted him to ask, "Sport?"

Grosevoir smiled in the way you might smile at a particularly doltish child. "Mr. Grant, I think you and your men know the score by now. Emperor Nero had it right: all the masses want is bread and circuses. Dole them crusts and treat them to weekly spectacles of blood and death and they'll forget all their earthly cares. So here it is, in stark black and white: the denizens of this preserve are the masses. Or the lions. This," he swept his hand in a wide arc, "is the circus. And you are the bread. Or the Christians. Whichever you'd prefer."

«««—»»»

Anton Grosevoir (though this was not the creature's true name, which was ancient, and guttural, and unpronounceable to the human tongue) had a vision. That vision was to repopulate the globe with the creatures of night and darkness whose numbers had dipped alarmingly over the past centuries. To this end he'd scoured the earth, seeking out those pockets and cubbyholes where such creatures lived, fed, and bred.

Orlock, the once-great vampire, was found dining on mice and bats in a crumbling monastery in Ipswich. The purest strain of werewolves were found in the Congo, preying on water buffalo populating the banks of the Ubangi river. Grosevoir uprooted a quarrelsome family of trolls living under a bridge in Strasbourg and a pair of Yetis wintering in the Altai mountains of outer Mongolia. He captured a clan of mentally-deficient djinn swirling around an office water cooler in Topeka, Kansas and a posse of goblins picking off freak-show performers in Phucket, Thailand. He secured many more monsters, most of whom defied logical description, wherever his dead-on instincts impelled him to search.

He told them his plan for a preserve. Most came willingly, acting out of self-interest or self-preservation. Those who refused were taken by force, subdued with the ease of an etymologist bottling a moth in a killing jar. Grosevoir transported them to his preserve and set them free.

Life in the menagerie was not always tranquil. Most of its inhabitants were loners or pack animals, and did not take kindly to sharing dominion. Boundaries were erected and quickly trespassed upon. Inter-species rivalries were common, the ensuing battles bloody. Inter-species breeding also flourished, enemies making strange but inviting bedfellows. This gave rise to some startling, and startlingly hideous, hybrids. Most of these did not live very long, which was a blessing.

It hadn't taken long for the preserve inhabitants to slaughter the local wildlife; maintaining ecological diversity was not a pressing issue with such creatures. They'd also murdered anyone hapless enough to reside within the preserve's boundaries. Every so often they were gifted with a trapper or wayward hunting party, but such occasions were few and sporadic.

Disharmony gripped the preserve. Infighting broke out among the inmates, threatening to scuttle Grosevoir's experiment before it had truly commenced. To quell the disunion, Grosevoir promised to supply a steady diet of "meat."

At first he'd chosen bums, welfare cases, and others down on their luck from the surrounding shanty towns, plying them with alcohol or the promise of a few dollars. Most of them came willingly, perhaps even happily, delighted to have their regretful lives wrapped up in such novel fashion. This had sufficed for a time, until the inhabitants started complaining about "inferior quality," "anemic blood," and a "gamey taste." The most common complaint was that the victims lacked vigor; *it's like they* want *to die*, one vampire grumbled.

Grosevoir's searches intensified. He sought out bar-room toughs, washed-up athletes, and men whose rampant insanity made for amusing sport. Again, the upswing in quality satisfied for a time before the inevitable complaints swelled: the victims were too few, too disorganized, too easy to pick off. Boredom settled over the preserve. Infighting picked up.

Fine, Grosevoir said to himself, petulantly. *They want dangerous thrills, then that's what they shall have.* The very next day he placed an advert in the Toronto Star:

HUNTERS NEEDED! SILVER FOX RANCH OVERRUN WITH GRIZZLIES. OWNER HAS LOST 300 FOXES. NEEDED: EXPERIENCED HUNTERS TO TRACK AND KILL MARAUDING BEARS. $2000 PER HEAD. TRANSPORT PROVIDED. BRING OWN WEAPON(S).

The men responding to the ad were the type Grosevoir had anticipated: lumberjack-vested and duck-booted, hairy and grizzled, not a full set of teeth among them. Those who had wives, families, people who would miss them were dismissed as unfit. Grosevoir settled on ten single men, adequate physical specimens with backwoods experience.

They'd performed rather well. The last of them survived for five days, until, starving and delirious, he'd stumbled into a cave of exultant goblins. The men even managed to kill a few werewolves (contrary to superstitious belief, almost all "monsters" can be killed by conventional means; bullets—enough of them in the proper locations—are lethal).

Grosevoir's efforts were met with an approval almost tidal in scope. *Yes, yes,* came the cries. *More of the same!* He set about gathering ever more innovative and challenging stimuli.

On a trip to Iraq—Grosevoir spent a lot of time in Iraq, Iran, Libya, Somalia, and other war-ravaged nations—he'd convinced a terrorist cell to journey to northern Canada under the pretense of locating a cache of nuclear warheads Uncle Sam had stashed there. They made exhilarating sport, with their guerilla tactics and ability to hide underground for days at a time, although their flesh possessed a pungent and unsavory flavor.

On another occasion, he'd been fortuitously on-hand at a prison-break in Magadan, USSR, spiriting away twenty of Mother Russia's most ruthless criminals. The men were unarmed and dressed in only prison coveralls, so he'd provided weapons and warm clothes. Lambs to the slaughter, yes, but well-armed lambs. He took a different tack with these men.

"This place is full of monsters," he informed the men in their native tongue. "If you can make it around the lake, I will transport you to a non-extradition location where you can live the rest of your life free from prosecution."

"Monsters," a prisoner scoffed. "You are as crazy as you are ugly, little man."

While the prisoners laughed, Orlock, an old and cunning vampire, swooped down from the trees, his form that of a giant bat. He plucked the offending prisoner off the ground with the ease of an owl plucking a field mouse and carried him, screaming, over the treetops.

Nobody laughed much after that.

That group had done exceedingly well. Not only did they kill three werewolves, a handful of zombies, and a careless vampire, two men actually made it around the lake alive. True to his word, Grosevoir transported them to a non-extradition location: an ice floe one-hundred miles off the coast of Barrow, Alaska. They froze to death in a matter of hours.

Since that time many more men had been brought to the barren and dangerous terrain surrounding Great Bear Lake. Very few ran the gauntlet alive. Those who did were rewarded with further suffering and, ultimately, death. The creature masquerading as a man is the great deceiver, spinning lies with the effortless grace of a spider spinning its thread.

Now it has trapped its greatest prize yet; men it knows, men it has fought, men with whom it has a score to settle.

Northwest Territories
December 9th, 1987. 2:02 a.m.

A rough-edged wind blew through the clearing, carrying the threat of snow. The men shivered. Grosevoir did not. He said, "I extend to you the same offer I've extended to those who've walked this path before you: complete the circuit around Great Bear Lake. Run from the creatures you encounter, or stand and fight. Any survivors receive full payment, plus the evenly-divided share of any who've died. In other words, if only one man survives, that man will walk away five million dollars richer."

Grosevoir delved into his pocket. When his hand reappeared, his palm glittered with shiny cylinders, which he scattered over the ground like bread-crusts to pigeons. "Silver bullets. Not necessary to kill lycanthropes, but rather effective. Five rounds, five different calibers, one for each of you." He reached into his other pocket and produced a vial of clear liquid, smiling in the manner of one granting a passel of fools an undeserved favor. "Holy water. Useful against most any supernatural minions. Use judiciously."

"Why are you doing this?" Oddy asked. "If this is a preserve, why are you giving us the means to kill your precious specimens? Like setting hunters loose in a zoo to shoot at caged animals."

Grosevoir chuckled. "It's not like that at all. These creatures are not caged, and they are a thousand leagues removed from harmless. These," gesturing to the silver bullets and holy water, "are an attempt, however feeble, to level the playing field. And remember: the chief aim of any preserve is rehabilitation. These creatures have grown weak, their survival instincts atrophied. When it comes time for their release, they must be strong, and cunning, and able to rule as they once did. Only the strongest *deserve* to survive. So think of your role as that of thresher, separating the wheat from the chaff."

"I don't buy your deal," Tripwire said. "Suppose we do make it out alive—you're just going to drop us where you found us with a bagful of cash? What's to stop us going to the cops, the fuckin' US military, telling them about the little rehab center you're running up here?"

"Get your head out of your ass," Zippo snapped. "Think you're going to waltz into the fuckin' Pentagon, ranting about vampires and werewolves and walking corpses? They'll have the men with butterfly nets on your ass before you can whistle Dixie."

"That's true," Grosevoir said. "Besides, anyone fortunate enough to survive has been happy to return to their boring little homes, their boring little lives, scarred but richer for their trauma."

"So you're on the level?" Zippo said. "Whoever comes out of this shitstorm kicking gets a one-way ticket back to civilization and the cash?"

Oddy could almost see the gears meshing inside Zippo's head, the hitman's mind playing more angles than a bagful of protractors. How did he see this going down? Did it end with Zippo boarding a heli solo, five million dollars wealthier? *Everything changes,* Oddy thought. *Allegiances shift, loyalties crumble. Only dead things stay the same.*

"Yes," Grosevoir replied with all the sincerity of an adder. "That's the deal."

Edwards was moaning almost constantly by now. White foam frothed the sides of his mouth. He spat up tatters of red, spongy tissue. *It's his lungs,* Tripwire realized. *Jesus.* Soon Edwards's eye would open. That eye would be red with burst blood vessels, and would reflect nothing but cold hunger.

"There's no hope for him," Grosevoir said matter-of-factly. "He's been bitten. Of course, he'd make a fine addition to the preserve, but his continued existence may pose a threat to you."

"What are we going to do with him?" Tripwire said.

"What *can* we do?" Crosshairs.

"Grease the poor fuck." Zippo.

"I suggest you get moving. The clock is ticking." Grosevoir.

"Who's going to handle it?" Oddy.

Before anyone could say another word, Answer unsheathed his K-Bar and stabbed Edwards in the neck. The soldier's remaining eyelid flew open like a window shade. One dead, red-threaded eye. Answer pulled the knife out. Brownish blood the consistency of motor oil pushed sluggishly from the wound.

"Jesus," Tripwire whispered.

Edwards bit at Answer's fingers. Answer jammed his knee down on Edwards's throat, forcing his mouth closed. He stabbed the knife into Edwards's forehead. It didn't go through. Answer found a large, flat rock and pounded on the hilt. The K-Bar slid into skull bone, through gray matter, out the other side into the snow.

Edwards gurgled. Edwards squirmed. Eventually Edwards died. Answer yanked the knife out and wiped it on his pants leg. He stood up. It was 2:33 a.m.

Oddy said, "Let's get humping."

《《—》》

Grosevoir remained perched on his rock, a cancerous black raven. "Carpe diem," he said, waving a stub-fingered hand at them.

Oddy was gripped by an overwhelming urge to take a potshot at the little gnome. The only thing stopping him was the knowledge any such act would be useless, and a waste of precious ammunition to boot.

"Here." He handed out the silver bullets, then held up the tiny bottle of holy water and said, "Any of you jokers take up the priesthood during the past twenty years? We could melt some snow, get you to bless it."

"I'm fully ordained," Zippo said.

Crosshairs, gullible: "Really?"

Zippo, smirking: "Oh, sure. In the church of *a-jackass-says-what.*"

Crosshairs, hook-line-and-sinker: "What?"

"I pegged you as more of a Hare Krishna myself, Zip," Tripwire said. "I can see you dressed in an orange dashiki at JFK International, handing out pansies."

Crosshairs, doggedly: "What church are you ordained in?"

"Are you deaf?" Zippo said. "*A-jackass-says-what.*"

"What?" Crosshairs cupped his hand around his ear. "Speak slower."

"You'd make a great Jehovah's Witness, Zip," Tripwire continued. "Preaching the Word door-to-door."

"Today's sermon," Zippo growled. "Silence is golden."

"Seriously," Crosshairs said to Zippo. "What church are you ordained in?"

This went on for a few minutes until Crosshairs was informed that Zippo had been calling him a jackass. Crosshairs made a face and, affecting a schoolmarmish tone, said, "Oh, real mature. A jackass says what and I say 'what' so I'm a jackass. You're *sooo* clever, Zippo."

When the men settled into silence, the bay of Great Bear became very quiet. The sky held a perpetually dour cast: a leaden-green surface of stained glass with a tarnished sheen to it, as though sluggish light were burning on the other side of the pane. Way off in the sky across the lake, the treetops glowed dully in the dirty light. Stars showed here and there, cold and distant. A raw wind blew across the iced-over lake. The men trudged through the freezing twilight before dawn, boots breaking through a crust of frozen snow into the loose powder beneath. Snow got into the gaps between boots and snowpants, melting down their calves in ice-cold rivulets. The surrounding tree boughs bent beneath their frozen white weight; some branches were encased in frozen layers of ice, snapping like breadsticks as the men brushed past. They came upon a snarl of wind-crippled willows and were forced to crawl beneath the lowermost branches like snakes on their bellies. Twigs whipped and snapped, lashing their faces, cutting into their hands through their mittens. "I'm gonna be spending that million bucks on doctor's bills," Tripwire muttered.

After a few hours of walking, it became clear they were following a rough path. Signs of previous passage abounded: a circle of ash-blackened stones forming a long-abandoned fire pit, a tumble-down pile of branches that had once been a bivouac, frayed lengths of rope descending from high tree branches where hunters hung their packs to keep marauding animals at bay. Here and there were small log shacks chinked with blackened seams of moss, lapped by birch bark roofs. Outside were trout and salmon nets, stacked firewood, pelt-stretchers. Most of the shacks had keeled over in the wind, supports rotted away though negligence or abandonment.

Zippo and Oddy entered a shack that still stood, hoping to find equipment or food. The interior was dark and dusty-smelling, log walls cracked and split and blackened by the heat of a central rock stove. Knives and fish hooks were stuck in the wood, also the odd nail with tattered clothes still hung in them.

The shack's occupant, what remained of him, was propped up in a corner where the log walls met. The man was maybe forty, although maybe younger, or older. It was difficult to tell. His jaw was in his throat, his upper lip and teeth were gone, his one eye shut, the other a deep black pit, his ears torn off and pinned to the wall with fillet knives. Frozen blood splashed the walls in a dark fan. The web of a trapdoor spider hung suspended from the man's upper palate, the tiny brown spider either dead or in a state of hibernation in the web's gossamer filament. The man's torn-off legs were draped over the shack's central beam by the knotted bootlaces, arms held out in front of him, fingers spread as if to block something from his vision. Innards lay in a frozen clump next to the rock stove, the flesh coated in a layer of crystallized frost, resembling strips of freezer-burned flank steak.

"Oh, man, Sarge," Zippo said. "This is…not good."

"No." Oddy tried to shut the man's blankly staring eyes, but the eyelids were frozen open. "Not good at all, son."

As the men continued on, they saw other signs of life that seemed even more cryptic and foreboding. Runic designs were carved into the bark of trees, some primitive as cave-etchings, others elaborately detailed. Words in a dozen different languages were cut into trees and etched into rock-faces, prayers and warnings to future travelers. This message cut into an oak tree with jagged, knifelike strokes: *HERE THERE BE TYGRES.* Another: *ONE-HORNED, ONE-EYED, TEN-LEGGED PURPLE PEOPLE EATER.* Heaps of stone markers, or cairns, were erected here and there; Oddy wondered how many bodies were buried in hastily-dug graves sunk into the dark inhospitable soil, the men who dug them spurred by a sense of duty to a downed comrade. These same men, long-dead themselves, had probably placed stones atop the burial mound to memorialize the man lying underneath in some small way. Every mile brought other signs standing as proof of Grosevoir's claim: a combat boot half-buried in the snow and stiff with frozen blood; what appeared to be a human ribcage and spinal column dangling from the crotch of a black maple.

They moved counter-clockwise around the lake. The sun passed behind a bank of low gray clouds. Rooting through his parka, Tripwire found a pack of Lucky Strikes. He sparked one and spindled the acrid smoke into his lungs. He offered the pack to Oddy. "I know you quit, but…"

Oddy took the pack. "Suppose this is a fine time to rekindle bad habits, son."

Tripwire's discovery prompted the rest of them to check their pockets. Crosshairs and Oddy found cigarettes and Zagnut bars. Answer found a fortune cookie, but the paper was blank. Zippo reached into an inside pocket and pulled out a roll of Benzedrine tabs. "Jackpot!" He unwrapped the foil tube and popped a tab. "Just what the doctor ordered."

Oddy grimaced. A lot of soldiers, Zippo and Gunner included, had picked up the benny habit in 'Nam. They claimed the drug helped them stay awake, or goosed morale, or just kept the darkness at bay for a few hours. Zippo on bennies was like the Tasmanian Devil on speed, Speedy Gonzales on Ritalin. A bad combo. Overkill.

"Go easy on those pink pills, son."

Zippo jacked another tab. "You go your way and I'll go mine."

They humped for six hours straight. The terrain took its toll. A line of fire lanced up Tripwire's spine. Oddy's blisters developed blisters. Zippo's wounded biceps burned despite the benny high. Crosshairs's legs were cramping constantly, though he didn't feel it.

They stopped for chow along the shore of a frozen stream. Answer broke a hole in the ice with his hatchet, dipping a pot into the clear water beneath. They boiled water for coffee and tore open dried food packs. The crackle and pop of twigs in the fire pit was the only sound as they ate.

"So," Tripwire said. "This is really happening."

"Doesn't seem to be any way around the fact," Oddy said.

"Who says we got to do this?" Crosshairs spat into the fire. "What's to stop us from laying tracks *away* from the lake, away from Grosevoir's rehab center for disadvantaged monsters—"

"I don't think we can," Answer said. "We're a good three-hundred klicks away from anything resembling civilization. We've got enough food to last a week at the outside, and," he cocked his ear to the silent woods, "I don't think there are many animals left to hunt. We've got no option. Grosevoir set us up good."

Tripwire said, "Sounds like you admire the guy."

"I'm not running anywhere." Framed by the parka's furred hood, Zippo's face was flushed, his eyes wild. "We've all killed before, right? Some more than others, but none of us are virgins. Now we got a chance to throw down on some fairybook freaks, fucks so sad-sack they allow themselves to be cooped up in the middle of nowhere by a humpbacked sideshow act." He placed a benny on his tongue and swallowed. "I'm looking forward to it."

As usual, Zippo was thinking short-term; just cruise around a lake, pop a few beasties, catch a heli back to civilization, easy as pie. But this wasn't 'Nam, where the worst-case scenario was you took a bullet in the gut and spent a few hours bleeding out, or got captured by the VC and spent a couple months dying of water rot in a half-submerged tiger cage. Out here, you got bit by a vampire and you run the risk of becoming one, spending your afterlife in this frigid wasteland. Or maybe you got bit by a zombie and end up wandering mindlessly over mile upon mile of frozen scrubland until you rot into a puddle of skin and fluids. Never was the saying, "there are things worse than death" more apt.

Crosshairs said, "Anyone got any strategies on how we get out of this alive?"

Oddy said, "Apart from moving as quickly as is humanly possible, no. We don't know where these creatures are hunkered, but they know we're here. Puts us at a distinct disadvantage. I imagine they'll attack quickly, try to pick us off before something else gets a chance."

Tripwire said, "But we know vampires can't come out in daylight. And don't werewolves only change during a full moon?"

"I don't think so," Answer said. "True lycanthropes—half-wolf, half-human—are in that form more or less permanently."

"Well," Oddy said, "we best be prepared."

He snapped a few branches off a nearby tree and set about sharpening the ends. Crosshairs emptied his cartridge clips and used a knife to cut an "X" into each bullet-head: not only were they now dum-dum rounds, they were marked with a Cross.

"Sarge, toss me that holy water," Zippo said.

Oddy passed the vial. Zippo unscrewed the cap on the flamethrower's fuel tank and poured half the vial in. He gave the tank a shake and flipped the vial back to Oddy. "Holy fire," he said. "The best kind."

Oddy finished whittling the stakes and passed them around. He checked his watch and said, "Let's get a few more miles under our belt."

They crossed the frozen stream gingerly, ice spiderwebbing under their boots. If any of them had cast a backwards glance, they may have seen that the trees on the far shore were carved with intersecting lines, one long, one short: Crosses. Had their eyes been more attuned, they may have seen the bulbs of garlic hanging in long garlands from many high tree boughs. There was no way they could see the perimeter of holy water that had been laid down on the ground, closing off some five square miles of land. There was no sign that read: "You are now entering Vampire Territory."

But indeed they had.

They hiked another seven hours. Shadows stretched across the landscape. By 4:00 a premature dusk had settled. Temperatures dropped and the men took to stomping their feet and rubbing their gloved hands together for what slim warmth the actions provided. Darkness obscured the path. Suddenly they were tripping over rocks and exposed root systems they'd previously managed to avoid.

Crosshairs became obsessed with the signifiers that officially marked nightfall. Was it night when the sun sunk from view? Or was it nighttime only when the sky had darkened completely, when the stars shone in sharp contrast to the blackness? Never had the distinction seemed so crucial.

The path fed into a small clearing. The trees were spindly and leafless, branches layered in powdery snow. In the upper reaches of one, the remains of a lightweight plane hung suspended by its tailfins like a criminal from a gibbet. Its wing coverings had fallen away, exposing fiberglass ribs and knotted electrical wires. Tatters of cloth hung in frozen strips from a lower bough.

Oddy suggested they stop. Zippo was the lone dissenter, declaring himself fresh as a fucking daisy and scorning the others as dickless wonders. Answer told Zippo to shut the fuck up. Zippo thumbed the pilot light on his flamer, thought better of it, swivelled away from Answer and set fire to the pile of kindling Tripwire had collected.

They squatted around the fire. Night had indisputably fallen.

"How far have we made it?" Crosshairs asked.

Oddy retrieved a map of Great Bear Lake. "We're making great time. If the lake ice holds, we can cross it instead of circumnavigating the inlet. We do that, I'd say we're a third of the way around."

Less than forty-eight hours and this nightmare will be over, Tripwire thought. *I can go home. Sleep. I'm so fucking tired—going to take a nap that puts Rip van Winkle to shame.* He stripped his gloves and warmed his hands by the fire. They were sweaty and pink and wrinkled, skin like a baby mouse's.

The skeleton of the lightweight plane rattled and shuddered as wind whipped through the empty cockpit. "Hell of a place to crash," Crosshairs said quietly.

"Should we set up camp?" Tripwire asked.

"We'd best keep moving, son."

"Yeah, but if we don't get some sleep, we're bound to—"

"Is anybody really going to sleep, knowing what's out there?" Crosshairs said.

"I'm with Sarge and the cyclops," Zippo said. "Sleep when you die. Who knows—could be soon."

"Son," Oddy leveled a finger at the benny-blitzed hitman. "I strongly suggest you lay off the attitude and the pills. You're dogshit for morale."

Zippo tore the foil around the tube of bennies and popped another into his mouth. "We ain't in 1967 no more." He unfastened the flame-thrower's straps and dropped it. "You ain't my boss. And if you don't take that big black finger out of my face—and I mean *right now*—you and I are going to have issues."

Oddy shrugged the H&K off his shoulder and laid it on the ground. Then he pulled the Webleys from his waistband and set them beside the machine gun. "If that's the way it's going to be," he said, "That's the way it's going to—"

The words weren't out of his mouth before Zippo bayed, "Yaaaww!" and clipped Oddy in the head with a roundhouse karate kick. Oddy dropped to one knee and Zippo hit him in the face with a front kick and tried for another roundhouse but Oddy caught his foot and pulled him down. They rolled around in the loose snow, breath coming from their mouths in white puffs, until Oddy got on top of Zippo, sitting on the hitman's chest and slamming punches into his face. The sound of flesh on flesh ricocheted off the trees, carrying across the cold, lonely expanse. Zippo struggled beneath Oddy's fearsome bulk; the hitman's body was pressed so deep into the snow it was as if he was buried.

"That's enough, Sarge," Crosshairs said. "You're gonna do serious damage."

Oddy stared down at Zippo and, in that moment, he *wanted* to do serious damage. He wanted to beat Zippo's mug until his knuckles split open and the bones poked through, beat Zippo's face until it wasn't recognizable anymore, just a shredded mess of raw tissue, broken bone and teeth. He was in the grip of something animal, something primal, something that resonated at the level of bone. He wasn't himself. He felt his fist rise, fingers curled into a tight fist and poised to hammer down on the dazed hitman.

"Jesus Christ," he heard Tripwire say, "you're going to kill him."

I know, Oddy thought. *I know, and I don't care.*

Then, like a cloud passing over the moon, the feeling lifted. Oddy's fist opened. He got off Zippo and extended his hand. "Here," he said. "Get your ass up."

Zippo's left eye was nearly swelled shut. He spat blood and took Oddy's hand. "Alright, boss," he said as Oddy pulled him up. "You're still big kahuna."

Oddy was beginning to reply when the noises began. Sly, creeping-cautious noises all around, drawing nearer. Noises like a thousand small animals—rats, sightless moles—skittering over a crust of frozen snow.

"Lock and load," Oddy whispered, shouldering the HK23. "Company's coming."

«« —»»

Abruptly, the noises ceased. The men stood, weapons drawn. Nothing.

"Wait for it," Oddy whispered. "Just...*wait.*"

A bony wisp of a man stepped from a copse of oaks. His flesh was the color of sun-bleached bones and his eyes, beneath dozing-caterpillar brows, resembled polished obsidian. He dressed in a manner Zippo would term "goth-fag chic": dark trousers of gabardine wool, white silk shirt, a cloak of black velvet. The cloak hung open to reveal a stringy body that looked to be assembled from twisted coat-hangers. He appraised the men with a slight smile, regarding the weapons trained upon him as if they posed no more threat than a child's toy pistol.

"Please, there is no need for unpleasantness." He raised his hands in the manner of a surrendering POW. His wrists were bits of drift-wood, fingers long and white, nails sharp and yellow. "May I sit?"

Oddy nodded. The man sat beside the fire, turning his palms to the flames. He grinned and shivered, as if the fire's warmth conferred some comfort. The snow beneath him did not melt.

"Who are you?" Answer's barrel did not deviate from the man's skull.

"My name is Orlock. And, as you may have guessed, I am a vampire."

"That's all I needed to hear," Zippo's finger tightened on the flamer's trigger—

"DON'T."

The voice was monstrous, a thunderclap at close range. The men dropped their weapons and clapped their hands over their ears, certain their eardrums had ruptured.

"I'm sorry," Orlock continued. "If you wish to resolve this situation... *aggressively*...you may do so in a moment. But first, please consider my offer."

A quick consensus was reached to let Orlock have his say.

"Thank you," Orlock said. "I'll spare you the history of my race—suffice it to say, some of the stories you've heard are true, others falsehoods. I am unsure of much of it myself. We are an old race, so old that nobody knows anymore how we came into existence, or when, or for what reasons." Orlock smiled. It was not a pleasant sight. "Our lives, as all lives, have benefits and drawbacks. So long as we feed, there is no limit to our longevity. I myself am several centuries old. There is no part of the world I have not traveled, no intriguing native custom I have not indulged in, no village virgin I could not bed. We are stronger than any human, our senses more attuned, our passions more fully realized."

Movement in the darkness. Orlock hissed menacingly. The movement ebbed.

"Of course, we have to kill." The old vampire grimaced, as if the admission caused him great pain. "Blood from any beast is satisfactory, although human blood is indisputably superior." The ancient thing smacked his lips. "The blood of a young, spry body is...narcotic. There is nothing like it—not drugs, not sex, not the joy of killing itself. It is an addiction. A terrible, terrible addiction."

Answer posed a most appropriate question: "If you're so powerful, why allow yourself to be imprisoned?"

Orlock smiled in the manner of one who is constantly amused by the curiosity of lower life forms. "A hierarchy exists between all things. The strong subjugate the weak, the rich exploit the poor, the cunning manipulate the foolish. One must learn to accept one's place in the order. And I am treated well enough to compensate for the boredom and solitude. I am provided wondrous sport."

Despite the vampire's apparent sincerity, Oddy couldn't believe such a self-interested, arrogant creature would willingly endure imprisonment. "Why don't you kill Grosevoir?" he asked. "Kill him and escape."

"Grosevoir, hmm?" Orlock chuckled. "Is that what it's calling itself nowadays? How European. Kill it?" The old thing's voice lowered, as though afraid of being overheard. "No. Not by me. Not by you. Not by any force living or dead."

Movement again stirred the fringing woods. Zippo swore he saw someone—a young woman, blonde hair, pale skin, eyes black, dressed in a shredded mackinaw and ice-glazed jeans—materialize from the darkness. Her neck was chewed up on the left side, as if some animal had been at it. A warning hiss from Orlock and she vanished like ether.

"In case you did not know," Orlock continued, "my brethren and I are one of the first obstacles you'll encounter on your journey around this godforsaken lake. Thus we have, how do you say…first dibs? Now, we are not greedy," he said, mixing lies and deceptions with the deft touch of a master alchemist, "and want no more than our fair share."

Fair share? Tripwire thought. *What the hell is he talking about?*

"There are others waiting for you beyond our confines," Orlock said. "None of them, you will find, are nearly so refined as I. They will not ask. They will simply take—quickly, greedily, and without mercy. This is your only opportunity to discuss your fate in a rational, gentlemanly manner."

"Get to the point," Oddy snapped.

"Very well. All I ask is this: a sacrifice. One of you, and only one. You may choose who goes yourselves." Orlock licked lips that resembled a pair of copulating maggots. The sight recalled a hungry borzoi. "Perhaps you'll want to surrender the weakest link, the man who lacks the stomach for what lies ahead."

Fear exploded like a mushroom cloud in Crosshairs's heart. Who was weaker than a one-eyed sniper with the cardiovascular endurance of an asthmatic octogenarian?

"So that's the deal?" Zippo asked. "Hand over one of our own with a bright red bow tied around his dick?" His tone made it impossible to tell if he found the proposal insulting, or outrageous, or acceptable.

"No need it be thought of as a death sentence," Orlock said haughtily. "As I said, you will see and do things you would never experience otherwise. You will live forever. Soon we will be released, once again free to roam the earth, regain our rightful place—"

Answer said, "—and the only drawback is you have to live by moonlight and drain some poor bastard dry every once in awhile, huh?"

Even the ancient vampire was unsure how to take Answer. "You don't *have* to become one of us," he said. "We could, as you said, 'drain you dry,' killing you outright." A shrug. "You are, after all, nothing more than food."

It was the most truthful statement Orlock made all night.

"Food." The word lodged in Oddy's throat like a string of gristle. *That's all we are to these things,* he thought. *Why is he bargaining, then? It's as ludicrous as a slaughterhouse owner bargaining with livestock. Unless the fucker takes some perverse pleasure in watching us cast one of our own to the wolves.* "And if we stand and fight?"

"Then we kill you all," Orlock replied.

Tripwire's mind skipped like a flat stone on a pond. Is this how it was going to end for one of them—diplomatic surrender to some bargain-basement Bela Lugosi? It was unthinkable, no different than surrendering to the VC without a fight. He glanced at Crosshairs, saw fear etched into every crease of the sniper's face. *He thinks we're going to give him up,* Tripwire thought. Something rose up in him then, something clear and true and defiant:

No. I won't give up my friend. I will not play the game by your rules. I'll die first.

He could only hope the others shared his resolve.

"This is your choice." Orlock kicked at the fire, agitated the men were taking so long to reach a decision. "This is your *only* choice. So. Choose."

Oddy knelt beside the vampire. Orlock smiled, mistaking his posture as one of supplication. Oddy stared into the thing's mineshaft eyes and saw nothing but hunger, and avarice, and capering amusement.

"Who will it be, young one," Orlock whispered. "Who dies so the rest may live?"

"Here's the thing." Oddy's smile was wide, and genuine. His hand moved somewhere behind his back. "Grosevoir said we can't be giving out no freebies. You blood-suckers got to work for your meal." Orlock frowned. Oddy said, "So, as far as your offer goes, I guess I'm speaking for everyone when I say—" he cleared a Webley from his pants, cocking the hammer as it made the short trip around his waist, jamming it up under the vampire's arrow-headed chin. "—no-*fuckin-way.*"

《《《—》》》

The physics at play when a .455 Webley round is fired at point blank range into a human head are quite elementary: the head more or less explodes. But, as Orlock was not human, the effect was slightly different, if no less dramatic.

BA-BOOM.

The slug punched through the vampire's chin at an acute angle on account of Orlock's turning away at the last second. The pressure of impact ripped Orlock's jawbone off with a sound like tearing burlap. It spun away from his face, a white horseshoe of skin and bone, landing in the fire pit. The bullet continued on, slightly flattened from impact, into the roof of Orlock's mouth and through his nasal cavity before exiting his forehead in a puff of powdered cartilage.

The vampire flipped over backwards, heels kicking twin spumes of snow. He sat up. His tongue flopped like an overfed flatworm, a neat hole punched through the center. Skin hung from his cheeks like ripped curtains. He made a noise deep in its throat, a growl of pain and rage.

Oddy shot him again. Orlock went down again.

Well, it's on, Zippo thought. *Let's see who else is at this shindig.* He unleashed a ripcurl of fire that threw the fringing wilderness into sharp relief. "Hail, hail, the gang's all here..."

They roosted in the trees like crows, hunched low, backs arched, ghostly hands grasping the branches on which they balanced. Their skin was universally white and their eyes universally dark, but otherwise appearances varied wildly. The woman Zippo had glimpsed earlier was perched beside a swarthy man dressed in moldering Middle Eastern garb; a turban unraveled messily from his head like bandages from a mummy's corpse. In another tree, a surfer-dude wearing board shorts and a Hawaiian shirt hugged a low bough. He looked a little like Eakins, the soldier who'd gotten his legs hacked to shit in that tunnel near Song-Be.

Zippo swept the flamer in a 180-degree arc. On the other side of the clearing a pair of vampires clung to either side of a scabby tree trunk. They appeared to have stepped out of a '50s sitcom: the woman's hair was done up in an outrageous beehive, she wore a blue-checked housedress, a frilled apron, and a pair of tortoiseshell glasses, the right lens shattered, strung around her neck on a faux-pearl chain. The man wore a plaid shirt, madras shorts, and beach sandals with a barbecue apron reading KISS THE COOK tied at neck and waist. They'd have looked ludicrous if not for the cold deadness in their eyes and the gaping, pink, fistulous caverns of their mouths. There were others, stewbums and honky-tonks and crewcut military joes, perhaps ten in total.

Orlock sat up. A massive chunk of his skull had been vaporized. His brain, white as cheese curd, glistened in the firelight. *Welcome to my world, you son of a bitch*, Crosshairs thought. The old vampire appeared disoriented. His tongue flapped and flopped. His hands clenched and unclenched in the air. He emitted obscene gargling noises.

The other vampires gawped in surprise. It was the first time they had sensed weakness in their leader. They attacked.

But not the men.

They attacked Orlock.

While living in Thailand, Tripwire once witnessed a feeding frenzy. He'd chartered a fishing boat, *Daydream Believer*, off the island of Phucket. At day's end, the crew gutted the day's catch on the deck, casting the offal overboard. Smelling blood, sharks came. Lemontails mostly, plus a few makos and tigers. They churned the calm waters of the Andaman Sea into a froth, snapping at the floating fish guts. When that was gone they fell upon one another, the stronger and faster devouring the weak and wounded. Tripwire was reminded of this brutal spectacle watching the vampires attack Orlock, thinking, *I am witnessing the law of the jungle in its purest form.*

The vampires set upon Orlock like animals, subduing him under the sheer force of their weight and numbers. The old vampire was still gargling. Zippo looked down at him. He was on his hands and knees. The beehive woman straddled his back with his head caught between her hands. She bit *into* his head, into the yawning hole Oddy's bullet had made. Gleaming clots of brain flecked her fishbelly lips. She smiled. Her glasses were canted at a ridiculous angle. A wet ripping noise as she tore off a patch of hair and scalp. Orlock shrieked. Beehive hooked a finger through the hole in his tongue, twisting and pulling and ripping it out at the root. It looked small in her palm: a tiny white tombstone. She threw it against a tree, where it stuck for a moment before falling to the ground.

These were not the vampires of the men's understanding. Where was the dark romanticism, the brooding mystery, the gothic beauty? These things were no more refined than a pack of dingoes.

The vampires flipped Orlock onto his back. Some held him down while others tore his clothes off. His body was cadaver-pale, limbs like splits of bleached wood, flesh hanging off the bones like bread dough off a dowel. His penis, childish in proportion, hung between quivering thighs. Tripwire watched the pretty blonde vampire reach between his legs and stretch it to excruciating tautness before snipping it off between her teeth. The old vampire howled.

Tripwire edged beside Oddy. "Got that holy water?" Oddy pulled the vial from his pocket. Tripwire held his hands out. A white phosphorus grenade was cupped in each palm. "Douse 'em." Freeing an arm, Orlock raked his nails across surfer-dude's face. They sank into surfer-dude's left eye, slitting the retina open. Surfer-dude's hands flew to his face like flame-stung moths. Surfer-dude's burst open eye drooled out of its socket. Surfer-dude's eye-jelly, black and syrupy, poured down his cheeks. Orlock slashed again, opening up surfer-dude's neck, digging inside the wound, yanking the esophagus out. It dangled to surfer-dude's breastbone like an obscene necktie.

The turbaned vampire clamped his teeth over Orlock's nose. It tore free with a dreadful splintering noise. Turban spat it into the snow and went back for more.

Oddy spilled holy water over the grenades. The other men assembled in a loose battle formation behind Tripwire. Answer pulled a stake from his pack and the others followed suit.

The man wearing the KISS THE COOK apron was pulling Orlock's stomach apart. The ancient vampire's flesh tore with sickening ease and a sound like old newspapers. He laid the skin-flaps across Orlock's ribs and dipped his hands into the chest cavity, squeezing and mashing as Orlock bucked like a bug on a pin. The organs KISS THE COOK tore free were desiccated, like withered pieces of fruit. He crushed one in his fist and it burst apart in a cloud of dust.

The holy water froze around the grenades, encasing them in a thin glaze of ice. Tripwire pulled the pins, whispered, "Fire in the hole," and lobbed them at the massed vampires.

They landed softly: Beehive's attention was drawn to the fist-sized holes in the snow for a brief moment before returning to the matter at hand. A white vapor-trail rose from the holes and a heartbeat later—

B-Ba-BOOM.

A momentary radiance followed by a lethal hailstorm of whizzing metal. The men shielded their mouths and noses against the deadly phosphorus fumes. The noise of the explosions gave way to a wild and horrified screaming, a sound so shocking in its intensity it seemed as though the screamer's lungs must surely burst from the strain.

The vampires, almost every one of them, had been struck by shrapnel. The effect was violent, bizarre, and instantaneous. Thick, green-tinted smoke poured out of every wound. It was as if a tiny woodsman had kindled a fire inside of them, stoking it heavily, until the resultant smoke was forced from any vent it could find. Smoke hissed from bloodless slits in chests and arms and legs; smoke billowed out of mouths and—cartoonishly, horrifically—from noses and ears; smoke surged out of a gash in surfer-dude's forehead with a steam-whistle's shriek.

The vampires spun in pain-maddened pirouettes. The internal combustion was so fierce that the hair of their heads and underarms and even their crotches burst into flame, crackling and glowing like piles of burning twigs. The pretty blonde vampire hacked up gobs of her lungs, the black, smoking clots spattering the snow.

Ironically, only Orlock avoided the shrapnel, on account of his position at the bottom of the pile. Amazingly, he stood.

"He's not going to be the next Barker's Beauty," Zippo said.

Indeed he would not: all that remained of Orlock's face were his eyes and upper palate, a few lonesome teeth, half an ear. The flaps of skin that had once sheltered the inner workings of his mouth caught the breeze like freakish sails. Viscera spooled out of the hole in his gut in petrified spaghetti loops.

He pointed at the men. A good many of his fingers had been bitten off, somewhat spoiling the effect. He said, "Glaaa…"

The monosyllabic moan acted as a rallying cry.

The vampires came at the men.

Zippo was a loner. Zippo was self-centered. Zippo did not have friends, he had business associates. Zippo knew who he was, and was generally comfortable in his skin. Hearing Grosevoir's proposal, he'd secretly hoped to be the only survivor left to collect the bounty. He didn't hate the other men. He wouldn't try to kill them, or see them abandoned. Yet, at the core, all they represented was a million dollars that could be his.

This mindset persisted up until the very moment the vampires came for his old unit members. Then it all changed. Suddenly he was twenty again, back in the jungles of Vietnam. Suddenly these men's lives had a value beyond mere dollar signs. A moment ago they'd meant nothing to him; now he would willingly go through hell for them. It was the kind of knee-jerk reaction he might make spying a child playing on the street in a speeding car's path—unpremeditated, almost thoughtless. It had little to do with friendship, or love, or compassion. It was something different altogether, and it functioned under the understanding that they were all in this together. Live or die, they did it together.

Zippo was unable to comprehend his feelings on such a profound level. What he thought as he stepped in front of his fellow mercenaries, shielding them, preparing to take the first hit, was elementary in its simplicity:

I will die for you.

Now. Here. This moment.

"Come get it," he whispered, and pulled the trigger.

The vampires hurled themselves at the wall of holy-water-laced flames with the heedless abandon of moths at a lit candle. Those who made it through were little more than flaming skeletons on the other side. Flesh sloughed off their bones in fiery gobbets, scattering their wake like glowing breadcrumbs. Fire licked from their eye sockets and shot from their mouths. Some retreated into the woods to lick their hideous wounds. Others were undeterred.

Beehive, her hair alight in a flaming spire, advanced on Tripwire. He backed away, fist clutching a stake. Flames gathered on Beehive's shoulders; her outspread fingers, webbed with fire, resembled blazing gloves. Tripwire stumbled on a rock and went down on his back. Beehive grabbed at Tripwire's neck; blisters swelled and burst on his throat. He screamed. She bent over him, mouth hot and necrotic …

Surfer-dude zeroed in on Oddy. His esophageal cord hung like a horrid pendulum, teeth very long and very white amidst the flaming wreckage of his face. Oddy snapped off a shot that spun him sideways. The vampire swayed like a three-sheets-to-the-wind drunk, left arm hanging cockeyed, bone shattered at the elbow.

Oddy cocked the Webley and fired again. The slug blew a flaming wedge out of surfer-dude's shoulder. He took a knee. He got up again. Oddy drew a killing bead. Surfer-dude dove, tackling Oddy at the knees, driving him to the ground. Surfer-dude's burning dreadlocks writhed like a ball of quarrelsome snakes atop his head. His nails punched through Oddy's pants, into the soft meat of his hamstrings. Bellowing, Oddy jammed the Webley into surfer-dude's mouth. The shot blew him upright, straightening his spine. Oddy saw the purpling night sky through the softball-sized hole in the vampire's throat and thought of Dade…

Zippo ran the flamer's tank dry. He shrugged it off and drew the Berettas. Answer flanked him; they stood back-to-back.

"Boy," Zippo said fiercely, "any of these blood-suckers get their teeth into me, I want you to put me down before I start changing."

"You got it."

"Knew I could count on you."

Turban and KISS THE COOK stalked in on them. Zippo pumped shots at Turban, slamming slugs into his belly and knees, bullets exiting in a spray of splintered bone. Answer's silenced Kirikkales made a *snick-a-snick* sound. A daisy chain of dime-sized holes spread across KISS THE COOK's throat.

Turban grabbed Zippo. His strength was immense: Zippo felt himself in the grip of a grizzly. The vampire's headwear unwound in flaming spirals around his head, burning with the smell of raw spices. Zippo brought his knee up into Turban's crotch. The vampire laughed, lips melting in ropy strings, hugging Zippo tighter. The hitman's ribs cracked. He angled one Beretta into Turban's crotch and squeezed off three quick shots...

KISS THE COOK batted a Kirikkale from Answer's hand. Answer raised the other pistol and fired. KISS THE COOK's right eye imploded in a spurt of yellow stuff resembling marmalade. The vampire twisted away. Answer shot him in the ear, tearing the lobe off. The vampire moaned. Answer shot him in the nose. The vampire mewled, smelling of Brylcreem and fireplace ashes. His shot-out eye was a deep conical hole, black and yellow. There was a light bubbling sound where his nose had been. Answer wasn't even breathing hard. He shot the aproned vampire through the cheek, blowing teeth between his lips. The vampire staggered. Answer took his stake and plunged it into KISS THE COOK's chest.

KISS THE COOK shrieked. KISS THE COOK shook.

Then KISS THE COOK exploded in dazzling fashion.

"Huh," Answer said.

Beehive was at Tripwire's neck. Her teeth brushed his skin. *I don't want to die*, he thought. *On the other hand, I don't want to live, if it means becoming one of them.* He clamped a hand over Beehive's face, fingers sinking into her flaming features. He pushed harder and the lion's share of Beehive's face came away in his hand, slipping between his fingers like fondue cheese. Beehive's jaws rattled and clacked like wind-up chattery teeth. She tried to say something but could not on account of her tongue being fused to the roof of her mouth.

"Blaa graaa lahhe," she blubbered. "Blaa gr—"

Tsst.

As soon as the vampires began to attack, Crosshairs had slotted his silver bullet into the Remington. His knowledge of the supernatural was sketchy—was silver good against werewolves? Witches? Bogeymen?—but silver struck him as a strong, pure metal, effective against any creature of evil. He saw Tripwire was in trouble: a faceless vampire was on his neck like a hobo on a ham sandwich. Crosshairs centered his breathing and—

Tsst.

There was no other way to describe it: Beehive's head flew apart. Fragments of skull bone exploded off in every direction like a flock of pheasants flushed from tall grass. Her headless body twitched atop Tripwire. He shoved her off and plunged the stake into her chest. It sunk to the hilt with sickening ease: like stabbing a warm loaf of bread. Beehive thrashed. Moth-like insects flew from the stump of her neck. She shriveled into ash and blew away, leaving only a faint outline in the snow. Tripwire staggered to his feet and went to help Oddy…

Crosshairs jerked the breech to insert a new cartridge. He did not see her slinking up behind him: blonde, petite, wearing a shredded mackinaw. He did not—*could not*—feel her nails tearing down the back of his parka, the noise of gunfire drowning out the sound of ripping fabric. Chill wind whipped up his spine. He felt nothing. He did not feel the razor-sharp nails cutting a vertical slash above his hipbone, deep and long and red. He did not feel the blood pouring down his back, pooling in the snow.

All he felt when she shoved her hand inside the wound was a dim sense of pressure. No pain. But he knew something was terribly wrong. Although the sensation of his organs being displaced was painless, he was keenly aware that, had the proper nerve centers been operational, he would be screaming like a motherfucker.

"What the—?" He spun on wobbly legs. She was squatted on the ground at his feet. Her hands overflowed with…*things.*

Red things. Deep purple things. Softly-shaped things that shone wetly in the moonlight.

A yellow tube ran between her fingers, dipping into empty space, rising again to connect to…*him.* He realized that the tube was his intestinal tract. His mouth opened. No sound came out.

She crammed one of his organs—a liver? a kidney? Jesus Christ, they all looked the *same*—into her salivating maw. She sucked greedily, like an infant. The organ changed color, purple to red to pink to peach to bone-white as she drained it of blood.

"Oh, Lord," Crosshairs whispered. "Oh, Jesus, no."

Crosshairs's legs buckled. An out-of-place odor—French vanilla?—filled his nostrils for a second before fading. His eyes were hard and dry, like marbles. He couldn't feel himself dying. This knowledge, the underhanded injustice of it, made him want to cry. "Give...give those back," he said quietly.

He shot the pretty woman in the belly. She bent forward, as if punched. He ejected the spent cartridge. His mouth was full of something. He turned and spat a pouch of black blood into the snow. He sat down and picked up some of his guts, trying to push them back inside, but they were slick and kept slipping through his fingers. He got some loops back inside but then the pretty woman crawled forward and tugged them out again. Equilibrium tilted madly. She started to suck on his intestine like it was a pixie stick.

"Those are mine," he whimpered. "I *need* them."

She said, "I'm sorry." She didn't stop sucking.

Schrutt was the sound Oddy's stake made as it sunk into surferdude's chest. The burning vampire made a queer noise and started to melt. His face softened and liquefied, running off his bones in gelatinous strings. His ribcage cracked open like a bomb-bay hatch, spilling warm guts onto Oddy's lap. Then the bones themselves melted, sagging like overcooked noodles before turning into a thick white paste that ran down Oddy's arms. It all happened very rapidly. Oddy stood. His parka and pants were soaked with the weight of molten vampire.

Zippo's face was purple from the hydrostatic pressure. Blood forced its way from his nostrils and ears and the corners of his eyes as Turban bear-hugged him. The vampire gibbered in a foreign dialect, breath stinking of tabouli and rotting meat. He tore a strip of skin off Zippo's throat and lapped at the gushing blood. Zippo hawked a blood-veined loogie into Turban's face. Turban squeezed tighter. Bones cracked. Zippo's body curved like a tightly-strung bow.

"Fuck you," he said through gritted teeth. "Fu...uuuck *YOU*."

Answer rose up behind Turban, bringing his stake around in a hard arc at eye level, burying three inches of Canadian maple in Turban's ear. Turban's eardrum punctured with the soggy decompression of a balloon popped underwater—*thop!* The vampire gasped. His grip on Zippo loosened. Answer tugged the stake loose. The tip dripped with gelid runners of brain and tissue.

Zippo brought the Berettas up into the gap now separating

Turban's body from his. He planted the barrels on either side of Turban's jaw and fired two pancaking rounds. The slugs cut an "X" through the vampire's skull, exploding from his burning headgear in a swirl of cinders. Zippo jammed the barrels further into the wounds, deeper into Turban's face, twisting, firing, twisting, firing. Slugs blew out of Turban's head every which way, muzzle flash lighting up the backs of his eyes like Japanese lanterns.

Answer stabbed the stake into Turban's back. The vampire let go of Zippo, who fell to the ground, puking strenuously. Turban staggered in circles, clutching at the stake. Then he gave up and exploded like a balloon full of lasagna.

Crosshairs fell to his knees. "Please...I need those..." The rifle slipped from his fingers. Even missing her chin, he was struck by the woman's beauty: smooth skin, nose tapering to a delicate point, eyes black as jewelry-display velvet. A small scar above her upper lip. Her mouth and chin and cheeks were smeared an oily red. *How did she end up here?* the sniper wondered. *Bad luck, bad karma, circumstances beyond her control?* He could not hate the woman. He sensed she was once a tender person, a compassionate woman who didn't like what she'd become. Crosshairs' hair was swept back, his prosthesis crack-glazed with ice. Tears rolled down his cheek to freeze on the underside of his chin in tiny clear globes.

"Please..."

She touched his face, finger tracing the seam where flesh met latex. Her fingertips left a sickle of blood on his face. "How did this happen?" she asked, shyly, as a child. She traced a fingertip over his lips, painting them blood-red.

He whispered, "I can't feel you."

She whispered, "I can't feel you, either."

Crosshairs's guts were a small red ball coiled between his legs. They were no longer part of him. None of it was. None of this was actually happening. This was all some movie he'd once seen.

She rested his head between her small, cold breasts. The edges of his vision were darkening. She unclasped the clips securing the prosthesis to his face. "I'm sorry," she said. "I can't help myself."

"Please," Crosshairs heard himself say.

"So hungry..."

Her teeth sunk into the soft flesh of the divot. Crosshairs raised his hand to her face, wanting so desperately to feel something, anything. He touched her cheek, her nose, the soft hollow of her eye socket.

"Please…"

Her teeth shifted inside his head, sunk deep into the gray matter. Then it happened.

Crosshairs's fingers felt…*cold*. He looked down at his hand and curled his fingers. He could feel the snow—feel every individual *snowflake*—on his skin. He brushed his thumb against his index finger. He felt every ridge and valley, felt the tiniest pressure, the wondrous friction of flesh on flesh.

For the first time in twenty years, Crosshairs could *feel*.

Sensation blossomed inside him, unfurling like the petals of some magnificent flower. Feeling sought out every outback and tributary of his body, reawakening long-dormant nerve centers. Crosshairs wondered if a Neanderthal man thawing out of a glacier would feel the same.

Her skin in his hand, the coldness of it like slate. His toes, warm and sweaty in his boots. Ice on the back of his neck, prickling the short hairs there.

Then…

The gaping, raw wound in his back. Her teeth in his head, in his *brain*, the terrible pressure of suction.

Pain, the glorious intensity of it, rocked Crosshairs to the bedrock of his soul.

A massive black hand fell over the pretty vampire's face, jerking her head back. Crosshairs watched Oddy pin her to the ground, knee jammed into her breastbone, and slam a stake into her chest. He twisted it inside her. Her body shriveled up and blew away like a burning leaf. Crosshairs gagged on blood in his throat. Pain ran a full-out blitzkrieg through his body.

"Pacify, son," Oddy said. He propped a balled-up sweater under his head.

"I can…" Crosshairs hacked up a wad of red. "I can *feel*, Sarge."

"Gonna be fine, soldier. Fine as cherry wine."

Tripwire joined Oddy. He paled.

"Jesus Christ. He's not gonna make it."

This time Oddy remained silent.

Tripwire knelt beside Crosshairs. "Want some morphine? One shot'll ease the pain. Two you'll go numb. Three to ease you out easy. You want?"

Crosshairs shook his head. "First time in twenty years, Trip—I can feel." His skull-divot overflowed with blood. "*Feel*."

Zippo and Answer reconnoitered.

"Oh, Christ," Zippo said, clutching his ribs. "We got to do something for him."

"I'm dying," Crosshairs said.

Oddy said, "Gonna be fine, son." It was a knee-jerk response and they all knew it.

"Don't bullshit a bullshitter, Sarge," Crosshairs said. He twined his hand with Tripwire's. It felt so good, so warm. Then his face darkened with fear. "It's just..."

"What's wrong?" Tripwire asked him.

"I don't want to end up like them..."

"I promise that's not gonna happen." Zippo unhooked a pair of grenades from Tripwire's bandolier. "Open your hands, if you can."

Crosshairs assented like a child. Zippo placed a grenade in each palm, closing Crosshairs' fingers around the clips. "I didn't mean it," he said. "About you being a candyass. That was the bennies talking."

"I know, Zip." Crosshairs's eyelids fluttered. "It's...it's alright."

The men geared up quickly. They had to keep moving. Oddy knelt beside Crosshairs and pulled the pins from each grenade.

"If I could call a med evac for you, I would. I'd call that fucking Huey down, load you onto it, watch it carry you away someplace safe."

"I-it-it's okay, S-Sarge..."

"You hold on as long as you can, son. When it gets too cold, or starts hurting too much, just let go."

"I c-c-can feel my f-feet, Sarge." Crosshairs waggled his toes as proof of this claim. The blood in his divot was thinly rimed with ice. "Feels so good, y'know? Just feeling."

Oddy kissed his palm and pressed it to Crosshairs's forehead. Crosshairs closed his eye and listened to their footsteps crunch through the snow, receding, getting farther and farther away.

Soon he was alone.

Or...not quite.

«««—»»»

"Go go go!"

The men crashed through the underbrush like crazed rhinos. They ran heedlessly. They ran as if simple distance might somehow erase all they had seen and done. They ran to beat the devil.

They did what soldiers did best.

Ran from the past.

"Go go go!"

Had they looked down, they would've seen shrubs growing at their feet. Had any of them possessed a knowledge of herbs, they might have identified the shrubs by their purplish, furred leaves:

Wolfsbane.

There was no way they could've seen the creature perched in a tree high above. A small, stunted creature who watched their progress with interest and amusement.

Watched with one large, red eye.

"Go go go!"

«« — »»

Neil Paris, who would later be known as Crosshairs, shipped out for Vietnam at the age of nineteen. He left behind a girlfriend, as most servicemen did. Her name was Maria, and they loved one another with a depth and breadth that thrilled and terrified them both.

He took her to Coney Island for hot dogs and birch beers at Nathan's. He remembered the ocean wind blowing through her hair, whipping it around her head, catching in her mouth, between her lips. He made all sorts of excuses to touch her. Being with her made the hard truths of the world bearable, even nonexistent; when he held her, he believed, however briefly, that there were no such things as hatred, or cruelty, or pain. And when she kissed him, he knew he never wanted to kiss anyone else again, ever.

She said she'd wait. She sent letters. In one she enclosed a sea shell. The young soldier, hunkered in a pillbox near Quoy Non, had licked it, tasting the brine. Although his mind tried to resist it, he couldn't help wondering who might have been with her when she collected it. He punched a hole through the shell and wore it on a strip of rawhide around his neck.

Nights in the jungle, blackness so absolute it became a living entity, he would dream of a reunion with her. She would be waiting at the bus station, hair tied back with a yellow ribbon. He would step off the Greyhound and walk to her, taking her head in his hands, kissing her small, sweet mouth. Her hands would slip around his waist, then up to encircle his neck. He would place his lips to her ear and say—these *exact words*, rehearsed over three Tours of desperate yearning: "Tell me anything. Tell me everything. I have crossed ocean and land to be with you. Help me forget. Help me remember."

Then the injury. Suddenly all those dreams seemed foolish. Maria wouldn't want him now, not with half his face blown off. He tried to imagine them together but found he could not: his face had become a black smudge she refused to look at. He knew what she would say: *I still care for you, but...* and he would let her off easy, for perhaps he might have done the same, had the situation been reversed.

She continued to send letters. They were forwarded to him at the institution in Coldwater. He would read them aloud to Eugene while he traced the cracks of his room with syrup. Letters full of love and compassion and infinite hope. But they were addressed to a man who no longer existed. He wrote back, long and searching letters on yellow foolscap, much of it lacking commas or periods—a furious outpouring of emotion. He would address the envelopes, stamp them...and burn them.

Better she thought he'd found someone else.

Better she thought him unfaithful. Better she thought him dead.

Help me forget. Help me remember.

Now, as he lay dying, his thoughts turned to Maria. In that still-ness, in that quiet, he wondered, Where was she? How was she? Had she found the love she so dearly deserved? Had she forgiven him? He thought of the way the wind caught her hair, the way her fingers traced his body in the darkness, his ribs, the fortune-lines of his palm...

Pain crested and ebbed, crested and ebbed, in great waves. He rode them, a ship in the storm. The moon curved upon the maples, brightening the ground, hardening the stars. The grenades in his hands felt weightless, blown-glass globes.

Just let go.

No. Not yet. Such a beautiful night.

Movement on the far side of the clearing. Something tottered to a standing position. Whatever it was, it looked horrible: naked and white, most of its face blown off or eaten away, guts hanging in a loose ball above a clean-picked groin.

"Glaaa..." it said.

"Glaaa yourself," Crosshairs croaked.

It advanced with aching slowness. Its guts bounced and slapped.

Just let go.

Not yet.

It fell at Crosshairs's feet. Its hands—one of them fingerless—caressed Crosshairs's flanks as if an exotic meat. It made a loud clicking sound deep in its throat, like a nun's clacker. Its eyes, the sole unscathed feature on its face, were alive with mindless hunger.

"Are you hungry?" Crosshairs said.

"Glaaa…"

It reached across Crosshairs's face and dipped a finger into the divot's pooled blood. It crammed the finger into the wet red hole in its neck.

"That's a filthy habit."

Its gaze lowered. "Glaaa…"

The finger dipped again, greedily. Crosshairs stared skyward. So wonderful, the stars in their orbit. "I want to forget," he whispered.

"Glaaa…" it said, predictably.

JUST…LET…GO.

Yes. Alright.

For a moment he was gripped with panic as his hands refused to open. Then the appropriate nerve centers received the appropriate messages and his fingers slowly unclenched. Grenade clips pin-wheeled before his eye on a spinning trajectory. It was one of the most oddly beautiful things he'd ever seen. Spinning metal. Over and over, and over and over. Beautiful.

Crosshairs smiled and said, "Let me take you away from this."

It was slow to comprehend. "Glaaa…?"

Then it saw the grenades. Its eyes widened in fear.

The breeze on my face, Crosshairs was thinking, *feels so fine. Feels like—*

BOOM.

The reverberation of the detonating grenades rose above the tree-tops, carrying for miles and miles.

V.
FOUR HORSEMEN

War Zone "D," South Vietnam
July 15th, 1967. 21:02 hours.

"Sit. Talk."

The fire spread. Blazing tongues licked at the overhanging palms, setting them ablaze. Flame unfurled across the jungle canopy like lit gasoline across calm waters. A huge black bird rocketed from a burning palm, wings and tail feathers robed in fire. It rose into the night sky, phoenix-like, before arcing into a tight tailspin, crashing in a shower of flaming plumage, withering and writhing as it died.

Answer sat less than five feet from the creature. Its burning flesh threw a pleasant warmth. Flies congregated on the stump of Slash's neck.

"What are you?" he asked.

"What do you think I am?"

"Some kind of monster."

The creature's long tongue reached out and licked its remaining eye in the manner of a gecko. "A monster? Perhaps. I've been called such before. But I do not see myself as one." A rueful smile. "Then again, I suppose no monster sees itself as one."

"If not a monster, then what?"

An expression of vexation crossed its face. "I am not exactly certain. You see, I have no parents—or, if so, I have never met them. I was not raised as you were, taught acceptable modes of behavior, shown my role in this world. Of course, I was born before even the most rudimentary societies existed, at a time when the Americas were no more than timberland and desert."

Answer crossed his legs and planted his elbows on his knees, resting his head on his balled fists. His posture echoed that of a young child listening, rapt, while his father spun a tale.

"Nevertheless," the creature continued, "I have come to some understanding of what I am, and my place in the world."

"And what's that?"

"I am War," it replied. "Or perhaps more properly Chaos. Anarchy. Discord. I am the living embodiment, the ultimate personification of these ideas." A scream rose above the fire's roar. The creature shivered delightedly at the sound. "Wherever there is anger, or strife, or suffering...I am *drawn* to such places, inexorably, like lead filings to a magnet."

Images flickered through Answer's mind in jerky, Nickleodeon-style stop-motion: Neanderthal men fighting with teeth and nails and blunt rocks; Genghis Khan and the Mongols cutting a bloody swath across the East, leaving fatherless children and ravaged women in their wake; Nero fiddling madly on the minaret while Rome burned beneath him; dead-eyed Jews being led to the gas chambers at Dresden, and Auschwitz, and Treblinka; soldiers fighting and dying in a foreign land for a cause they would never fully understand. The images held a single commonality: in the background, or on the periphery, swathed in shadows, a form watched, bearing witness and urging humanity on to greater atrocities.

"Why?" Answer said. "Why do you *exist*?"

Chaos shifted. The smell of pork barbecue, unpleasant given the setting, wafted off its body. It said, "Every living thing has a reason for existence, be it to provide the world beauty, or to create great things, or to see beyond the borders of what is to glimpse what could be. But the most important role any of us can play is to maintain the balance."

"Balance?"

Chaos nodded. "The nature of balance is of utmost importance. When an infant boy is born, an old man must die. Whenever a tree is struck by lighting, a sapling must grow in its shadow. Any act of kindness must be equalized by an act of malice. Love offset by hate. Happiness neutralized by despair. Order balanced by...me."

"Then you are a monster," Answer said, "because Chaos is evil."

Chaos issued a choked gurgle that in some alternate universe may have passed as mirth. "This from a species responsible for such suffering and bloodshed as I could only *wish* to wreak. When you have lived as long as I, you come to understand very little in this world is truly good or evil. It is a matter of shades, of degrees. If I am evil—and yes, I am—it is simply because evil is my nature. But my evil is a necessary one."

"Why?"

Chaos smiled, a thin and almost imperceptible motion of its glowing lips. "Something once told me, long ago and in another world, that the most truthful of all stories in this universe is one in which something horrible happens for which there is no explanation. There is only one essential truth, and it is this: things happen because they happen. Bad things. Sometimes good things. All things. With no rhyme or reason." A hut toppled in a shower of swirling sparks. "And what is so evil about chaos, anyway? Does it not represent ultimate free will, total empowerment, absolute self-determinism? And what is so evil about war? Yes, it brings out the worst in men—but it also brings out the *best*. Comradeship, heedless self-sacrifice, heroism of the highest order: war effects such actions."

Through the foliage to their left came voices. Answer heard Tripwire say, "Shit, Sarge, half his fuckin' head's missing…"

"So tell me," Chaos said, "if I am indeed the truest mode of social behavior, the shape that humanity naturally tends towards when freed from the shackles of ordered society…am I not Truth?"

"Truth in Chaos," Answer whispered. Did it not make perfect sense?

Chaos took a step forward. Its eye was shiny and red and huge, the pitiless eye of a predatory bird. Answer felt, for the first time he could remember, a sense of kinship with another living thing. Chaos reached out and touched his face. The texture of its digits was as smooth as polished porcelain. It took Answer's chin and pulled his gaze upwards, locking it with its own.

"Are you going to kill me?"

"No," Chaos said. Its expression suggested that killing him would be sacrilegious. Like killing a son, or an heir. "You will live. You and the others. They will live because they are creatures of combat, and their lives will echo with the chaos of this night and this war for the rest of their lives." It stroked Answer's cheek lovingly. "For you perhaps a higher purpose exists. Not yet; you are too young. But someday…perhaps."

"When?" Answer was on the verge of tears. "*When?*"

"That I cannot say. Nothing is for certain." Chaos's flaming shoulders shrugged. "Que sera, sera."

Chaos turned and walked away. Wounded though it was, its myriad limbs still moved in perfect sync, like gears in a precision timepiece.

"Don't go," Answer said. Tears shined in his eyes. "Please...stay."

Chaos disappeared into the fiery jungle. Flames leapt to greet it and Chaos spread its arms wide to receive them. Then it was gone.

Answer got up. He considered pursuit, dashing headlong into the flames, catching up to Chaos, or dying in the attempt. His life, whatever slim value system he had previously operated under, was obsolete. Duty, valor, sacrifice: such ideals seemed trivial now.

Whatever will be will be...

He turned and walked in the opposite direction, following the voices of his unit members...

"Shitcan that talk, dogface," Oddy said. "Where's Answer?"

"Here, Sarge," Answer said, melting out of the foliage. Crosshairs lay on the ground with a blood-soaked blanket wrapped around his head. Zippo gave him a look that said: *Where the fuck you been while this shit's been going down?*

"We got a med evac rendezvouz one klick down this speed trail," Oddy said. "Answer, scout ahead. Trip and me'll hump Crosshairs. Zippo, you tail."

They raced down the speed trail as if the devil himself were in pursuit. Five pairs of eyes scanned the darkened jungle; four fearfully, one in hopeful anticipation.

"Go go go!"

The landing site came into view. A Huey waited. Dylan's "Like A Rolling Stone" pumped out of the cockpit speakers at a pitch capable of vibrating teeth from gums. They lifted Crosshairs onto the chopper's honeycombed aluminum floor before hopping in themselves.

"Motherfuck." Tripwire's body shivered against Oddy's. "What was that thing?"

"Don't know, son," Oddy replied through gritted teeth. "Hope to Christ it's dead."

The door gunner was the same kid who'd ridden shotgun on the drop-off. He said, "Where are the other two?"

Oddy shook his head.

"Oh," the kid said.

The Huey flew directly over the village, which was now nothing but a flaming scalp in the darkness. Oddy leaned into the cockpit. "Get on the horn," he told the pilot. "I want a napalm drop on that village and outlying area. Give me as wide coverage as I can command."

The pilot said, "That village is burning merrily all on its own."

"Don't lip me, son. Got no patience for it."

The pilot flicked the com-link toggle on his headset. "A-303 team leader requests scar line on coordinates fifteen-twenty-two-niner."

"*Roger*," came the reply.

"What's the problem, Sarge?" the pilot said. "Some of 'em get away?"

"Precautionary measures."

"One hell of a precaution."

Minutes later a phalanx of F-4 Phantoms buzzed the Huey. The incendiary *whoosh* of the napalm drop was audible for miles around. *Please God*, Oddy thought. *Let that be the end of it.*

«««—»»»

A-303 Blackjack was disbanded after the mission. Oddy and Zippo returned to the States, followed shortly thereafter by Crosshairs. Tripwire set off for Thailand.

Answer stayed.

There was no reason for him to return: no family, no girlfriend like the one Crosshairs was always yakking about, no factory job waiting. But there *was* a reason to stay—he knew, on a bone-deep level, Chaos was still out there.

Waiting. Watching.

He fell in with a group of Green Berets working Night Recon. The Greenies were *baaad* motherfuckers, most of them jungle-mad. Answer fit right in.

They worked night patrol. Answer applied camouflage—green stripe, black stripe, green stripe, black stripe—until his body was colored with the jungle. He slipped through the darkness like water, like oil, soundless, centerless. Answer *became* the jungle. He lost himself in the land, and in doing so located himself. His Truth. He stopped carrying a weapon, except for his K-Bar. He didn't need a gun anymore. He had become part of the terrain, indistinguishable from the trees and the dirt and the water.

At night in the jungle he felt as close to his own body as was humanly possible: his blood moving, his hair, his skin, his heart pounding with the rhythm of the land. He felt the roots beneath his bare feet and wished they might grow up into him, anchoring him in place, connecting him to the land. Sometimes, out in the darkness, he slipped into a kind of daydreaming state. He dreamed of dead bodies, acres upon acres of them, piled atop one another like split logs. He dreamed of armless, legless, headless corpses, fields of little rag dolls pulled apart, liquid, stuffed with streaming redness, flowing out and away. He dreamed of bloated rats skittering over and into the piled carcasses like ants trundling in and out of their hills. Vietnam—the bloodshed and madness and *chaos* of it—became him. He crossed to the other side. He was part of the land. He became shadows and nightmare. He wore a necklace of human tongues.

He was watching and searching.

He was waiting to be found.

Northwest Territories
December 8th, 1987. 1:20 a.m.

Once, during an R&R stint in St. Petersburg following a string of Midwest bank jobs, Oddy went scuba diving. It struck him that the pastime had much in common with his Tours in Vietnam.

Men were not meant to breathe underwater.

Men were not meant to go to war.

Submerging for the first time, his heart hammering inside his wetsuit, taking that first lungful of compressed air…so unnatural. Dropping to the ocean floor, staring into the silty water, wondering what creatures might emerge from it…unnatural. Nitrogen entering the bloodstream, blossoming in every ventricle…unnatural. But after a while you got used to the unnaturalness of the situation. Came to enjoy it, even.

Same rules applied in Vietnam. The first time he'd waded through a rice paddy with an M-16 raised overhead…unnatural. First time he'd set an M-14 toe-popper under a pile of wet leaves and dropped a Twinkie beside it…unnatural. The first time he'd killed a man, blowing a moon-roof in the back of his shocked yellow head…so unnatural. But by that time he'd dipped far enough beneath the waves he'd entered that fathomless realm where there was no right or wrong, only grim survival.

Dangers abound in both cases. Free divers who spend too much time at great depths suffer aseptic bone necrosis from years of residual nitrogen bubbles trapped in their marrow, bones left fragile as honeycombs. Soldiers who spend too much time in a warzone suffer shellshock and night sweats; their minds become fragile as honeycombs—or worse, hard as obsidian. But these are the prices to be paid by those who live and breathe at those alien depths where the wild things are.

Now, as he ran through the night, Oddy was struck by how *natural* the situation felt: the weight of a gun in his hands, the blood and pain hammering his calves and thighs, adrenaline spiking through his heart. He was in the eye of madness. Where the wild things are. And he belonged.

How long have I been running? he wondered. Felt like forever. His legs burned as if the veins were shot full of carbolic acid. Answer flashed up the path ahead of him, Sig Sauer sweeping the fringing bushes. Zippo and Tripwire brought up the rear. The land stretched before them, endless and dark and menacing.

"Hold up."

Answer stopped and turned. His gun tapped his leg with the irritability of a man late for an important meeting. Zippo and Tripwire caught up.

"What's the problem?" Zippo said.

Oddy pulled the map out. Answer snapped a flare alight.

"We've been running like headless chickens," Oddy said. "My bearings are shot." He pointed in a westerly direction. "Lake's over there. If we cut across this inlet, we'll shave off half a day."

A distant explosion swelled across the treetops. Tripwire bowed his head in recognition of what the sound meant. *And then there were four*, Answer thought.

"We hoof it down to the lake," Oddy said after a moment, "slap on the snowshoes, and hightail it across the ice. How much ammo we got?"

"The flamer's toast." Zippo spoke like a boy whose puppy had been run over. "Got five magazines for the pistols."

Tripwire checked his pack. "One more clip, plus whatever's left in the one I'm using. He fingered the bandoliers crossed over his chest. "Still got enough explosive to blow a hole in the world."

Oddy said, "Answer?"

"Couple hundred rounds."

"And I got two belts for the H&K." Oddy smiled wearily. "After that I guess we're using our bare hands."

Zippo leaned against a tree covered with brittle moss and frozen white flowers. Slowly, like a drunk sliding down an alley wall, he slid down the trunk, hitting the ground with a groan.

"Zip?" Tripwire came over. "You okay?"

"My fucking ribs," he said. "Busted a couple, I think."

Tripwire unzipped the hitman's parka. Beneath his thermal vest, the left-hand side of Zippo's chest was lumpy, as if shards of broken glass had been inserted beneath the skin. The hitman shifted. Things ground inside his chest, bone against bone, bone against organ. His torso felt like it was packed full of thumbtacks.

"Yeah," Tripwire said. "Three greensticks, maybe more. Also a dislocated shoulder."

"Do what you do," Oddy told him.

Tripwire cracked the M-5 kit. He loaded Zippo up on streptomycin for the pain and penicillin to stay infection. "I could give you morphine, Zippo, but you'd be fuzzed out of your mind." The hitman shook his head, grimaced, and said, "No morphine." Tripwire removed Zippo's thermal vest and braced his left shoulder against the tree. Zippo's dislocated clavicle bone pressed against the skin, the knob looking like a gold ball.

"I'm gonna pop it back in," Tripwire said. "It'll hurt like fuck."

"Get to it."

Instructing Oddy to keep a firm grip on Zippo's right shoulder, Tripwire went behind the tree and gripped Zippo's left shoulder from the opposite side.

"One…two…*three*."

Jerking hard on his shoulder, Tripwire popped Zippo's shoulderbone back into its socket. It re-located with a crisp *pop*. Zippo screamed. Tripwire wrapped the hitman's chest and shoulder in Ace bandages before helping him into his vest and parka.

"You going to be okay?" Oddy said.

"You lead, Sarge," Zippo said, "and I'll follow."

"Let's get at it, then."

They cut across a steep downhill grade leading to the lake's shore. Great Bear stretched for miles, covered in a white pane of snow. The trees of the far shore were pinprick spires. The men pulled on the snowshoes and set off. The snowshoes took some getting used to: to compensate for their width, the men were forced to adopt an awkward bowlegged gait. Their breath puffed out in great white plumes. It had been over twelve hours since they last rested.

Tripwire pulled up beside Oddy. He shook two Luckies from the pack, lit them, passed one to Oddy. "Absurd, isn't it?"

"What's that, son?"

"Us. Here. Life. The universe." Tripwire exhaled smoke through his nostrils, smiling.

"Hmmm," Oddy said. "Yeah. Absurd."

"But don't you also feel a bit like…I don't know, like this feels so…"

"Right?"

"*Exactly*," Tripwire said, clapping his hands together. "I feel *right* out here. I mean, no question I'm scared as shit—but it's not *bad*. It's like I belong here, and this was something I was meant to do. And it's wrong, I know—Christ, Crosshairs is gone—but I can't help it." He looked away, ashamed of the admission. "You know?"

"Sure I know, son. Think about what brought us together in the first place—the fact we're good at destroying things. The army saw it before we saw it in ourselves. We were born into this, born to fight and to kill…and, on some level, to enjoy it." He took a long hard drag on the Lucky, inhaling so deeply its coal flared like a neon sign. "If the war hadn't found us, we would have found the war. And if not 'Nam, then some other conflict."

Tripwire puffed contemplatively, cigarette smoke curling around his manicured fingernails. He'd had them done a week ago at an East-LA esthetique, clipped and filed, the cuticles buffed. Now there were bits of a vampire's face underneath them. "Some shitty birthright, isn't it? Like we've been bred, bred from the *cradle*, to be what we are." He looked at his hands, detached, as if they were not a part of him. "And isn't it strange how we all came? None of us married, no families, all of us needing, for one reason or another, to accept Grosevoir's proposition."

Oddy licked his thumb and pointer finger and extinguished the cigarette's heater between them. "You think it's fate, son—destiny?"

"I didn't mean it like that. It's just, I think, could be—"

"I think it's fate. No other way to explain it."

After a moment, Tripwire said, "Yeah. So do I." There was a grimness to his voice, and his shoulders slumped under the weight of the inevitable. "More of us are going to die before this thing's over, aren't we?"

"I don't know, son."

Somewhere on the lake's far side a great noise arose. The men turned their heads. In the distance, carrying over the lake's frozen plate, the sound of snapping wood. Not twigs. Not branches, even. *Trees.* They were being broken low, near their bases, two-foot-thick trunks shattering like dandelion stalks.

"Jesus Christ…" Tripwire whispered.

A massive shape moved through the forest skirting the lake. Silhouetted against the permanent dusk, its immense frame towered above the trees. Its arms, which may or may not have been covered in matted fur, swung loosely at its sides. Its legs, each twice the size of a stabilizing support on an offshore oil rig, covered two-hundred yards in a single stride. Birds massed in a loose halo above its head; its hand occasionally rose to brush at them in an agitated manner. Although it was difficult to tell, Oddy thought he saw human-sized creatures clinging to the massive beast's back, sides, and chest. They scuttled across its shoulders or rode the hillock-sized knobs of its spine or simply clung for dear life wherever purchase could be found. Zippo craned his neck upward in an attempt to take in the thing's head. He saw two red pits, each the size of a swimming pool, where its eyes should be. Its smell carried across the lake: wood sap, smoke, carrion. The men stood stock-still, willing themselves invisible, until the shape ambled from view.

"Of all the times to be without a camera," Zippo said finally. "Ripley's would've paid big money for a snapshot of that thing."

They hiked for another hour before breaking for grub. The portable stove had been lost during their flight from the vampires, so they tore the dried food packets open and ate the contents with their bare hands. Dehydrated shards of beef cut the insides of their mouths, rock-hard kernels of corn shattered between their teeth like jawbreakers, bullion powder gritted on their tongues. Zippo cracked open four tins of fruit salad and passed them around. The men ate greedily, silently, hands and mouth smeared with sweet syrup.

"Sarge," Tripwire said once they'd finished. "You tell me to, I'll get my ass up and hoof it until I keel over dead. But I really wouldn't mind a bit of a rest."

Oddy glanced at Zippo out of the corner of his eye. He was looking pale and had been coughing up gobs of blood throughout the meal. "Okay. We got good sightlines here—nothing's going to sneak up on us. Take a break."

Answer retrieved four flares from his pack. He snapped them alight and set them around the encampment. Tripwire collected the empty fruit salad tins.

"Give me your fishing rigs," he said.

Tripwire took the tins and the fishing line and walked out to where the flares had been set. He scooped a hole in the snow, into which he deposited a tin. He unhooked four grenades and tied fishing line to the pins. Then he placed the grenades into the tins and played line out until he was back with the others.

"A little boobytrap," he said. "We see anything coming, I yank the line, pull the pin, and…" he placed his fist in front of his mouth, made a *pop* sound, and opened his hand. "…boom."

"Nice idea," Answer said. "But won't the explosions crack the ice?"

Tripwire frowned. "Hadn't thought of that."

Oddy said, "Well, we can all swim."

They stretched out on the snow. Oddy was somewhat alarmed to find he could not feel his feet: his toes felt like knobs of wood knocking against the insides of his boots. Frostbite, or just poor circulation? Fuck it. If he got out of this alive he'd have them chopped off and replaced with solid gold prosthetics. *Goldfoot*, he thought. *James Bond's newest adversary.*

"So," he said, "what are you boys spending your take on?"

Tripwire smiled. This was a variation on a game every dogface and flyboy and ground-pounder played in 'Nam. The game was called "What Are You Gonna Do When You Get Home?" For some soldiers it was all about food: they were going to eat a garbage pail full of French fries, a rain barrel full of soft shell crab, a T-bone steak the size of a manhole cover. For others pussy was the passion: they were going to fuck homegrown bush till their jimmies waved a white flag.

For Oddy it was music. He'd just wanted to crank up the Hi-Fi, a little Chubby Checker or Ray Charles' "Can't Stop Lovin' You," snug on a pair of headphones and float away with the tunes. For Tripwire it was movies: sitting in the balcony Aladdin theater with a tub of hot buttered popcorn, feet cocked up on the balcony rail and some old film—*The Maltese Falcon* maybe, Bogart as Sam Spade—flickering on the screen. And, if he was lucky, perhaps there'd be some sweet young thing to throw his arm around. Heaven. The purpose of the game was simplicity itself: it provided hope. And in 'Nam, hope was the most valuable currency going—sometimes it was enough to get you through. Not always. But sometimes.

"How does this sound, Sarge," Tripwire said. "I take that dough and make the porno to end all pornos. We're talking A-List cast— Seka, Marilyn Chambers, Amber Lynn, Annie Sprinkle, Linda Lovelace, the whole starlet constellation." Tripwire cracked his knuckles against his chin, warming up. "Here's the setup: the year is 2020. The world has been ravaged by nuclear destruction. The only survivors are a group of super-hot models who've constructed an impregnable fallout shelter—"

"The fuck are supermodels doing building fallout shelters?" Zippo said.

"You're watching a movie with your pants around your ankles, tugging at your pud, and you're going to give a shit about logic?" Tripwire shot back. "Now, five years have passed since Armageddon. The chicks are down to their last can of SPAM, clean out of tampons, horny as fruit flies. They've been dyking it out for years and are starved for pole. Lo and behold, a knock on the door."

Oddy said, "That pizza they ordered five years ago?"

"Better. A platoon of marines searching out any survivors. But the fallout has mutated their bodies in the most interesting way: their cocks are *massive*."

"How fortunate for them," Answer said.

Zippo said, "If that's what radiation poisoning does, I'll start hanging around nuclear test sites."

Tripwire said, "We're talking foot-long hogs here, thick as pop cans—"

"Ah, come on," Zippo said. "No man's got a hose that big."

"You kidding?" Tripwire said. "Couple weeks ago a kid walked into my office. Face like a fucking bear trap, wicked case of acne and little niblet teeth like mongoloids got, but then he doffed his pants and—" Tripwire held his hands a jaw-dropping distance apart. "—to his *knees*. I mean, I don't got a pussy and *I* was scared."

"Oh," Zippo said. His hand dropped to his crotch and gave it a self-conscious squeeze.

"So," Tripwire continued, "the soldiers tell them Earth is uninhabitable. The chicks say no problem, 'cause they've built a spaceship capable of light speed—"

"A fallout shelter *and* a spaceship," Oddy said. "These are some *super* supermodels."

"You'd think they'd have spent their time inventing more effective vomiting techniques," Zippo said. "Or perfecting the art of walking and chewing bubblegum at the same time."

"I'm ignoring you," Tripwire said. "So they hop into their space shuttle, which is decorated tastefully, with a lot of lounging chaises and throw pillows and balloons—"

"But of course," said Answer.

Oddy said, "How could it be otherwise?"

"Christian Dior eat your heart out," Zippo said.

"—and, as the only remaining humans, their duty is to propagate the species—"

"It's a hard job, but someone's got to do it," Oddy said.

"Fucking in zero gravity? Going to be fluids floating every-where!" Zippo.

"—Cue a giant orgy. I'm talking constant, enduring fucking. Every orifice. Rotating partners. A sea of thrusting, moaning body parts. *Caligula* will have nothing on this flick!"

Oddy said, "What are you calling this opus?"

Tripwire considered. "How about *Intergalactic Space Sluts*? Or maybe *2020: A Space Orgy*?"

"Tough choice. They're both so classy," Zippo cracked.

"Ah, fuck it." Tripwire threw his hands up. "You jokers wouldn't know class if it yanked your pants down and blew you. What are your plans, Zippo—got any?"

"Whores," Zippo said. "Whores and cupcakes, a million bucks' worth."

"Well, son," Oddy said, laughing. "Gonna end up with a lot of fat-assed whores, I thi—"

From the darkened forest a feral howl arose. Moments later it was answered by another, this one from a different location. The sound ricocheted across the inlet, prickling the hairs on their necks.

"I don't suppose there's any chance that'd be your garden-variety timberwolf," Tripwire said.

"Don't suppose so," Oddy said. "Let's get back on the hump. Zippo, how do you feel?"

"Like a bag of smashed assholes."

"Maybe we should hunker here." Answer swept his arm to encom-pass the broad, flat landscape. "Like you said, nothing's liable to sneak up on us. If we got to fight, might as well be on our own terms."

"You've got a point," Oddy said. "And I've got a feeling we're surrounded, anyhow."

Another howl arose, a long and shuddering and lonely sound that went out across the cold night air. The men's blood chilled. They knew that sound. It was in their blood, that sound, an echo from far away and long ago, when all the world had been forest and jungle and primitive man had fled in terror before the pursuing pack. It echoed over the barren vista, unchanged over the eons, infused with the looming threat of the hunt.

Zippo retrieved the silver bullet from his pocket. He rolled the smooth cylinder between his fingers. One shot. He ejected the Llama's magazine and slotted the silver slug in.

"Don't put it on top," Oddy said. "Don't know about you, but my first shot's most often my wildest. I don't zone in until the fourth or fifth. Plus, regular bullets don't much affect these things—they'll charge right through to give you a clean close shot."

Made sense to Zippo. He ejected four bullets, inserted the silver one, and re-loaded the rest. The others did the same. Oddy spun the Webley's cylinder and snapped it home with a flick of his wrist, scanning the darkened terrain. What he saw was disturbing: in places the snow appeared to be *moving*. It wouldn't stay still, and each time he refocused it would shift, hillocks becoming ridges becoming flat land again. The movement was furtive and sneaking: it possessed a pattern and connection just beyond Oddy's capacity for understanding.

There was only one certainty.

It was getting closer…

«« —»»

Excerpt from *"Never Cry Wolf,"* by Farley Mowatt (1963):

> *I have lived amongst the wolves of the arctic tundra for some months now. They see I pose no threat, and have come to accept my presence as a matter of course. Fall slips into winter, and their appearance adapts to suit the season. Their pelts, previously iron-gray, have changed to a creamy-white. This, I suspect, is a natural camouflage, aiding their pursuit of the nomadic caribou herds. It is effective, to be sure: in the gloaming they are nearly impossible to spot. They are one with the land, ghostly specters who live only for the hunt, for the kill…*

«« —»»

"…spotting something over here." Answer pointed in the opposite direction. "Indistinct, but…something."

"Something here, too." Tripwire.

"Ditto." Zippo.

Oddy stared skyward. The full moon was up by now, he knew, but hidden behind a bank of black cotton clouds. He willed the cloud cover to lift; he *needed* that moonlight. "Steady on those booby traps, son," he whispered.

Tripwire knelt close to the ground. He'd wrapped the fishing lines around the index and middle fingers of each hand, both of which were trembling. *Steady, baby*, he told himself. *Keep your shit wired.*

The acid burn of anticipation smoldered in Oddy's arms, his hands, his finger squeezed around the H&K23's trigger. He squinted. Something was out there. Odd movements, odd shapes. The whole landscape seemed to stare in at him—a watched feeling—and his eyes followed the forms that slid through the whiteness. Every time he pinned one down, every time the foreign contours began to coalesce into some recognizable silhouette, it melted into shadows again.

"Getting a bit flaked here, Sarge," Tripwire said.

"Keep your head. Fortune favors the brave."

It was their eyes that ended up giving them away: specks of slitted red glowing like well-stoked embers. Their brightness was such that they left lingering contrails wherever they moved, the way sparklers held by excited children do on Fourth of July nights.

"I got a bead," Oddy said, nodding to a spot perhaps ten feet past one of Answer's flares. He let loose with the Heckler and Koch. Bullets stitched a path across the snow, slugs slamming through the ice, gouts of water spurting up through the holes.

He didn't hit a thing.

A growl arose from somewhere close by. Zippo jerked his head back, half-convinced a slavering jaw was within an inch of his neck. Nothing was there. A smell wafted across the unbroken expanse to where they hunched: a scent of fevered hunger, insistent as death.

Zippo snapped off a shot that kicked up a puff of snow. *What good's a clean sightline*, he thought, *if you can't see what the fuck you're shooting at?* For the first time since 'Nam, Zippo was scared: that sickeningly familiar sensation of fire-ants crawling at the back of his throat…

"There!" Answer said. His finger pointed to a shimmering shape near one of the booby traps. He said to Tripwire: "Hit it!"

Tripwire jerked his arm up, hard, like a bodybuilder performing a biceps curl. The fishing line tightened across the ice in a seismic wave of crystallized snow, then went slack as the grenade pin pulled free. The clip made a dull metallic sound ricocheting off the tin's insides.

Oddy couldn't tell which was louder: the grenade detonating or the lake's surface shattering. The sounds were different—the concussive thunder of high-explosive versus the ear-splitting whipcrack of ice cracking down deep fault lines—but equally deafening. The frozen surface trembled and the clear ice beneath Zippo's feet spider-webbed and then went milky and opaque. Fist-sized shards of ice rained down and a swell of water surged over their boots. When the cordite cleared they could see a jagged-edged hole the size of a VW Minibus. Ringing the hole were chunks of meat clung with white fur.

I got it, Tripwire thought savagely. *I got one of the fuc—*

Howling with rage and pain, it charged. Though the explosion had torn its rear right leg off, it still moved with chilling speed. Its remaining limbs, girded with thick roping muscles, flexed with svelte animal power. Its ears were pinned back to a bullet-shaped head and its eyes glowed a hideous baleful red. Muzzle was black as coal, teeth long and sharp as ivory daggers. Slaver ran between them in long viscid runners. The men saw all this in the split-second it took to cover the twenty feet separating them.

Then it was in their midst.

Oddy swiveled with the H&K23 slung low. The werewolf lashed out with its foot. Razor-sharp claws cut deep into the back of Oddy's hand, just below his knuckles, cleaving flesh and severing nerves. Blood sprayed from the wound to sheet his face. The machine-gun skittered along the ice and out of reach.

The werewolf's paw pistoned out towards Tripwire in a murderous upwards sweep. His fevered mind saw, in that fractured second, the battered watch around its wrist, the tiny TIMEX logo written in orange.

Takes a licking, his mind raved and then a paw tipped with heavy claws ripped a scar-line into his armpit, continuing through the junction where shoulder met arm. Pain sung along the raw gash as Tripwire spun with the blow's force. In the process his arm flailed upwards...fishing line arced across the ice...the faint *tic* of a pin detatching...

BOOM and the ice tilted madly beneath them. Ice chips sprayed like smashed teeth. There was another gaping hole now, to the left of the first, with a three-foot ice bridge separating the two. Chunks of ice and slush pelted down; a sharp wedge struck Answer on the shoulder and his right arm went instantly numb. The smell of wet gunpowder mixed with the wet-dog odor of the werewolf.

A buzz-saw of blood spurted through the vent in Tripwire's parka and in his head things were exploding with dim popping noises, underwater fireworks. He fell down hard on his ass and the ice cracked beneath him. He felt as if he were sitting on a crust of spun sugar that could melt, or shatter, at any moment. Then the werewolf was towering above him, blood matting its jaws, canines like sharpened hooks, and all else was forgotten. He fought back the urge to bare his throat like a whipped mongrel.

A combat boot came down on Tripwire's hand. Biting back a scream, he craned his neck to see the boot belonged to Zippo, and that Zippo's gun was drawn and pointed at...*him*.

The werewolf's head slammed into his chest and Zippo's gun barked simultaneously. The bullet passed through the werewolf's skull and exited from the underside of its chin, burrowing into the ice between Tripwire's spread legs. The werewolf jerked as if stung but its jaws kept gnashing. Zippo's lips were moving rapidly. He was counting off the bullets as he ran through the magazine.

OnetwothreefourFIVE—

The silver bullet spun from the cylinder to punch a neat hole just above the werewolf's left eyebrow. It reared with a shocked howl. There was a gaping crater on the underside of its jaw. Tatters of fabric hung and swung from its jaws—the front of Tripwire's parka looked as if it had been shoved through a wheat thresher.

Then the most amazing thing happened: silverish tendrils began to spread outwards from the wound. They opened out across the werewolf's face, entering its mouth and snout and vulpine ears, before racing outwards across its limbs. This was accompanied by a sharp tinkling sound which Zippo associated with rapidly-freezing water. Within moments the creature was encased in a network of silver threads. Its front paws were raised above its head, teeth bared, hunched in pre-attack. Zippo shot it and the thing exploded like a tennis ball that had been immersed in liquid nitrogen and thrown at a brick wall.

"Sorry," Zippo said, taking his boot off Tripwire's hand. "Didn't want another grenade going off."

"S'okay."

"Get bit?"

Tripwire looked down at his chest. He shook his head.

"You got the devil's luck, then—"

"Over *here*!" Answer hollered.

Two sleek shapes rushed out of the darkness at a dead heat. Tripwire saw that they were maybe thirty feet from a booby trap. He wasn't sure the ice could withstand another explosion. But what choice did he have? Ignoring the searing pain in his shoulder, he jerked his arm across his neck in a throat-slitting gesture to detent another pin.

The grenade went off just as the werewolves reached it, the force of the explosion propelled them high into the air. Answer steadied himself as the ice pan see-sawed beneath him. Tracking the airborne werewolves, their white bodies stark against the purple-black sky, he selected a target, raised his pistol, and started firing. The fifth slug punctured the lycanthrope's sternum and silver tendrils burst instantly from the wound. It twisted midair, clawing its body, movement slowing as the threads unfurled. Then the motionless body was hurtling downwards at him. Answer fell back against the ice and it buckled inwards under his weight and icy water bubbled up through hairline cracks to soak his hair. He fired at the plummeting mass, which exploded like a pane of glass. Slivers of flash-frozen werewolf cut into his face and hands like razor blades.

Zippo snapped off four shots at the second werewolf before it hit him square in the chest. Air whoofed out of him in a bloody-tasting gust as he was knocked to the ground. His skull hit the ice and he dropped his guns. The force of impact propelled them across the slippery plate of ice. The werewolf's head was cocked at the predator's deadly questing angle and it was all Zippo could do to keep its jaws from his throat. He got his thumb up and jammed it into the werewolf's left eye. The retina popped like a bath bead and his thumb sunk in to the knuckle. The wolf's jaws snapped in pain and rage, taking three of Zippo's fingers.

The ice pan tilted. Ice water surged over Zippo's collar and down his back. Oddy watched them slide past. He couldn't take a shot without the possibility he'd hit Zippo.

They struggled for a moment longer, perched precariously at the ice's edge, before toppling backwards into the freezing lake.

Cold hit Zippo like a closed fist. It was near-paralyzing, and for a moment his heart stopped. They tumbled over and over in the dark water. His hands were snagged in the rough matted hair of the werewolf's head and he could feel the heavy bone of its skull beneath. Gunmetal-tasting water surged into his mouth and nose, invading his ears in thin icepick streams. He twisted and struggled against the werewolf, matching its animal ferocity with his own will to survive. His legs kicked as his boots and pants grew heavy with water. His lungs burned for air. His head thumped against something hard and he had no idea whether he'd hit the ice shelf above or the rocky lake bottom below.

The werewolf's paws raked his legs and suddenly the water was slightly warmer with his blood and his body slightly colder with its loss. Someone had thrown a flare into the water and greenish light spread in a mellow orbit above. The water's surface shimmered. Zippo reached upwards. The stumps of his bitten-off fingers left a cloudy red wake. Blood flowed like cold mud through his veins. The werewolf slashed frantically, trying to free itself now. *No way, José,* Zippo thought grimly. *No way I'm going down alone.*

A shape entered the water above them, swimming downwards with powerful strokes. Zippo's oxygen-starved brain was shutting down. He felt something thick and muscled pass by his face. The werewolf's head jerked back.

The water trembled. A brief flash of light—muzzle flash—lit the werewolf's destroyed face and, behind with his huge arm wrapped around its neck, Oddy. He pulled the Webley's trigger and another slug tore through the werewolf's head, exiting in a red haze, spinning away into the dark water. The creature's paws continued to claw at Zippo, ripping deep into his flesh, severing muscles and tendons.

Oddy chambered the silver bullet and jammed the barrel beneath the werewolf's chin. The flattened slug detached a massive portion of its skull and silver threads spooled from the wound. Moments— hours? days?—later, Zippo felt its limbs snap away like driftwood. Then Oddy's hand was hooked around his collar and dragging him up.

They broke the water's surface together. Oddy pulled Zippo to the ice's edge as steam rose off their bodies in smoking eddies. Zippo sucked in great lungfuls of air and then, like a fratboy who'd drunk too much too fast, vomited a stream of blood and bile onto the ice.

"Help him out," Oddy told Answer.

Answer laid flat on the ice, anchored himself as best he could, and offered Zippo his hand.

"Easy," he said. "Easy."

Zippo's hand felt like cold slate. Answer pulled him out of the water and rolled him onto his back. His thighs were flayed open to the femurs. Blood spread in a red pool beneath him. His face was pale with shock and his teeth chattered uncontrollably.

Answer retrieved a syrette of morphine from the med-pack. "You want?" he asked Zippo.

"Y-y-yeah."

He jabbed the syrette in Zippo's chest and depressed the plunger.

"A-ano-another."

Answer did as asked.

"A-ann-anno-another."

"It'll kill you," Answer said. He had no personal stake in the decision. "You want?"

Zippo nodded…then, slowly, shook his head. "Not yet."

By this time Oddy had pulled himself onto the ice. He'd only paused to strip off his parka and boots before diving in after Zippo. Now he shrugged off his sopping sweater and pulled the parka on. His feet, which he was now certain were frostbitten, he shoved back into his boots. He picked up the Webley and worked the cocking mechanism. It was frozen stiff. He hurled it into the water.

"We got another one," Tripwire said. He pointed with weary desperation at a spot just beyond the final booby trap.

"Hunker low," Oddy said. "and blow it."

Tripwire jerked his arm back in a motion one might use to bring a leashed dog to heel. The final booby trap went off. A gaping fissure ripped the length of the ice, and a large plate broke away. When the smoke cleared the men were left on a floating crescent surrounded by deep black water. The only escape point was a narrow ice bridge that had somehow withstood the explosions.

Their packs and spare clothes were soaked. Dried food packets floated on the water, tinfoil squares bobbing on the slight waves. Each of them was wounded. Each of them was bloody. Zippo dry-heaved helplessly. Blood streaked his teeth.

"Look," Tripwire said.

A single werewolf was hunched on the ice bordering the water on the far side. Smaller than the others, but sleeker, like a ballistic torpedo. It crouched on lean haunches and regarded the men with baleful red eyes. It seemed content to sit and wait.

They gathered around Zippo. Blood ran in sluggish rivulets from his legs and his front teeth had been knocked out. His hair was stuck to the ice in an uneven black fan. Tripwire reached two fingers into his mouth and scooped out pooling blood, afraid he'd choke on it.

"I-I'm f-fuh-fucking d-duh-done, Sarge."

"Lay still, son." Oddy felt for a pulse. There, but very weak. He asked Tripwire, "How's that arm?"

Tripwire gingerly parted the rip in his parka. Something winked back whitely from the wet redness. He had a sneaking suspicion it was bone. "Deep, but clean."

"You losing blood?"

"A bit."

"My b-buh-belt," Zippo said. "T-tor-tourniquet."

Tripwire said, "You sure?"

"T-th-the fuh-fuck I nuh-need ih-ih-it for?"

Oddy carefully stripped off Zippo's belt, looping it around Tripwire's shoulder and cinching it as tight as he dared. He looked at Answer. "How about you?"

Answer's face was a mess of long shallow scratches, some precariously close to his eyes. Blood trickled in torpid rivulets from the wounds, tracing the curve of his brow and collecting along the ridge of his upper lip. "I'll be fine."

Oddy performed a brief self-inspection: left hand useless, the back of it shredded, tendons and sinews looking like frayed red yarn. Most of his toes, and perhaps his feet, would have to be amputated if and when he got home. The only way to survive was to keep moving. But that meant—

"G-g-go." Zippo grabbed Tripwire's hand and squeezed. His grip was weak, like an old man, or an infant. "G-guh-get the fuh-fuck ow-out of hu-hu-here."

"Can we pick him up," Tripwire said. "Carry him?"

"He's dogmeat," Answer said. "He knows it and we know it."

"Zip that fuckin' lip, son."

Answer turned away.

"Huh-he's ruh-right. I-I'm duh-done."

They all knew it was true. But you just don't say those things. Not to a fellow soldier. Not to a fellow *human being*.

"Give him the rest of the morphine," Oddy said.

Tripwire uncapped the last two syrettes and curled them into Zippo's palm. He positioned Zippo's thumb over the plungers. "Just jab and push," he whispered.

The lone werewolf sat licking its chops. Answer said, "What are we going to do about that one?"

"See any more?" Oddy said.

"No."

"Is it going to attack?"

"Not us and not now," Answer said. "It's waiting."

"For what?"

"For us to leave. Then it'll take him."

Tripwire pulled the DeLisle's clip and ejected all the bullets except one. He slotted the silver bullet in on top and slapped the clip home. "Here," he placed the gun in Zippo's free hand, "one shot for that thing, and one more...for whatever."

"W-wuh-whatever, huh?" Zippo said. Tripwire scooped more blood out of his mouth. It was cold, like jelly. "Tuh-take my g-guns."

Tripwire retrieved the Llamas as Oddy crouched beside Zippo. The hitman's eyes were almost closed and lake water had frozen around his ears and nose and lips. Oddy breathed into his palm and pressed it to Zippo's forehead.

"Can you feel that, son?"

"N-nuh-no."

Oddy breathed again, deeper this time, and reapplied his palm. Suddenly it was very important, suddenly it was *crucial*, that Zippo feel this warmth.

"F-fuh-fucking a-ah-amazing, ih-ih-ih-isn't i-i-it?" Zippo's lips were sticking together from the blood. Oddy wet his thumb and wiped them clean. "V-vuh-vamp-p-pires and wuh-wuh-werewol...and...a-an..."

"Last of the big game hunters," Oddy said quietly. "That's us."

Zippo smiled, a subtle upturn at the corners of his mouth. "It's n-nuh-not so bu-bad, Sarge." He was thinking about Kazuhito Kawanami, the yakuza boss he'd killed. Thinking about how Kawanami had nodded, and sipped his drink, and accepted death with quiet dignity. "C-cu-cu-cold, b-b-buh-but o-o-o-okay..."

"One hell of a life we chose for ourselves, son. Hell of a life."

"W-wu-wouldn't h-huh-have it a-any other w-wu-way."

Oddy pressed his palm to Zippo's forehead a final time. The hitman's flesh was cold, rubbery. "We've got to go now, son. I'd've done anything to see this go down some other way."

Zippo's eyes opened then, fully. Oddy was struck by the piercing blueness of them and, in that moment, he appeared almost childlike. "A-ah-anytime. A-a-anyw-wu-where. A-any-h-hu-how."

Then his eyes clouded over again, and closed. His chest rose and fell in shallow swells.

The men gathered up what supplies they could. The ice splintered alarmingly beneath their feet. Oddy hefted the H&K23. His back screamed mercy and he dropped it. He still had one Webley and fifteen rounds. It would have to do.

Tripwire stopped beside Zippo. Blood ringed the hitman's body like a chalk outline around a corpse. His eyelids were fluttering. "Remember," he said, "just jab and push. It's that easy."

Zippo mumbled something unintelligible.

The ice-bridge looked about as narrow as a gymnast's beam, although it was more accurately the width of a city sidewalk. The ice was transected with hairline cracks. There was no way to tell how much weight it could withstand.

"Put your snowshoes on," Oddy said. "Disperse the weight."

Tripwire and Answer did as advised, though neither relished the prospect of trying to swim with them on.

"Jack be nimble, Jack be quick," Tripwire whispered, and set off.

The ice cracked. The ice groaned. But the ice held. Tripwire made it across, then Answer, then Oddy. The werewolf had not moved. *Why fight when patience will bring an easy meal*, it was no doubt thinking.

The forest resumed to the west. Dark shapes moved within the tall pines, watching, waiting.

"Let's get humping."

«««—»»»

Shshshshsh…

Daniel Coles, who, as a man, would earn the nickname "Zippo," could not tell if the sound came from the dim and fading world around him, or was an internal echo within the darkening corridors of his own mind.

Shshshshsh…

Opening his eyes required a colossal effort. Above, the sky was a blissful, muted purple—the most beautiful purple he had ever seen. *Gorgeous*, he tried to say, but no word came out. He swallowed blood and coughed, his eyes never leaving that sky. The stars shone brilliantly. Although he had no knowledge of astronomy, their order made some kind of elemental sense to him.

Shshshshsh…

The pain resonated at a distant level, like a cathedral bell ringing many blocks away. He stared down at his body. It was a testament to his beatific state of mind that the sight did not disturb him: the flesh flayed open and the stiffly frozen tatters of fabric peeling away from horrific wounds like dead birch bark from a tree trunk. His legs, bent at awkward angles, looked like stogies that had been crushed in someone's pocket.

"*Shshshshsh...*"

Something was moving through his hair. A hand. A woman sat beside him, stroking his hair. She was, without question, the most beautiful woman Daniel had ever seen. Her skin was the color of burnt caramel and it glowed in the dusk. She was naked but seemed neither cold nor self-conscious. Her breasts were small and her ribs visible. It looked as if she had not eaten in quite some time. But her body, the leanness of it, the ropes of muscle running long beneath smooth brown skin, realized some kind of essential symmetry.

"You're hurt very badly." Her voice was rich as cream and honey.

"Y-yuh-yes."

She asked his name.

"Daniel," she repeated, "such a nice name."

Her hair and eyebrows were shockingly white. And if her face was slightly too long, the angle of her jaw slightly vulpine, Zippo neither noticed nor cared. Her eyes, though too close-set, flashed with colors he had never seen, nor could put a name to.

"You are going to die soon, I'm afraid." She scratched behind her ear. Not with her hand but with her foot, in the manner of a dog.

"I cuh-could h-have b-buh-been r-ri-rich." She had stopped stroking his hair. He wished she would do it some more. "A muh-muh-million b-bucks."

"That would have been nice, I suppose."

Tripwire's gun was nowhere to be seen. Zippo couldn't have shot her, anyway.

She bent down and pressed her lips to his ear. "I can help you." Her breath was sweetly bitter, like fresh-mown grass. "Would you like me to try?"

More than anything in this world.

"Y-yuh-yes."

"Alright."

Her mouth moved further down and her breath warmed his throat. Then her teeth—small and white and very, very sharp—were biting into his flesh, saliva mingling with blood...

...he felt himself moving, pulled across the ice on a bier of flexible saplings. The bier hit a rut and pain, thick and fibrous and sickening, hammered down his legs. He passed out…

…in a dark, warm place. In the darkness, noises. A sound like trickling water. Another like the spirited play of puppies. He touched his face to find it matted with a layer of coarse fur. A beard? How long had he been here…

…he was in a cave. To his left a fire flickered, casting strange shadows on the rock. The woman crouched between his legs. She was licking his wounds, cleaning away the blood and pus with her small pink tongue…

…terrible fever dreams. Every man he had every killed appearing before him as they had at the moment of death. Kenny Webb, the first man he'd killed for money, twenty-one years old with powder burns frosting the bullet hole in his neck. The father-and-son Viets, the look of utter hatred on their faces the moment before he'd flamed them in that tunnel outside Song-Be. The dreams deepened, darkened, spiraled. Now he dreamt of the great caribou herds, the scent of them, a crystal-clear sense-memory of their flesh, their taste…

…in the cave again. Small creatures at play near the fire. Some were wolf kits, some young children, some an uneasy combination of both. Beneath a fine layer of white hair his legs were slender and scarred. Jagged scabs healed along their length. She appeared at his side. Firelight etched the contours of her face and reflected off her kaleidoscopic eyes.

"Who?" he said, pointing at the wolf kits.

"Mine alone," she said. "My mate was killed by the black man."

"Why did you save me?"

"Because you are a hunter."

She pressed her lips to his cheek…

…and then he was outside under a full moon. She was at his side. She was as beautiful, or more so, in lupine form than she was as a human. Her fur was white as snow and her body radiated grace and power. Wolfish yips emanated from the cave, interspersed with childish laughter.

"Young mouths to feed." Her voice was a guttural growl.

He stared at his feet. They were longer now, and furred. His nails were dark, and hooked, and very sharp—*claws*. There were dark pads on the underside of each foot and he barely felt the snow beneath them. His mouth felt crowded with too many teeth. He tried to stand but his spine had acquired a streamlined curvature that made moving on all fours more comfortable.

So he did.

He could hear things he'd never heard before: it was as if someone had cranked the volume of the world to full blast. His nose was alive with scents more tantalizing and more deeply-textured than he'd known to exist. He opened his mouth to speak and a howl tore out of his throat. To his new ears it was the most natural sound in the world.

She loped off into the forest. He followed, marveling at the coiled strength of his new body. Soon they were running together at speeds that were breathtaking, exhilarating. He caught the scent of something small and quick-footed ahead, sensing its stark fear, and realized he'd never been hungrier in his life.

He ran as fast as his new legs would carry him, the taste of blood strong in his throat. She ran beside him, her body a sleek white blur. Their quarry juked ahead of them, desperate and afraid. They veered easily, a unified motion, locked on their prey.

The creature who had once been Daniel Coles unleashed another, gleeful, howl.

He was hunter once again.

VI.
THREE AMIGOS

Northwest Territories
December 9th, 1987. 4:43 a.m.

Nothing existed except the path.

Sometimes it described a flat, straight line. Other times it climbed, or wound, or dipped only to rise again. They followed wherever it led. Their focus narrowed to a single overriding intent: constant forward motion. If their minds were to deviate from this goal for even a split-second, there was a chance, and a good one, they would fall and never get up again.

The snow began to fall sometime earlier. Big wet flakes clung to the men's sweat-slick hair and melted in thin streams down their backs. Their feet sank down into the new snow, and soon chunks of ice clung to their fatigues and bootlaces, as though to the fur of a dog. It was, Oddy noted with worming melancholy, the consistency of snow he'd always wished for as a child: moist and packable, perfect for snowmen or forts. He recalled a time when, as a child, he'd packed a rock into a snowball and thrown it at a neighborhood boy he'd suspected of stealing his toboggan. It had burst against the boy's cheek and the rock left an inch-long gash under his eye. His toboggan re-appeared on his doorstep the next day. That was the first time Oddy realized that violence and intimidation were a form of currency and that sometimes the only way to avoid being stepped on was to wield the bigger boot.

As the miles unwound under his feet, Oddy found himself thinking about his father, who'd also been a soldier. Oddy's father enlisted in Roosevelt's war on May 3rd, 1942. He took a jerry slug in the throat and, after three months recuperation in Poland, was medically discharged. Sick of the flag-wavers and flag-burners, he grew his high-and-tight haircut out long and bushy, finding work at a pulp mill in Montana.

Oddy didn't believe his old man slept a single peaceful night in the fourteen years he knew him. Like Oddy, he kept a Barlow knife under his pillow, a .45 Desert Chief in the drawer beside the bed. Like Oddy, he rose at hourly intervals to walk the perimeter of his house. Oddy would hear him get up, stab his feet into slippers, make a brisk circuit. The height of Oddy's bedroom window allowed him to see his father's head and neck move past. During the final circuit he'd look in on him. Oddy remembered the first pale light of dawn cutting through the backyard cedars to silhouette his father's head, a dark and featureless disc, except for the eyes, white and glassy, animal. Other times his father disappeared into the attic, where he kept his footlocker. Oddy once poked his head through the trapdoor to see his father in his dress blues. Standing stock still, tunic buttoned to the neck, a fruit salad of combat citations pinned to the left breast. Standing at attention, staring at the naked roofbeams, before fingering the dimpled scar on his throat. The man snapped off a four-fingered salute at nothing, no one.

The day of Oddy's fourteenth birthday, his father bought him a Remington 30/30 with a seven-cartridge clip, red bow tied around the walnut stock. He packed lunch and supper, filled a thermos with hot chocolate, and the two of them hiked deep into the seed lot flanking their property. Father and son rambled over snow-topped rocks and down a rocky daw, across frozen streams lying flat and silvery against the sun, boots crunching through mid-winter hardpack. A sharpshin hawk wheeled low into the blue strip of sky over a stand of poplars, legs trailing a brown curve of mouse.

Listen now, Oddy's father said after they'd set up a blind. *Deer are skittish and temperamental creatures. You'll only get one chance.* He lifted his arm and jabbed a thumb into the meat below his armpit. *Here. Behind the front legs. Bullet ruptures the lungs, lungs fill with blood, deer suffocates. Got it?*

He chambered a round in the breech and handed Oddy the Remington. It was incredibly heavy. Oddy said, *Did you learn that in the war?*

Learn what?

Where to shoot something so it dies.

The older man stared up into the big safe sky. A good man, Oddy's father. Never hit his son or wife, never catted around, gutted it out in the pulp mill's stink and heat to provide for them. Nothing extraordinary. Just a kind, decent man. *The war taught me a lot of things,* he said. *Most of it was...useless.* He smiled at the sky, as if he'd come to a sudden revelation. *It's a sucker's game, son. Pointless. Never get involved.*

Two months later he shot himself. Head-shot with the .45 Desert Chief while sitting in front of the television, test pattern casting multicolored bars across the broken remains of his face. A note pinned to his chest: *If I had it to do all over again, I would.* Oddy remembered finding a curved sliver of bone deep in the carpet years later, a tiny splinter of his father's skull.

Oddy turned to Tripwire and said, "You know, the greatest joy of my father's life was his garden. He'd plant these rows of tomatoes and sugarsnap peas, peppers and carrots. He was always fussing with fertilizers and humus to, y'know, get the most out of the soil. I remember him down on his hands and knees, working the earth with a mattock, awaiting those little sprigs of green..." Oddy's eyes rose to the sky above, to the puffy night clouds, moon the size of a dime. "I'd never seen him more alive, more at peace. My father was a gardener, man. I mean, he was a soldier, but what he should've been was a gardener. But we hardly ever end up where we should, do we?"

Tripwire didn't reply. He wasn't being rude; he simply lacked the energy for conversation. He stumbled, took a knee, located some internal wellspring of strength and determination, stood, and continued on. He was panting helplessly, like a boxer at the end of a marathon bout. Sweat drenched his clothing and filled his eyes, freezing his lashes, blinding him. His stomach and chest were heavy, as though filled with wet stones. He felt like an egg pressed between cement blocks: the slightest pressure, the tiniest tap, and he'd shatter into a million messy pieces. The branches of the trees on either side of the trail joined overhead, and he felt as though he was groping through an endless tunnel. Shadowy shapes moved in the trees all around him. He retained the awareness that they might be nothing more than figments of a sleep-starved mind, and this kept him from firing wildly into the dark.

One foot, two foot. Left foot, right foot. Red fish, blue fish...

While his body applied itself to basic locomotion, Tripwire's mind was free to wander. Memories flooded in and out with no clear sense of purpose or direction. He remembered fucking a whore in a Saigon brothel. A child had sat beside the bed, watching her mother thrust and moan. He remembered taking the whore's hair in his fist and pulling as hard as he could. He'd needed to hear her scream. He'd needed the *girl* to hear her mother screaming. He didn't know why he'd done that. Forty-eight hours earlier he'd knelt on the bank of a Mekong bay with a fisherboy's headless body in his lap. But he still didn't know why he'd done that thing to that woman.

He remembered another time he'd come across an American soldier in a bamboo plantation outside Than Khe. The man—the name stamped on his dogtag necklace read "Richardson"—had been captured by some sadistic NVA's, who'd cut the bamboo at ground-level and lashed Richardson down over it, naked. By the time Tripwire came upon the clearing, the bamboo stalks, which grew at the rate of two inches per day, had grown nearly through the poor bastard. He remembered the stark greenness of the bamboo sticking out of Richardson's pale chest and the plugs of tissue on the ground around his body, reminding Tripwire of plugs of dirt dotting a recently-aerated soccer field. He remembered the sly displacement of soil as bamboo pushed up through the earth, through Richardson—the fucking stuff grew so fast you could *hear* it. He remembered how one stalk had grown up through the man's testicle sac, skewering one of his balls like a cocktail olive on a plastic sword. But somehow the man was still alive, alive and staring at Tripwire.

Richardson motioned with his eyes to his fatigues, which lay in a crumpled ball five feet away. Tripwire rifled the pockets: a toothbrush, dental floss, a set of brass knuckles, a rabbit's foot (oh the fucking irony), two lambskin condoms and, in the breast pocket, a letter. "Is this what you want?" Tripwire said. Richardson nodded as best he could. All around the bamboo kept growing, growing.

Tripwire unfolded the letter and read the first few lines: *Dear Kevin, I hope all is well. Sally took this picture of me at the beach and she thought I should send it to you.* Tripwire looked at the photograph paperclipped to the letter. The girl was a tall, big-boned blonde. Seventeen years old, Tripwire guessed, long white legs and blue eyes and skin like vanilla ice cream. "Do you want me to write to her—tell her what happened?" he asked. Richardson nodded again, but his eyes said something different—*don't tell her I died like this*, those eyes said. *Tell her I died a hero*. Tripwire promised he would. Then he shot Richardson in the skull with a Swedish grease gun he took off a dead VC.

He never wrote the letter. Ten minutes after shooting Richardson, he pulled it from his pocket, tore it up, and scattered the pieces to the four winds. *People die*, was his thinking at the time. *Boys die out here all the time, die anonymously and without regard, and why should she know while a thousand other girls and mothers and fathers will never know?* And he didn't want to lie. *Your boyfriend charged a VC machine gun nest, took down eight of them before one of the sneaking slant-eyed fucks nailed him.* No. He wouldn't do that. It would be a validation of something he no longer believed in. So he ripped up that letter, the envelope with its return address, and tossed them into the sky.

But now, thinking back, he knows he should have written that letter, let the pretty big-boned blonde know what happened to the young man she had loved so many years ago. Lied, if he had to, because sometimes lies are okay, if they offer peace. But he did not write that letter. He ignored a dying young man's last wishes.

Don't go down that road, skip. The voice in his head belonged to Freddy Achebe, his cameraman. *The past is the past. Leave it there. Doesn't matter now.*

But Tripwire realized, with bitter clarity, that it *did* matter. Of course it mattered. It mattered in the spaces between people, and it mattered in those sunless and empty spaces within every one of us. It mattered. And it hurt like hell.

Left foot, right foot. Hup-one, hup-two, load on up and break on through…

Why didn't he write that letter? Why did he hurt that poor woman? *Why?*

Tripwire leaned over suddenly and retched into the brush, exhausted, moaning helplessly as his stomach spasmed. His feet were on fire, the pain nearly unbearable. His throat and tongue seemed covered with wooly felt. He didn't know how much longer he could go. He knew if he slipped on the snow he would probably stay where he fell and not get up, staring up at the few stars visible through the naked tree branches, breathing hoarsely until his breath stopped altogether.

Answer slammed a flare alight and held it above his head. An umbrella of reddish light spread to illuminate the fringing firs. Obscured forms shrunk away from the light. Something with spidery limbs beyond numbering and flesh that glittered like wet fish scales skittered through the underbrush to his left. To his right another creature tracked steadily: segmented and cylindrical, trunk the circumference of a wine cask, pale and greasy as tallow. A massive maggot.

Beyond these two were others, the sound and smell and surge of them unmistakable.

But they did not attack. They *wanted* to; Answer was sure of it. But something prevented them from doing so.

Twenty years ago, Answer had walked into the Green Beret hootch the day after A-303 Blackjack was disbanded. On a pike in the hootch's center was the decaying head of a cougar. Next to it, on another pike, was the head of a Viet boy. The boy's face was badly burned, and there were flies at his mouth and nose. Off in the gloom dim figures lounged on hammocks. Jangling tribal music came from a tape deck encircled by black candles.

Answer went out with them the next night. A low fog was sliding down from the mountains and, somewhere in the dark, music was playing. It was a chaotic, discordant sound, without rhythm or form or progression. It was the music of the jungle, and Answer soon realized it existed only inside his head.

After a while he broke away from the Greenies. He set off on his own, charting a private path. Sometimes he'd go barefoot to feel the soft soil underneath his feet. He went deep enough into the land and deep enough inside himself that he vanished from sight completely.

Alone like that, isolated from humankind, the realization dawned: There were no sides to be taken, no profound ideals worth fighting for.

There was no good. There was no evil.

There was only Chaos. The elemental Truth of Chaos.

He began to kill people at night. He ignored the color of their skin and the cut of their uniforms. It didn't matter. He wasn't killing Gooks and he wasn't killing Yanks, although many nights he killed both. He'd cut their tongues out, if he could, and strung them on a loop of tungsten wire around his neck.

Never had he felt so alive and so *right* as he had during those jungle nights. That was, until now, with these nightmare creatures flanking him left and right.

Now and then, he felt the same: perfectly at home.

"Sarge?" Tripwire said. "Any idea how far we've come?"

Oddy shook his head. "Lost the map." His shoulders slumped slightly. "My sense of direction is all screwed up, anyway. All we can do is keep moving forward."

They lapsed into a protracted silence. There was only the sound of their boots crunching the hard-packed snow, their labored breathing. All the trees looked the same. The land described an end-lessly-repeating loop, like a möbius strip. It was impossible to tell if they were breaking new ground or re-tracing old paths.

Oddy caught his reflection in the Webley's nickel-plated cylinder: skin ash-gray and eyes deeply sunken in their sockets, stubble fuzzing the hollows of his cheeks, slashes of dried blood streaking his face like war paint. He seemed to have aged fifteen years in the past few days. His feet were now so frostbitten he felt as if he were walking on stumps of oak.

"Either of you got the time?" he asked. His own wristwatch currently resided at the bottom of Great Bear lake. "The date?"

Tripwire hiked his sleeve up and looked at his Seiko. The watch-face was shattered, black liquid crystal seeping through the cracks to stain his fingers. He threw it to the ground and said, "Mine's busted."

"Answer?"

"Don't carry one."

"Of course not."

They walked and walked. How long and how far became unknowable. Day blended into night. Snow blindness set in and after awhile all they could see was an endless expanse of white. Time stretched and became liquid, simultaneously inconsequential and of greatest possible importance. One foot in front of the other. And when they could go no further…take another step.

At some point the path bellied into a circle of bare earth ringed by tall trees. At the far side was a jumble of snow-covered branches—the skeleton of a bivouac? In front of it was a ring of snow-topped rocks—an abandoned fire pit? Oddy was rocked by a heady rush of déjà vu.

They walked to the clearing's center. Tripwire's foot snagged on something. He cleared snow away with the toe of his boot.

It was a parka. A blood-soaked parka, frozen rigid. A parka just like theirs.

Heart hammering, Tripwire cleared away more snow. Beneath a crack-glaze of blood, a name was sewn over the breast:

EDWARDS.

Behind them and around them arose a sound of stamping limbs and the crick-crackling of alien joints and the snuffling of seeking snouts…

Off to the west, seemingly within spitting distance, was the hill upon which they had been dropped. Beyond was the purple-hued sky that a Labrador helicopter would soon cleave with its dual blades.

They were so close.

So god*damn* close.

"And isn't it true," the repellently familiar voice came from behind them, "how all things that come around do so surely go around?"

«««—»»»

Anton Grosevoir hunched on the ground. His knees were spread and his arms hung between them, fingers brushing the snow. With his stubby arms and fat legs he looked for all the world like a bullfrog coiled to hop. He wore a vanilla suit, which remained as clean and unrumpled as the day they'd first met.

Oddy's guts contorted with rage and for a moment the outline of his world, every plane and contour, was etched in cold blacks and reds. He curled the fingers of his good hand into a fist so tight the fingernails left bloody half-moons in his palms.

"And oh how *spectacularly* you went around," Grosevoir continued. "My tranquil little preserve looks like a slaughterhouse at quitting time!"

"Crosshairs and Zippo are dead," Oddy said.

"I know." Oddy may as well have told him the time of day for all the emotion he exhibited. "Damn good thing, too. What's the use of maintaining monsters that don't earn their keep?"

Tripwire's fingers tightened around the Llama's butt. "A deal's a fucking deal. We made it around. You've got to take us home."

"You're finished?" Grosevoir's fingers traced strange designs in the snow. "As far as I can see, you've made it exactly as far as that unlucky fellow." He pointed at Edwards' parka. "The hilltop is your finish line, and that remains a ways off yet. And—" he inclined his head towards the treeline, where the noise of massing bodies had reached a fever pitch. "—there are rather a lot of...*things*...who'd prefer you didn't leave."

Oddy knew they possessed neither the strength nor ammunition to withstand another assault. "This place has taken two of my men," he said. "Two of my *friends*. And we're badly hurt. But if we turn and face whatever it is waiting in those woods, I promise you we are going to kill a lot of them." He brandished the Webley with more conviction than he truly felt. "So why don't we call this whole fucking thing a draw?"

Deformed shapes swirled in the air above the men's heads. For a moment Tripwire mistook the spectacle for a particularly gruesome phase of the northern lights, until the air coalesced, attaining a splintered permanence, and a shoal of faces swam out of the sky. Their aspect was hideous: eyes ripped of eyelids or punched from their skulls outright, noses bitten away, lips freakishly swelled and Negroid, tongues long and lolling and eaten through as if by parasites. Grosevoir waved his hand irritably and they broke apart into nothingness.

"A draw?" he said. "No, I can't have that. It smacks of failure and compromise and business left unfinished. It goes against my nature."

"And what nature is that?" Tripwire said. "What *are* you?"

Grosevoir said, "What do you think I am?"

"You're no different than the things you keep—a monster."

"No," Answer said quietly, "not a monster. It is…Chaos."

"I am that exactly."

Oddy said, "What do you mean, you're Chaos?"

"I am that which causes havoc, pandemonium, anarchy. It is my role, my position in this world."

Having been forced to accept the existence of zombies and vampires and a thousand other monstrous manifestations, their minds easily assimilated this new revelation.

"Why all this, then?" Tripwire said. "This preserve, the monsters, us—how does it fit?"

Chaos stood and stretched. It dipped its head and regarded them out of the tops of its eyes. "Ask yourselves this: what is it such creatures inspire? Unrest, disharmony, terror…chaos. You've heard stories of medieval villages disappearing in the span of a single night, or men driven to madness by unseen apparitions, or sightings of such things that rational minds must dismiss as untrue. These are not myths, or delusions, or the ravings of lunatics. They are the truth. They happened." It ran its small pink tongue across its small gray teeth. "There is always a truth, and that truth is to be found in the woods surrounding Great Bear Lake. But that truth is so unthinkable, flying in the face of all logical thought, that people refuse to believe—at least their rational minds do. But deep down, in those places where dark speculation takes root, an ember of belief is always smoldering.

"These creatures represent the unknown threat. They are the monsters under the bed. They are the dark shapes circling endlessly beyond the light of humanity's fires. At their best, they create confusion, and insanity, and primitive fear. They aid and enable chaos. In this way they are, and always have been, foot soldiers in my cause. So you see how I have a vested interest in their health and continuance."

"But why *us*," Oddy said. "Why the letters and why the lies and why the whole goddamn front?"

The snow stopped, but the wind had picked up. It skated across the ground and wormed through the vents in their clothing to graze their many wounds. Chaos walked behind them, touching the napes of their necks with one cold fingertip. Oddy withdrew from its touch, as did Tripwire. Answer did not.

"I wanted my denizens to be challenged," it said, "and knew you would fill that need. As to how I knew you would fill that need…" It returned to its position facing them. The eye patch had been removed. The skin underneath was wet and raw, as if the wound had been inflicted only moments ago. "Do I really need to tell you?"

"No," the three men said in near-unison.

And how long *had* they known? In their hearts and in their minds and in their souls—*known*. Had they been tricked? Really tricked? Or had they merely been tricking themselves?

"I looked different then, I know. This," he swept his hand down his chest, "is strictly for civility's sake. It's so difficult to secure a table at a decent restaurant looking as I did in Vietnam."

"And that's it?" Oddy said. "Because twenty years ago, when we were fucking *kids*, we hurt you—revenge, pure and simple?"

"Not the only reason," Chaos said. "But one of them. I have lived a long time and, sad as it is to say, have become somewhat petty. But if simple vengeance was all I wanted, I could've killed you all long ago."

Chaos's true shape shifted beneath the skin of its human form. The flesh rippled like water stirred by a slight breeze and something tore wetly. It said, "A time comes for all things to change. This body—my adopted body—is getting old and infirm. Its previous owner gave it to me willingly, as they all have. This particular body belonged to a freak show performer. The fellow bit heads off live chickens and had gotten into the nasty habit of killing a single child in each and every village his sideshow toured through." Chaos cocked his head to the side, as a dog sometimes will. Oddy found the gesture jarringly familiar. "You see, his nature was the same as mine. I am always on the lookout for such specimens."

There was another tearing sound and the skin of Chaos's head split down the center. The wound was red and raw-looking, the skin spread an inch wide. Something was pushing its way out.

"I made this man the same offer I made all of them: become the vessel of Chaos. Your body becomes mine, my powers yours. You will live beyond all natural bounds. The only pain you feel will be the pain of others. Most importantly, you will exist at all times in those places where bloodshed, and disharmony, and anarchy reign."

Chaos's forehead split wider and a sharp V-shaped wedge of bone forced its way through the wound. It looked like an axe-head, or a shark's fin.

"The time for change has come." Its voice was no longer human. "I need a new vessel. That is why I brought you here. To make a choice."

Chaos's false face loosened, then folded, then began to fall away. Gaping tears at the eyes, the ears, the neck. *Like an old, rotten t-shirt ripping*, Tripwire thought. *Or a snake shedding its skin.* Then, horrifically: *Or like a baby being born.*

Chaos's old face fell off. Underneath was another face: sharp and white and hard as bone, a little bloody, one blood-red eye and a mouth wide enough to devour entire worlds.

"Now," it said. "Choose."

Tripwire's mind reeled. The proposition was ungodly, unthinkable. *Become one with...that* thing? No. Never. He'd die first. The proposition was somehow insulting, given all they'd seen and done in the previous days—he'd gone through hell just to surrender? Rage welled up within him, vast and wild and bitter.

In the sky to the south a faint thrum arose. Oddy squinted his eyes into the gloom. He could see, or thought he saw, a pinprick of dark movement, growing slightly larger with each passing moment.

"No," Tripwire said. "Not me. Not ever. Fuck you." He pulled a pistol from his waistband and brought it to bear. "*Fuck* y—"

The sound was so whisper-soft that Oddy nearly missed it. *Tsshshsh*, like trembling waves lapping a sandy shore, or a deep-tongue kiss.

Tripwire's neck—his pale slim neck—had a K-Bar knife sticking out of it. A hand was wrapped around the hilt. The back of that hand had red hairs growing on it. Oddy's eyes followed the hand to where the arm met the shoulder, across to the clavicle, and up to a pair of eyes he'd stared into a thousand times without ever really understanding the thoughts that turned over behind their cold and lifeless blue.

"The world needs a little Chaos, Sarge," Answer said. "You see that, don't you?"

Tripwire made a dry hacking noise. His eyes reflected a wretched bewilderment and Oddy recalled a fawn he'd hit while driving to Poughkeepsie and how the animal had died without dignity or shelter, how it had died lacking the awareness of what had killed it, or why. They had been the eyes of a creature awakened to the hideous serendipity of this world when it was too late to do anything about it. Tripwire's hand jerked up and grabbed at the knife but all he did was cut his fingers and make Answer jam the blade in further.

The distant thrum to the south grew louder. The black dot in the sky attained a recognizable shape.

A Labrador helicopter.

Answer pulled the knife out of Tripwire's neck. Tripwire staggered back and Oddy caught him before he fell into the snow. His body was rigid; the muscles and tendons of his neck and shoulders pulsed against the skin like twisted mangrove roots. Blood pumped out of the slit in his neck, the brightest red Oddy had ever seen. He pressed his hand over the wound even though he knew it was useless. Blood pushed between his fingers and down his arm and the dying warmth of it made him want to throw up.

You fucker, he thought. *Oh you fucking motherFUCK…*

"Blegghh," Tripwire said. His face was white and his teeth were red and his eyes were focused on the helicopter with a sort of terrified sadness, like a marathon runner who is approaching the finish line only to find he ultimately lacks the strength to cross it.

"Blegghh." The sound came out with so little force, was so pitifully meaningless. It filled Oddy with crushing sorrow to see the man who had kept him sane through the madness of Vietnam robbed of the simple ability to express his dying thoughts. Something blossomed inside Oddy in that moment, flowing dark through his arteries, vile and slippery like heavy black oil in a crankcase.

Oh you fuck oh you goddamn motherfucker….

Answer wiped Tripwire's blood on his pants and approached Chaos.

"I looked for you," he said. "In the jungle."

"It was a busy time for me," Chaos said. "Are you ready?"

"Yes."

"This is going to…*sting*."

Chaos began to change—began to melt, to streamline. The shape of its skull elongated, as if it had been made of wax that was softening and starting to run. Its body transformed into something that resembled hot tar, molten and malleable and deepest black. It surged forward, a long thick rope pushing its way into Answer's wide-open mouth. Answer struggled against the intrusion, gagging, clawing at the inrushing blackness. Oddy saw, for the first time, a real and definable emotion flash across those ice-blue eyes, and if that emotion could have somehow been translated into words, those words might have been *oh dear god what have I done?*

As Chaos entered Answer its shape changed. Gibbering faces appeared along its dark length, human and beast and others whose aspects were in no way analogous to anything ever glimpsed in this world; nightmare limbs, claw-tipped and sucker-dotted, pulsed from the amorphous mass only to melt into the blackness again. Then, for an instant, Oddy believed he nearly saw what shape Chaos really was, and his heart froze in his chest, leaving him gasping.

The helicopter touched down on the hilltop.

How long would it stay?

"Blegghh," Tripwire said again. And then, mercifully, he was dead. He died so quickly he didn't even have time to shut his eyes.

FUCKER FUCKER MOTHERFUCKER—

With the thumb and forefinger of his right hand Oddy closed Tripwire's eyes. He set the body down with as much gentleness as his clumsy arms were capable of.

Answer stood ten feet away. His lips and cheeks and the inside of his mouth were sheathed in blackness. Only he wasn't Answer anymore. His eyes, previously blue, were now completely red. On the other hand, he wasn't *not* Answer: physically he was unchanged and his eyes, though a different shade, still radiated the same chilling deadness.

"You wouldn't believe it, Sarge," he said, voice slightly breathless. "You wouldn't bel—"

He said no more.

Because that was when Oddy pulled the Webley

...FUCKER...

the sound of the hammer cocking like some great cosmic gear turning over

...DIRTY MOTHERFUCKER...

and shot him square in the face.

Answer's head rocked back in a spray of black and red. His arms flew upwards like a giddy rider awaiting a roller coaster's plunge. His back bent at a ludicrous angle and his arms pinwheeled for balance: he looked like a man perched on a high-rise ledge caught off-guard by a sudden gust of wind. Then he fell backwards to land with a puff of snow.

«««—»»»

Oddy never got the chance to view the result of his marksmanship. It was as if the crack of his pistol had signaled the start of some desperate race as the creatures who'd lain in wait burst into the clearing and made a reckless beeline for him. He got a good look at the leader of the pack, an apparition straight out of a madman's fever dream: the legs of a giant crab and the elongated neck of a giraffe terminating in the flattened head of a Portuguese Man O' War, bulbous green eyes set atop insectile stalks and its mouth packed not with teeth but with bone, sharpened knuckles of bone chattering a skeletal calliope.

Oddy turned and ran faster than he'd ever run before. His feet skimmed across the snow so quickly he couldn't be certain his boots left their indentation in the snow. Fear and exhaustion fought against one another; fear was winning at the moment.

He reached the base of the hilltop. Something buzzed past his skull. There was a wet ripping sound and Oddy raised his hand to the stump where his ear used to be. He dug his feet into the hillside, unable to feel the ground beneath him, and started to climb. Noises gathered beneath him, clickings and gurglings and the sob of hungry infants.

He snagged his foot on an exposed root and something snapped below his Achilles tendon and for a moment nothing and then pain roared up his leg, through his belly, through his neck. It seemed to rip the top of his head off and he puked a gut-wrenching stream into the snow but he never slowed, never gave pain the upper hand. He was thinking of Gunner and Tripwire and Crosshairs and Slash and how he owed it to them to reach that fucking whirlybird; he couldn't save them but if he could save himself then maybe, somehow, he'd be saving them all. The concept made no sense but it was all he had and he clung to it like a drowning man to a life preserver.

There was a snapping whiplike noise and sudden pain sang up his arm. Oddy stared down at his left hand to see that now, in addition to the stripped tendons, his ring and little fingers were gone. *Well, at least I can still make a peace sign*, he thought madly. He glanced over his shoulder at the creature who'd done it: small, the rough size of a monkey, the skin of its head peeled off in tiny ribbons that danced and circulated around its raw face in the manner of streamers tied to an oscillating fan. Its limbs were filament-thin threads, the purplish tendrils of an anemone, thousands upon thousands, lashing out to lick at his lower extremities.

He spun awkwardly and fired. Through dumb luck or benign providence the slug struck the creature's center and sent it tumbling backwards, filaments licking uselessly, where it was trampled by the advancing horde. Oddy's peripheral vision was a blur of bizarre movement and streaking shapes, things beyond description, things nearly beyond *conception*, things his tautly-stretched mind rebelled stridently at the very existence of. Pain blossomed in his skull, a great burst-open flower, making his eyes water. He ran on senseless feet, legs pumping, arms pistoning, blinding blood in his eyes. The helicopter was ten feet away. The lowered gangway yawned like an open mouth.

The time it took him to cross those remaining ten feet was a little under three seconds. Yet those scant moments unfolded into a lifetime inside his head. Unconnected images sprang, unbidden, into his mind: his mother chopping onions over the sink, the sun streaming through an open window to touch the blackness of her hair; a package of cigarettes, his father's brand, half-open on a folding TV-tray, droplets of blood flecking the cellophane wrapper; a pretty girl on a city bus who had touched his knee and so he had touched hers and something had passed between them but now all he could recall was the narrow outline of her bra-strap beneath her blouse and the smell of her body like fresh-picked spearmint; the draft letter held in his twenty-year-old hands, his clean and unlined and somehow innocent hands, the letter's folds machine-straight and the words stark on the bright white page; a dark trench in the jungle's heart, the stink of terrified young bodies and tracer fire snapping overhead; Dade's face blown wide open and his limp body rolling across the freeway. And he wondered, idly but earnestly, what his mother was doing right now, at that exact moment, who she was talking to or what thoughts might be occupying her mind as her son fought for his life in a place as foreign and remote as the dark side of the moon…

The gangway made a hollow metallic sound as his boots struck it. Oddy thought it was perhaps the most wonderful sound he'd ever heard. He pounded up the ramp, overbalanced, and toppled forward into the cabin. Gunmetal-gray pain exploded like shrapnel in his leg and ear and skull; slivers of shooting light spun through his vision like formations of tiny burning sparrows.

"Go!" he screamed. "Get the fuck out of here!"

The pilot—who, through some heroic feat of inattention, had failed to take note of either Oddy's scrambling ascent or the monstrous daisychain attending him—turned to regard the cabin. The man he saw—black and filthy and wild-eyed, blood squirting from his hand and his head and a thousand smaller wounds besides—looked in no way like the man he'd dropped off seventy-two hours earlier.

"Where are the others?"

"Gone!" the bloody black man said with a rising note of hysteria in his voice. "Dead! *GO!*"

"All of them are dea—?"

It was then the pilot saw something fly through the gangway breech. For a moment it was just a blur—either that, or the only way his eyes and mind could cope with such a creature's existence was to blur it out. But the blur rapidly fused into a solid shape and his heart trembled in his chest.

The first thing that came into focus was the texture of its flesh: red and shifting, dimming and brightening like embers in a gusting wind, lumpen and pustulent and shimmering under the cabin's bright lights. Next was its method of locomotion: a pair of wings, now nothing more than a black-boned exoskeleton, the ribs hung with moldering rags of flesh, and at its rear a fish-like tail, also fleshless, slashing the air. Then its head swam into clarity and the pilot recoiled as if slapped: petals of burning-ember flesh peeling back—no, not peeling back but blossoming outward, like some cancerous flower—to reveal the smallest of faces, wrinkled and wizened and aged beyond all fathomable bounds, a shriveled walnut face, tiny blind eyes and a mouth like a wound, sharp needlefish teeth and the sound of its body cutting the air was horrid, the sound of a dying child's screams.

The black man raised his pistol and fired almost casually. The flying thing was knocked against the cabin wall and a gout of ichor plastered the dull metal behind its body.

"Stay or go," the black man said. "Your choice now."

"Jesus," the pilot whispered as the thing made a slow descent down the hull, leaving a shiny wake of itself behind. He thumbed the gangway switch.

A pneumatic hiss and the gangway began to rise. Oddy struggled to a sitting position and leveled the Webley at the narrowing slit of darkness. His ears—his *ear*—rung with the concussive pistolfire and deeper inside his head there was another kind of ringing, huge and thudding and furious.

Come on…

The barrel trembled. He bore down hard. It stabilized.

Bring it if you want bring it if you may oh can you just BRING IT…

Shapes lashed and cringed in the murk outside, getting closer. The gangway rose: now five feet from closed, now four…

"Holy fuck!" the pilot screamed as something slammed into the windshield. Blood and slaver exploded across the glass. The thing, small and toothy and determined, slammed into the glass again. Again. Again. The pilot jumped with every impact. The windshield splintered, then a big section of it went milky with cracks. Lacking any practical method of defense, the pilot switched on the windshield wipers, which, in slapping against the creature's flanks, only enraged it further.

The gangway was two feet from closed, one and a half…

Come on come on come the fuck ON…

A thick cable shot through the gap. *No,* Oddy realized quickly, *not a cable. A tentacle.* It was a tentacle, and there was a neat grid of suckers on the underside of its mucous-coated length. *No,* Oddy realized in an apoplexy of horror, *not suckers. Faces.* Each of the disks he'd assumed were suckers was indeed a twisted, screaming, sickeningly human face. The tentacle thrashed against the honeycombed metal grate and some of the faces burst open like overripe fruit. Shapes proliferated in nauseating abundance outside the helicopter, flukes and scraps and scabs, a whirlwind of colors and textures and scents. Oddy fired through the dwindling aperture; the bullet whined off the hull and out into the darkness. Then the gangway snicked shut. The tentacle, neatly severed, writhed on the floor like a cleaved earthworm.

"Now!" Oddy screamed. "Now!"

"The fuck you think I'm doing?" the pilot screamed back.

He pulled hard back on the steering yoke and the Labrador started to ascend. Then something *thwapped* against its side with massive force: as if a giant redwood had been felled on top of them. Oddy was hurled against the airframe. His skull connected with a metal rib and his vision blurred. An explosion barked overhead and sparks jetted down around them. The windshield broke inwards and pellets of Saf-T-Glas sprayed the pilot's face. The hull groaned and there was a sound like a beer can crushed underfoot and the lights flickered, then winked out. They flickered on and Oddy saw the pilot fighting the joystick, trying to stabilize the helicopter as something dark and gelatinous squeezed through the windshield hole.

Oddy shook his head clear and staggered aftwards. The pilot was bug-eyed looking at the amorphous black shape expanding into the cockpit, billowing out of the hole, a shiny dark bulb. Oddy jammed the gun into it—the barrel dimpling its skin as if it were an over-inflated innertube—and pulled the trigger. It exploded with a wet *plot*, spewing noxious matter that burned their faces and hands. Oddy stumbled back and his ass hit the tape deck and suddenly "Manic Monday" by The Bangles reverberated throughout the cabin, Susanna Hoffs singing *Just another manic Monday; wish it were Sunday*...

Oddy clubbed the Webley's butt into the console and her voice cut out abruptly.

The pilot flicked his stinking hair out of his eyes and bore down on the yoke with as much strength as he possessed. Things were pinging off the underside of the hull and the sound reminded Oddy of how Charlie would fire at low-flying Hueys in hopes of rupturing the fuel tanks but he knew this pinging was not bullets but claws and teeth and other appendages that defied all laws of nature and sense. Something slammed into the cockpit beside his head and the metal buckled inwards in a riotous outline of the thing that had struck it. Looking at that indent, the utter *senselessness* of it, Oddy's heart sped up and his saliva glands spurted bitter juice into his mouth.

The Labrador's propellers labored heavily and the helicopter began to rise again. Then the back end jerked down alarmingly, like a bobber that'd been hit by a big fish, and canted upwards again. Oddy imagined an accumulation of monstrous limbs wrapped around the landing gear, bearing the helicopter down.

This is it, he thought. *Moment of truth*...

The engines whined. The tachometer redlined.

A point of perfect tension was achieved: the moment when, during a tug-of-war, one team's resolve slips and they tumble, headlong, into the dirt...

Please please oh please God...

...and then the Labrador was hurtling into the sky as if shot from a sling. Oddy and the pilot were thrown violently forward. The pilot's head hit the console and for a gut-churning moment Oddy felt them lurch downwards again. Then the pilot shook away the cobwebs and steered the chopper into a stable ascent. Wind whistled through the hole in the windshield. It was sharp and stinging but also pure and cool and wonderful.

Oddy slumped into the co-pilot's jumpseat. Beneath him, in the rapidly-darkening forest, he saw, or believed he saw, Answer.

He was standing at the bottom of the hill. Behind him, creatures hunched around Tripwire's corpse. Oddy could not tell if they were eating him, or simply tearing him to shreds and scattering the pieces for what savage pleasure the act afforded.

Answer was smiling. Half his face was destroyed, a mess of bone and red muscle tissue that resembled prime beef, but his mouth was intact and smiling. He raised his arm, casually, chummily, and waved goodbye. All around him were milling and massing and shambling atrocities that made many of the things Oddy had seen during the past few days, the werewolves and vampires and zombies, seem like pleasant daydreams. And there was Answer standing amongst them, perfectly in his element, arm upraised, waving, waving goodbye.

Farewell—for now?

Oddy leaned back in the jumpseat. He didn't say anything. The pilot didn't say anything. There was nothing to say. Cold air whipped through the cockpit and Oddy sucked shallow lungfuls. He was aware, vaguely, of an inability to feel any of his extremities: not a single finger or toe. The seatback and armrests were sticky with blood. He wondered if he was dying, and if it would hurt very much. On the heels of this came the realization that perhaps death wouldn't be such a terrible thing—after all he had seen and done, what horrors could death possibly hold in store?

Thousands of miles from home and hovering on the brink of death, Oddy closed his eyes. Warmth suffused his body. He recognized it as false warmth, shock warmth, but he didn't care. He simply relished it, the elemental comfort of it.

He drifted down through black levels of unconsciousness and, as he approached that final black river, he had a dream. A dream so real that he smiled as he sat in the middle of that blackness with the forest unfurling below him like a dark green sea.

They lay on a beach somewhere in the South Pacific. Tripwire, Crosshairs, Gunner, Zippo, Slash, him. They wore cutoff camos and their young skin was bronzed from the sun. There was a bucket of cold Singha beer. Zippo grabbed a handful of ice and rubbed it on his chest and, playfully, tossed it at Crosshairs, whose face was whole and undamaged and smiling broadly. Tripwire was saying something, telling a story, his hands describing animated shapes in the air. Gunner and Slash watched him, pointing, laughing. He sat somewhere to the side, facing a setting sun, its fleeting warmth tingling his smooth dark skin. Although he could not see his face, he knew he too was smiling. Smiling because it was good to be with your friends, good to know that times of conflict are followed by times of serenity, good to know that the storm shall surely pass and the sky shall surely clear...good to find that safe warm place in the sun.

Sitting in the jumpseat of a laboring helicopter, far from everything he knew or ever cared for, Jerome Grant sat in a widening pool of his own blood...smiling.

VI.
ONE TIN SOLDIER

Somewhere in the Mediterranean Sea
November 12th, 1988. 7:54 p.m.

It was once only the noble qualities of Odysseus I saw reflected
in myself.

Courage. Self-sacrifice. Leadership.

Now only one similarity remains:

We're both the only member of our crew to return home alive.

The frigate is a 120-footer, *Monkey Sea*, based out of Key Largo.
Its hold is laden with eighty tons of rock salt for delivery to Syria.
The captain tells me we are close to the southern coast of Albania, but
as to exact longitudes and latitudes I cannot say. The waters of the
Mediterranean are of the deepest and clearest blue; so perfectly blue
it is impossible to chart the horizon's curve, tell where water ends and
sky begins.

I am sitting on deck with my back against the bulkhead, watching
the prow cleave the water before it. A deckhand brings me a cup of
Turkish coffee. It is hot and sweet and its spiciness tingles my tongue.
Warm crosswinds blow off the Albanian coast, carrying with them the
scent of seaside commerce.

As the ship carries my body forward, the slow rolling motion of
the waves carries my mind back...

The pilot dropped me on the helipad of the Yellowknife general
hospital. Just rolled me down the gangway like a sack of dirty laundry
and hit the friendly skies. I was unconscious at the time, though I do
recall a sensation of tumbling over and over, shirts in a dryer. Imagine
the E.R.'s surprise to see the big bloody black fellow lying in the

middle of a painted white "H" while his mysterious good Samaritan dwindled into a tiny dot in the sky. Thinking about that scene, it always makes me laugh!

They hustled me to the O.R.. I was intubated, ventilated, aspirated, ablated, even inoculated—some doc thought I'd been attacked by wild animals and contracted rabies. They sucked the bad blood out and pumped good blood in; I drained the blood bank of O-positive. I was EKG'd and EEG'd, transfused, stitched, and cauterized. I had machines breathing for me and purifying toxins for me and for all I know moving the mail for me. Every so often I'd swim up through the haze to see doctors and nurses clustered around, the light harsh on my eyes and their tools glittering wickedly. I distinctly remember a blue-masked doctor saying to a nurse standing beside him: "He pulls through this, I owe you dinner."

I want to believe she ordered the Lobster Newburg and a bottle of Dom.

Other times I spiraled down into a deep, deep darkness that pressed upon my body with a profound weight and I knew I was very close to death. There were no bright lights or harp-strumming angels; thankfully I didn't smell any brimstone, either. Just this solid blackness. And it's my best guess that's all death really is: this blackened consciousness where, for a while at least, you retain some awareness of who you were and the life you lived…then nothing. *Zzzzap*: a light bulb fizzling out.

Tell you this much: it compels you to live for the moment.

I mean, Carpe-*fucking*-Diem, you know?

When the fog lifted I found myself in a white bed in a white room with a window that overlooked a snow-covered field beneath a cloud-swept sky. For a minute all that whiteness had me thinking I'd gone blind. Then I saw my hand and the contrast assured me that my sight, at least, was undamaged.

My other hand was covered under layers of bandages but I could tell, just by looking, that it was useless to me. My feet, also heavily-bandaged, had a squared-off look confirming the fact that each and every one of my toes resided at the bottom of a medical waste bin. My face felt like it'd been submerged in an acid bath. I remembered, faintly, a struggling blackness bursting all over it. My right leg was set in an air-cast and elevated in a complex pulley system. My body—and I'm talking every square *inch*—ached like an abscessed tooth.

A nurse came in. She had a cup of ice chips for me to suck on. I wondered if they'd taken my tonsils out, too. She conducted herself in that efficient manner nurses have, as if she'd woken that morning knowing in advance every move she'd make during the remainder of the day. She tapped the IV bag hung above my head and unkinked the tube feeding milky solution into my left forearm and examined my raggedy fingernails and clucked her tongue and she smelled, pleasantly, of fabric softener.

"Do you know your name?" she'd asked.

I told her I did. She nodded her head expectantly.

"Jerome Grant, nurse."

"Do you know where you are?"

"No, nurse."

"My name is Vera. You are at the Yellowknife general hospital. Do you know how you got here?"

"No, Vera," I lied.

She told me a helicopter had dropped me and taken off without a backwards glance. She told me I'd been operated on for nearly twelve hours, and that one of the doctors was forced to cancel his trip to Fort Simpson for the Iditarod.

"You had us up around the clock, Mr. Grant. You're lucky to be alive."

I wondered if she'd said it so I'd feel obligated to thank her…for doing her job?

"Thank you, Vera."

"Oh, now." She waved her hand around her head, as if trying to shoo away a fly. "It's just….oh, you're welcome, then."

She gave my pillow a brisk fluffing and asked if I needed to use the little boy's room. A bedside machine beeped in time with my heartbeat and I wished Vera would turn it off.

She said, "Were you up north somewhere?"

I nodded.

"Doing…?"

"Hunting."

"By yourself?"

"Yes."

"And you got lost?"

"Yes."

"You aren't the first. Treacherous woods up there."

Vera, you have no idea.

"Who dropped you off?"

I shrugged. "A kind soul who took pity on a wayward traveler."

"And he left you in a heap *why*...?"

"He didn't want his secret identity revealed?"

"Seriously, Mr. Grant, why—?"

"Vera? It's Jerome. And I think I'll use the bathroom now."

I didn't have to go but I didn't want to answer any more questions. Questions are dangerous things: sometimes blindly, sometimes falteringly, but somehow instinctively, they have a way of leading you back to the truth. And the truth was something I didn't want to face.

They kept me for two weeks. Call it a re-education period. I had to learn to walk again, for starters. My leg was fractured, not broken, so I was able to put weight on it within a few days. But my toes, one-quarter of the space I'd grown accustomed to balancing on, were gone. It's difficult to explain what it's like to walk without your toes. The closest comparison I can draw is this: imagine standing on the ledge of a building with your toes dangling over the edge and a strong headwind kicking up. Can you feel it—the loss of equilibrium and that involuntary urge to rock back on your heels, the constant sense you'll overbalance and fall face-first into empty space? That's how every step felt for me. And when they took the bandages off my injured hand and I saw those three sorry-ass fingers...Christ, it reminded me of those shiny metal pincers kids use to pick up stuffed animals at the arcade.

Still, plenty of folks have had it worse than me—Helen Keller would've slammed me as a pussy.

These were the choices: curl up and die or deal with it.

And I don't even know how to curl up and die.

The doctors tried fitting me for prosthetics but I said piss all over that plan. Instead I wadded newspapers into the toes of a pair of sneakers and started staggering around. And fell. And fell. And, just to shake things up a bit, I'd fall some more. My knees were scraped raw on the tile flooring; at night the healing flesh would knit itself to the sheet and come morning the nurse would have to strip the sheet off like peeling an industrial-sized bandage. Afterwards she'd dress my wounds and help me on with my sneakers so I could shamble out into the hallway...where, inevitably (and, were you to ask the charge nurse, often comically) I'd go ass-over-teakettle again. Got so bad I seriously considered gluing a spring to my forehead so I'd bounce back upright every time I fell forward. But the nurses were encouraging and the physiotherapist supportive, and I needed to prove it to myself so eventually I got the hang of it.

The first few nights were the worst. I mean, *every* night is pretty damn bad—that's another thing I've learned to live with—but those first few…bad, bad times.

The door to my room. That *damn* door. I was always watching it. In the darkness of my room, the only light came from the narrow gap separating the bottom of the door from the floor. Just that tiny slit of light bleeding under the doorframe and spreading weakly across the tiles. And a hospital is a busy, busy place—code reds and code blues and code yellows, a rainbow of codes, nurses and unit aides rushing up and down the ward at all hours of the night. I'd listen to their footsteps and every time the slit of light—*my* slit of light—was darkened by the length of a passing shoe, I'd flinch. Every…single…time. At night that unbroken stretch of light became everything to me…man, it became the whole fucking *world*.

Worst of all was this repeating…vision, I guess you'd call it. I'd be lying there, blankets tucked up under my chin, and the door opens. The harsh light of the hall streams into the room and I squint and shield my face. A figure stands in the doorway. I can never make out features: only the stark outline of a body carved in shadow, every angle and curve of it repelling the light so utterly that it seems as if someone has taken a pair of shears and cut it, the utter blackness of it, out of the light. In the black hole forming its head, to the left side, a red pit glows balefully. I hear this voice, so familiar and at the same time completely inhuman, and that voice is saying: "The world needs a little chaos…"

And that's when I'd start to scream. Long, wracking screams, so loud I'd end up hoarse the next morning. I've never screamed like that, before or since. Dawn would come and with it a sense of humiliation and shame…but there was no room for shame during those first few nights. Terror was king, those nights.

Sometimes Vera would come to me. She'd press a cold cloth to my forehead and my arms would find their way around her waist and pull her to me, needing her warmth and her permanence and her sweet, clean smell. I remember saying things to her between the sobs and screams: confessions, I think, of all the terrible things I'd done to others, of the people I'd killed, some of whom deserved it but most of whom were just in the wrong places at the wrong times or whose ideologies disagreed with those of my government. Confessions of a man who felt his purpose on this Earth was to lead others to their deaths.

"Shhhh," Vera would say. "It's alright, now."

Once, when it got really bad, she kissed me on the forehead, and again, on the cheek. There was nothing sexual in the gesture: it was just one human being comforting another human being in the most essential way they knew how. And it's a big world, you know? A big, fucked-up world. But it's acts like that—just the briefest and most instinctive acts of kindness and warmth—that somehow make it just a little bit smaller, and little bit safer, and a little bit more beautiful.

They released me on Christmas eve, thinking there must be someplace I'd rather pass the holidays. I spent Christmas in a Greyhound bus driving through Saskatchewan. Christmas dinner was a hot hamburger sandwich at a truckstop outside Regina. Boxing Day found me washed up in Pittsburgh, standing in front of the same P.O. box where, one month and a lifetime ago, I'd received the letter that had set it all in motion.

I inserted my spare key and opened the box. My heart skipped a beat. Another letter.

The frigate captain descends from the bridge to sit with me. He is older, perhaps sixty, his accent impossible to place. A certain sadness expresses itself in the lines around his eyes and the set of his mouth. We have reached an unspoken agreement: our pasts are our own. In his hands he carries a silver flask and two small cups. He sets the cups on the deck between his spread legs and pours them full from the flask. He hands one to me. We click rims and he says:

"May you live in interesting times, friend."

"And you."

The liquor is very smooth and leaves a taste of burnt lemon on the tongue. He pours another cup. I don't protest. He knows a lot of people in Syria. The type of people I need to meet. He says they'll sell me whatever I need—automatic rifles, rocket launchers, stinger missiles—and offer me safe passage into Iraq. He said they'd fight alongside me, if the cause—and the price—is right. *It's amazing*, he says, *the kind of loyalty the American greenback can buy.*

I told him I didn't need anyone fighting beside me. I've taken enough young men down that dead-end road. This is the last time I will go to war, and I will go alone.

The envelope in the P.O. box was white and inside was a small strip of paper. Two sets of numbers were typed on it. One of them was a telephone number; the –011 prefix identified it as European. The other was a string of eight numbers.

I walked across the road to a bank of telephone booths and dialed the number. An automated operator told me how much change to insert. There was a series of distant clicks and snaps and, after a single ring, a pleasant female voice said, *"International Bank of Stockholm, how may I help you?"*

"I…I don't know," I said.

The woman laughed. *"Do you have your access number?"*

"No, I—" Then I saw the strip of paper in my hand, the eight-digit string below the telephone number. I read it off.

There was the sound of a keyboard being tapped. Then, *"Alright, Mr. Grant, how can I serve your needs—will you be making a withdrawal?"*

I felt like I'd been stabbed in the gut. I braced my hand on the booth's scarred Plexiglas.

"H-how much do I have?"

"Five million dollars," she said. *"A little more now, with interest."*

I staggered and fell forward, ringing my head off the booth. The receiver slipped from my fingers to swing on its flexible metal cord.

Distant, tinny: *"Mr. Grant? Are you alright?"*

It was the only promise the fucking thing ever kept, one it knew would hurt me more than any bullet. One last dirty trick.

I steadied myself and picked up the receiver. "I'm here."

"Is everything alright? It sounded like—"

"I'm fine. Bobbled the phone."

"Alright. Now, would you like to make a—"

"Withdrawal. Yes, I would."

"And how much would you like?"

"All of it."

I donated the money, in one lump sum, to the International Coalition for World Peace. It was the largest single donation the organization had ever received, and I was assured it would help a lot of people. When their press rep asked me who to thank for such generosity, I gave her the names of the Magnificent Seven, and Grosevoir's. There was a press release, and the story made quite a few papers.

I want to believe, wherever that thing was, it read the article.

And I want to believe the irony ate its fucking guts.

The question that remained was: What do you do when the whole world falls apart? It had been hard enough to get my life back on track after 'Nam—and *now*, after *this*? Forget about it.

Still, I tried. I had money stashed from the Keybank job and with it I rented a one-room apartment near the Pittsburgh Public Library. Every day I'd rise at eight o'clock following a dreamless sleep, shit, shave, get dressed. I'd eat breakfast at a diner facing the library and, at nine o'clock sharp, cross the road and walk inside. There were sections of the *Post-Gazette* threaded onto long wooden dowels and I would take the World News section and sit in a faintly urine-smelling chair facing the wall. I would read the section front to back, even the adverts—*Losing your hair, or lost most of it? Call DeOliviera Hair Care Systems, Inc.*—and set it back on the rack.

Afterwards I would sit and stare at the wall. The wall was white pigmented concrete and I'd stare at it, all the tiny perforations and cracks on its surface, losing myself in the emptiness. My major focus was to think of nothing, to let the wall's whiteness sink into me and render my mind as blank and whitewashed as it was. I became very good at it: hours passed, my stomach rumbled and joints ached, day passed into night and yet I noticed none of it, gone and away in that cold white world. Then the lights would be clicking off and on, twice, to signal closing time.

I'd eat supper at the same diner and walk home. By the time I reached the apartment my boots would be wet from the slush, the wadded newspapers in the toes a cold, sodden mess.

I would draw a bath, strip down, and slip into the steaming water. I bought a radio and plugged it in and set it on the sink's ledge. I never turned it on. Sometimes I would try to lose myself in the bathroom tiles as I did in the library wall, but the faded floral pattern and corridors of dark grime marred the necessary whiteness. That's when my mind would wander, spiraling in an ever-tighter orbit like water circling a drain, approaching that center of perfect darkness. There was nothing good down there: only misery, and recrimination, and slowly-creeping insanity.

But I couldn't help myself from probing that darkness, in the same way I'd probe a rotted molar with my tongue. And, sooner or later, I'd probe deep enough and peel away enough layers that I'd end up screaming, screaming and thrashing in the water with my toeless feet rattling against the porcelain while my next-door neighbor hammered his fist on the wall telling me to shut the hell up.

Once, and only once, I found myself holding the radio in front of my face, the red numbers flashing *12:00* six inches above the water. The cord was black with a white stripe running its length and a sticker near the plug read CAUTION: TO PREVENT ELECTRIC SHOCK MATCH WIDE BLADE TO WIDE SLOT AND FULLY INSERT. I switched it on. "Sweet Dreams," by the Eurythmics. Then my hand lowered until the radio's plastic casing broke the water and suddenly Annie Lennox's voice resonated waterily and little bubbles rose from the speaker holes to burst on the bath's surface. I wondered how long it would take the water to find a live circuit...

...and, as I watched those pinprick bubbles break the water's surface, I thought about a time in the jungle during those small still moments preceding an engagement. Tripwire had asked, "Sarge, if my ticket's punched, you think I'm going to hell?" My initial reaction had been anger: "Shitcan that lip. Nobody's getting their ticket punched." Then, after the firefight: "We're soldiers, son. Soldiers don't go to hell. Soldiers kill other soldiers. We're in a situation where everybody involved knows the stakes. And if you're going to accept those stakes, you've got to do certain things. Simplicity itself. We're soldiers. We follow codes. Orders. There is dignity in that. Honor. So, no, son, you wouldn't have gone to hell. Soldiers don't go to hell..."

...and then my arm was rocketing up, the radio pulled clear of the water, spinning end-over-end to smash against the wall.

Soldiers don't go to hell.

But maybe cowards do.

The next day I woke at my regular hour and walked to the library. I grabbed the World News section and sat in my urine-stink chair.

And that's when I saw it.

The headline read: "Iran-Iraq War: Blood in the Streets of Kuwait." It was accompanied by a quarter-page color photograph; a street scene. The road was a narrow stretch of dirt tamped flat by an endless procession of feet and scooter tires. On either side stood squat buildings—or, more accurately, their remains. They resembled sand castles in the midst of being washed away by an advancing tide. Chunks of brick were strewn haphazardly about, crumbling walls pockmarked with bullet holes. To the far left, a tattered and charred Iraqi flag was caught in mid-flutter on a twisted flagpole.

A pair of bodies lay amidst the rubble. Their limbs were bent at angles that would've been physically impossible had they been alive. There was an uneven ring around one of the heads, tinted a slightly darker hue than the red dirt it was lain across. In the right foreground a young boy, maybe fourteen, crouched behind an overturned Jeep. He was firing an AK-47 at something or someone off-frame.

If that had been all the photograph depicted I would have turned the page.

But it wasn't.

A lone figure stood in the doorway of a gutted building. He was not hunched over or cowering; instead he leaned, one hand casually pocketed, against the doorframe. It was a posture suggestive of complete comfort and ease: a director watching an expertly-orchestrated action sequence playing itself out. Sunlight streamed through shell-holes in the building to veil his face in muted yellow tones...

But there was no mistaking the shock of curly red hair.

Or the oh-so-familiar smile touching the corners of that delicate upturned mouth.

Or that cold, red, utterly unfeeling stare.

Answer. Chaos.

Two emotions swept through me, starkly conflicting: hate and love. Hatred for Answer, or whatever he had become, and, on a higher cosmic level, hatred for whatever forces were at work to necessitate such realities as war, and violence, and evil. But, cresting in a surprising wave, was the opposing emotion.

Love.

It slammed together in my head with all the crushing weight of epiphany: I loved those men. Gunner and Slash, Crosshairs and Tripwire and Zippo—*loved*. There was no shame in the admission, only the unshakeable certainty that I *should* love them. It was not the love of a man for a woman, or of a father for his child. That is an elemental love, love expressed at the depth of bone, and blood, and soul. The love I felt for those men was one of circumstance: the element of choice did not exist for us. We did not choose one another but instead were thrown into a situation that forced us to place our trust and our lives in those we fought beside. Soldiers in a warzone enter into a pact, whether knowingly or unknowingly: whatever goes down, whoever goes down, they all go down together, as a unit, live or die.

So, yeah, I loved those men. It was a reckless and extreme kind of love, but love all the same. Perhaps the only kind I've ever really known.

I set the newspaper back on the rack and walked out the library's front doors.

I would never return.

A Greyhound took me from Pittsburgh to Macon, Georgia, where I spent the day with an old friend. Another Greyhound brought me to Key Largo. I took a motel room a few blocks from the seaport. The next morning I walked the pier and made casual enquiries. A longshoreman pointed me towards the *Monkey Sea*. I met the captain and we struck a handshake deal: seven-thousand dollars for passage to Syria and safe entry into Iraq.

Now, nearly three weeks later, the frigate is a thousand knots from the Syrian coast. The captain drains the flask's final drops into our cups.

He says, "And what of you, friend—a toast?"

I consider. "Well, Ernest Hemingway once wrote, *It's a fine world and worth fighting for*. There was a time when I only agreed with the second part." I tip the cup back, swallow, and stare out into the darkly cycling sea. "But now I'm pretty much in total agreement."

The captain claps me on the back. "You are a good man. I will see you in the morning." He stands, legs wobbling slightly, and disappears belowdecks.

When I was young, fifteen or sixteen, I used to think war was the Great High: I'd thumb the pages of *Soldier of Fortune*, those grainy black and white photos of Special Ops soldiers with their faces smeared in greasepaint, legs shoulder-width apart, rifles crossed over their chests; or that famous snapshot of an unidentified unit cresting a hillside at twilight, their bodies silhouetted against the setting sun, their posture bowed but resolute as they passed into enemy territory. And all I was thinking then was *yeah, gimme some of* that *shit*. It was about kicking ass and taking names, killing 'em all and letting God sort them out, living hard and going out in a blaze of glory.

But, after a few Tours in 'Nam, I came to see war as the Great Lie: your country wanted something and their country wanted something and everyone was feeding lies and misinformation to get what they wanted. And all the memorials and the monuments and the medals and the American flags waving outside shopfronts on Veteran's Day—that was all part of the lie. Those things only shrouded the one stone-cold fact, which was this: some soldier, some fucking *kid*, dying alone in the middle of a rice paddy or a shallow trench, this kid who was playing high school ball and chasing tail six months earlier now dying with parts from the inside of his body strewn about the outside of it, dying in the mud and the shit and the sick-*fucking*-twist of it was that he had no idea *why* he was dying, no comprehension of the forces that had brought him there, far away from home, to die. All he knew was he was cold, and in pain, and that once, at some far-off time, he was deathly afraid of being thought a coward, a boy who'd refused to do what was best for his country. Look into the face of any man dying in a combat zone and all you'll see is confusion. This *what the fuck am I doing here* look—because it is then, and only then, that they're able to peer beyond the ropes and the pulleys and the scaffolding and see war for what it really is: a horrible, stupid lie.

But now I know differently.

War is not a lie.

War is Truth. The purest Truth in this world.

War is the truth of human nature. The basic law of man. The truth of *life*. It's a fight, man against man, and if you are going to defeat that other man, defeat him completely. Leave him there, dead, on the ground. The laws of beasts and the laws of man are interchangeable at their most basic level—they are the laws of the jungle, survival of the fittest. The refinements of civilization take us away from that basic truth, but war pulls us back. It reaches deep inside and grasps at the roots of who, and what, we really are. It is jungle law, primal law, a law that calls for winners and losers and leaves no room for compromise. It is war's ability to tap that fundamental state of mankind that gives it so much power; of all fundamental human endeavors it goes deepest and, in going deepest, goes the furthest toward the truth.

And now I know.

War is Truth.

But there is no beauty in this truth.

It is a cold truth, a hard truth, an ugly truth, and I want nothing to do with it.

I walk to the ship's bow. The wind and the booze and the lack of toes combine to unsteady me and I reach, blindly, for the railing. My fingers catch the metal rail and I pull myself up. Christ, I feel so feeble. Weak and infirm, an old man where a young man once stood. Doesn't matter. I'll be strong enough when the time comes.

Bluegills ride the wave of water pushed by the frigate's shovel-shaped prow. Their bodies are lean and tapered, resembling ballistic torpedoes. They move just below the waves, quicksilver flashes, leaping out of the water occasionally, tails flickering, droplets of water spraying. They don't care where they're going or remember where they've been. They are content to be moving. Content with the simple pleasure of forward motion.

I am a born leader. Give me a unit or a crew, five or six men, and they will follow me anywhere. And I think war—*Chaos*—needs me, and men like me. We are the enablers of chaos. The spark. When a young man is going into a situation where he could lose his life or take the life of another, he is not thinking about the inspiring speeches of photogenic statesmen or the safety of the free world or the red, the white, and the blue. All he is thinking, then, is how scared he is, and how lonely, and how far he is from home. He looks to me, or someone like me, for strength. And I give it to him in the form of a reassuring hand on the shoulder and the words, "You're going to pull through, son. You're going to make it. Just go hard, bear down, don't look back."

And they do.

So you see how I give chaos a recognizable face and a familiar name and all the force of conviction. A front line agent of chaos, if you will. I possess the ability to lead men into the unthinkable, again and again. In this way I am every bit the instrument of Chaos as any of those creatures I encountered in the woods of northern Canada. A monster. The realization sickens me. And yet it is who I am, who I have always been.

A monster.

I am reminded of the old parable of the scorpion and the frog. The scorpion needs to cross a pond, so he says to the frog, *Take me across on your back, because I cannot swim.* The frog says, *But you're a scorpion. You'll sting me. No I won't,* the scorpion says, *I promise.* Halfway across the pond, the scorpion stings the frog. *Why did you do that?* the frog says as the poison works its way through its system. *Now we'll both die. I'm a scorpion,* it replies, *and you knew that when you picked me up.*

Sometimes you've got to ask yourself who you are—the scorpion or the frog.

Sometimes you'll find you're both.

And, like the scorpion, maybe I can't help what it is I am. Except this one time.

I see it, in my mind's eye. Answer. Chaos. See it squatting in a filthy Iraqi bunker, surrounded by bones and blood and shit. Waiting for me. It is dark in the bunker but candles are burning, hundreds of them, in every corner, on every ledge. Things are moving at the periphery of my vision, beyond the light of the candles. Darkness prevents me from giving them a name or a species. I don't believe they are human. I hope they aren't.

Chaos squats naked in the swimming light of the candles. Its body is half human and half beast, and this seems perfectly right to me. One of its legs is humanoid, but withered and lacking muscle tone—an invalid's leg. The other is that of a quadruped, a stag or elk, heavily furred and tapering to a cloven hoof. Its remaining eye is huge and compound, a miniature disco ball; candlelight arcs off each individual facet. Its hair is red and curly, a feature that feels at once so right and so totally wrong.

"Here I am," I hear myself saying.

"I knew you'd come," the creature says. "You are my finest achievement. You and others like you."

"And I have come. But not for the reason you think."

Does an expression of unease flicker across its face?

I think it does.

I say, "I know what I am."

Then I part my jacket and let it see what I've hidden inside. Watch its septic red eye expand in recognition.

"But that doesn't mean I like what I am."

Beneath the cot in my cabin is a crate. In that crate, beneath a layer of dried hay, are sixteen sticks of dynamite. I picked them up in Macon, where I stopped to visit Deacon, the man whose life I saved by taking the life of another. Deacon, an ex-demo expert, knew people who knew people and in this way I laid my hands on enough explosive to level half a city block. I purchased a nylon vest, the kind fly fishermen wear. At night, sitting here on the deck, I have carefully sewn sixteen long, narrow pockets onto its chest and back. The dynamite fits snugly.

It fits.

Questions, questions, always questions.

Can I kill it? Can Chaos *die*? What would the repercussions be? Can the world exist without Chaos? And most terrifying: If I do kill it, what might appear in its place?

Doesn't matter. My mind is set. The score needs to be settled.

I am unwilling to bend on this. Do I always have to answer violence with violence, take an eye where one was plucked? Am I incapable of turning the other cheek? Maybe so. In the end we always return to what we are. In the end, we find our truth.

Embrace it, I say.

Embrace it, hold it, never let it go. If we are defined, as individuals and as a species, by those deep-seated drives that make us who we are, then it is only a fool who fights that definition. There must be love. But there must be hatred, as well.

And there must—*must*—be vengeance.

The ship carries me forward. I go willingly. Like the fish swimming below, I relish the simple pleasure of forward motion. Soon the Syrian coast will come into view.

Yes, people can change.

But sometimes the old ways, the true ways, are the best ways.

And I am coming.

Coming to show you the truth inside the lie.

PATRICK LESTEWKA is the pseudonym of Canadian writer Craig Davidson. *The Preserve* is his first book. His collection *Rust and Bone* is set to be followed by a novel entitled *The Fighter*.

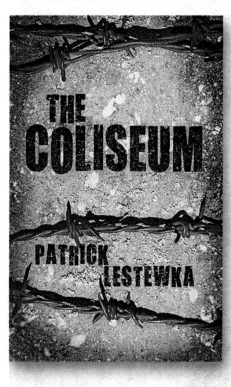

Deep in the Canadian back country a new experiment in extreme penal punishment is underway. Although officially known as the Innuvik Penitentiary, it's more widely known as:

THE COLISEUM.

On October 15th, 1993, the first twenty prisoners were unleashed. These were the worst of the worst. Brutal criminals, psychopaths, lunatics, call them what you will.

Today there is a batch of new fish.

• Harlan Rudduck, called The Beast, and boy is he, physically and mentally. A brutal and ruthless killer sentenced to battle the other beasts haunting the inside of a prison Hell wouldn't even want.

• Albert Rose, a simple and meek man who buries himself in his work. Then one day he loses his job and then finds out an awful secret about his wife. Now he's about to find out what happens when you kill the wrong man.

• Jackson Cantrell, a brilliant and charismatic man. Good qualities unless you're also a complete psychopath working for the Lord. It began with convincing his brother to jab his own eyes out with a fork to "see the light." And now, after sending 487 of his followers to meet their maker, Cantrell's manic faith is about to be tested as he and his fellow inmates are unshackled and released into The Coliseum.

How long will they survive? What became of the original 20 prisoners? And what the hell is breeding in the deep, dark recesses of...

THE COLISEUM!

NECRO PUBLICATIONS • 5139 MAXON TER. • SANFORD, FL 32771
407-443-6494 • dave@necropublications.com
WWW.NECROPUBLICATIONS.COM
ACCEPTING PAYPAL, VISA, MASTERCARD, CHECKS AND MONEY ORDERS

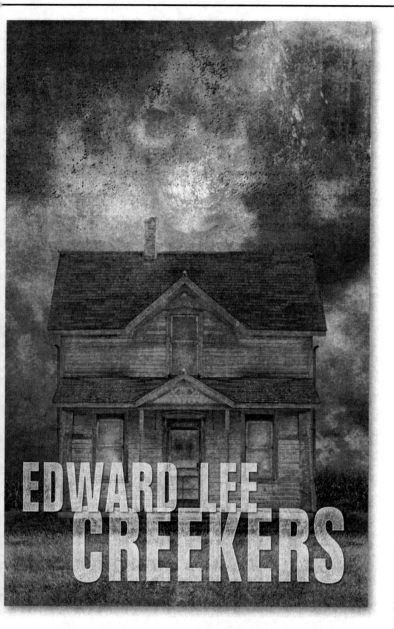

Following on the heals of his critically acclaimed collection, DEAD SOULS, David G Barnett offers up the beginning of what will hopefully be a long series of novellas and shorts centered around the new battle for heaven. These first three tales are fast-paced, funny, raunchy and poignant. Barnett's world comes to life with horribly flawed characters that you will like or hate, but won't soon forget, abominable creatures and visions of Heaven and Hell that will begin to paint the way for more tales to come.

OF ANGELS FALLEN

They rescued him from the streets and with their help he has become the world's greatest assassin. So much death, so much blood, but it all ends after this one final job. Just one more death and Mal will finally get what was promised him so many, many years ago.

Jonas White is a powerful man, an empire builder. He commands adoration and respect from everyone who meets him. He is a good man, does good things. But now he's also a marked man. He knows destiny is banging on the door. What will happen when he opens it?

Two men fated to meet each other on one cataclysmic evening. An evening when secrets will be revealed, loyalties will be tested, old grudges settled and new ones made. This is just one stop along a long road. A road that leads back to where it all began so very long ago.

DADDY DEMON'S DAY OUT

He wanted revenge for an atrocity committed so many years ago. Back when his world collapsed around him with a single knock on his door.

But that was then and this is now and revenge is at hand. Years of planning, years of blasphemous dealings and terrible actions have led to this moment. He has worked for decades to be able to summon the demon of revenge and now he's ready. Tonight he will demand the demon grant him his one wish and all of this will finally be over.

But Travis Burnsfield will soon find out that the demon of revenge has other plans for the evening. Plans that involve Starbucks, cheese steaks and a trip to the infamous Painfreak where many creatures go, all with very different hungers—especially one creature's hunger that can be sated with the sorrow of a tired old man who only wants revenge for something taken from him so very long ago.

THE SLEEPERS AWAKEN

The old man hadn't been here in... Well, he couldn't really remember. But what he did know was that it had changed. Changed so much. His heart was heavy at seeing the destruction and knowing what it all meant. But he didn't have time to mourn. No, he had to move on.

He had placed them here so long ago, but over time he grew careless and forgot to keep track of them. But the time has come for him to track them all down. Things had changed and now he needed their help. It was time to seek out the others and awaken them...awaken his army. He only hoped they wanted to be awakened and wanted to help him. It would take some time. But after all, time was all he had right now.

NECRO PUBLICATIONS • 5139 MAXON TER. • SANFORD, FL 32771
407-443-6494 • dave@necropublications.com
WWW.NECROPUBLICATIONS.COM
ACCEPTING PAYPAL, VISA, MASTERCARD, CHECKS AND MONEY ORDERS

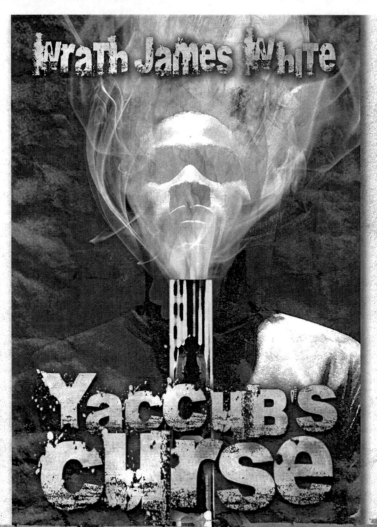

CPSIA information can be obtained
at www.ICGtesting.com
Printed in the USA
LVOW12s2135110416

483154LV00012B/126/P

9 781889 186665